throwing stones

robin reardon

IAM Books
www.robinreardon.com

THROWING STONES

Copyright © 2015 by Robin Reardon

Cover and formatting by: Sweet 'N Spicy Designs

Praise for *Educating Simon*

"I love Simon Fitzroy-Hunt! He's a perfectly-realized character — extreme, but never exaggerated; flawed, but always relatable. An excellent book." —Brent Hartinger, author of *Geography Club* and *The Elephant of Surprise*

Praise for *The Evolution of Ethan Poe* (2012 ALA Rainbow List; winner of five categories in 2011 Rainbow Awards)

"Mesmerizing, drawing readers into Ethan from page one, endowing him and all the characters with great depth, and building a slow-burning tension." — Publishers Weekly

*For Havah, who opened my mind to new ways of thinking
and for whom, whatever the question, the answer is love*

The first principle is that you must not fool yourself—
and you are the easiest person to fool.
– Richard Feynman (1918-1988)
Nobel Prize, Physics, 1965

The hardest thing of all is to find a black cat in a dark
room,
especially if there is no cat.
— Confucius

Chapter One

So we were pulling up to that traffic light where the road from Brad's house comes to a T with the miracle mile. Windows were down to let in the warm, early October air. Brad was driving my truck—a reward for the padded wheel cover he'd bought for it—and the traffic light turned red before we got to it. Brad's fingers were drumming on the steering wheel with a song on the radio. I forget which one.

And as I looked to my left I saw a familiar red truck, perched high on over-sized tires and about to tear through the intersection in front of us, with Lou Dwyer behind the wheel. His partner-in-crime, Chuck Armstedt, had his arm hanging out of the window, pounding on the outside of the passenger door. He looked over, saw us, and shouted.

"Faggots!"

I couldn't be real sure whether there was an "s" on that or not.

I looked at Brad. His face was hard, and he was watching the truck fly past. Then he looked at the light, then at the sign that said "No Turn On Red," then at the traffic, and before I could say anything he was through the red light and off after the red monster.

"Brad, hey guy, not wise. Really not wise."

Brad didn't say anything right away, just pushed forward. Then, "Honestly, Jesse, aren't you fucking sick and tired of those assholes? Wouldn't it be great to make them answer for something once in a while?"

"Just not sure now is the best while. And this is my truck you just ran the red light with."

Brad ignored me, and I know him well enough to know there's not much I could do to get him off his high horse. It's one thing for *him* to challenge these guys; he's big, wide receiver on the school football team. I'm not puny, or timid, but I'm not Brad's size, either. And Lou and Chuck are kind of used to being aggressive bullies. That's how Brad and I got to be friends, way back in grade school; he stood with me against this same friggin' pair of goons. But we're not eleven any more.

The road is four lanes, two in each direction, and Brad passed and changed lanes and passed again until he was right behind the red monster. Ahead of us, I saw Chuck raise his hand and flip us off. Brad didn't flinch, and after another quarter mile or so, Lou pulled into a large parking lot where a car dealership had closed up shop a few months ago. He made a sharp turn to face the road and waited, engine idling. Brad stopped about fifteen feet away, facing the other truck, and he was out before I could undo my seat belt.

Lou and Chuck didn't get out of their truck. The windows were up, now. Brad marched over to the driver's door and reached for the handle, but the door was locked. He threw the side of his fist against the door so hard I expected there to be a dent, but there wasn't. Inside the truck, the two jerks were laughing like hyenas.

Brad took a step back as I came up beside him. "Assholes!" Brad shouted. "Shitheads! Get out, or stay there like the cowards you are!"

Lou and Chuck just kept laughing, almost like Brad was talking in gibberish. Brad got up onto the running board and started to bang on the window with an elbow. Suddenly the truck lurched forward and swerved around mine. Brad jumped off, picked up a stone, and heaved it. It bounced off the rear bumper as the truck tore out of the parking lot and back onto the road.

I raced back to my truck and climbed behind the wheel.

THROWING STONES

I didn't want to risk Brad going after them again; it wasn't worth it. Brad's body thudded against the closed door beside me, and he pounded once on it before walking around to the passenger side. He threw the door open and climbed in, still furious. His fist hit the dashboard.

"Hey, Brad, knock it off. Just because you can't pound on them doesn't mean you can damage my truck."

His back hit the seat hard. "Fuck!"

"Ditto."

So goes much of my life, these days. It's been like this, more or less, ever since I decided to stop hiding, stop lying, and come out. It was Brad I told first.

We were rockhounding—hunting for crystals and minerals—in the Ouachita National Forest, the southeast corner of Oklahoma, in late August. Just over a month ago now. This was the first time I'd gone with Brad, the first time I'd done it at all. It's something Brad used to do with his father before Mr. Everett was in that accident in the mines. Mining's big around here, and it seems like somebody gets hurt badly every year. Last year it was Brad's father. He can still drive, still gets around okay, but his left leg doesn't work very well. He's on disability, and he uses a cane to walk.

Anyway, the day I came out to him, we were walking along through the woods, Brad in the lead and headed for this spot he knows about, when he said, "You seem real quiet today."

"I guess." I'd spent the better part of the ride from town, beside him as he drove his mom's car, thinking that today might be the day I'd tell him. It had been weighing on me more and more, especially since he'd started going out with Staci Thompson, and he kept trying to get me to double with them. Truth be told, every time I thought about it, I felt guilty. Ashamed. And I needed to know how much of that shame was coming from lying to my best friend and how much was coming from inside me because of what I

3

was lying about.

"You're not pissed at me or anything, are you?" I could tell he tried to make it sound like that was almost funny, but I heard the doubt underneath.

I stopped walking, and he turned to face me. Trying hard to keep my knees from shaking, and mostly failing, I said, "Can we talk for a minute?"

He let his pack fall from his shoulder onto the ground. "S'up?"

I let the backpack he'd given me, the one his dad used to use, slide to my feet. "If there were something about you that was really important, and I didn't know what it was, and it was on your mind a lot and you didn't tell me, I'd probably be pissed when I found out you'd been keeping quiet about it." I watched his face for any kind of clue, but I didn't get one.

"Dude, spit it out. What's on your mind?"

"I'm gay."

Nothing happened for maybe twenty seconds. Then Brad lowered himself slowly until he was sitting on a rock just off the trail. Head bent forward, he ran a hand through his hair. There were so many things I wanted to say. Like, *We're still friends, right?* Or, *You don't hate me, do you?* Or, *I've wanted to tell you for so long.* But mostly, *What now?* All I could do was wait.

Finally he looked at me. "How long have you known?"

"A while. Couple of years, anyway."

"Jesus, Jesse! Since we were fourteen? How could you not tell me?"

"It's not something that just spills out, you know? It's not like, 'I'm thinking of becoming a doctor,' or 'I really do like math after all.'"

"Yeah, but—Jesus! I'm your best friend, man!"

My breath caught. Would this really be the worst of it? That he was pissed I didn't tell him sooner? "Yes. You are." That was the best thing. He'd said it in the present tense.

But he was still staring at me. "See, now, I'm feeling like I need to get to know you all over again."

I shook my head. "I'm still the same. Maybe—maybe it's like now you need to see me in a pickup truck, where before you might have pictured me in an SUV."

He leaned his elbows on his legs and looked off to the side at nothing. "Jeez." Then he looked at me again. "So this explains why you haven't asked a girl out in, like, six months."

"Actually, I've never asked a girl out."

"Then—"

"*They* asked *me* out."

After the stunned look left his face, he started laughing. "Oh, man! Wish I had known that. What a pisser." His grin faded slowly, and then he said, "So d'you still like the same things? Or have you hidden a whole bunch of stuff from me?"

"No, man! I still like the same things. I still wanna do this today. And," this is one thing I needed to be really sure he understood, "I still feel the same way about you I always have. I've never wanted—you know—that kind of relationship with you. I already have the relationship with you that I want. Nothing's changed between us as far as I'm concerned."

He sat there a bit longer, looking at me, and then he stood, came over to me, and hugged me. I hugged him back, so hard, and then it was over.

He picked up his pack. "You wanna do this? Then let's do it." He marched off, and I followed, a grin on my face I couldn't have rubbed off if I'd tried. I would have followed him all day if that's what he'd wanted.

Probably I should go into how I came out to my folks. And what made me think it was time. It was after I told Brad, the weekend after my birthday, which had been

September ten. And it had a lot to do with what happened on my birthday.

My present from my family had been the best one ever, thanks mostly to by brother Stu. My dad and I always had an odd relationship. It hadn't been a bad one, I don't mean that, but it's kind of like we didn't ever talk about anything important. His relationship with Stu was totally different.

Stu's three years older than me, but he was still living at home to save money while he took a few courses in something called automotive service technology at a vocational school in McAlester. He was also working at Dad's garage, Bryce Motors, for some number of hours each week. Someday he'll partner with Dad in the business, probably inherit it eventually, and Dad didn't want him "knowin' just what you read in books."

Sometimes I've wondered if Dad and Stu talk when they're working together, repairing cars and trucks. I picture them there, each working on a different vehicle, making the occasional comment, followed by silence, followed by another comment, and so on. Some of the comments would be about the work, some of them would be about life in general, and they wouldn't be having even that much conversation if they weren't both working in the same place on the same kind of thing. Me, I'm not interested in the inner workings of vehicles. So it's like there's no platform for my dad and me even to begin to talk. We don't care about the same things. We don't have anything much in common.

Stu and I have always been different enough from each other that we've managed never to step on each other's toes. Growing up, I'd never leeched onto him and made a pest of myself, and he'd never felt the need to keep me in check by lording anything over me. We'd always had separate rooms. The shared bathroom had brought up a few conflicts, but nothing serious. I hadn't been in his shadow at school, and I'd kept such a low profile there generally that nothing I did had caused him any serious embarrassment. No one had ever referred to us as the Bryce brothers, or anything like that. And by the time my seventeenth birthday rolled around, we'd established a kind of friendly respect. Or that's how I'd thought of it before my truck had appeared on the scene.

My folks had promised me I could have my own car once I'd passed the license requirements, and that had happened at the end of July. I never expected to be given a set of wheels, just like that, but that's what happened.

We celebrated my birthday the Sunday before the tenth. Instead of waiting until after dinner to give it to me, as soon as our after-church lunch was over, Stu handed me a wrapped box while we were all still sitting at the kitchen table.

Stu was grinning. "This is all you'll get this year, bro. From everyone. Including Patty."

Everyone... including Patty Arnold, the girl Stu will probably marry. I almost replied that it had better be a great present, in that case, but I just unwrapped it. Inside the box was a remote key entry to something made by Dodge.

OMG. The best present ever. Positively the best. No doubt. I was on my feet without knowing I had even stood up. "But—what is it?"

Grinning from ear to ear, Stu pulled a folded piece of paper from his pocket and handed it to me. There was some printing, but my eyes focused only on the image of a silver pickup truck. Gradually I began to take in what Stu was telling me.

"It's a two thousand eight Dodge Ram 1500. Six-cylinder, three-point seven liter engine. Standard transmission with four-wheel drive. Silver, with gray interior. Eighty-two thousand miles."

I was still staring at the paper when I heard Dad say, "Stu worked on it himself, Jesse. It's been his project for the past six weeks. He even changed the timing belt himself."

I glanced from Dad's face to Stu's. It had been Stu who'd taught me to drive a stick shift; Mom can't, and Dad seemed too nervous with me at the wheel, so Stu had stepped into the breach. And now… "You did that for me?"

He looked torn between *Aw, shucks* and *I did good, huh?*

Grinning, Mom said, "Stu worked so hard on that truck that Patty started to complain that she had to go to the garage to remind herself what your brother looked like!"

I dropped the box—key securely in one hand—and wrapped my arms around Stu, then Dad, then Mom. Left to my own devices, I wouldn't have gone for a pickup, especially this one with no back seat. But both Dad and Stu drive pickups, so I knew that this was the vehicle they wanted me to want, and—hell, it was mine! My eyes watered, and I didn't really want them to see that. "Where is it?"

Dad said, "At the garage, waiting for you. We can all go over, and you and Stu can drive it home. He'll show you all the bells and whistles."

Instead of driving Stu home, I drove us out to Wister Lake, right out onto Quarry Isle. I parked as far out toward the point as I could, getting a huge rush out of the sound it made as I hit the remote lock, which of course I didn't need to do here, but what the hell? Stu and I sat on the rocks overlooking the lake and stared out over the water.

I broke the silence. "Thanks, man. Really. This is something special."

"Sure thing."

The time Stu had spent on it, and however much money he'd been able to put toward it—this spoke to something deep. Sitting there, silent, just enjoying the moment together, this picture of who we were brought up a conflict I'd been feeling more and more over the past few months. I'd always seen this secret I carry—being gay—as something Stu would never have to deal with, or at least not as long as I lived at home. I felt sure it would be something he'd never want to know, never want to hear. And yet now I felt a strong pull to tell him about me. To let him know this really, really important thing about me. Suddenly I wanted him to know who I was beyond what he can see in day-to-day encounters. It's one thing to share a bathroom with a guy. It's another thing to know that you're different on this oh, so basic level.

Sitting there, I tried imagine what words to use. And then it hit me how much it would hurt him to know it.

After my birthday, after getting the truck and feeling so great about that, it had begun to weigh really heavily on me that I was lying all the time. I was hiding from everyone but Brad. It felt so wrong, more wrong than it had ever felt before. And it began to seem as though the way I was hurting the people I loved was the opposite of what I'd worried about at the lake. I was trying to protect people by lying to them. Now it was the lying that was hurting everyone. Including me.

I'm not sure why I had decided to tell Brad first. Maybe it was that he seemed like a good test case. It would have hurt like hell to lose his friendship, but losing my whole family? That would have been worse.

I'd been doing all kinds of online research, about how homosexuality is just as natural and normal a condition for people and animals as heterosexuality is, how marriages between men were proving to be more stable than straight marriages, all kinds of stuff like that. I'd printed reams of it out, hoping against hope that I'd have a chance to show it to my folks.

I'd tried it out on Brad one day after I'd told him about me. We were in a booth at The Flying Pig, that place where you can get sodas and stuff served like cocktails. I had a Market Pig— which was Coke with, like, three different syrups and skewered pineapple in a wide glass with a tall

9

stem—and a large order of fries I was sharing with Brad. He munched on fries as he scanned my printouts. I asked him to start by looking over my summary document, which he did, and then he skimmed some of the more detailed information on the other pages. After a few minutes he pushed the whole pile toward me, a dribble of ketchup on one corner.

"This would make a great school paper, Jesse, but in the end I don't think it will matter all that much to anyone who's already made up their mind that being gay is bad. Facts won't matter to them."

The red stain felt like my blood. I'd been counting on keeping things on as rational a basis as possible, and I wanted the weight of this research to make my case for me.

But he was right. What my family would care about would be how it made them feel that their son was gay. Dad and Stu would feel sick to their stomachs just thinking about it. Mom would be sure that I'd lead a miserable life, and she'd assume that she'd get no grandkids from me. What would matter most, perhaps, would be knowing that I wouldn't be able to stay in Himlen. I'd have to leave. I knew that, already. Everything about this news would make them sad, or sick, or angry, or all three. And it could all be wrapped up in one ugly package: I was a disappointment to them so huge that it would make them want to scream.

And not all the research was good. One disturbing thing I found had nothing to do with facts or studies. It had to do with family. Somehow, last year, I'd missed this video that had gone viral. A guy in Atlanta named Daniel Pierce decided he was going to come out to his folks, and he was so scared of what might happen that he used his phone to record the whole thing. Then he posted it.

It was horrible. They screamed at him, they wouldn't listen to anything he had to say, and then they threw him out. The good news for him was that after he posted the video, people from all over the place started sending him

money. He got so much that he told people to send any
more donations to this home in Atlanta for queer kids
who've been disowned. I read an article where the director
of that home said that about half of the kids in the southeast
who come out to their parents get kicked out of their own
homes. *Half the kids.* And I wondered, what was it about
the southwest?

Whatever, after what Brad said, I was afraid I'd have to
put my plans on hold. But then, after a particularly moving
sermon at church the Sunday after my birthday, a week
after I got my truck, I decided to go ahead. The sermon had
been all about love, really, even though as long as I've
known Reverend Gilman he's been saying plenty of
unpleasant things about gay people ruining traditional
marriage. But that Sunday he quoted Matthew, where Jesus
says to love God with everything we are, and to love all
people as much as we love ourselves. Reverend Gilman
pointed out that we must know ourselves in order to love
God with all of ourselves, and we must love ourselves, or
loving other people has no meaning. He quoted First
Corinthians, where St. Paul says that he's nothing without
love. All knowledge, all wisdom, all faith even—all of it is
nothing without love.

By the time the sermon was over, and we all stood to
sing a hymn, I realized that this was how I'd tell my folks.
Love is everything; all else must bow to that. So I didn't
need my research. I didn't need facts and data and studies. I
just needed love, and I needed to call on love before I told
them. Up to this point in my life, I believed my family
loved me as much as I loved them.

After lunch, Stu headed off to fetch Patty for a picnic or
something. I was glad Stu wouldn't be home when I talked
to my folks; I was outnumbered as it was.

Dad was still at the table with the last of his coffee, and
Mom was loading the dishwasher. I needed to get this
started before Dad headed downstairs to the family room to

watch TV or work on stuff for his business or something. I kept telling myself, *Say something! Anything! Just get it started!* But I could barely breathe. I tried to take a deep breath and failed. I told myself I couldn't lose my parents' love. I told myself again. I took another breath and it seemed okay, but then my hands started shaking, so I clasped them together so hard my knuckles hurt.

Dad pushed his coffee mug away like he was about to get up, and with a massive effort I pulled myself together enough to say, "Mom? Dad?" My voice was so squeaky I sounded like someone else. Mom didn't even hear me over the water running in the sink. But Dad looked up.

"Jesse? Is everything all right?"

Mom looked around at that. "Jesse, what is it?" She grabbed a towel to dry her hands.

I cleared my throat; it helped a little. "I need to talk to you." I put my hands in my lap so no one could see how white my knuckles were or how much I was shaking if I didn't clench my hands. I had my parents' attention, that's for sure. They looked worried. Probably I did, too.

Mom sat in the chair across from me. "Jesse, what is it? You're scaring me."

I tried to smile, but even my mouth was shaking by then. "Sorry. I don't mean to. Um, first, I want you to know—" This is such an awkward thing to say. No one ever just blurts it out like this, but I needed to set the stage. I clenched my hands harder and looked down at the placemat on the table: blue and white weave, fringe on the edges, a few odd specks of something caught among some of the fibers.

Dad was losing patience. "Know *what*, Jesse? What are you talking about?"

"I want you to know that I love you. Both of you. And Stu, and Patty. And I know you love me." I looked up at them. "That's very important. That you know that. And I need to tell you something about me that I know won't change that, even though it might be hard for you to hear. Even though you probably won't understand it."

Silence. I took two or three breaths, closed my eyes, opened them again. I didn't even try to breathe. And for the second time in my life, I said, "I'm gay."

I had intended to keep my eyes on theirs, to watch for their reactions, to see whether there was shock, or horror, or anger, or what. But I couldn't. I couldn't look at them. I looked down at my hands, and then that seemed wrong; looking down made it seem like I was ashamed, and I was determined not to be. So I looked up again, but I couldn't really settle my gaze on anything. Then I saw Mom's hand fly to her face, covering her mouth. Her eyes were huge, strained wide open.

It seemed like an eternity before anyone said anything. Finally, Dad said, "Who told you that?"

That made no sense. Now I could look at him. Now I wasn't shaking nearly as much. "No one. No one told me anything. It's just something I know."

"I don't see how you can know something like that. You're too young."

I shook my head, hard. "It has nothing to do with how old I am, Dad. And anyway, other guys know they're straight. They go out with girls, because that's what they want to do. I don't want to do that."

Mom found her voice. "Jesse! You're not going out with boys, are you?"

"I'm not going out with anyone. Dating is not the point. It's not the dating that matters, it's what I know about myself."

Dad was starting to get angry. "Well, you got one thing right. I sure as hell don't understand."

"Gene! Language, please."

"Diane, this goes beyond language. Do you understand what our son has just told us?"

They stared at each other for several seconds while I

held my breath again. Would Mom let him drag her into antagonism? Finally she said, "I don't think we *can* understand it. I think we need to give this some time, let things settle, and then talk about it again later."

Dad looked like he had something unpleasant to say to that, but Mom interrupted him. "It won't do any good to get angry, honey. If Jesse is right, yelling at him won't help. And if he's just confused, he'll have to find his own way out. We can help, but we can't pull him out."

Dad crossed his arms on his chest and glared at the refrigerator.

Mom said, "Jesse, sweetie, how long have you felt like this?"

"I've *known*," I corrected her, "a long time. A couple of years, anyway. And I suspected before that." That floored them, I could tell; she was probably sure I'd say it had been only a few months or so.

I glanced at Dad; had he softened at all? Didn't look like it. Suddenly he stood, and the chair went flying behind him. Without another word he tromped downstairs. Mom and I sat still, silent, not looking at each other, until I heard the television.

"Jesse, I honestly don't know where we go from here." Mom's voice sounded sad.

"If it will help, I have lots of information I can give you. You know, to help you understand what it is and what it isn't. Because there's a lot of misunderstanding out there, and I think probably that's all you and Dad have, because you've never needed to know anything else. But now you need to. So tell me if you'd like to know more."

"What kind of information?"

Deep breath, Jesse, I told myself. *Take it slow; don't get excited.* "Like, I can show you scientific proof that this is a natural condition. Lots of animals are gay, not just people. And marriage equality is working. So far, they're seeing that—"

"Oh, Jesse… gay marriage? Do we have to go there?"

"I—it's just a point I need to make." Something about the look on her face made me stop from making that point. This hurt. She wasn't even going to let me make my case? "Mom, this is real. I'm real. I need you to understand."

She nodded, looking down at her hands on the table. "It's like I said, Jesse. We need time. Especially your father, and Stu. You've known for a while. We're just finding this out now, suddenly."

"Don't you think it would help if you knew more about it though?"

"Maybe. Maybe. Just not all at once, Jesse. And—I don't think we should tell your brother. Not right away, at any rate."

"You're all going to start hating me now, aren't you?" My tone was sharp; I was getting pissed.

"Oh, Jesse! Of course not."

"And you were totally right to say that it won't do any good to yell at me. It would do about as much good as yelling at Stu for being straight. You couldn't force him to want to be with a guy no matter what you did. And no one can force me to be straight. Including me, by the way. Not that I want to." I was pretty sure that last statement surprised her. So I added, "In case you were wondering."

She didn't take the bait. "Well, I think we all need some time. You hang onto that information for now, Jesse. We'll just have to see." She dropped her head onto her hands, massaging her hairline. "I don't know. This is so unexpected. I don't know what to do."

"You don't have to do anything, Mom. I'm still me."

"I need time to think."

I got up rather suddenly, my chair scraping across the floor, and headed upstairs to my room. I needed time to think, too, but once I was sitting in front of my sleeping PC it was obvious my brain wasn't my friend for this situation. I was at a complete loss. I thought about texting Brad, maybe going driving with him someplace, but I would be really shitty company.

Suddenly I was at the window, looking out at the gray afternoon, pissed that here was a chance to have what I've always said I wanted: a real conversation with my father. I'd even given him a topic. And what did he do? He clammed up and went to hide in the basement.

I pounded a fist on the window frame. And again. And again.

"Jesse? Are you all right?" Mom must have heard that from downstairs.

I was out of my bedroom in a flash. "Fine, Mom." Down the stairs to the living room. Down the stairs to the family room. The TV was blaring an ancient rerun of some cop show. Dad, slumped into his recliner, stared at the screen, obviously not really taking it in. I walked past him and sat on the couch, my eyes on him, not the TV. He said nothing, like I wasn't even there.

"Dad." He didn't move. "Dad, we have to talk. We don't usually talk about much of anything. This is important."

He hit the remote's mute button, stared at the screen for a few seconds, and then turned so suddenly it startled me. "You wanna talk? I tried to talk to you. I tried to teach you what I know. You were never interested. Maybe it wasn't good enough for you, I don't know. All you wanted to do was play computer games, and then cook, and then go traipsing around hunting for rocks. You think I wanted only one of my sons to value what I do? My business is growing, Jesse. It's going to take two people to run it. I wanted that to be you and Stu, both. But, no, it's not what you're interested in. So what *are* you interested in, will you tell me that? Besides cooking all the time."

I blinked stupidly at him, struggling to remember the last time he'd tried to engage me in his business. It must have been a long time ago, and I didn't remember being aware that that's what he'd wanted. And since when did it bother him that I was becoming a great cook? He sure ate all the stuff I made. Before I could say anything, he was talking again.

"I just don't understand you, Jesse. I've never understood you. I've tried. Oh, I've tried hard. Well, maybe this is the reason. Maybe you've just explained it all to me."

"That's not fair!"

"What? What isn't fair?"

"I've tried to talk to you, too, y'know. You think I'm not interested in what you care about? Well, you've never been interested in what I care about, either. It's not that I'm gay, Dad. That's not the problem. It's that we're different."

We glared at each other, and I was sure each of us was tallying up complaints about the other.

I was faster. "You say you wanted me to help out with the garage. Well what about helping Mom out? 'Cause I do a lot of that. I'm interested in cooking, sure. But I'm not always in the mood for it. But whenever she needs help, I'm there. Other times I volunteer when I see she's busy or tired, whether it's what I want to do right then or not. I go shopping for her, and I clean up sometimes. Stu never does any of that. I'm not saying he should. I'm saying *I do*. Her job isn't any less important than yours."

I couldn't have said where that came from. Who knew having an argument with my father would bring up resentment I hadn't even known about?

"Don't you tell me I don't take care of your mother. She has all the time in the world to play piano, and teach, and spend money on those—those things she collects."

The words could have been worse, but the tone? It took me a minute to grasp what "things" he was talking about, but very quickly I knew he meant Mom's collection of Hummel figurines. She *loves* those things. She's collected them for years. There's a special locked case in the living

17

room with the most expensive ones in it. And suddenly I knew, beyond any doubt, that he hated them. Or at least he dismissed them, considered them a waste of money and time. I think he'd barely stopped himself before saying, "those *stupid* things she collects." Or maybe even a worse word than *stupid*.

If he had contempt for something Mom felt passionate about, I didn't want her to know. For sure, I didn't want her to find out because of me, because of what I'd set in motion today.

"Keep your voice down!" I hissed at him, like he was the child and I was the parent. "You do what you want, too, y'know. Cars might be more functional, but that's what you chose. You could have been a miner, or a farmer, or a friggin' insurance salesman. Mom chose to be a mother, but that's not an interest. It's a life. You chose to be a father. And then you chose what interests you. Mom deserves the same."

More glaring, neither of us knowing what to say now that we'd come so far from the subject at hand. Or maybe we'd come *to* it. And it wasn't about cars or Hummels, or even about being gay. I'd already hit on it. I decided to go back to it.

"The problem you're having is that we're different. If I'd been a girl, no problem. But I'm a boy, so I have to be like you."

"And that's a bad thing. Being like me." His voice dripped sarcasm.

"No! Stu's like you, and he's a terrific brother, and a great guy. But, Dad, I'm *not* like you. That's not a bad thing, either. And being gay is just one way that's true."

"Oh, there's a lot more to that one, my boy."

"Yes. There is. And I didn't tell you before because I already felt like you didn't know me very well, and this would prove it. I don't want that to be true, Dad."

"What's true is that this gay thing makes no sense." He

18

was avoiding the real issue. He didn't want to admit that he doesn't know me at all, that he's never tried very hard, beyond hoping I'd be like him.

"Y'know, Dad, not everything that makes sense is going to make sense to you."

That got to him. He leaned forward, his voice low and threatening. "It makes no sense to *anyone* that any *man* would want to touch another man. There's no way that works."

"It doesn't work for you. I get that. But you need to get this: It makes no sense for me to want to touch a woman. And there are lots of people like me."

"Did it ever occur to you that there's a problem with that, and they all share it? Like some kind of disease?"

Oh. My. God. I couldn't believe he went there. "Did it ever occur to you that you didn't choose to be straight?"

He stood. He was trying not to shout. "I didn't *choose* it, because it's how men *are*! It's how we're supposed to be!"

I stood, too, but my voice was quiet. "And I didn't chose to be gay. Because that's how *gay* men are. You have no more right to manhood than I have. And I don't have to be just like you to be a man." I headed for the stairs.

"Jesse! Get back here!"

I stopped on the third stair. "Why? So you can tell me some more about how every man needs to be just like every other man, and how we all need to be just like you?"

His fists were clenching, his face was red. Nothing good was going to come of more talk, now. I turned and continued upstairs.

Mom was standing near the bottom of the flight to the second floor, and *her* face was *white*. I knew she'd heard it all. I froze, and then she moved toward me so fast it was a blur. She wrapped me in her arms and sobbed. Squeezing tears from my eyes, I hugged Mom tight, surprised that I had to bend down a little to drop my head on her shoulder.

Again, as though I was the parent, I said, "It's okay, Mom." But I really didn't know if it ever would be.

I headed upstairs, grabbed my keys, and thundered down again. I didn't know where I was going, but I had to get out of there.

I pointed my truck west toward Wister Lake, the same place where I'd driven with Stu. The whole drive I was thinking that even though I wasn't looking forward to breaking my news to him, it felt wrong not to. Mom had said to keep quiet, and I'd been glad to hear that at the time. Now, I wasn't quite sure what we were afraid of. How much worse could it be?

But I knew it could be lots worse.

Sitting at the edge of the water, throwing stones at nothing, it occurred to me I'm in a kind of limbo. Purgatory. My church doesn't talk about those places; we're not Catholic. But I know about them anyway. They represent an unpleasant kind of in-between state, not one thing and not another, and there's not much to indicate when things might change or which direction they'll go in. Could be heaven, could be hell. Or it could be right here forever.

I'd thought I was in a bad spot before, lying to everyone I cared about. But at least things had been calm. I'd been accepted. I'd been a part of the family. That was all changed, now. Maybe I should have kept my fucking mouth shut. Maybe I should have just gone on lying. I can't even remember, now, why I'd thought it was going to be such a great idea to tell my folks. It didn't do them any good, that's for damn sure. And it sure as hell wasn't doing me any good.

What was I thinking?

Love. It was *supposed* to have been about love. The kind of love God feels for us, and we feel for God, the kind we're supposed to feel for everyone.

Yeah, that was working out great.

THROWING STONES

Life at home pretty much sucked after that, starting with Sunday dinner. Mom walked around like there were eggs rolling around the floor and she didn't dare step on one. Dad walked around like he was trying to smash every single one of them, all the while clenching his jaw so hard he might just pulverize some teeth.

Something had to change. I didn't know what, but I had to get out of limbo, and I decided I had very little to lose by making my research available. So before I left for school Tuesday I put my printouts into a folder and set that on the back of the piano in the living room, where I knew Mom would find it at some point. I was pretty sure she had a student coming for lessons that afternoon.

When I got home from school, she was in there with a student, and I took a good look at the back of the piano. My folder was gone. So at least she'd seen it.

No one had said anything since Sunday afternoon about the bomb I'd dropped, but even Stu had noticed that something was wrong. Dinners were the worst, with Dad not able to bring himself to look at me, and Mom going around with a fake smile and a faker tone of voice, trying to act as though everything was normal.

I thought for sure the shit would hit the fan over dinner on Wednesday, because Dad was pissed as hell about something that had happened at the garage that afternoon, and it seemed likely that my issue would come tumbling out of the mess. Stu had been in McAlester, so he hadn't been with Dad when a man named Mr. Holyoke brought an old Toyota sedan in for a refurb.

There'd been something hanging from the rear-view mirror, something with three oval parts in a circle, all balanced, that Dad had thought looked Irish. There's a little Irish in our heritage, so Dad asked Mr. Holyoke about it. And he got an earful of information he didn't like.

21

"It's this heathen thing," Dad said. "It's not even Christian at all. He says it sometimes means earth, sea, and sky, and sometimes it's body, mind, and spirit. But then—get this—he says it also stands for the three life phases of some goddess. Can you believe that? Virgin, mother... I forget the third. It means old lady."

"Crone?" Mom volunteered.

"Yeah. That was it. Anyway, I told him to take that thing out of there. God knows I didn't want to touch it. I could tell he didn't want to, but finally he did."

Stu was obviously in agreement. "Maybe you should have found a Catholic priest to do an exorcism."

I wasn't about to stir things up or draw any attention to myself by asking any more about it, though the image of my own father afraid to touch that symbol got stuck in my head. My dad never seemed to be afraid of anything. What did he think would happen to him? It puzzled me.

Anyway, nothing happened to enlighten Stu about my issue that night. But it was only a one-day reprieve. Because all through dinner Thursday, Stu kept looking at me from under his eyebrows, and I couldn't quite tell whether he was worried or pissed. Maybe both. And then he'd glance at Dad, or Mom, like he might read something on their faces and be able to figure out what was going on that he didn't know about. It felt like a balloon that's being blown up to its maximum capacity, and the air is still coming into it, and you know there's going to be an explosion, and you just hope your face isn't too close when it happens.

Finally Stu couldn't take it any more. "What the heck is going on around here? Will someone tell me?" He sounded angry, almost as though he'd already asked Dad or Mom, and they'd refused to tell him. Then he looked right at me. "Well?"

I shrugged and leaned over my plate. Mom had said not to tell him yet, and I was trying to honor that. Truth be told,

I wasn't that anxious to go into it, anyway. I was regretting having said anything to anyone. Except maybe Brad.

After dinner, Dad was downstairs as usual. Mom was in the kitchen as usual. I was trying to do homework as usual and failing. I had left the door open so I'd hear anything that exploded. And suddenly I heard Dad's and Stu's voices, far enough away that they seemed to be coming from the basement family room. At first I couldn't understand the words, but I could tell Stu was pissed. Then there was a second or two of silence. Then, "Are you shittin' me?"

I got up fast, and from the top of the stairs I could see Mom in the doorway between the kitchen and the living room, obviously listening to the same thing I was hearing. She saw me and glanced up, looking as worried as I felt.

I headed downstairs, and Mom reached a hand out to me. I can't remember the last time she held my hand. We moved closer to the staircase that led down to the family room.

Dad's voice was low, mumbled, but I could tell he was unhappy.

Stu's words were very clear. "How can you let this go on? What are you going to do about it?"

Now we could hear Dad. "There's nothing *to* do, Stuart. I've looked this up. He can't help it. And he can't change it."

"Bullshit! You hear about it all the time, people getting fixed."

"No one seems to stay fixed. Or almost no one, and even those who do mostly don't say they've been changed. They just change the way they live, not the way they are."

"Then make him do that!"

"You wouldn't."

"What?"

"What if someone told you to marry a guy?"

I stole a glance at Mom. Was I hearing this right? My

23

father was on my side after all?

She whispered, "I found the information you printed out. I read it and gave it to him." I stared at her, wanting to know more. And she told me, "He's not happy about it, sweetie. You can hear that. But he's accepted the reality of it."

"And you? How do you feel?"

She sighed. "Resigned, for the moment. Give us time, Jesse."

Meanwhile the fight went on downstairs. Stu ranted on about how of course no one would ask him to marry a guy because that would be unnatural and sinful into the bargain. "He needs a good talking to by someone like Reverend Gilman."

"That would just make matters worse. And it would also be letting this shame out of the family. I'm not going to do that, and you keep your own mouth shut. Do you hear me?"

Okay, so Dad was not exactly on my side. But at least he wasn't siding with Stu.

Stu. How was I going to win my brother back? Especially since as soon as the word "shame" had come out of my dad's mouth, I'd felt it. And I'd been trying so hard not to.

"I have a good mind to take that truck back again!"

"Stu, knock it off. You aren't the only one who gave it to him."

"But—he's traipsing all over creation in it! Christ, for all we know he's having gay sex all over it! God!" There was a sudden slam, and Mom jumped; Stu had hit something, evidently.

I whispered to Mom, "I'm not having 'gay sex' anywhere." Mom squeezed my hand and then let go. She headed for the stairs, the ones that go down into the hell my brother was creating right now. I started to follow, but she shook her head. Maybe she thought my presence would escalate things. In a few seconds, I heard her voice from the basement, not shouting, but definitely pointed.

"Stuart, your brother loves you. He loves all of us. And we love him. Now you stop this horrible talk, right now. If you don't want to take the time to learn about what it really means to be gay, that's up to you. But as long as you don't know—and you obviously don't—then you lose the right to condemn it. You don't get to condemn your own brother, especially when you don't understand him. Do you hear me?"

Mom doesn't often talk like this to anyone. And she was doing it for me. If she could be strong, so could I. I headed down.

I stood at the bottom of the stairs, one hand on the railing in case I needed support. "You're all talking about me, but you're not talking *to* me." I looked at Stu. "Mom's right, you know. Up to now, you've been the greatest brother I could have. Don't change that."

"*You've* changed!"

"No, I haven't. I've been gay as long as you've been straight, which means my whole life. Just because you didn't know it doesn't mean it wasn't true. And now I think you can see why I didn't want to tell you. Now you know why I felt I had to lie to you about who I am. I just decided to stop doing that."

He stood there, clenching his fists, grinding his jaw. He looked from Dad, who'd essentially told him to simmer down, to Mom, who'd told him he was just plain wrong, to me. "So you're all ganging up on me, is that it?"

Mom jumped back in. "You need to cool down, Stuart Bryce. You need to get your head out of your butt and see what's going on here. Your brother needs our support, not our anger. And you'd better figure out how you're going to give that to him, and soon." She turned and grabbed my shoulder. "Come on, Jesse. Let's give your brother a chance to calm down before he does something he'll regret.

He's already *said* a few regrettable things."

Stu and Dad watched as we headed upstairs. Mom didn't let go of me until we were in the kitchen. She sat me down and took the chair across the table.

"Jesse, I know you want this to be all right. And maybe it will be. But we have to get over some hurdles. One of them I don't know if there's any getting over. It's what your life will be like if this thing is real. How hard it will be for you, out there in the world. I know gay people get hurt all the time, for no reason other than being gay."

I wanted to argue with her, tell her my life would be as good as anyone else's, but it was already looking like that was only an unrealistic dream.

She wasn't done. "Being gay is not something the rest of us ever heard anything good about, and we've heard lots of bad things. Maybe they were wrong, but it's all we've ever heard. And you've known about this for a long time. You need to let us thrash around for a while. You need to let us say some things we'll regret later. You need to let us feel some things that will take time to stop feeling. Do you get what I'm saying to you?"

I nodded and looked down at my hands on that blue and white woven placemat.

"We love you, Jesse. You were right about that. If we didn't, this wouldn't be so hard for us. But for a while, it might not feel like that to you. I'm sorry about that, but I don't see how it can be helped."

"So I have to just keep loving everyone, even though they're horrible to me."

"We're not all horrible, Jesse. I'm not, and you heard your father tell Stu to knock it off. And I'm sorry, but— yes. You're going to have to forgive us even before we ask you to. Even before some of us know we'll *need* to ask. It's our job to love you even though we don't understand what we've learned about you. And it's your job to love us before we manage to show that love in the way you want us

26

to." She waited until I looked up at her. "Can you do that? Do you love *us* enough?"

I swallowed to clear the lump in my throat. "I can do that. But maybe you'll need to be a little patient with me, too. Because right now I sure don't feel a whole lot of love from downstairs."

We looked at each other for a few seconds, and then she did her best to smile. "Good. Now, I'm guessing you have some homework to finish."

She was right, though I wasn't able to do a terribly good job with it. My mind bounced all over the place, wondering if there was really any hope that they'd come around. Especially Stu.

And then there was me. *I* needed to come around. I had to get to a place where there was no shame in me. Not for being gay. Not for being me.

Chapter Two

Things at home got into a pattern that wasn't great, but it was more or less manageable. Things at school got worse. Brad swears he never said anything to anyone, and I believe him, but to me it seemed clear that my status had changed from being someone who was a little odd but mostly okay to being someone to act oddly around. And suddenly Lou and Chuck were not just obnoxious. Suddenly they were obnoxious in a very specific way, calling me "faggot" every chance they got. This was about the time Brad chased the red monster and threw stones at it.

The week after our close encounter with Lou and Chuck, the second week of October, something happened that made me start a whole new career. Stalking.

If I think about how this got started, I have to say that it was at least a little inspired by how much I had pulled away from the kids I'd grown up with—gradually, over the course of a few months or so, but steadily. I was never one of those kids with scads of friends, so it wasn't like I had a whole lot of people to shed. But when I realized I was gay, knowing what my church had always said about that, believing that nobody else around me was gay, expecting the worst of the worst if anyone found out, a kind of fear set in. The more I dreamed about boys, the greater the fear was that someone would find out. It might have made sense to try and cover for this by dating girls, but I was terrified they'd figure it out because I wouldn't be able to act like other guys they'd been out with, or like they'd expect a guy to act. This meant that the only times I'd gone out were when girls had asked me, and it had been only because I'd been afraid of what they'd think if I'd turned them down.

So maybe it was this pulling away from what was most familiar to me that made me look in another direction. Maybe it seemed safer.

There's this community of people on the east side of the two-lane highway that heads south from town. All my life, I've heard it referred to as the village, and the people who live there have been called a variety of things, all of them ugly. Freaks has been the most common term, but there've been others: vampires; weirdoes; goblins; gremlins. These folks follow some weird kind of religion, and they don't go to our church. Their kids do go to our school; Himlen's a pretty small town, and the village isn't very big. Even so, the townie kids don't socialize with the village kids.

Mr. Holyoke and his family lived in the village. Aside from being afraid even to touch it, I hadn't been surprised at my Dad's reaction to that "heathen" thing he'd made Mr. Holyoke remove from his car. I mean, pretty much everyone I know who lives in the town would have a similar reaction to talk about goddesses and crones and the like, and it all goes along with the town's basic attitude about everyone in the village, like the Holyokes. They're terrified of something. I just don't know what.

And I've never known how the fear got started. I mean, they pretty much keep to themselves out there, and as far as I know they've never caused a problem in the town. Except for that woman last year who marched back and forth in front of the town hall at Christmas, protesting the use of her tax dollars to support churches and then rub her face in it when the government put up a manger scene. Sometimes she was joined by one or two other people from the village, or they were there instead of her to give her a break, but she was there on and off for a couple of weeks. After a while, town kids started throwing things like eggs and tomatoes and things like that at her. One kid, Roger Hastings, stood there for something like five minutes and threw rocks, but then she started throwing them back. That's when the police hauled her in, saying it was for her own protection. But they never did anything to Roger. And that lady was back again the next day, with four other villagers.

Sometimes it's hard to tell which side starts things like that, but I have to say I've never heard the villagers call the townies names. And as far as I know, they've never thrown the first rock.

But back to my stalking career. This one day at school, phys ed class had ended, showers were about over, and I was in a rush to swipe away enough water so I could get dressed and leave; the boys' locker room—a pressure cooker for males desperate to prove they're male—is not a safe place to be when the other guys know you're gay, or if they even suspect. Lou and Chuck weren't there at the time; they were a year older, seniors, and had a different period for phys ed. Even so, I was keeping my head down as usual while keeping an eye out for anyone approaching from any direction, and who should walk close by me but Griffin Holyoke.

I didn't have any reason to think he'd attack; nobody from the village had ever picked on me in any way. But as he passed by me, something about him—the way he walked maybe—made me go hard. I held the towel strategically while my eyes followed him.

I'd seen the tattoo he has on his back before, but never so clearly. It's all in black. Just below his waist, tree roots begin. The trunk starts at his waist and follows up on either side of his spine, and the branches—no leaves—swell out across his shoulders with a few delicate tendrils disappearing into his dark hair, which he dyes black and wears a little below collar length. His skin is pale, so the ink stands out starkly. And he's pretty tall, so the thing is impressive.

For some reason he turned and looked right at me. His

eyes were as green as leaves in spring. I still haven't gotten that look out of my mind. Not that I want to.

After that, I began to notice everything Griffin did. Like, who he hung out with (Ronan Coulter, another village kid), where he sat in the classes we shared, where his locker was, what route he took to walk home, all that kind of thing. I even started to pay more attention to some of the other village kids. Ronan didn't interest me; he'd always seemed kind of aloof, like he thought he was superior or something. But I was encouraged to new efforts by a paper another one of the village kids read in English class.

We'd been assigned to write a five-hundred-word essay about Halloween, and some kids were chosen at random to read theirs. When the teacher called Silver Shaw's name, everyone turned to look at her. We all knew she was a freak, and she dressed the part: long, pale hair with no style to it, clothes almost like a born-again hippie—lots of cotton, or hemp, or whatever. Canvas shoes that she covered with galoshes in rain or snow. By all rights, she should have been painfully shy, or at least terrified of the townie kids who loved to make fun of her and her people. But she seemed almost oblivious to taunts, which made her kind of scary, despite her harmless demeanor. Or maybe it's that a lot of the townie kids were convinced she was a witch and they were afraid to cross her.

As she read, the first thing that caught my attention was that she described time as a great circle, with our lives going round and round it. She said that Halloween—which she referred to as Samhain—is the beginning and the end of each circular year, and as such it looks both backward at the past and forward to the future. And on that night, you can step out of time, and this gives you a view of the entire year. She also said that your costume—and from what she said, this meant everyone, not just kids—should be chosen carefully so that it gives you a chance, in that place out of time, to experience life as some other person, or some other creature. She said the best experiences are from taking on a persona that can teach you something about yourself. It lets you see yourself through different eyes.

This was going to be my last year dressing up for Halloween, and I'd chosen a kind of hip-hop outfit, just because I thought it looked cool. As Silver spoke, I remember thinking that was a pretty piss-poor choice. All it would do, at most, would be to make me feel cool for part of one evening. Would that teach me something about myself, other than the fact that I have to pretend to be someone else in order to feel cool?

It wasn't long after this that I was following Griffin, per usual, as he and Ronan left school. I liked driving my truck, but I lived close to the school, there's the cost of gas, and driving would have meant I couldn't follow Griffin, who was always on foot.

Ahead of Griffin and Ronan, I could see Lou Dwyer and Chuck Armstedt, poised like wrestlers about to do battle, but not with each other. They faced a solid wooded fence gate, set back from the road by maybe five feet and forming a U shape from the rest of the fence at street level. It's where the people who own the house put their trash bins when they're full. Lou had a large piece of burlap, maybe a potato bag or something. I was kind of surprised to see them there, on my walking route home from school. Lou's red truck is their usual method of transport for any route, no matter how short.

Griffin and Ronan were about to cross the street so they could walk past without getting close, but whatever those jerks were focused on caught Griffin's attention, too. He stood behind them silently for a few seconds and then walked forward, startling the hell out of Lou and Chuck. That's when I caught up with them and saw what everyone was looking at.

Trapped against the solid wood of the fence, on its toes, back arched and ears flat back on its head, was a black cat, warning all on-comers with an eerie, gravelly wail. Whatever came near it was going to catch hell. I knew immediately that Lou and Chuck were planning to capture it and use it in some gruesome seasonal prank. It's no secret that anyone with a black cat should make sure to keep it inside around Halloween to save it from the horrors it would be subjected to if caught by someone like these guys, so you wonder about anyone who would let their black cat roam around right now.

All of us watched as Griffin approached the cat, slowly but fearlessly, kind of sideways, his eyes on the ground rather than the cat. He crouched down, waited maybe five or six seconds, and then just picked it up, calm as you please. It was one of those "Don't try this at home" moments. The cat looked wildly at everything, but it didn't scratch or bite, didn't try to get off of Griffin's shoulder. And he walked right past those goons—and me—as though we weren't even there. Ronan gave me a heavy stare for some reason, but I couldn't think why; it isn't like I had anything to do with this cat-napping attempt, or with Lou or Chuck either, for that matter.

Ordinarily I would have expected Lou and Chuck to jump on anyone who thwarted one of their evil plans. But there was something about Griffin at that moment, his fearless attitude or his self-confidence, that kept harm at bay. Ronan wouldn't have been much of a deterrent for these guys, so I doubt they felt outmatched.

Chuck mumbled, "Fucking freak. Bet he's got something planned for that cat himself."

I barely heard Lou say, "Fucking vampires."

I ducked my head a little to avoid any perception of my own involvement one way or the other, and as I hurried along I noticed Lou's red truck; it was parked a little way down the street. And then I heard Lou's voice once more.

"Fucking faggot."

And scene.

I couldn't guess how long Griffin would carry the cat, or if he'd take it home; obviously it didn't belong to anyone who cared about it enough to keep it safe. But I felt certain that thanks to Griffin, no one was going to torture that cat for Halloween.

On Halloween, a Friday, dressed in the hip-hop outfit that now made me feel kind of stupid, I went out trick-or-treating with Brad and his friend Phil Ahearn (who's also on the football team), but I faked feeling sick after about ten minutes. I went back, doing my best to avoid being seen by Lou and Chuck, who were cruising around in Lou's truck, no doubt looking for opportunities to perpetrate pranks as gruesome as possible on short notice.

I had a plan in line with my stalking career. I very much wanted to know what Griffin did on Halloween. In my mind, all the villagers dressed up like ghouls or something like that and danced around—what? A bonfire? A slaughtered black cat?

I knew driving right into the village was out of the question, so when I got near the left turn off the highway I slowed down and peered through the darkness at the sides of the road. Almost directly across from Woods Way, which is the street that leads into the village, I saw a pullout. When I turned onto it, I realized it was actually a narrow track that kept going past a small bit of woods and out toward fields that are part of a farm. I pulled my truck in between a couple of trees off to the side, killed the engine, pulled the key out of the ignition, and sat there. And sat there. I couldn't hear much of anything from inside the truck, and I couldn't see much, either, with no lights nearby. But I sure as hell could feel my skin crawling. It wasn't like there were bugs on me. It was more like they were crawling around just beneath the surface of my skin, where I couldn't see them. I started to wonder what they would look like, how gross they would be, whether they would bite, whether they were poisonous. In one swift motion I opened the door and jumped out, and without giving myself time to wonder what might be in the woods around me that might be gross or deadly, I practically ran across the highway and into the village.

There were no street lights or anything like that in the village. By the time I got close enough to see the houses, I had bats in my belly. I mean, how sure was I, really, that Griffin *didn't* have something nasty planned for that cat? People talked about the freaks doing some pretty wild things, anything from eating hallucinogenic mushrooms to sacrificing aborted fetuses. Sometimes there was talk about sex orgies. So my plan, which was to figure out where they were all gathering and spy on them, could mean I would see all kinds of things, some of which might give me nightmares. And, of course, the more horrible the acts were, the more trouble I'd be in if I got caught. So I was practically shitting myself by the time I got near the houses.

I'd never been this close to where they live before, and I was amazed that the houses all looked so normal. I guess I'd been expecting something creepy, dark buildings with lots of gables and odd angles, sagging porches, that sort of thing. But it was just houses on a long, narrow, curved street winding around a sort of town green in the center. And in the middle of that town green was a building lit up like there was a party going on.

Glancing fearfully over my shoulder, I crept around to the side of this building the least visible from any other structure. The windows were just a tiny bit too high for me to peer in comfortably, so I scrounged around until I found a rock I could stand on. It was heavy, and I had to heave and roll it to get it into position, and then of course it was a little wobbly. But it worked.

Inside, there were maybe forty or fifty people—hard to tell for sure—adults and kids. The place was lit by candlelight and lanterns, so details were hard to make out.

My expectation that they would be dressed as witches or ghosts or creatures of the night turned out to be totally off-base. At first it looked like they were all just people. But then I began to notice that something was off, and the first solid clue was that for the most part, the women were taller than the men. Then I noticed that the women seemed awkward in their motions. And finally it dawned on me that the "women" were really men dressed as women, and vice versa. I pulled sharply away from the window, fell off my rock, and hit the ground hard. When I stood I had another shock; there was a tall girl standing a few feet away, staring at me.

"Jesse."

It wasn't a girl. And, obviously, it was someone who knew me. He wore a wig of long, blonde hair, and he had makeup on, not a lot but enough that I could see it in the light from the window. I just stood there, mouth open as though waiting for flies to walk in.

"It's Griffin." OMG. The fly trap opened wider. "Do you want to come in? I, uh, see that you're in costume."

Was he making fun of me? His tone of voice was so close to facetious. But then he said, "You know, you could have dressed as Rob Lowe, or maybe James Dean. You kind of look like a young version of a combination of them. Join us?"

Finally I found my own voice. "No! I mean, no, thanks. No, I, uh…" There was no way to pretend I was there to do anything other than spy.

Griffin smiled. "We're pretty harmless. Honest."

"Why… why are you dressed like that?"

"It's like Silver said. We're experiencing what it's like to be seen as something other than what we are. And maybe see out of our own eyes in a new way." He watched me flap my mouth open and closed a few times. "You could come in as you are, you know. You don't have to cross-dress. It's just a party. And you already know some of the other kids."

I shook my head and repeated, "No, thanks. Um, thanks anyway. Uh, have fun." I turned quickly to get away and tripped right over that rock I'd rolled over to the window, and the scrape on my chin from where I hit the ground was with me for a couple of weeks afterward. Stumbling to my feet, I threw one more glance at Griffin. He stood where he was, and I could tell he wasn't laughing at me. He was smiling, but that was all.

My truck was to the west, but instead of turning left from the meeting house I went straight, maybe because the edge of the woods on the north side of the clearing where the houses were would provide some cover. Once I was safely behind a tree, I couldn't quite bring myself to leave. Seeing Griffin dressed like that, made up like a girl, had shocked me at first. But as the image lingered—and it lingered, all right—the shocked feeling morphed into something more like fascination. Still a little creepy, but I felt a tension, almost a quivering feeling. It was not altogether unpleasant.

I rubbed my chin and felt for moisture; not much blood, I decided, just a bad scrape.

Calmer now, I reasoned that if practically everyone was at the party, there wouldn't be a lot of people in the houses. I decided to walk around a little in the dark and get more of a sense of the place. I'd looked at it from Google Earth, and all-told there were about fifteen houses, different shapes and sizes. Now that I was here in person, I could see that lots of them had the dead and dying remnants of what must have been vegetable or flower gardens where townies would have had a front lawn or a back yard.

By the time I'd made a full circuit of the area, I'd discovered that on the far side of where the houses were, opposite the entrance from the highway, there was a huge field. Part of it had been planted, evidently with corn, but there was a large area in the northwest corner near where

I'd hidden that was open. And in the middle of this was an unlit bonfire, dead cornstalks all leaning into a peak. From where I stood, I could hear slight rattling as a light breeze toyed with the tattered, dried leaves of the cornstalks.

I sat on the ground, leaned against a tree, and let my mind wander. What, exactly, did I think I was doing here? Why had I come? True, I'd been haunted by Griffin's image, by the very idea of Griffin, ever since that day in the showers. I had no way of knowing whether Griffin might feel about me the way I felt about him, though after that Rob Lowe/James Dean comment, maybe it would be reasonable to feel encouraged. And he might have started to cotton to the fact that I was kind of fixated on him. I just wasn't sure why my fascination had started. I'd known Griffin most of my life, or had at least been aware of him. But it was only recently that I'd begun to dream about him.

My favorite dream, which I'd tried to reconstruct (without success) as I'd fallen asleep almost every night since I'd had it, was climbing the boughs of that tree on Griffin's back. In the dream, he was even taller, and strong, and I believed he had the answers to questions everyone else was struggling even to frame: Who am I, *why* am I, what am I doing here, what should I do with my life, what happens when it's over? I climbed the branches, and the tree that was Griffin seemed to go on and on. I didn't tire, climbing, but I did begin to feel more and more driven, as though the tree were growing at a rate barely faster than I was climbing. But finally I reached his neck.

I could make out in stark detail the silver metal bits he wears poked through holes all up his left ear, from the spider on the lobe (which seemed alive in the dream) to the tiny feather, to the skull, and finally, close to the top, a silver spiral that pierced the ear in three places. I bit into his neck, just a little, and his head arched back, mouth open, eyes shut, a kind of ecstasy apparent on his face. He turned toward me and opened his green eyes. My hands gripped his hair, and our mouths clamped onto each other, desperate, seeking.

And then I was awake, a wet mess in my pajamas and tears in my eyes.

I swore into my pillow, mourning the end of the dream, wanting more than anything else to get back into it again, to a place where Griffin's body and mine could merge in some magical way I didn't understand but very much wanted to experience. Rolling onto my side, I pacified my cheated dick with my hand. There was no way to pacify how I felt.

Suddenly the party noise grew louder, and I realized that the door had opened, and people were pouring out through it. From here, I couldn't pick Griffin out, or Silver Shaw or Ronan Coulter, but it almost looked like a perfectly normal crowd—small clusters forming and reforming as different conversations started up. Several people carried a small pumpkin or a gourd, carved with different versions of a grimacing face, each with a burning candle inside.

I hid behind my tree and watched as the crowd moved away from the meeting area and toward the bonfire waiting to be lit, and they formed a large circle all around it. Then they began chanting something, I don't know what, in relative unison. Sounded like nonsense words. It left me feeling totally creepy, and the bugs were back under my skin again. After a couple of minutes, the people holding the pumpkins approached the teepee of cornstalks and gently tossed the burning faces into the center, and within seconds fire nearly erupted from inside. Everyone stood, silent, watching the fire grow. After a few minutes, they joined hands and began to walk slowly around the fire, and chanting began again, in English this time. I caught only a few phrases:

Welcome, Samhain, dark twin of Beltane... Summer's end... Death of the old year... Chaos ... Doorway for the dead.

Then a low, tuneless humming began. The villagers walked and hummed and walked and hummed, trance-like, for a long time. My gaze followed the smoke as it rose above the fire. Once my eyes adjusted from the glare of the fire I could see the dark bowl of the night sky, stars twinkling across it, like some kind of blue-black velvet cloak decorated with diamonds.

When I looked down again I saw the villagers embracing each other, two at a time. Suddenly they weren't just costumed party-goers. Something told me that what I was seeing was an exchange of real warmth, maybe even love. Now there were no more bugs, and no more worry about danger. Now there was no more fear. Instead, there was a sadness that felt really deep. I felt painfully isolated, like that warmth was not something I had access to, a sense of belonging that I don't have anywhere—not here, not at home, and certainly not in the church I go to every Sunday with my supposed family. It hurt. It hurt a lot.

Eventually all but three people left the fire, and they took up positions beside it with buckets, full of something that was probably water. I stayed for several more minutes, watching the silent sentinels who stood by the dying fire. It seemed likely that nothing much more was gonna happen tonight, so I headed home.

The next day, someone found the mutilated body of a black cat beside the high school's main entrance. On the other side of the door was a crude face with huge vampire teeth, drawn in blood. And under it—also in blood—were the initials GH.

My clandestine visit to the village haunted me as strongly as my dreams about Griffin. I couldn't bring myself to believe that he'd been responsible for the dead cat. After all, I hadn't seen anything like that, not even remotely, when I'd spied on the villagers' Halloween celebrations. Maybe some of what I'd seen had made me uncomfortable, but I couldn't exactly say it was in a bad way. Plus, if Griffin *had* killed that cat, why on earth would he draw vampire teeth on that face or sign "GH" on it? One thing was certain: I wasn't afraid. I wasn't afraid of the village, or the people in it, or what they did when townies weren't looking. I wasn't afraid.

Put all this together and it was probably unavoidable that I'd go from being fixated on Griffin to being obsessed by him. Any time there was a school function, I looked for him. I even scoured the crowds in the bleachers at the football game on Thanksgiving, not really expecting to see him; the village kids didn't participate in the school's extra curricular activities.

Dad and Stu, of course, were thrilled that it was a home game. Stu went to Himlen High, like me. He was even on the football team—which I'm certainly not—though I don't recall that his performance was more than average. As far as I know, he's not planning to leave Himlen to go anyplace; if he and Patty do end up getting married, someday their kids will go here. So he's still kind of invested in his alma mater.

It was not my choice to go with Stu and Dad to the game. I'd have preferred to stay home and work on Thanksgiving dinner. But the event is seen as just this side of some kind of rite of passage, even for those not on the field. And I suspect that in Stu's mind, if he could get me to take football seriously, there was some hope of getting me to be a real man after all. It would have done me no good to list the football players and other athletic professionals who'd come out as gay in the past couple of years.

Dad had pretty much given up by this point, I think. Not Stu. I saw him cringe any time I did or said something

41

he considered "too gay." Like, cooking. He thinks guys shouldn't cook, evidently. I'd made pies the night before the game, and that probably gave him the creeps, so he made a big fuss about my going to the game. Sometimes it's just easier to go along.

I got bored somewhere in the middle of the first half and told Dad I was gonna go talk to some kids in my class (a lie; not many kids in my class talk to me these days, or maybe it's me who doesn't talk to them, and Brad was on the field). Telling myself that I wasn't lonely and that I actually enjoyed this marginalization (another lie), I wandered around the uninhabited top rows of the bleachers for a bit, examined the overcast sky in vain for rain, examined the crowd in vain for a sign of any Holyoke, and eventually I worked my way down to the ground and under the bleachers.

Had I known about the show down there, I would have descended sooner. There were three couples, all boy-girl (of course), in different corners from where I was, making out big-time. A few articles of clothing had body parts more on them than in them. At first, this carnality captured all my attention. But then I noticed there was someone across from me, sitting on the ground at the other end of the bleachers, also watching the show. Griffin Holyoke.

He saw me looking at him and grinned. As I watched in disbelief, he got up and came around the edge of the space toward me, careful not to call attention to himself or disturb any of the activity. He leaned against the other side of the support post I was leaning on, and although we both looked at the show, all my attention was on him.

Maybe five minutes went by, and one couple was—I swear—very close to ultimate consummation, when I heard Griffin's voice, low and silky. "It's amazing how fascinating something so repetitive can be. Don't you think?" And he turned to look at me.

My eyes caught on the silver ring pierced through his

right eyebrow. Not having a clue how to respond, I just shrugged.

He said, "Not a big sports fan?" I shook my head. "Me neither. I just come for *this* show."

"You what?"

He smiled and jerked his chin toward the couples. "Never miss a game." He watched my face as I tried to keep my eyes from widening too obviously. "You had enough yet? Wanna go someplace we can talk?"

Did I ever. We sat on the ground behind the bleachers, the sounds of the game present but not front-and-center, and shredded grass blades. I couldn't think of anything to say, and my pile grew faster than his. Finally he leaned back, elbows supporting him from behind.

"I don't want you to think it's a problem or anything," he told me, looking around at nothing in particular, "but I know you hung around on Samhain, after I saw you."

"Samhain? Oh, right. Halloween." He didn't sound mad...

"You can ask me about it if you want. I don't mind that you're curious."

I was more curious how he knew I had hung around, but I decided against going there. I thought back to that night and my thoughts landed on the fire. It wasn't especially odd that someone would have a bonfire on Halloween, but what I'd seen had been more than a bunch of people having a fun fire. I didn't know how to ask about the feelings that had caused me so much pain, so I asked, "What was that chanting about, at the fire?"

"Fire is transformative. It changes one kind of matter into another through energy. Samhain is the border between one thing and another, so the fire represents the transformation. And, of course, it's the end of harvest season, when the old corn stalks have done their job, and cold weather is coming on. Now that we have corn, what we need is warmth. So fire transforms food production into heat. We were expressing gratitude to corn, and to fire."

I was actually a little surprised that he was prepared to be so specific about this stuff. So I asked another question. "But I heard something about chaos, and a doorway for the dead."

He nodded. "It's like the Christian tradition, All Saints Day. Only the church changed it from All Souls Day, which is what it used to be. It's a brief time, a few hours, between what was and what will be, for the dead to walk with the living."

Okay, creepy. "And the chaos?"

He laughed. "Well, it's a pretty chaotic picture, don't you think? Dead people walking around with the living? And when the time is up, things have to go back to normal again."

I was almost afraid to ask this, but it seemed unavoidable. "Do you know who killed that black cat on Halloween? The one they found at the school?"

"As a matter of fact, I have my suspicions. But I don't know for sure. All I know is it wasn't me."

That was a relief, even if I hadn't believed he'd done it. But there was a related question I needed an answer to. "And, do you, like, worship the devil, or anything?"

He scowled. "Shit, Jesse, you saw everything we did on your Halloween. That would have been the time for that kind of ridiculousness. Did you see or hear anything about a devil or a demon, anything like that?"

"Well... no."

"Exactly. Pagans don't even acknowledge this concept you refer to as 'the devil.'"

"So, but—are you Christian?"

"No. *Pagan*. Paganism predates Christianity. And Christianity stole a lot of the Pagan traditions and rituals when it was busy trying to convert everyone in Europe. The whole evergreen thing? The Yule log? Giving presents and singing carols and picking bright red holly berries? Those are all Pagan traditions. Christians stole them." He sounded almost like there was anger in there someplace. I didn't think it was directed at me, exactly, but I didn't want him to be angry.

I went back to Samhain and did my best to sound like I had taken what he'd said seriously. "So, have you ever seen any of the souls who came through the doorway?"

He relaxed again. "Not me, no. Not yet, anyway. But my sister did. Last year, Gramma came to her. Selena— that's my sister—was thinking of moving to San Francisco. She'd fallen in love with Parker Harrison, and Parker's parents had kicked him out when he came out to them. He moved to California, and he asked Selena to go with him. Gramma told Selena she should follow her heart. So she did."

This made no sense to me. "I thought Parker Harrison was a girl."

"Parker identifies as gender queer. He grew up as a girl, but he transitioned in his late teens. Now, people who meet him for the first time see him as a man."

"Transitioned? Like, sex change?"

Griffin shook his head. "No; just started living life as a man lives life. Clothing, typical actions, haircut, that sort of thing."

I still wasn't able to make a lot of sense out of this. "How does Selena see him?"

"As Parker." I thought he'd say more, but he didn't.

"I don't know what that means. Is Selena gay or not?"

Griffin's smile was cryptic. "She's bisexual. As she puts it, 'I fell in love with the person, not the plumbing.'"

Wow. Like, wow. And I thought my situation was uncommon. My idea of bisexuals was that they want everything, so one person would never quite be enough for them. Maybe this made sense for Selena, then; Parker was kind of both. "Your folks don't mind?"

"Mind what? That she moved away?"

45

"About her being bisexual."

One side of his mouth curled up in a half-smile. "You Christians. You get upset over the silliest things."

I could feel my heart beating faster. If Pagans were so open about this, and if Griffin was gay, there was hope for me with him. But even if the townie kids knew about me, that didn't mean the village kids would know, what with that line of demarcation between our respective groups being so sharp. In fact, saying something about me seemed like the best way to find out about him. It was an opening, and all I had to do is say, *You know I'm gay, right?* But I hesitated too long, and it got awkward.

My next thoughts were to wonder whether the Harrisons were more upset that Parker was gender queer or that "he" had taken up with a freak. Because even if Griffin were a girl I know my folks would not want me to get involved with him, because he's a freak. But instead I moved to a related but safer subject. "So, under the bleachers there. You, uh, you come here a lot?"

He laughed at my facetious use of the cliché, and I relaxed a little. "Sure. Sex is great. I'm still trying to understand why it's so fascinating, and how the spiritual aspects come into it. Dad says I'm still too testosterone-poisoned to see through the fog of cum, and it will be a while before I can balance things out."

Wow. His dad talks to him like that? Really? I set that aside in favor of something he'd said about sex that puzzled me. "Okay, you'll have to explain that to me. I mean, I get the idea of being with someone you love, but—spiritual?"

"Sure. It's like… well, my dad says it's like being so close, not just physically but also spiritually, that during the physical act, there's this compelling desire to actually become one being. And, I mean, as Pagans, we see the diversity around us, but really we see it all as only part of the picture. Because we're all one with the Goddess, ultimately. Well, in my kind of Paganism, anyway; not all

Pagan practices revolve around a goddess figure. But anyway, the spiritual part of sex is like having a taste of that feeling—of being one with everything—but with one person at a time."

That feeling I'd had in the dream, when Griffin and I had kissed, washed over me in a huge wave. Maybe that was the spiritual aspect. But I wasn't about to bring that up, and I wasn't prepared to discuss goddesses, either. So I stayed with what I could connect with.

"Man, I can't believe you and your dad talk about it like that. Or at all. I mean, when my dad told me about, you know, the birds and the bees, he didn't go into a lot of detail, and he didn't talk about anything spiritual. I think he mentioned love, but that was it."

"What a weird expression. 'The birds and the bees.' What the hell is that supposed to mean, anyway? It's just avoiding saying what you're really talking about. Sex is good, Jesse. Sex is something you should want. Something you should enjoy."

I had to ask. "Have you ever done it?"

"Only with myself, so far. But when I'm eighteen, my dad says he'll to talk to me about what my mom taught him."

This blew my mind on so many levels I wasn't sure which one to focus on. I landed on the angle that seemed to spell disaster for my hopes. "You mean, about sex with a woman?"

"Of course. Well, of course, for me, that is. Interesting that you would ask. Are you—are you more interested in sex with a man?"

So he didn't know. *Do it fast, Jesse. Just rip off the Band-Aid.* "Yes."

He nodded. "Good to know."

It seemed like he genuinely hadn't been aware before I'd told him. This didn't say much about what the other kids knew, though; Griffin didn't exactly hang with the townie

47

kids. "And… you don't mind?"

He laughed again, and I was beginning to really love that sound, even if he was interested in women, not men. Not me. "Not as long as you don't try and make out with me, no. In fact, it lessens the competition. Every guy who's gay is one less guy I have to compete with for straight girls."

At this point the sounds of the half-time show—the school band sounding vague about the actual notes—registered in my brain. And, evidently, in Griffin's, too.

He clambered to his feet. "Think I'll head home. Mom could use some help getting ready for dinner. You?"

I shrugged. "I'd rather do that, actually." Hell, maybe I just would, game or no game. I stood as well. "Yeah. Think I'll head home. I love cooking."

"I can give you a lift. I drove myself over. Got my intermediate last week."

"Great! Yeah. Thanks. My brother made me ride over with him and my dad. Is it your own car?"

He nodded, and I pulled out my phone and texted Dad to tell him I'd meet them at home; I figured he'd put up less of a stink than Stu at my abandoning this sacred ground prematurely.

Griffin and I walked together to his car, a blue Toyota sedan that had seen better days, and it seemed like my feet weren't quite touching ground. Maybe we'd never be, you know, lovers or whatever it's called, but we could be friends. Hell, we were well on our way to being friends. I couldn't have said why that should matter, now that I knew he'd never feel about me the way I felt about him, but it did. Part of it might have been that the Pagans accept gay people. But part of it was that I'd felt haunted by that bonfire I'd witnessed, and by that feeling of belonging that they all seemed to have. A feeling I've never had. A feeling I never expected to have.

I did feel a little guilty about walking out on a game

Brad was playing in, but he could give me a blow-by-blow account of it later. I didn't usually go to games anyway.

On the short drive to my house, Griffin chatted easily about having Selena and Parker come for the holiday. "Parker will probably feel kinda weird, being back in his home town and not able to see his folks, but I think being with us will be better than not coming at all. And we're his family now."

The idea that the Holyokes would circle the wagons around their daughter's gender queer partner so protectively stunned me. And there didn't seem to be any tension at all among the villagers around the fact that Selena had taken up with a townie.

I asked, "What will you do to help your mom? Do you cook?"

"Ha. She won't let me near the stove. I've ruined more pans... Don't know why I'm so bad at it. I get distracted, I guess, and things get away from me. She has me wash pans and utensils when she's done with them, set the table, that kind of thing. You cook, you said?"

"Yeah. Better than my mom. I like to, you know, just throw things together and see if they work."

"Really. And your mom didn't teach you to do that?"

"No way! 'Season to taste' sends her into a tizzy." He laughed, and then there was silence. So I said, "Last night I made two pies. Pumpkin and apple."

"Well, I couldn't do that, but it doesn't seem like it would take an expert."

"Ah, but you haven't tasted my lard crust. And I started with an actual pumpkin, not a can. And the pumpkin pie recipe is mine."

"Yours? What does that mean?"

What did that mean? I don't really use a recipe; I just smell and taste and add stuff. To answer his question, I told him about my first pumpkin pie. "Whenever my mom was cooking, I'd always try to stick my finger into whatever she was making, and she'd always try to stop me. So this one time, when I was about nine years old, I got a taste of pumpkin pie batter from the bowl. Before she could yell, I told her it needed more spices."

I glanced at Griffin to be sure I hadn't lost him. His eyes were on the road, but I could tell he was listening. "She said, 'Fine. You just put in whatever you think it needs.' Probably thought this would teach me some kind of lesson. And she stood back while I added some cinnamon, tasted, then some clove, tasted, more clove. Some nutmeg. She tried to draw the line when I reached for the cardamom. 'I don't even know where I got that stuff! You can't put it in the pie!' But I did. And it was really good. So instead of having the worst pumpkin pie ever, we had the best."

Griffin's laugh was so real, so honest. That's the best way to describe it. And I loved that I had brought it out of him. But he didn't say anything else, and like some third grader desperate for Teacher's attention, I told him more. I couldn't stop myself, even though we were at my house.

"I made cranberry sauce last night, too. Started with raw berries. I used only half the sugar the recipe called for, and I added vanilla. My own idea."

He pulled up along the side of the road and grinned at me. My eyes caught on his and I almost didn't hear him say, "Get in there and have your way with the stuffing, then. Save it from the mediocrity of a recipe."

I was about to get out when I noticed something hanging from the rear view mirror, and my dad's angry rant about heathens and goddesses crashed into my brain. So this was the very car Dad had refurbished. I nodded toward the symbol, which looked like three pointed ovals overlapping, each pointing in a different direction, with a circle joining them together at the widest parts of the ovals.

"Griffin? What's that?"

"Depends on who answers." He stopped; I wanted him

50

to go on.

"I'm asking you."

"Then it's virgin, mother, and crone. My Paganism sees the Goddess as representing life in all its aspects, from innocence through to wisdom."

"*Your* Paganism?"

"Remember I told you that not all Paganism is centered around the Goddess. Mine is."

"You mean, people in the village see it that way?"

He shook his head. "No. I mean me. We don't all have to worship the same. We're not like the rigid Judeo-Christian traditions. And, by the way, this symbol? We call it the triquetra. It was ours, first. Christianity adopted its mind-body-spirit symbolism and called it the trinity."

I didn't want that resentment I'd heard earlier about Christianity stealing Pagan traditions to creep in again. Stepping out of the car I said, "That makes sense, actually. Okay, well, see you Monday."

I pushed the car door closed and watched him drive off, praying that my need for his attention hadn't seemed as obvious to him as it had to me. Praying also that he didn't hold me in any way responsible for the thefts Christianity seems to have committed.

Mom was surprised to see me. "Home team doing so badly you couldn't bear to watch?"

I didn't tell her I had no idea what the score had been when I'd left. "Nah. I'm just not that fond of seeing guys run around in lumpy costumes bashing each other into a pulp over some ball that isn't even a ball. It's an oval. What's with that, anyway?" I didn't care about the ball being oval. I just wanted to distract her from thoughts about why a red-blooded Oklahoma boy wouldn't love football. At least she appreciates my talents in the kitchen, and she's never discouraged me from using them.

I asked, "What can I help with?"

She was pulling things out of the fridge. "You can peel the potatoes and get them into some water." I lifted the top off a casserole dish on the counter. "Leave that alone, Jesse. It's extra stuffing. It goes into the oven as soon as the bird comes out."

So of course I tasted it. "Needs more rosemary. And sage. And salt."

She grinned. "Up to your old tricks?"

"Let me try?"

She stopped what she was doing to look at me. "Jesse, do you understand how traditional this meal is? And how important it is to your whole family that it's pretty much the same every year?"

"I get that, yeah. I don't have anything radical in mind." And I didn't need reminding how important "traditional" ways of living are to everyone around me.

She took in a deep breath, let it out slowly, waved a hand in the air. "All right. But I'm warning you, your father will be bullcrap mad if you ruin it."

While I doctored the stuffing, Mom peeled the potatoes, telling me about this bottle of port Dad had bought. "I don't know what he was thinking. He heard someplace that it was a great thing to have after Thanksgiving dinner. He'll probably have half a glass, and so will I, and the rest of the bottle will go to waste. Stu won't like it, and you're not getting more than a taste."

Port. Interesting. Stuffing stuffed back into its casserole, I told Mom I'd be right back, and I went to where Dad keeps his bourbon. Beside it was a bottle of ruby port. I opened it and tipped just a tiny taste into my mouth. Rich, just slightly sweet. I took a larger sip. Heady. I'd had red table wine a few times, but this was altogether different. I went back into the kitchen, grabbed a small jar, back to the port, and poured maybe half a cup into the jar for an idea I had concerning our dinner. By the time Dad reached for the bottle later, we'd have finished eating already, and I would have explained where the missing port had gone.

The last thing I did before sitting down to dinner was to fetch a cobalt blue bowl, one of Mom's favorite pieces, and I put the whipped butternut squash into it. The deep blue, bright orange contrast was gorgeous.

Of course, everything was a success. Even Dad asked for seconds on the cranberry sauce. Then, as he poured gravy over his third helping of stuffing, he asked Mom, "Diane, what's special about the gravy this year? It's different. I like it a lot."

This pissed me off. Dad knows that whenever anything "special" happens to our meals, I'm the one who made it that way, not Mom. She's an adequate cook. I'm going to be a great cook, and he knows that already.

Instead of repeating anything from that horrible day when I'd come out, instead of saying, *See? This is what I meant when I said you don't care what I'm interested in,* I said, "Dad, why don't you ever ask *me* a question like that? Why won't you ever give *me* credit? You know damn well that I'm always making changes to our recipes, and you always like it."

Before Dad's glare or Stu's could turn into one of our full-on battles, Mom stepped in. "Jesse, language. And temper. Please."

All the male members of the family breathed audibly for several seconds, and then Mom said, "*I'll* give you credit, Jesse. Please tell us what you've done to change today's recipes."

I let out one more noisy breath and spoke to Mom rather than Dad. "You know that bottle of port Dad brought home? The one you're worried will go to waste after tonight?"

Her eyes widened. "You didn't."

"I put it in the gravy. Before I put the cornstarch in.

53

Only about half a cup. I boiled it a few minutes so the alcohol would burn off."

"And what magic, pray tell, did you work on the cranberry sauce?"

She was amazed I'd halved the sugar; the vanilla made it taste sweeter than it was. I'm not even sure where all these ideas come from. I've wanted to try the cranberry sauce idea for a while. But port in the gravy? I hadn't even known Dad had bought port until today. The only thing I could figure was that it felt sort of like I was trying to impress someone who wasn't even there.

Chapter Three

If I'd thought that the friendly chat Griffin and I had had on Thanksgiving was going to translate into being buddies at school or anywhere else, I would have been wrong. He didn't avoid me or anything, but nothing changed in the other direction, either. And I don't think it was just me; that is, I don't think that my being afraid he'd see me as needy made me avoid him. It just wasn't any different.

It was about a week before Christmas vacation that Brad didn't come to school for two days in a row. One day, no big deal. But two, without hearing from him? So at lunch Friday I sent him a text.

S'up u OK?

I heard nothing back all afternoon, and my after-school phone call went right to voicemail. So I called home to let Mom know I was going over to Brad's. I didn't much like going to his house since the accident; with Mr. Everett hanging around the place it felt gloomy and sad. Even Brad's younger sisters tended to hide out upstairs in the bedroom they share, if they were home at all.

Mrs. Everett's car and her husband's truck were in the driveway; Brad doesn't have wheels of his own. As usual when I go there, I went around to the back door and knocked. Of course, typically Brad would know I was coming, and he'd be listening for me, maybe even in the kitchen. No one answered, even though I could see that there were lights on, so I knocked a couple more times before I gave up and went to ring the front doorbell. No answer on the first ring, so I stepped back to look at the windows. There was a light on in Brad's room; WTF?

This was feeling really weird, now. He doesn't answer my text, he doesn't take my call, and now, even though there must be someone at home, they're ignoring knocks and doorbells? I was getting worried. So I rang the bell again. And again. Then I heard a mans' voice, no doubt Mr. Everett, yelling something.

Finally Mrs. Everett came to the door. She had her hair kind of brushed forward, and she was wearing sunglasses, of all things. Indoors, in December? She didn't speak.

"Is Brad home?" I asked, feeling like maybe this had been a bad idea. I could hear the drone of the television; no doubt Mr. Everett was in his usual chair, staring at it.

"I'm sorry, Jesse. He can't see you right now."

Behind her, I caught a motion near the top of the stairway, which I could just see from where I stood. It was Brad, with a cast on his left arm. He didn't come all the way down the stairs.

"Let him in," he said, his voice sounding odd, strained.

"Brad—" Mrs. Everett seemed reluctant.

"Let him in, damn it!"

I don't think I've ever heard Brad swear in front of his mother before. But rather than yell at him, she glanced toward the living room, where I know the TV is, like something might come flying at her from that direction. As she turned her head, I saw that the side of her face was all bruised. Speaking of TV, I've seen enough of it to know that sunglasses over bruises usually mean something's happened that the person wants to hide, and the way she'd turned toward the living room left me with no doubt about what had happened to her. But what about Brad?

Mrs. Everett stepped aside, maybe thinking letting me in would be less dangerous than having Brad shout swear words. I headed up the stairs as quickly as I could, not wanting to find out whether Mr. Everett wasn't happy about something. Brad said nothing until we were in his room, door shut firmly. We stood there staring at each other for maybe ten seconds before he spoke.

"Sorry I didn't text you earlier. Didn't know what to say." Which is also probably why he didn't answer my call.

"What's going on?" I didn't want to assume, though it seemed pretty obvious.

Brad moved toward his bed, I think about to throw himself onto it like I've seen him do so many times before, but at the last second he must have realized the broken arm would be a problem. So he sat on the edge of the mattress. I sat in his desk chair.

He kept his voice low. "Mom doesn't want anyone to know, so don't go talking about this."

I shook my head.

He let out a long breath, and then, eyes on the fingers of his right hand as it twitched nervously on his thigh, he said, "My dad was hitting my mom. I tried to stop him. He shocked me with that fucking cattle prod and pushed me down the cellar stairs."

All that, and my mind landed on one thing: "Cattle prod?"

"His cane. You've forgotten he uses a zap cane?" Brad's sounded antagonistic.

"You never told me it was a—what is a zap cane, anyway?"

Brad heaved a sigh. "Sorry. I'm a little on edge, as you can imagine. A zap cane is basically a cattle prod. When you turn on the juice, it shoots some outrageous number of volts into anyone it touches."

"Christ. Like, a Taser or something?"

"A lot like that, yeah."

"But—why? Why can't he just use a regular cane?"

"He had one at first. But one day he was at the liquor store, buying more beer, when that bum who hangs around everywhere—Stokes? Harry Stokes?—decided it would be fun to knock it out from under him. I thought he was gonna burst something, he was so mad. It was the first time I was actually a little afraid of what he might do to us at home. But instead of beating on anyone, he ordered the zap cane."

"Jesus."

"Anyway, Sally called the cops when she heard me thudding all the way to the bottom of the cellar stairs. She and Terree had locked themselves in their room when the shouting started."

"So… is he out on bail, or something?"

Brad shook his head. "Mom wouldn't press charges for hitting her, and she made me hide in the basement when the cops got here so they wouldn't see me. Then she had her sister take me to the hospital. Called it an accident."

Even though Brad's kind of big, his dad is bigger. I wouldn't want him hitting *me*. So I asked, "What d'you think the chances are it'll happen again?"

Brad got up and paced the room a few times, waving his right arm in the air. "Who knows? Pretty damn good, I'd say. It started after the accident, and it's gotten worse and worse since he ran out of beer."

Oh, yeah; I'd forgotten that Brad's house had sometimes smelled like whatever it is that makes beer smelly. Mr. Everett used to make his own, in the basement he tossed Brad down to. It must be harder for him to go up and down the stairs now, and I'll bet he can't carry anything.

My brain was dancing around, trying to come up with something to say. Like, *What are you gonna do if he hits her again?* And, *Does he ever hit your sisters? Has he hit you before?* Or just plain, *What the fuck are you gonna do?* Rather than stare at Brad while these questions bounced around my brain, I glanced over to the shelf above his desk where he keeps his best rockhounding specimens. Many times I've picked one of them up to watch it catch the light. My favorite is this clear quartz spear-like thing, maybe three inches long with six sides, coming up to a sharp point, stuck at about a ninety-degree angle from a mass of cloudy white rock. But this wasn't the time to be focusing on pretty things.

"Man." I looked him, shook my head. "D'you know what set him off?"

"Everything sets him off!" Brad glared at me, his right hand clenching and unclenching.

"So this has happened before? Or, some of it, at least?"

He sat down again. "It's never been this bad. And if he does that to her again, I swear I'll kill him."

I nodded; what could I say? "Does anyone at school know?"

"Just about the broken arm. I'll be back at school on Monday." His voice took on a sarcastic tone. "Can't have anyone suspecting anything, can we?"

"Just four more days of school. Next Friday starts Christmas break." I was thinking that would be good; he wouldn't have to be at school and pretend all was well. But I wasn't thinking it through.

"Don't remind me. It means I won't have someplace to go all day."

"You could come to my house. We can watch movies, make popcorn, play video games."

"Thanks, maybe some of the time. But I need to be here when Mom is. Watch out for her."

"He doesn't hurt Sally or Terree, then?"

Brad froze. "He'd fucking better not."

"Can you take the batteries out of that cane when he's not using it?"

"He takes it everywhere. Never loses sight of the thing. And it doesn't use batteries; there's a wall charger."

"Then hide that."

"Don't think I haven't thought about it."

"And…?"

One side of his mouth turned up; at least I got a half smile out of him. "If only. But he didn't hit Mom with the cane. That's only part of the problem."

"Anything I can do?" I didn't know what else to say.

"You can tell me what's going on at school. Anything interesting happen?"

We talked for a while longer, and then there was a quiet knock on the door, and it opened. Mrs. Everett said, "Supper, Brad. Probably time you went home, Jesse. Isn't it your suppertime, too?"

"Yes, ma'am. I'll head out right away."

She left, Brad and I stood, and he surprised the hell out of me my wrapping his right arm around my neck. We had one of those hips-apart-two-slaps-on-the-back kind of guy hugs.

Brad said, "I'll see how things are here tomorrow. I think Mom's working at the restaurant through supper, and I'll have to help the girls get supper ready here, but maybe I can come over for a bit, earlier. Be good to get out of here."

"Just give a holler."

"Remember. Don't say anything. Not even to your folks."

"Promise. I'll just tell them about the 'accident' in case you can come over. The cast, you know."

"Right."

On the way downstairs, we both practically tip-toed. I peeked into the living room and saw that Mr. Everett was still glued to the TV, a beer can in one hand. Purchased beer. He didn't look toward me, so I decided against saying anything and maybe setting him off. Mrs. Everett was in the kitchen, and it felt odd not to call to her on my way out. I just said, "See you," to Brad, quietly.

On my way home I tried to imagine sitting down at the dinner table with someone who had beaten my mom, zapped me, and thrown me down a staircase. Things weren't great at home, for sure, but they could be worse.

Mom was in the kitchen when I got home, and I gave her a hug.

"What's this for?" she asked, a smile in her voice.

"Just because. I'll go wash my hands. Need any help with dinner?"

"You can mash the potatoes if you promise not to add any secret ingredients."

"Aw, what's the fun in that?" But I did mash them. And I didn't add anything she wouldn't have put in.

That Sunday, sitting in our usual pew with my folks and Stu (who made a point of not sitting beside me), I sent up a prayer. It was part thanks for my mom and part supplication for Brad, for his dad to calm down, for his family to get together again. Maybe my dad wasn't violent, but I could sure understand what it felt like to have your family in a shambles. I looked over at the pew where they sat, glad that at least Mr. Everett came to church with them, hoping it wasn't just for appearances. Maybe his injury would keep him from tramping through the woods with Brad in search of crystals, but he could still be a good father if he chose.

All the good feelings I'd had praying for Brad's family went flying through the clear parts of the stained glass windows by the end of the sermon. Reverend Gilman, in his infinite wisdom, decided to launch his rant from recent news items about the rights of gay people to marry. To support his anti-gay position, he started with Genesis where God's busy creating Eve out of one of Adam's ribs, and when he got to that bit about a man leaving his father and mother to go be with his wife, he swept the congregation with the kind of scowl that demands agreement. Now, I'd never really thought about this before; probably I've been too cowed generally by what the Bible says about homosexuality. But suddenly it hit me that these verses made no sense. I mean, the only father Adam ("man") has is God, and he has no mother at all. So—who the fuck is he leaving? And how did this verse get stuck into the middle of a story where it has no meaning?

In a kind of epiphany-like alertness I turned toward my parents, hoping for—I don't know for what. But what I saw was my dad, nodding away as if to say, "Right on, Rev! Amen! Give those homos what for!"

I shrank into myself, feeling like I'd been slugged in the gut.

When I was little, my idea of Jesus was that he was full of love that he wanted to share with everyone. Love that came from God. But I swear, the older I get, the less loving it feels here, in church. And the more isolated and alone it makes me feel.

We have this six-foot artificial Christmas tree that we drag out every year and piece together, and then pull apart to store away in January. It's not as bad as it sounds, though, because every December it's like welcoming an old friend, and every year I get better at fixing it up (read: decorating it) so that you don't notice the fakeness of the bristles. This year I used a double strand of tiny white lights, twisted together and hung so that they created a clear spiral from top to bottom. Then I hung all the red ornaments from the wires to exaggerate the spiral. The other ornaments—no red ones—I hung in size order, smaller ones near the top, colors all mixed up. It would have been better if I could have bought a whole bunch of new ornaments, but at least Mom let me buy the light strands. And as always, Stu put the tree-top angel on. Patty said it was the prettiest tree she'd ever seen. I think she overstated things a little, but it was a nice thing to say.

I liked Patty; she always treated me like a person, not just her boyfriend's younger brother. Which is probably why I'd been wondering whether Stu had told her about me. Dad had told him to keep the "shame" in the family, but

Patty was practically family and likely to be legally so before another year went by. How would she react? Would she be more like Stu or Mom? And was I an idiot to hope she'd react even better than Mom had?

Two days before Christmas, Stu was working at the garage with Dad when Patty showed up at the front door with a plastic shopping bag, and I let her in. She had on one of those knit hats that look like animal heads, and hers was a tiger—orange with black stripes, yarn whiskers, perky little ears complete with the white spots on the back. It should have looked awful over her red hair, but somehow the way her short hair flipped up from under the lower edges of the hat, and the freckled face that makes Stu call her his little pixie, brought the look together in a way someone else might not have been able to pull off. She looked adorable.

"Stu's not here," I told her.

"Good! I was looking for you, anyway. Can we go downstairs? I need your help with something." She stopped in front of the special case where Mom keeps the most expensive Hummel pieces she's bought over the years. "What does Stu think of these, Jesse?"

"Stu?" I shrugged. "No idea. I don't think I've heard him say anything one way or another. Why?"

"Just wondering what his thoughts might be about spending money on this kind of thing. You know, something that doesn't put food on the table or pay the bills. Well, let's get downstairs."

Deciding against repeating what Dad had said about the Hummels, I set her question aside as something a girl might ask about a guy she was thinking of marrying, and followed her.

Patty emptied the shopping bag onto the ping pong table and then picked up a beautiful navy-blue box. Smiling at me, she opened it. "This is my present for Stu. What do you think?"

It was a gorgeous watch. His typical watch needed to survive working at the garage, so it was practical but not a thing of beauty. Patty's gift would be something he might wear to his wedding.

"It's great. Really. But—what do you want me for?"

"I need your help wrapping it. I mean, I can wrap it, sure, but your presents always look so special. Would you do that for me?"

She pulled out a few different kinds of paper, different colors and styles of ribbons, scotch tape, even scissors. I sorted through the stuff, which wasn't bad, decided which paper and ribbon to use, and said, "I'll be right back."

Upstairs I searched the tree until I found the ornament that looked like a tiny clock, a red-painted box with a white face and green ivy-leaf hands that actually move if you push them with your finger. We'd had it for years, and one year the hands had fallen off. Stu had repaired it.

Back downstairs, Patty chatted about the plans she and Stu had for New Year's Eve while I worked on the wrapping, carefully folding tape back onto itself before placing it so it wouldn't show. Making sure my huge bow was securely in place, I tied the clock ornament around it.

Patty loved that touch. "That's perfect!"

As I cut a small rectangle of paper from the scraps and folded it in half, I told her about how Stu had fixed the hands. Then I had her write, "To Stu from Patty" on the paper and taped it onto the other side of the bow so that it could be opened and read.

We both looked at the final product, admiring it, and then she gave me a big hug.

I think it was the hug that made me brave enough to find out whether Stu had told her about me. "Can I ask you something?"

"Anything, Jesse. You know that."

"I—Has Stu said anything to you about me?"

"Like what? You mean about presents? You know I

couldn't say anything about—"

"No. Not that. Um... Look, forget it."

"Jesse? What is it? You look worried. Or sad. Maybe both. Please. Tell me."

I looked at her carefully. I saw concern. And—this was the clincher—I saw love.

"Has he told you I'm gay?"

He had not. I could tell immediately. She seemed stunned. Then, "No, Jesse, he hasn't." She took my arm and led me over to the couch. "How long has he known?"

"I told my folks back in September. A few days later, Dad told him."

I took another good look at her face. She was gazing across the room, obviously thinking something, remembering something.

"That explains a few things," she said. "I mean, about Stu. About some of his behavior, which has puzzled me a few times lately." She took my hand in hers. I was surprised, and I wasn't. It felt warm. It almost made me cry.

"How are *you*, Jesse?"

How was I? What a difficult question to answer. "I'm all right."

"How is it at home?" It was almost like she already knew.

"Mom's doing her best. Dad doesn't like it. He and I never got on all that well, anyway."

She nodded. She didn't ask about Stu; I figured she already had a pretty good idea. "Is there anyone you can talk to when things get tough?"

I shrugged. "My friend Brad knows. He's cool with it."

"Well, you can talk to me. You can talk to me about any of it, Jesse. I want you to know that."

I tried to say Thanks, but my voice wouldn't work.

"Do you want to talk about it now?"

I shook my head, and she let go of my hand and wrapped me in another warm hug. "You let me know if you want to talk, Jesse. Truly. Now, I have to dash. I have a few errands to run."

After this conversation, I had to reassess what had been going on with the kids at school. Believing that everyone was judging me, looking oddly at me, I had actually begun to suspect that Stu had somehow let the cat out of the bag. Brad had told me he hadn't even told Staci, and I'd believed him. That left the probable leak being Stu and the possibility that he was so angry about it that he'd made sure that I would suffer both at home and everywhere else, despite the shame. But if he had told anyone other than Patty, wouldn't he have told her, too? I strained my brain to try and recall when things had started to change at school. The only concrete thing I could come up with was that Lou and Chuck, Lou in particular, had started calling me faggot. Why that had started, I couldn't say, but I couldn't recall that I'd ever denied it. Just remembering how it made me feel caused me to cringe. So, what if they'd called me that in front of other kids, and I'd cringed, and I hadn't denied it? Would that have been enough to make people wonder?

It might have. It just might have.

The only thing that made my life seem less sucky was what had happened at Brad's house; it seemed worse than what was going on at mine. So the day after Christmas, I picked him up early in the afternoon for a long drive, to get him out of that house. He climbed into the passenger seat, sullen and hunched, staring straight ahead through the windshield. It must have pissed him off royally that he couldn't reasonably ask to drive. With standard transmission, the cast on his arm would get in the way enough that I wouldn't have wanted him to, and maybe he knew that.

"Let's get outta here," he grunted.

I figured, you know, things weren't great at his house

today. I headed south toward where we'd gone a few months ago. We weren't hunting rocks today, but it was a good drive.

Neither of us spoke for a few miles, and for some reason I found myself remembering the first time I'd shown Brad my truck, before I'd come out at home, before my world went berserk. Brad's really into the mechanics of vehicles. I'd parked in his driveway, and when he'd come out of the house he'd gone straight over to the truck.

"I gotta give this baby a good look."

Brad had circled slowly a couple of times around the truck, touching the paint here and there, running his hand inside the fender, bending down to check the exhaust configuration.

"Pop the hood," he told me, so I did. "Holy shit. Looks like Stu cleaned this engine out with a toothbrush. There's nothing here but pure truck."

He poked around a little, testing one thing and then another. Then he said, "This is a nice piece of work, Jesse. You're so god-damned lucky. Hope you know that."

That had felt true, once. Anyway, we'd made an arrangement that he could drive the truck sometimes, and even borrow it once in a while, if he helped with the upkeep. And he seemed determined—even delighted—to keep it looking and running as well as it had the day Stu had finished his work on it.

But he couldn't drive it today.

Brad asked, "Where are we going, anyway?"

"Thought I'd turn onto Holson Valley Road, maybe take a few of the back roads off that. If you wanna get out and look around, fine, or we can just keep driving. Sound good?"

"As long as we'll be gone for a while, it sounds great."

Maybe a quarter of a mile later, I said, "I'm not prying, or anything. Just want you to know that. But if you wanna talk about anything, you know..." I let that trail off.

He waited about ten seconds and then said, "Yeah. Thanks." But he said nothing else.

I was pretty sure I could keep him away from home for hours. I had plenty of gas, and I was fine with silence if that's what he needed.

Rather than stay on Route 270 all the way to Holson Valley Road, I turned west onto a road that's more of a track than a road and followed Cedar Creek for a while. Eventually it swung out onto Holson, and I drove west until Brad pointed toward a dirt road off to the right.

"Turn in here."

It was a different track from the one we'd gone down the time I'd come out to him. We bumped and jolted along until we came to a spot Brad pointed at where I could pull out of the way of anyone else crazy enough to drive down this path. I let the engine idle while Brad decided what he wanted to do next. Did he want to talk? Did he want to run farther into the woods and scream? Finally he opened his door and jumped out. I killed the engine and followed.

Brad headed through the trees and then down a slope, following a narrow trail that I wouldn't have known was a trail at all. There were rocks everywhere. The footing was pretty bad; you couldn't keep going without stepping on some of those rocks, and they were not all exactly stable.

The slope ended in a kind of marshy area, and we had to step carefully to avoid going up to our ankles in partially-frozen muck. Nothing looked like a trail to me at this point either, but Brad seemed to know where he was going, so I followed him as we climbed uphill past umpteen loblolly pines and along the base of a huge outcropping of jagged rock that towered over us on the right. We followed below a kind of low ridge for a bit, and then Brad turned to his right again, facing the ridge, and stopped. He seemed to be scouring the area for something.

Suddenly he pointed. "There."

"What, there? I don't see anything."

"See that opening?"

I squinted into the gloom. "I think so," I lied.

"That cave is one of the first places I looked for rocks. Didn't find anything big, but it's where I got hooked." I half thought he might move toward it, but he didn't.

I looked harder. "Any reason I can't get closer?" Maybe I'd be able to see it if I did.

Brad chuckled. "Go ahead. But make sure the owner isn't at home first."

"And that would be…"

"Well, the last time I was here, I was on my back on the ground in there, chiseling chunks of rock away from the wall, when the homeowner showed up." Brad looked at me, grinned, and nodded back toward the cave, which I still couldn't see. "I heard this low, nasty growl, and when I looked toward the entrance I was face to face with a bobcat."

Bobcats aren't very big, but they're notoriously ferocious and afraid of absolutely nothing. I turned fully around to see if one might be creeping up on us and stepped on a large flat rock that wobbled under me. I steadied myself and glanced nervously around for any signs of motion between the trees, listening for snapping twigs or crunching leaves on the forest floor.

"It won't do any good to watch for a bobcat, Jesse. You'd never see it before it sees you."

"What did you do when it saw you in its cave?"

"Threw a few rocks at it to get it to back off, then high-tailed it outta there." He turned back to the cave. "If I hadn't been in its cave, I wouldn't have been worried. They tend to avoid people. But once Dad and I saw a bear not far from here. It didn't come too close, 'cause we shouted and waved our arms."

I decided against checking to see if the bobcat was at home. "Anyplace else you wanna see? Look for some rocks, maybe?" I wanted to get away from this spot but wasn't sure that anything else would be safe, either. Standing still here was making me nervous.

"Give me a minute."

While he was considering things, I leaned over and brushed dead leaves off the wobbly stone. It was just a slab of something dark gray, less than an inch thick, a couple of feet long and maybe eighteen inches across. Mildly curious and still waiting for Brad, I heaved it over. In the middle of the underside, embedded deep in the gray, was a mixture of several oblong bits of bright white rock.

"Brad? What's this?"

"Just a slab of limestone. That thing in the middle is called a breccia. If the embedded stones were smooth instead of angular, it would be a conglomerate. Looks like white quartz." He leaned over it for a closer look. "That's an unusual formation, all the quartz in the middle of the slab like that."

"Something you might want to take?"

"Almost. It would be a royal hemorrhoid to get it out of here."

I bent over, got a good grip, and tested the weight.

"Hey, Jesse, not like that. Squat down, and lift with your legs."

That worked better, to be sure, but it was still heavy as sin. I decided against lifting it up completely; I wasn't even sure I could.

Brad exhaled loudly, looked up into the treetops, glanced into the distance ahead of us, and turned toward me. "Let's go back to the truck."

I did my best not to appear to be hurrying, but the idea of bears gave me prickles on the back of my neck.

Brad said nothing on the way back to Holson Valley Road, and he gave no indication about where he might want to go next, so I just continued the way we'd been going. He said nothing as we approached the intersection with Route 271. I pulled over to the side of the road a couple of hundred feet from the corner. It was almost three o'clock. I looked at Brad, but he was staring out the window. I figured, you know, I had promised him I'd keep him out. So I headed toward Sardis Lake. There are lots of little off-shoot roads from Route 2 along the eastern shore, and I headed toward my favorite one. It didn't have the best view, but it was one almost nobody else ever drove out to.

I drove all the way to the end of the road and put the truck in neutral, admiring how well the heater was working. Brad was just staring forward. I asked, "Wanna get out and walk a little?"

He opened the door, climbed out, and headed toward a few trees that blocked the view. As I followed, I noticed how the way he had to hold his arm made his gait a little awkward. He's such an athlete; I'll bet it kills him to feel like his body isn't working right.

I caught up with him at the shore, and we stood there staring out across the water for a good five minutes, saying nothing. I was straining my brain for a discussion subject when he said, "Do you mind if we just drive?"

So we drove. I knew that silence was the best thing for him right then. Or, at least it's what he wanted. But I felt so useless, like I ought to be able to say something helpful, or get him to talk about things.

I pulled into his driveway around quarter of five. "Do you want me to come in with you?"

"What for?"

It seemed obvious to me that it would be in case his father was on another bender and he needed help. I wasn't sure what "help" might mean, but I was willing to do what I could. But if he didn't want me to…

I shrugged, and he got out. He was about to close the door, but he stopped half-way. "Jesse? Thanks. For today."

I nodded. "We can do it again whenever you want."

When I got to my house, Patty's car was parked out front. Not terribly unusual, except that Stu was still at the garage with Dad. As I reached for the handle of the kitchen door, even before I turned it I heard sobbing. Inside, Mom and Patty were at the kitchen table, and I saw it was Patty crying.

Mom stood and wrapped me in a hug.

"What's going on? Is Stu all right? And Dad?" I'd always thought of them as safe from the kinds of things that happen to miners, the kind of thing that happened to Brad's father, but maybe that was ignoring reality.

"They're fine, sweetie. They're at the garage." Mom pulled away just far enough to look at me. With one hand she stroked the side of my head, and then she hugged me again for a second or two. Patty blew her nose and seemed like she was trying to calm down.

"So—what's happened?"

"Sit down, Jesse. Can I get you something?"

"Mom—"

She let out a long breath. "It's a friend of Patty's. Mary Blaisdell. She was—she was attacked this afternoon, behind that gas station out on Route 270, the one that's way back off the road closer to the fields." She stopped, like that was going to be enough. It wasn't.

"Attacked? What does that mean? Is she all right?" I didn't know Mary very well, but I did know she was a close friend of Patty's. And Brad and I had driven right past that gas station on our way out of town earlier.

Patty said to Mom, "You might as well tell him everything. He's going to hear it, anyway."

Mom rubbed her fingers along her hairline and gave me a heavy look. "She was raped, Jesse. And Mr. Ward tried to stop it. He got killed."

"Mr. Ward? From the village? My God! Who did it?"

"They've arrested Harry Stokes."

Harry Stokes. The bum who had knocked Mr. Everett's walking cane out from under him, which had prompted the purchase of the zap cane. This guy had all kinds of things he'd need to answer for.

Patty's voice was quiet but sharp. "They should have arrested him years ago." She blew her nose again. "He's a drunk, and he's always hanging around places. Mary told me he kept coming into the IGA and buying just one cheap item so he could stand in her line and say things to her. Like, when did she get off work, or he had something he wanted to show her and when could they get together. Or he'd comment on how tight her pants were, or how sexy her hair looked. Mostly she ignored him, but sometimes she had to call the manager over."

This didn't surprise me, from my limited information about him. It seemed like a bit of a leap to rape and murder, but not a huge one.

I asked, "What happened to Mr. Ward?" Wren Ward, his daughter, was in the class behind me at school. What effect would this have on Griffin and his family? In that close-knit community, everyone would at least know everyone else. Mr. Ward's death would leave a gaping hole in the next bonfire circle.

Patty plucked another tissue from the box beside her.

Mom said, "Harry Stokes had a gun, Jesse. He shot Mr. Ward."

I tried to gauge Patty's stability and decided to ask her, "How did you find out about it?"

"The police came to talk to me. They said they're talking to her family and close friends. Something about establishing background information. You can bet I told them about that low-life pestering Mary at the store."

"So, why was she there?" Everybody knows that station is used mostly to refuel farm equipment. Mr. Ward was probably doing exactly that; several of the villagers earn their living by farming.

"She was just using the restroom! Sorry. Didn't mean to shout."

I turned to Mom. "Was she alone?"

"Yes. I think she told the police that she's been sick, and she needed a restroom in a hurry. Harry grabbed her as she was coming out."

"And Mr. Ward tried to stop him?"

Mom's voice took on an odd note. "It would seem so, yes."

Patty sounded bitter. "He failed."

"Well, yeah," I said, "but he died trying." Freak or not, that had to count for something. But no one said anything else. I pushed away from the table. "I'm real sorry, Patty. Um, I'll be upstairs, Mom. Let me know if I can help with dinner."

"Actually, you can. Do you mind putting it together? It's easy. Hamburger meat fried up and mixed with that rice package over there," she pointed to the counter beside the stove, "and maybe some salad?"

"Sure."

"Jesse, don't do anything creative. We just need comfort food tonight."

I poked around in the fridge and found enough normal things to add to the meat and rice, and a few other things to add to the salad, so it could at least be interesting comfort food. While I was frying up the meat (secretly throwing in a small handful of cumin seeds), I tried to think whether I had any way to contact Griffin. I could probably find his land line, if his family had one; I didn't have any other number.

After supper I texted Brad with the news. He hadn't heard.

Poor Mary, he replied to my information.

Poor mr ward too, I responded.

Yeah I guess

That was my second clue that whatever genuine sympathy Mr. Ward was going to get would come from the villagers. And from me.

THROWING STONES

The next morning I searched the web for cell phone listings, and I had to create an account someplace but I did get a number for Griffin. His house had just a standard address in Himlen as far as anyone looking at it on the screen would know. It didn't say "The Village." Because of my stalking Griffin last October, spying on their Samhain celebrations, I already knew there was just one street, Woods Way, that meandered around a bit, completing a giant, twisting loop that eventually fed back out onto the highway.

I created a contact entry for Griffin on my phone, but then I sat there staring at it, not quite able to bring myself to use it. Texting *seemed* harmless enough, but we hadn't had any real contact since Thanksgiving.

Around eleven I grabbed my keys and headed downstairs, sort of pretending to myself that all I wanted was a short drive in my truck. I told Mom I was doing just that, and she flagged me down to give me a list of a few things she needed at the supermarket. "Thanks, Jesse. Drive safe!"

I put off the grocery run till later and headed south. Of course. I slowed as I approached the left turn that led into the village, but I didn't take it. I kept going, but maybe two minutes later I pulled over to the side of the road and let the engine idle while I tried to gather enough courage to go back and make that turn.

Someone in an SUV pulled off the road ahead of me, and a friend of my mom's got out, Mrs. Chambers. I lowered the window as she got close. "Jesse? You okay?"

"Sure. Just, you know, contemplating which direction to go."

She smiled and nodded. "You have a nice day, now. And drive safe." And she was off. This "drive safe" phrase is one I've never paid any attention to before. I'm sure people have been saying it to each other in my hearing all my life, but of course until I got my truck they'd never said it to me. I talked myself down from the position of *How do you think I would drive if you didn't tell me that?* to figuring, you know, it was just standard small talk, not unlike the perennial "Have a nice day," which she'd also said. Still, it put me in mind of those signs hanging inside car windows that say *Baby On Board,* like I'd aim for that vehicle if that sign weren't there. Maybe they make one of those signs that says *Nobody On Board;* that's the one I want. I watched Mrs. Chambers drive off, put the truck in gear again, and turned back to the road that led into the village. This time I took it.

Once I got near the houses I started looking for numbers. Some houses had numbers I could see, and some didn't. I did notice a spot at the far east end of Woods Way where a path led into the trees, and I figured it must be the path to where those secret meetings take place, the ones where the villagers are said to do unmentionable things.

The Holyokes' house was number twelve, which turned out to be a two-story house, painted blue, with garden remnants instead of a front yard. I saw Griffin's car in the driveway. I'm not sure why, but I drove right past, back out to the highway again, and pulled over. My breathing was a little fast, and I could hear my heartbeat in my ears.

WTF? What's the big deal, Jesse?

And what kind of a big deal would it be to my folks if they knew I'd visited the village at all, for any reason? For that matter, what was drawing me here, anyway? There was no longer any question of Griffin returning my feelings. Did I even still have them?

I took several deep breaths and then asked myself what I would say to Griffin if I found him. As I thought my way through several imaginary conversations, my gaze fell on a collection of mailboxes at the edge of the highway, which I realized must be the mailboxes for everyone in the village. Most of them had been bashed in—no doubt by kids riding by with baseball bats—and pounded out again. So even the Post Office won't go in there? The mailboxes have to be way out here on the highway? I wheeled around fast and headed straight for number twelve, not letting my mind circle back on itself again.

I was about to knock on the front door when someone from the inside opened it. It was a woman, probably Griffin's mother, her dark brown hair in a short, stylish cut that surprised me. Guess I'd expected something more along the lines of Silver Shaw.

"Oh!" she said and stopped suddenly, a canvas bag on one arm swinging forward and then back, a casserole dish in her hands.

"Are you Mrs. Holyoke?"

"Yes. What can I do for you?" She seemed more surprised than either friendly or unfriendly.

"Is Griffin home? I'm Jesse Bryce, a friend from school."

She started to answer, but then she looked past me. "He's right behind you, actually. Griffin, can you see what Jesse needs? I have to get these things over to the Wards'."

Stepping down from the door to the ground, I turned to face Griffin, who looked at me like he wasn't quite sure he remembered me, and that if he did it wasn't necessarily in a good way.

His tone didn't sound friendly. "What are you going here, Jesse?"

I blinked like an idiot and shifted my weight once or twice. What *was* I doing there? "I, uh, I heard about Mr. Ward."

His response seemed to have been pulled right out of my own head; it's what I would have said in his place. "And?"

"And, well—I guess I just wanted to say I'm sorry about what happened."

His voice took on even more of an edge. "Who do you

77

think Mr. Ward is to me? Why aren't you offering your condolences to Wren?"

I was starting to get a little irritated. "I don't know Wren very well. And I thought you and I were friends."

"Did you." Not a question. "So, just because someone in the village dies, you show up at a house here—any house will do, really, because of course we're all the same to you—and you think that's appropriate."

"Look, what's your problem? All I wanted to do was say I'm sorry."

Griffin breathed loudly through his nose, like he was trying to control his temper. He turned his back to me, his hands clenching and unclenching, and then he turned his head sideways and said, "It's just that I'm sick of being treated like this."

"Like what? Like a friend?"

He turned fully around again and ran a hand through his hair. "If you're serious about that, then you're the only one."

I didn't know what that meant, so I shook my head and lifted my arms out sideways. As I let them fall back down, Griffin walked past me and sat on the steps to his front door. I turned to face him and waited.

"All right, I guess you couldn't know… The police were here, asking questions like why was Allen at that station, how well did he know Mary Blaisdell, why would he have gotten involved—it was almost like they thought he must have been pissed because Harry Stokes beat him to it!" Griffin's voice, his face, everything about him made me think something was about to burst into flames. "I'm so fucking sick and tired of being treated like some kind of freak, just because we don't hang signs on our front doors every Sunday morning saying, 'See y'all in church!'"

I'd seen signs like that. It hadn't occurred to me before this minute what they implied, which was that of course everyone would be in church on Sunday morning, because of course everyone was a church-going Christian. But

Griffin had told me on Thanksgiving that the people here in the village aren't Christian. And this disconnect hadn't ever occurred to me because why? Because I happen to be one of the majority? One of the church-going Christians? Because until it affected someone *I* cared about—that would be Griffin—it didn't matter?

I sat down beside Griffin, maybe a foot away from him, and we both stared at the white house across the way, no doubt neither of us really seeing it. Then a black cat trotted out from around the side of the house, came up to Griffin, and wound around his ankles. Griffin reached down rather absent-mindedly to rub behind its ears.

His voice low and tender, he said, "Hey there, New Moon."

This was the cat, I was certain, that he had rescued from Lou and Chuck last October. And I'd been right; Griffin hadn't hurt it. "I remember that cat," I said.

"Do you." His voice had that edge back, and I'd had about enough of it.

I stood and faced Griffin, who still sat on the steps. "Okay, look, I just came out here to see how you were. I know you're all pretty close out here, so I figured that if one of you got killed it would affect everyone. I know you better than I know anyone else in the village, so that's why I drove here. And I guess there's nothing else, so I'll be on my way."

His attention was back on the cat as though to ignore me pointedly, so I turned and walked toward my truck.

"Jesse?" I turned, pissed but willing to listen. "Sorry. It's just that everything dark between your people and mine is darker than ever at the moment. Everyone here is on edge, and I'm taking it out on you because you're here. I'm sorry, but I can't help it. And yes, I think you'd better leave."

It was everything I could do not to leave rubber on the road as I drove off. And I got almost all the way home

79

before I remembered the groceries Mom wanted. I pulled into the parking lot at the supermarket and sat there, staring through the windshield at nothing.

Everything's "darker" now, is it? Well, maybe it wouldn't be so dark if Griffin had accepted my visit for what it was, which was an act of friendship. It wouldn't be so dark if he could have acknowledged that I was concerned about his people, or at least about him.

But—this wasn't about me, really. I'd made it about me, perhaps, driving out there with very little I could actually say and feeling insulted by the reception I'd gotten.

Maybe I should look at this from Griffin's point of view. Someone he knows really well was just murdered by a townie who raped another townie. And from what he said, the police didn't exactly treat the Wards like victims in this crime, but more like Mr. Ward shared the guilt in some way.

And then there's the cat, New Moon. Griffin had rescued that cat from Lou and Chuck, and Lou had called him and Ronan Coulter "fucking vampires." It hadn't been Griffin who'd planned something gruesome for the cat, not Griffin who'd actually tortured another one. But *he* was the vampire?

So maybe I'll cut Griffin a little slack, here. He did apologize, after all, even if he couldn't suddenly be friendly after that. And, really, we hadn't talked since November. So maybe he was right that I shouldn't just assume we're friends.

But I want to be.

Why? Was it just because of that dream that I still wanted to dream again? (Though, to be honest, at this point it's more that it was about kissing another guy, any guy, rather than the fact that that guy was Griffin.) Or was my wanting to be friends just an unhealthy curiosity about what the "freaks" are really like? About what the insides of their houses hide, now that I've seen that the outsides look pretty normal? And if they don't go to church on Sunday, what *do* they do to worship as Pagans, besides dance around burning cornstalks at Halloween, or Samhain, or whatever? And what is it about Paganism that makes being gay okay when the Bible—Old and New Testaments, both—say it's not? When my scripture says I should be killed for it?

Selena had been home for Thanksgiving with her... what, her partner? Was she here now, at Christmas? Thanksgiving isn't a religious holiday. Christmas is, but for Christians only. Would the fact that most of the country has holidays right about now be enough for Selena to come home?

So many questions. Surely, I could answer some of them, myself. Or find the answers. So I picked up Mom's groceries and headed home.

"Have a fun drive, Jesse?" Mom was cutting the remains of our Christmas roast into smaller pieces, probably making some version of leftovers for tonight's dinner. I half wanted to stay and work with her, make some suggestions. But the Internet was calling to me.

"I saw Mrs. Chambers," I told her, tucking the new carton of milk behind the nearly-empty one in the fridge. "I pulled off to the side to decide where I wanted to go, and she thought I might be having car trouble, I think. Anyway, she says 'hey.'" She hadn't, but it seemed appropriate to say she had.

"And where did you decide to go?"

Was she suspicious? I glanced toward her, but she looked casual enough. I took a nanosecond to debate what to say and decided to take a risk: truth. "I drove into the village, just to see what might be going on."

"Going on?" Not so casual any longer.

"You know, after what happened yesterday."

She set down the knife she'd been wielding on the beef and turned to face me. "Jesse, why did you do that?" She didn't wait for an answer, which was good, because I didn't have one. "Your father and I don't want you going in there."

Somehow, this was an even stronger admonition than I'd expected. And the look on her face was—what? Horror? Was that too much to say? Then I recognized it: fear. She was terrified of the village.

"Why not? What do you think they're gonna do to me?" It was tempting to tell her I'd been there on Halloween, at night, alone, and nothing bad had happened.

"It's just not a good idea, Jesse. You'll have to take my word for it. Don't do that again."

"Fine." I think she kind of wanted to ask me what I'd seen, but she didn't. And it wasn't fine, but I had to say that or start an argument I wasn't going to be able to win. So telling the truth had failed me a second time; the first, of course, was when I stopped lying about who I am.

Upstairs I fired up my laptop and searched "Pagan holidays" and got pages and pages of results. It seems there are eight main holidays, called sabbats, four major and four minor. Samhain is major, and Yule (on the winter solstice) is minor. Yule was on a Sunday this December. So, while I was in church with my family, what was Griffin doing? Was there a service, or a ceremony? Was it like the famous Yule log? And did they go to "church" eight times a year to my fifty-two?

According to the Internet, there are ceremonies for various moon cycles as well, all optional. And how many celebrations, and what they look like, depend on the— what, denomination?—of Paganism you follow. What I couldn't figure out was when they went to some gathering that equated to Sunday church for me. And I couldn't find anything that seemed to pass for scripture in Paganism, outside of this: An it harm none, do as ye will. Were they really that free? It sounded like anarchy to me.

I was in the middle of saving a bunch of links for future

reference, like how the obscene-sounding word "wortcunning" just has to do with knowing about medicinal plants, when I got a text message. It was from Griffin. So he must have looked up my number, too.

Really sorry about earlier will you forgive me

Forgive him? I can't remember whether anyone has ever asked for my forgiveness. Mom mentioned the word once about how my family and I need to treat each other while they get over my being gay, but no one had asked anyone else for it yet. Maybe a few times someone has asked me to accept an apology, but—forgiveness? But what could I say?

Sure

And then I added, *When is the funeral*

There was a pause that went on so long I almost asked if he were still there. Then,

Wed nite

Where?

Another pause. *Not a public place. Just us. c u at school*

Just us. Meaning just the villagers. I was pointedly not invited. And the place was certain to be that spot in the woods, at the end of that path that I now knew how to find. I couldn't help wondering whether there was any significance to the funeral being on New Year's Eve, but there was nothing indicated on December thirty-first or January first on the Pagan calendars I'd downloaded.

Paganism was not making any sense to me.

Brad's dad drove him over early in the afternoon and dropped him off so we could watch a movie. He had a DVD of *Gravity* and didn't want to watch it with his sisters around, so we headed downstairs with some popcorn and drinks. As I set up the DVD player I asked if his dad was calmer lately.

"He had a talk with Reverend Gilman. Guess there was

83

some repentance there."

"So things are better at home?" I didn't look at Brad while I fussed with the audio-visual setup; didn't want him to feel like I was interrogating him.

"Better, yeah. You haven't seen this yet, right?"

"Right." Guess he didn't want to talk about his family life. At least there had been an improvement, which must mean Brad wasn't feeling like he had to be around all the time in case more shit hit the fan.

We settled onto the sofa to watch the movie. At one point, Mom called to me from upstairs and asked me to turn down that "horrible music."

Brad wasn't happy about that. To me, he said, "The soundtrack on this one is half the fun."

I kept wanting George Clooney's character to shut up and stop making Sandra Bullock answer him and waste oxygen, which she was supposed to be running out of. The idea of being totally helpless, though, floating in outer space like that with no one around who could help? That hit me kind of hard. It reminded me of my more lonely moments, like when I'd driven Stu out to Quarry Isle and had felt so connected to him and so absolutely unconnected at the same time. Or like sitting in church, which is supposed to be about love and connection, and all I felt these days was isolation because of what the church says about people like me.

Brad got into the tension of the movie, I think; he was kind of wired and crazy by the end, and after it was over he hooted and hollered, no words, just a lot of noise, bouncing around the room despite his cast, like he was the one floating in space. It made me want to grab him and hold on, to let him know he wasn't alone, and maybe to convince myself I wasn't, either. Before I could decide whether to do that, Mom yelled down to make sure we were okay, and Brad settled down again.

I wanted to talk about the murder of Mr. Ward, but I

wasn't sure how to open. I landed on the way I had found out about it. "Patty—Stu's girlfriend—was really close to that girl who got raped."

"Mary Blaisdell?"

"Yeah."

"Did you hear about the effigy?"

"What effigy?"

Brad scratched around the edge of his cast. "It was left on a pole in front of City Hall, sometime that night. It was an effigy of Allen Ward."

"What the fuck? But—why? He wasn't the one who did anything wrong! That was Harry Stokes!" This made no sense to me, no sense at all, even from people who hate the "freaks."

"Yeah. It does seem a little over the top. I dunno, maybe someone thought that if Mr. Ward hadn't interfered, the only thing Stokes would have gotten in trouble for would have been the rape. Not the murder."

"D'you think there's any question about whether Stokes is guilty?"

"Dunno." Brad's voice took on a heavier note, and he said, "Um, change of subject, here."

"Okay. Shoot."

"Well... I want you to know it wasn't me. I never said anything." He stopped.

"About what?"

"About you." He stopped again and looked down at his hands, fingers twining together nervously.

"What *about* me?" But I was pretty sure I already knew what he meant. So I said, "Fuck it. I know what you're saying. But who are you saying it about?"

He didn't look up. "The team."

"Shit. So I'm a topic of discussion for the entire football team? Is that what you're saying?"

"I wouldn't say 'a topic of discussion.' But, yeah, they all know. They asked me about it." He stopped again, but this time I waited him out. He looked up and added, "I told them we're still best buds. I told them it didn't make you any different from who you've always been."

We stared at each other while I took this in. Then I said, "When did this happen?"

"Right before my dad went all Terminator on Mom and me. Don't know why I didn't tell you sooner."

"I guess you had your own problems to deal with."

"But, hey, it's good news that you didn't know, because it means they aren't treating you any different, right?"

"Well, if we're talking about the football team, they never treated me in any way at all."

"Okay, well, that's still the case, then. And there must be lots of other kids who know. And you haven't felt ganged up on or anything, right?"

"I have been getting odd looks in the locker room and the showers. But, really, I kind of already suspected some of them have known for a while."

"Yeah. I guess you were right, before."

I let out a long breath. "Thanks, man. For sticking up for me. I know that's going to help a lot."

"So, anyway... Hey, any more popcorn?"

Guess we'd about talked that one out by now. "I think there are brownies upstairs." I knew there were; I'd made them, from scratch. "How about a couple of those?"

I had another dream about Griffin that night. He was larger than life, and he looked as much like a girl as like a guy. There was a meeting deep in the woods someplace, and instead of a funeral for Mr. Ward, Griffin and Silver Shaw (who was also large but definitely a girl) presided together over some ritual with words I couldn't understand. There were other villagers there. They all chanted these strange words in eerie-sounding voices as Griffin and Silver bent over something that glowed deep red, working together in some way I couldn't see. The chanting got louder, and suddenly Griffin and Silver stood up, and out of the red glow came Mr. Ward, alive again.

I was already sitting up in bed when I woke up, and for some reason the phrase "will you forgive me" was bouncing around inside my head. I couldn't connect it with the dream. My association with the concept of forgiveness was with Christianity and the Lord's Prayer. But Griffin is Pagan, not Christian. And I don't recall any Christians ever asking me for forgiveness, or asking for it, myself.

Chapter Four

New Year's Eve. Time for Mr. Ward's funeral, to which I'd pointedly not been invited. Maybe it was being told I couldn't go that made me want to be there so badly. Whatever the reason, after dinner I went up to my room, not sure what the funeral timing would be but knowing Griffin had said "Wed nite." Stu headed out around quarter of seven to get Patty for some event at the church, and not long after that I headed downstairs. I could hear the TV rumbling from the family room, so I figured Dad was down there, watching sports or maybe one of his cop show reruns. Mom was at the kitchen table, reading a magazine. I stopped at the bottom of the stairs and watched her for a minute.

Sometimes it would occur to me to wonder whether she ever wanted to have a real job. You know, something she got paid for. I mean, sure, she got some money from teaching piano to a few local kids who'd rather be doing almost anything else. It wasn't like there were a lot of career opportunities around here. She worked for Dad's business, doing bookkeeping types of stuff. But Himlen's a pretty small place, largely fuelled by work in the coal mines, with most everyone else in transportation or farming. There's lots of good ol' Oklahoma corn. OK corn.

Mom must have sensed my presence, and she lifted her gaze to me. As I moved toward her she looked back at her magazine. "Finish that book report, Jesse? School starts up again in a few days."

"Mostly." I could tell the question was pro forma, so I

didn't go into details. "Um, think I'll go for a drive. Feeling a little cooped up."

She looked up. "Everything all right?" Her gaze got intense suddenly, and she folded the magazine around one hand. "You're not—you're not seeing anyone, are you, Jesse?"

Her tone, and the look, got my back up. "You mean like, a date? What if I am?" *Stupid, Jesse. That was stupid.* Quickly, I added, "No, Mother, I'm not 'seeing anyone.' I said I'm going for a drive, and that's what I'm doing." Even though that was a lie. But truth wasn't getting me anywhere lately.

"Well... drive safely. There are lots of idiots out on New Year's Eve. And don't be too late, or I'll think one of them has crashed into you."

I left before she could say more.

When I got near the left turn off the highway I slowed down and located that spot across the road where I'd parked for my Halloween spying adventure. Skirting the edge of the woods south of the village, I didn't see anyone on the street, and although I wasn't close enough to the houses to peek into any of them, it looked like there were people inside them, including Griffin's. When I got to the path into the woods on the far side of the village, I found a large tree near the entrance, pulled out my phone, turned the ringer off, and waited.

Maybe half an hour later, people started to gather in the building where they'd had the Samhain party, and at first I thought maybe that was where they'd hold the funeral. I was disappointed; I was both longing to see something more sinister and afraid of seeing it. But then they started to file out of the building and head toward me. Some of them had torches, thick sticks with some kind of cloth or something on the ends, covered in pine pitch to judge by what I could smell as they filed past my hiding spot. They walked slowly, single file, and once they'd all gone by me I followed them into the woods, my stomach in knots.

After a few minutes the path fell steeply and ended in a clearing where the villagers formed a large circle and stood quietly. From behind a tree again, above the clearing and a hundred and fifty feet or so away, I could see their faces pretty well in the light from their torches. They were standing in a loose circle around some shapes I had trouble making out in the dark. It looked like there was a tree stump, maybe two feet high, with a large, flat, dark stone balanced on it. All around the stump were lots of smaller flat rocks, piled haphazardly but covering the ground completely. The whole area, rocks and stump, was about six or seven feet in diameter.

Scanning the people who stood around the "altar" or whatever it was, it took me a minute to locate Griffin. He was not holding one of the torches, and with that dyed black hair I might have missed him entirely despite the fact that he's tall if the torchlight hadn't glinted off some of the silver metal he's pierced through himself. A man standing next to him—his father, I assumed—carried an urn that must have had Mr. Ward's ashes in it.

A woman named Eleanor Darling started speaking from her place in the circle. I'd never net her, but I knew she had some kind of authority here. She was tall, kind of old, wore her hair long, all down her back. It was silver gray with dark streaks. She wasn't Silver Shaw's mother, but she looked like she could have been.

"We create a sacred space in memory of our brother, Allen Ward." Eleanor's voice was gentle and clear. "May the Goddess be with us as we acknowledge his return to her."

Then Ronan Coulter stepped out from the crowd and walked across the flat rocks toward the stump. After brushing leaf litter and twigs off of that long rock balanced there, he started a small fire and then went to stand back in the crowd again.

THROWING STONES

Wren Ward, Mr. Ward's daughter, stepped forward from the circle, her mother behind her, hands on Wren's shoulders. Wren was a year behind Griffin and me at school, so she was probably around fifteen. Her brown hair caught flickers of light from the flames. Mr. Holyoke sprinkled some ashes onto Ronan's fire, and everyone watched in silence as he scattered the rest among all those smaller rocks.

Wren tried to say something. She got about as far as "Do not stand," before her voice caught and she couldn't go on. Mrs. Ward looked like she was going to speak for Wren, but then she covered her mouth with a hand, obviously trying not to cry.

Suddenly Griffin was by Wren's side, towering over her. He took her hand, watching the fire. He repeated her words and kept going, and after a couple of lines her voice joined his. Together they recited this poem.

Do not stand at my grave and weep.
I am not there. I do not sleep.
I am a thousand winds that blow.
I am the diamond glints on snow.
I'm sunlight on the ripened grain.
I am the gentle autumn rain.
When you wake in morning's hush
I am the swift uplifting rush
Of quiet birds in circled flight.
I am the stars that shine at night.
Do not stand at my grave and cry;
I am not there. I did not die.

They stepped back from the fire, Griffin still holding Wren's hand. Then four different people, two men and two women all holding torches, stepped out from the circle and closer to the fire, equal distances from each other. One of the men spoke first.

"From the East, the spirits of air bring us bright, loving memories of our brother. When sadness approaches, we call upon Air to lighten the weight with the love that never dies. Blessed be!"

I tried to work out whether he was at the eastern compass point, pretty sure he was. Then one of the two women, the one on his right, spoke.

"From the North, spirits of the Earth remind us of the cycle of life. There is birth, there is life, there is death, and there is renewal. Earth gives us the strength to trust in life and life again. Blessed be!"

"From the West," the next woman said, "spirits of water flow gently through us. They open our hearts and allow our tears to be the water of healing and renewal. Blessed be!"

The second man completed the circuit. "From the South, the spirits of fire are with us. They bring warmth, helping us keep the love for our brother alive, overcoming the cold that might fool us into thinking love itself is lost. Blessed be!"

As the "south" man finished, all four people stepped back into the main circle. Eleanor's voice started up again, and immediately everyone around the circle joined in.

In silence you will sing your truest song.
When your body returns to earth, you will truly dance.
From earth's highest point, you will begin to climb.

Someone had brought a small drum, and they started a light, steady beat. Then someone else joined the rhythm with what sounded like a pair of wood sticks. The sounds seemed to cast a gentle veil around the funeral circle, leaving me out. Then everyone laced together, arms on each other's waists, and they all swayed almost imperceptibly. Someone began a humming sound, no melody to it, and others picked it up, though not all on the same note, very much like at the Samhain bonfire. It was hypnotic. I felt myself start to rock back and forth with them, outsider though I was. This exclusion almost hurt, like what they had down there was something wonderful I was denied. It was pretty much exactly the same feeling I'd felt at their Samhain bonfire—a sense of belonging I've never felt. One I didn't think I ever would feel.

I couldn't tell whether there would be more to the ceremony, of course, but when everyone was ready to leave I'd be right in their return path. Trying to decide whether to leave, I wondered what would happen if I was discovered spying this time. Griffin had known I'd stayed at Samhain, and evidently that hadn't been a problem. But he was the one who'd told me I wasn't welcome here. And this ceremony was much more private than Samhain had been. I wasn't just spying, now. I was intruding. And I was the one who wanted to be friends?

I did wonder why no one had talked about Mr. Ward—what he was like, what he'd done, how he'd died. Maybe they were going to do that now, but if I got caught it would ruin everything. Whatever "everything" might be. For sure, given how pissed Griffin had been to see me appear on his doorstep a few days ago, he'd really hate me if he knew what I'd done tonight. Ashamed, and still feeling hurt and deprived, I turned as quietly as possible and headed back toward my truck.

I didn't get caught, so Griffin couldn't have known about my transgression concerning the funeral. Even so, I was a little worried when, after classes on Friday the third week of January, I got a text from him. I was at my locker, figuring out what to leave and what to take home with me, when my phone played the "constellation" tone, which I'd assigned to Griffin in honor of the night sky at Samhain.

Q for u can u meet at caf

I finalized my book choices, hefted my bag, and headed toward the cafeteria, a little nervous about what he might want to meet for. I couldn't have said what had changed, but although I was still kind of fixated on the village in general and Griffin in particular, I wasn't feeling that—I don't know, that lust any more. Something about him still fascinated me, but I was no longer feeling the urge to kiss him.

Griffin wasn't at the door of the cafeteria when I got there, so I dropped my book bag and leaned against the wall to wait. And I waited, and waited. Maybe ten minutes went by, and I was just thinking of texting him when I saw Griffin coming up the hall. He was walking oddly, almost limping, and his hair was a mess. As he got closer I could see that his face was bloodied, and obviously it would look all bruised before too long. His jacket was torn at the shoulder. And his hands had something red on them, but it wasn't blood. It was… paint?

"What the fuck, Griffin?"

"Had to clean something off my locker. Again."

OMG. I knew someone had scrawled the word "Vampire" on his locker a few days after that cat had been found dead last October, though I didn't know for sure who the culprit was. And now it had happened again? But—that wasn't all that had happened. "And the rest of it?"

He walked/limped into the cafeteria and moved off to the side. "Never mind, Jesse. It's not your battle."

"But—shit, man! Who did this to you?"

"It's just the same fuck-ups who keep painting my locker. I caught them at it today," he dropped his bag like it weighed more than it probably did, "and paid a price. Listen, I know I was rude to you when you came out to see me after Allen Ward was killed, but—well, the fact remains that you did it. So you can say no if you want, of course, but I thought you might like to know we're making a labyrinth in the village in his memory. So if you'd like to contribute any material, you'd be welcome to do that."

I did my best to ignore his battered condition and my rising fury at what had caused it. What did he say? A labyrinth? Like, a maze? It wasn't a term that had turned up during my online research. "Material? What kind of material?"

"The path is made of bricks, with flat stones to set them apart, so we're looking for anything like that we can set into the ground. Around the outside there'll be standing stones. So anything like that would be welcome. We've got a good start on it, but there's still lots of work to be done. We want it to be ready by Imbolc."

I wasn't sure what a standing stone was, but I figured I could look that up. And it seemed less mysterious than what I decided to ask about. "What's Imbolc?"

"Sorry. Imbolc is the sabbat of lights and fire. It's when the grove releases dead and dying things, including old resentments and anger. It's kind of a spring celebration of life returning, life renewed, that kind of thing. We celebrate it early in February. It's particularly appropriate this year."

Yeah, right; one of those Pagan holidays. Sabbats. I almost didn't want to ask, but I really did want to know: "And, 'the grove?' What's that?"

"Again, sorry. You probably haven't heard that term. You folks always say 'the village,' so we do, too, but for us it just means the physical location. The community itself, the Pagan community, is called the grove."

I wasn't sure what to say next; actually, I'd mostly forgotten what the question was, the one *he* had asked *me*. So I just stood there like a dummy.

Griffin hefted his pack and grimaced with the effort. "It's okay. You don't have to contribute. I just thought you might like to."

"No, wait. I do. I mean, I'd like to. I just need to think of what to bring. And, um, when? Where, all that?"

"Tomorrow. Sorry for the short notice. The site is on the far east side of the village, the opposite side from the road to the highway. There's a large open space there. So just show up anytime, really. Late morning? Early afternoon? Something like that. When you get to my house, text me, and if I'm over at the site I'll come get you and show you where to drive with the stuff."

We nodded at each other, and just before he turned to walk away, he said, "By the way. I don't like being the one to tell you this but... well, you should see *your* locker."

I made a B-line down the hall, and even before I got to it I knew what the writing would say. I'd been right: FAGGOT in big, red letters.

I stared at it, not moving, for maybe a couple of minutes while I thought about what to do. Brad had already told me the football players all knew, and Lou and Chuck have been shouting this at me since September. What they'd written on Griffin's locker was false. What they'd written on mine was unacceptable, but it came from truth. I decided to beat Lou and Chuck—who, I was positive, were the "artists"—at their own game.

Back in school after a trip to the hardware store, I used a graffiti remover to rub and scrape away the red FAGGOT. Then I picked up the can of purple spray paint I'd bought and, at a rakish slant, in big, bold, gorgeous letters, I wrote: GAY.

In bed that night, I didn't even feel like jerking off. I was thinking of Griffin, but not only did he not affect me that way any more, but also what I felt was a kind of frustrated fury because of what happened to him. Because of what my townie classmates did to him, what they seemed to be always doing to him. I could stand tall and proud and call myself gay; it took guts, and I was already thinking maybe I'd been a little hasty this afternoon, thinking maybe I wouldn't let on I'd done the work myself. But Griffin couldn't stand tall and proud and change "vampire" to anything good. Maybe he could stand tall and proud and write, "Pagan" on his locker, but somehow I knew that would be very different, and somehow even harder.

THROWING STONES

After he'd been beaten up, he'd had red paint on his hands. But, unlike me, he hadn't needed to make a trip to the hardware store to get stuff for paint removal. Which told me that this happened to him so often that he kept the stuff right in his locker.

I hated the word "freaks" for the people in the village. Or of any of the other derogatory words townies use. In my own head, I could refer to them as Pagan and know that was truthful and—coming from me—not insulting at all, but I couldn't use the term around most people and not have it misinterpreted. This seemed profoundly unfair.

As I was about to drift off, I heard Mom's voice in my head: "Your father and I don't want you going in there."

Why not? Really, why not? So Dad thought they were heathens. So what? He thought I shouldn't be gay, and that ain't changin'. As for the "heathen" bit, it wasn't like that was dangerous. I went to church with my family every friggin' Sunday. The villagers weren't Christian, but no one had ever done or said anything to try and pull me away from Christianity. Their houses all looked pretty normal, and Mrs. Holyoke looked like anyone's mother. Okay, so they had an unusual way of celebrating Halloween, and their funerals don't look anything like the one I'd been to when Brad's grandmother had died last year, but no one had invited me to either of the Pagans' gatherings. They weren't pulling me in; I was invading. But not so that I could lose my soul, or whatever my folks were afraid of.

At no time had I seen anything that looked like a goddess, or a devil (a concept Griffin says doesn't even have a place in Paganism), or a dead baby, or even a dead cat. No upside-down crosses, no brooms parked anywhere, no cauldrons steaming with eye of newt, or whatever Shakespeare had his witches brewing.

Griffin's piercings are Griffin's because he wanted them, not because of being Pagan, and the only places he has them are his ear and his eyebrow; I've seen him naked

97

in the shower. His friend Ronan doesn't have any. I've never seen any evidence of anyone taking drugs, or being high on something, or even being drunk. And, for God's sake, Mr. Ward had *died* trying to help Mary Blaisdel.

This was going to be one of those things I would decide for myself. And my decision was to "go in there." Suddenly it had changed from being something I just wanted to do for myself into a kind of mission I *had* to do for—for what? Justice? Truth? Humanity? Paganism?

For love. I had to do it for love.

Everyone was surprised to see me downstairs for breakfast Saturday. Often I'd sleep in and then make something for myself, just about in time for lunch. But I had some rockhounding to do before heading over to the village.

I had debated asking Brad if he wanted to go with me today, but somehow telling him I was gay seemed to make more sense than telling him I was going to help the villagers build something neither of us had ever heard of, for reasons he wouldn't understand. For reasons I could explain even to myself, let alone to Brad.

On the drive down to where I'd taken Brad in December, which is where I was headed first, I reviewed in my head what I'd learned on the Internet. Standing stones would seem to be stones of various sizes, longer than they are wide, that are set in the earth so that they literally stand up. They're used to mark locations deemed important for one reason or another. Like Stonehenge, though standing stones for some purposes can be small enough for me to lift. I'd look for a few of those. And labyrinths are not mazes. They're kind of the opposite, in fact. Mazes have dead ends and paths that don't really go anywhere. Labyrinths come in lots of different patterns, but they always lead you all the way in and all the way out without trying to get you lost. The idea seems to be that you'd spend the time thinking about something important. A kind of meditation, I suppose.

I managed to find the spot where Brad and I had parked last time. As soon as I was out of the truck I started scouring the ground for rocks that could be used for standing stones, ones that weren't too heavy for me to lift. I found one almost right away, a boring color but a really cool shape—flat-ish on one end with spikey points on the other. Even though it was thin—probably shale—it was almost too heavy for me to lift, but I managed it, thanking Stu silently for including a rubber bed liner for the back of my truck. But then the only rocks I found were either not useful as standing stones, or they were too big for me to manage on my own. I figured I could drive around some and maybe find a few more later. First, I was headed for bobcat country.

It felt a little creepy, heading out alone toward the place where that cave was, and I made a couple of mistakes trying to follow the trail that doesn't look much like a trail. The sky was full of high thin clouds, but I could see the sun well enough to keep track of it, so I didn't get too lost. Eventually, feeling more nervous with every step, I approached where Brad and I had stood that day. What I was after was that flat, gray rock embedded with the mixture of other rocks that Brad had declared not interesting enough to be worth the bother of bringing home. Taking it for the labyrinth, then, would not deprive Brad of anything he might care about.

I'd hefted the slab a few weeks ago, so I knew it was not going to be easy to retrieve. But I had a plan.

As I had expected, I could barely lift the stone. Once I got it to the truck, I was pretty sure I'd be okay, but getting it there was not going to be any fun. The first thing was to get it into an old backpack I'd brought from home. The stone was a little too long for the pack, so I couldn't zip the pack all the way up, but I'd anticipated this and had brought an old flannel pajama bottom to cover the exposed end of the stone.

With the stone wrapped up as well as I could get it, I tied a rope to the pack's straps, took a deep breath, turned toward the way out with the rope over one shoulder, and hauled.

My plan worked pretty well, though I had to be really careful in places where the path got rocky. At least I didn't get lost on the way back; that would have been the worst, having to haul this heavy thing any farther than absolutely necessary. Even so, getting it up the slope to the truck—a slope that hadn't seemed especially steep until now—was a Herculean effort. I was glad no one was around to hear me grunt and swear and grind my teeth. I had to take a good long breather about half-way up, which gave me time to wonder what the fuck I was doing this for. Who was I trying to impress, anyway? Was I deluding myself to think I didn't have a crush on Griffin any more? But I turned back to my task; I'd got the thing this far.

At the truck, I remembered what Brad had said about how to lift it, using my legs rather than my back, but it was still quite an effort. I decided to haul it in instead, from inside the truck. Of course, the pack got caught on the tailgate, and by the time I managed to overcome that I was done in.

Back in my seat behind the wheel, I saw it had taken me nearly an hour to fetch this stone. I leaned my head back and let my overused muscles relax, and the next thing I knew it was thirty-five minutes later. And I still wanted to find a few more standing stones.

As the engine roared to life, I thought back to when Stu had shown me the printout with the photo of this truck, and I'd been thinking that I wouldn't have chosen a truck. Shows how much I knew.

I collected three more stones farther along the track that

THROWING STONES

I was pretty sure would be good for standing stones, and by then it was well past noon.

When I got to the village I had to squeeze past a commercial truck at one house where they were getting a piano delivered; Woods Way is kind of narrow. Past the meeting house and across the field, I could see lots of people working, no doubt where the labyrinth was being built. I saw no sign of Griffin or anyone else at his house, so I pulled out my phone to let him know I was here.

Griffin appeared from the east, the direction of the field, and I climbed out, noticing how dirty he looked; he'd been working hard today, too. His face was bruised, for sure, and his left eye was swollen half shut, but his mood was decidedly better than yesterday.

"You've missed lunch," he said, "but I'm sure there are lots of leftovers. Hungry?"

Thank God! Or maybe the Goddess. "I am, yeah."

He walked around to the back of the truck. "Great wheels, Jesse."

"Thanks. My dad owns a garage, and my brother did the refurb." I almost cringed, remembering the confrontation between Griffin's father and mine over that symbol. Whether Griffin remembered or even knew about that incident, I couldn't tell.

He took his eyes off the truck and looked at my face. "They love you a lot," he said, like he was sure, and I thought, *They used to*. Then he peered into the truck bed. "Holy crap! Jesse, these are fucking fantastic stones! Where did you get these?"

I shrugged like it was nothing. "Do you know Brad Everett? He goes rockhounding, and I go with him sometimes."

Griffin sprang into the truck bed like some kind of gazelle; guess the rest of him didn't get as much grief as his face yesterday. He hefted a couple of the standing stones. "Man." Then he turned to the pack. "This one's special?"

"Take a look if you want."

He pulled the flannel off and unzipped the pack. The side with the breccia was face up. Griffin ran his fingers over the center where those white quartz pieces were embedded. But he wasn't just looking at it, not just touching it. It was like he was communing with it.

He packed it carefully up again and climbed back out. "Jesse Bryce, I think you have found *the* stone."

"The stone for what?"

"For the center. We've collected a lot of rocks—you'll see in a minute—but nothing this perfect. I can't wait to show everyone! Let's head over."

Griffin had me drive over the ground to where a large group of people were working in what must have been one of last year's corn fields. I knew the village owned lots of farmland all over, so maybe this small field near their houses was where they grew the stalks they used in bonfires. Griffin made a bee-line for one huge man I didn't remember seeing before. The guy was stripped to the waist despite the cold, but he was working so hard I could see where lines of sweat had run through the dirt he was covered in. It took me a minute to work out that he was maybe forty or so.

"Jesse, this is Todd Swazey. He's our blacksmith and all-around superman. Todd, meet Jesse Bryce. And then come see what he's brought us in his truck."

Todd started to reach his right hand toward me, but then he laughed and shook his head. "You don't wanna shake my hand just now, kid!"

He was right; it was filthy. He rubbed his hands on his dirt-caked jeans and looked toward my truck.

"That's yours?" he asked. "Gorgeous." He strode toward the truck and went right to the back. If Griffin had looked like a gazelle jumping in there, Todd looked like a gorilla. He hefted the slabs of slate and nodded. "These will work." Then he opened the pack.

For a moment he froze. Then he looked at Griffin, then at me, and then he shouted, "Eleanor!" He stood and cupped his hands close to his mouth. "Eleanor! Stones!"

Across the open space, on the far side of the shape they were building, I saw Eleanor's tall frame. She turned her head toward us, looked around, and called someone's name. The guy who'd been with Griffin the day New Moon had been saved from torture and death, Ronan Coulter, looked up. Eleanor gestured to him, and they both headed toward us, meeting up about halfway. Eleanor was looking at Todd. Ronan's eyes were on me.

When they got close, Eleanor said, "What do we have here, Todd?"

Todd bent over, picked up that heavy slab like it was made of wood, held it face out so Eleanor could see the white quartz, and then set it down carefully. She stared at it for maybe fifteen seconds and turned to me.

"You brought this?"

I nodded, and Griffin said, "This is Jesse Bryce, Eleanor."

The next thing Eleanor said made me uncomfortable. "You're of the town, Jesse." It wasn't exactly a question, but she looked like she wanted a response.

I was feeling pretty ashamed of my people just now, with Griffin's bashed-up face right in front of us, but I said, "Yes, ma'am."

"Do you know anything about stones?"

"No, ma'am." At least, not enough to speak up about this one. Somehow I could tell breccia formations would be only part of what was important here.

She smiled. "Then you don't know what you've just done. Ronan, what do you see?"

Ronan looked at the stone. "Limestone. It contains many other types of rock materials and acts as a repository for more individual energies. Like this white quartz, which is useful in healing rituals to direct negative or excessive energy away. It helps us to connect to the divine and to grow in the areas of intuition and spirituality. And in this case," he looked at me at this point, "embedded in a spiral pattern, it forms the symbol for eternal life."

Eleanor turned to me. "Jesse, I think it's likely that you have not been schooled in the importance of the last thing Ronan said. Has Griffin told you why we're creating this labyrinth?"

"It's for Mr. Ward. Because of what happened."

"It's because his physical body is no longer with us. But the spiral, reminding us that life is eternal, is especially important in this case, precisely because it's the physical death of Allen Ward that has inspired this effort. Do you understand what I mean?"

"I think so." Actually, and to my complete surprise, I really did get it, even though I hadn't noticed until this moment that the white quartz breccia did, in fact, form a spiral pattern. What Eleanor couldn't know—at least, I didn't think she could—is that I had witnessed Mr. Ward's funeral ceremony. Or, at least enough of it to pick up on the idea of life renewing itself.

She looked closely at me. "Yes. I think you do. Then you can understand why this particular stone will be perfect for the center of our labyrinth."

"I know the difference between a labyrinth and a maze." It was kind of like being with Griffin in his car, last Thanksgiving, when I'd been desperate to impress him. I felt a lot like that now.

Ronan called me out on it. "Why would you even bring that up?" His eyes, light gray with black rings around the outside of the irises, looked almost eerie on someone with such dark hair. They drilled into me.

Maybe I'd been a little too eager to prove myself, here, but why was he challenging me? "Not everyone knows the difference, you know."

"Everyone here does."

THROWING STONES

Todd had managed to get the stone out of the truck with a lot more ease than I'd had getting it in. On his way to where he wanted to set the stone, off to the side and out of the way, he walked between Ronan and me, almost as though he wanted to break up any negativity. Ronan followed him, and as Griffin led me over to where lunch remains were waiting, I watched Todd set the stone down. Ronan leaned over it, stroking it tenderly.

I filled a plate with vegetable lasagna and a rich egg dish with lots of cheese and bits of zucchini and red peppers, and I took a huge hunk—that's the only right word—of absolutely the best bread I've ever had in my life, thick salty butter in chunks all over it. There were thin, metal plates and forks, no paper plates or plastic anything. There was water, and I downed a metal cup full of it to get over my thirst before moving on to spiced cider. Griffin sat with me, explaining what everyone was doing on the work site. Quite a bit of the path was already paved. Griffin showed me a paper with the shape of the labyrinth they were constructing.

"It's a goddess labyrinth, sometimes called Baltic," he told me. "We're doing only seven circuits. Sometimes they have as many as eleven."

I examined the design on the paper he was holding. "It looks kind of like a ping pong paddle."

He eyed it for a few seconds. "I guess it does. Never thought of it like that. Probably because we're all so used to these patterns, and we knew what it was before we even saw it. Anyway, your stone could go on the part that looks like a paddle handle, but it sounds like Eleanor wants it in the center."

I set my plate on the ground, wondering if it would be rude to ask for more bread as I scanned the work site, trying to imagine it finished. Almost directly across I saw Ronan and Eleanor looking through the collection of stones, all of mine included now, no doubt trying to figure

105

out which should go where. Maybe Ronan felt me looking at him, because suddenly he looked up, right at me, and glared. He didn't look away, and that made me uncomfortable, so I did.

"I don't think Ronan likes me," I told Griffin.

Griffin was following the labyrinth pattern with a finger and didn't look up. "Oh, he'll get over it. I think he'll like you just fine. Give him a chance."

"He criticized me earlier, and now he's glaring at me. What did I ever do to him?'"

Griffin looked at me briefly and then over toward Ronan and Eleanor. "You're of the town. He probably expects the worst. I did, the day you drove out here unannounced, even though you'd been friendly enough on Thanksgiving."

"Yeah, about that. It seemed like we made some kind of connection, and then by the time we were back at school it was like it never happened."

"Remember that I approached you first, under the bleachers there? Maybe I didn't approach you after that, but you didn't approach me, either. I was waiting to see what you'd do. To see if you'd be brave enough to cross that line. Because, really, it's the town that starts the conflicts, not us."

So, he'd been waiting for me? Had I been waiting for him? I rolled my metal cup between my palms, staring sightlessly in front of me. Then I said, "And if I had been? Brave enough, I mean?"

"Well… you were brave enough to drive out here after Allen Ward was killed." He was silent for a few seconds. Then, "Bringing these stones here today… how much grief is this going to cause for you?"

I let out a laugh that was more of a snort. "Depends on whether I tell anyone what I'm really doing today."

He nodded. "And that's how things go, Jesse. I couldn't approach you at school. It wouldn't cause me any grief at home, but it would have made things even worse for me at school. And it would have been unpleasant for you in both places. I'm not saying you should have approached me again, just that you'd need to be really sure that's what you wanted to do."

"Why did you talk to me on Thanksgiving?"

"Why did you spy on us at Samhain?" My back started to stiffen, but then he said, "I'm not saying it was wrong, as long as you weren't doing it just to spy on the freaks. And yes, I know that's the word town folks use."

"*I* don't."

"I'm glad. So what I was trying to figure out on Thanksgiving was why you had come out here that night. And I got the sense that you were not doing it for the thrill of it. It seemed like you were genuinely interested."

"How could you tell?"

"I couldn't be entirely sure right away, of course. But you came here alone. More often, when people of the town want to make life difficult for us, they run in packs."

He waited to see if I had anything to say to that, but I was too busy feeling ashamed of belonging to the people who join wolf packs to attack those who've done nothing to hurt the wolves. So he continued his explanation.

"After Samhain I asked Eleanor about it, and she suggested talking to you alone. Which is what I did. And it was a good conversation, but then it was up to you to keep it going. You didn't. So when you drove out here weeks later, right on the heels of having the police be so—I don't know, antagonistic, maybe? I wasn't inclined to be welcoming."

"I remember."

"I also asked Eleanor before inviting you to contribute to the labyrinth. We need to be super careful about interacting with town folk. I think you can understand why. So let me ask you outright. Why *are* you here?"

A question I'd asked myself, more than once. "I'm not

sure I can describe it. I don't understand who you are, here in the village, or why you do what you do, or even *what* you do, really. But I keep feeling like I want to know more." I glanced at his face. He wasn't looking at me. I decided to take a risk. "At first, I think it was you. I had a crush, or whatever, on you. But even though I don't feel like that anymore, there's still something—I don't know."

I couldn't quite tell what he was thinking, or if he might not be happy about what I'd said. I swallowed the last of my cider and stood up. Griffin stood, too.

"So," I said to him, a challenge in my tone, "you probably just want me to leave so you can get on with your sacred task."

His eyes bored into me for a few seconds. "As a matter of fact, this *is* a sacred task. Everything we do is a sacred task. And no, you don't have to leave. If you want to stay and help, we'd welcome you. But I'm not going to ask you to stay. You'd have to do it because you want to. It would have to come from you. And you wouldn't have to think of it as sacred, but we would want you to think carefully before telling anyone about being here. Anyone of the town, that is."

"Fine. I'll stay, then." I felt almost as though he'd dared me. But also it was like I had something to prove. Maybe that I could be brave, at least away from school. Away from the pack.

His smile put everything back on a friendly footing and made me feel good about my decision. "Great! I'll turn you over to Piper, then. She's our project manager. Come on."

As we walked, he told me that Piper was Eleanor's daughter, and that she was married to Todd the blacksmith. Her hair was mostly hidden under a green bandana. She was studying some plan or something as we approach and didn't bat an eye when Griffin introduced me, though she must have known I wasn't of the grove.

"Good to have you, Jesse. How about if I put you under

Cory over there? He's heading up the shovel brigade. Just walk over and introduce yourself, would you?" She smiled at me and then looked back at her work plan or whatever it was.

Cory was maybe twenty, tall and slender like Griffin, but with light hair. A green dragon tattoo climbed up his left forearm. He put me to work immediately, digging to a depth of a few inches between lines of string that connected markers set in the ground to indicate the path of the labyrinth. I had a shovel, a hand-held gardening fork for digging out unwanted stones, and a wheelbarrow to cart the dirt to a place across the field.

Before long I had to shed my jacket, and the work was strenuous enough that I almost wanted to strip my shirt off as well. A couple of times I took a short break and leaned on my shovel, and one time I spent a minute or so watching Ronan over near the stones, helping Eleanor sort them into different piles.

My wheelbarrow was half full when Cory sent me over to the tables where lunch remnants were still laid out, telling me to drink some water. I took advantage of the fact that there was still some of that bread left. While I was chewing on it, Ronan appeared beside me. He took some water and bread, too, and I was thinking I should either come up with something to say or go back to work, when Ronan broke the silence.

"That's a beautiful stone you brought. The limestone and quartz."

An olive branch, perhaps? I didn't want to cave too easily after his unfriendly treatment earlier, but I did want to show that people of the town could be friendly. If I could prove it to Ronan, perhaps they'd all believe me. "Thanks. I got it at this place where a friend of mine goes to look for crystals and things. Will it really go into the center?"

"Yes, I think so. It will be perfect there."

We munched and sipped in silence again, looking out

across this very large field. For the first time, it hit me that the labyrinth wasn't in the center of the field; it was off to one side. Also, it was in the middle of last year's corn planting, though the old stalks had already been cleared away from the work site. So I asked, "How did you decide where the labyrinth should go? Why is it in the corn field?"

"This is where Talise Alexander sensed the best energy."

"The best energy? What does that mean?"

Ronan turned toward me. "Griffin says you're not like the others. He says you were angry about what happened to him, and you're actually interested in what we do here. Is that true?"

He was maybe an inch shorter than me, but his question, which sounded like a challenge, made him seem larger. It was as though he had all the power of the grove behind him. And as for the question itself—well, I'd just told Griffin it was true. And it was, to a point, at least. Though I wasn't quite sure what that point was. But I said, "Yes."

"Is that why you followed us into the woods for the funeral?"

My jaw dropped. How could he know? It had been so dark, and the light from the torches and the small fire Griffin had made would have meant it was much easier for me to see them than the other way around. Even if Ronan had seen someone hiding behind that tree I'd used as cover, which was very unlikely, he wouldn't have been able to tell who it was. I struggled to cover my guilt. "What makes you think I was there?"

"See, now I can't trust you. If you were truthful, you'd just answer my question. Instead, you're trying to make me doubt what I know to be true." He set his water cup down on the table behind us and started to walk away.

I called out, "Wait!" He stopped, but only his head turned a little toward me, not his body. "How did you know it was me?"

"I sensed your energy. Make what you will of that."

He started to walk away again, but I wanted him to explain. "Ronan, wait. What does that even mean?"

This time he turned fully around. "I'm not going to try and explain that to you. You're not ready." He walked toward me and stopped a few feet away. "But if you really want to know about the field, if you're truly interested, then I'll tell you that. But only if you can convince me that you're not here just to observe us as though we were a freak show at some circus."

"I can do that," I said, scrambling to organize my brain cells so I could repeat some of what I'd learned. I started with a confession. "I was here at Samhain. I watched from other there," and I pointed to where I'd stood watching the fire, "while you opened the doorway for the dead. I know Samhain is a major sabbat, and Yule—which was December twenty-first—is a minor one. I know that Imbolc is coming up soon and that it's got to do with lights and fire and releasing old things and negative things, and it's about renewing life. And," I tilted my head just a tiny bit here, "I know the difference between a labyrinth and a maze."

Speaking of sensing energy, I could feel a kind of tension between Ronan and me. There was anger there, or maybe it was just challenge waiting to be met. I didn't know. All I did know was that it made me want him to stay right where he was and talk to me.

Our eyes locked, and for several seconds I wasn't aware of anything other than some connection between us that I couldn't identify. He lifted his chin a little, which broke the spell. "I knew about Samhain, too. I'm glad you included that just now."

Right; Griffin had known that I'd stayed after he'd discovered me at the meeting hall. So it was Ronan…again with the energy? What was with that, anyway?

He said, "All right, then. But don't go talking about all

this to anyone not of the grove. Just because you're open to it doesn't mean others are. Do you agree?"

What could I say but, "Yes."

He turned to gaze across the field and gestured with an arm as if to take it all in. "Talise doused with an aventurine pendant, and this is where she said the labyrinth needed to be. Aventurine is a stone with strong positive energy, and it's good for releasing old patterns and disappointments so new growth can take place. So this spot will be good for celebrating Allen Ward's life and also appropriate for Imbolc."

"What does 'doused' mean?"

Ronan looked around and then pointed toward a short, plump woman carrying used plates away from the food tables. "Talise is our best douser. For the labyrinth, she set her intention based on what we all decided—that was to find the most powerful positive energy. Then she made a large pendulum using a stone heavy enough to give a clear response even as she walked all over the field. And on the night of January fifth, during the cold moon, she tranced and walked around holding the pendulum. This is where it responded. We'll dedicate it on January twentieth, in the dark of the moon, even if we're not quite finished with the construction. The new moon is the best time for new beginnings."

Honestly, every time I spoke to one of these people I lost track of how many questions arose. I managed to connect "new moon" with "dark of the moon," perhaps helped somewhat by the name Griffin had given that black cat. So I asked, "Cold moon?" Had it been especially cold on January fifth? I couldn't remember.

"Each full moon has a different name. The first one in January—there could be two, but that's rare—is called the cold moon."

"Oh, okay. And—tranced?"

"She went into a trance state so she'd be as receptive as

possible to energies from the field, or from any other influence that would let her know when she'd found what she was looking for. Or, maybe, when she should avoid some spot."

His eyes were back on mine, and for a few seconds I was tongue-tied. Then I asked, "What do I have to do to be ready for you to tell me about sensing my energy?"

"I'll let you know." And he walked away, leaving me standing there watching him until I remembered that I need to get back to work.

By the time I headed over to the spot where I was to dump the third load of dirt I'd collected in my wheelbarrow, I realized it was after four and probably time for me to be gone. I grabbed my jacket and then located Griffin to tell him I was heading out.

"Thanks," he said. "Really. For the stones, and for staying to help. You did a lot today. After we get it all finished, maybe you'd like to come see it? You could even walk it, if you like."

"Sure. I'd like that."

Before I hopped into the truck, I did what I could to clear rock debris out of the bed. I had nothing like a broom, so I decided to take my shirt off and use that; it was easier to wash than the jacket. It worked well enough, though there were still some signs that I'd been carrying something around.

I was putting my shirt back on, just about to step behind the wheel, when I decided to turn and look for Ronan. He was watching me. He'd probably *been* watching me. I almost raised my arm to wave, but something stopped me. Somehow that casual gesture seemed wrong.

I had intended to go right home from the village, but somehow, even though it was getting late and Mom might be hoping I'd help her get dinner ready, I drove out to my

113

spot again. Wister Lake. The wind had picked up, whipping the water into little peaks and making the air feel really chilly. I didn't care. Just like after I'd come out to my folks, I sat there throwing stones into the water. Each one hit with an impotent plop and disappeared into nothingness.

Something was eating at me. But what? I'd just had a really great day, being with people who didn't care whether I was gay or not, helping them do something for Allen Ward that I hoped would go a little way toward neutralizing the apathy and worse from the town about that whole event, and—I wanted to believe—deepening my friendship with Griffin. Now I had to go home again, where people did care that I was gay (and not in a good way), but at least I wasn't living a lie there anymore.

That's when I realized what was bothering me. I'd created another lie. I'd directly disobeyed Mom, not just by going into the village, but also by staying there all afternoon. And I'd have to come up with something about where I'd been all day in case I got the third degree over dinner.

Damn it! I didn't want another fucking lie. But I knew I couldn't tell them about the village, especially right on top of coming out. I wasn't sure which would be worse, but I was determined to limit my revelations to one, at least for the time being.

So I thought, maybe I shouldn't go back to the village again. Maybe I should just hang out with Brad until after high school, when I might go to college or I might just move away.

Hell, maybe I'd move into the village like Parker.

I picked up a rather large stone and heaved it, and I killed my elbow. I got up, hugging my right arm against my body with my left hand, and walked up the narrow shoreline, feeling decidedly sorry for myself. How far away would I have to go, how far behind me would I have to leave my home, in order to be myself? What was this

114

shame thing that my dad feels—hell, that *I* feel about being gay—this shame that disappeared completely when I was with Griffin?

With this second lie now weighing on me, I decided I'd keep my head down about everything, starting that night at dinner. I didn't get home in time to help prepare the meal, but Mom asked me to help with last-minute stuff, using a tone of voice that let me know that I'd arrived home after she had been expecting me. Tough shit; I hadn't said when I'd get home, it wasn't my job to feed anyone, and if there was something about cooking that made my father and brother—who were sitting at the table expecting to be waited on—think of me as less than a man, maybe I should just stop doing that. I did the things Mom asked me to do, but I was sure my attitude let her know I wasn't any happier than she was.

She tried to cheer up the sour mood at the dinner table by asking questions about everyone's day. Dad and Stu are not chatty people, so even though Stu had spent the day someplace with Patty, he didn't exactly make a speech about it. When Mom turned to me, I did my best not to lie outright and also to keep my head down as planned.

"Drove around. Looked for places to hunt for rocks." For some reason I couldn't have explained, her questioning me got my back up. Shouldn't have; she wasn't any more insistent than she'd been with Dad or Stu; I knew she was just desperately trying to get a conversation going. It didn't help to know that.

"Really?" she asked. "All afternoon? Why were you so late?"

I looked down at my plate, stabbed a piece of steak, said, "Lost track of time," and shoved the meat into my mouth. I *had* lost track of time. I'd just happened to be in the village when that happened.

Lies of omission were going to be my friends. Or at least my companions.

I got through the Monday holiday (Martin Luther King Day) somehow, mostly by hiding in my room doing homework or watching stuff on my PC, and driving around. It was so, so, *so* tempting to drive back into the village and work on the labyrinth again. I must have driven past Woods Way on the highway six times. Partly I wanted to be in there to be with my new-found friends, and partly I wanted to distract myself from what was going to happen at school once everyone saw my locker. I went back and forth eighty-eleven times about whether to pretend astonishment and fury over that purple word, or whether to own it and say "Fuck you" to anyone who had a problem with it. Or with me. I didn't come to a decision.

Chapter Five

Back at school Tuesday morning, as I approached my locker, there were a few kids standing in front of it. They saw me, turned away, and walked quickly toward something else. Anything else. I forced myself to hold my head up, pretending not to care about them and to take no notice of the purple letters.

But then something snapped in me. Friday's paint job had been done on a whim, on the heels of feeling ashamed of what "my" people kept doing to Griffin and "his" people. And although I'd had a few difficult moments over the weekend, knowing there was going to be some kind of hell to pay this week, it no longer felt like a whim. It felt like the first step on a journey I needed to take. And it was my way of announcing that journey. Like, I'm gay. Get over it.

Half-way through home room, the office secretary appeared and handed something to the teacher, Mrs. Sawicki, who caught my eye and beckoned me to the front. I was pretty sure I knew this was going to be about my locker, and not knowing how long it would take I grabbed my book bag and followed the secretary back to the principal's office.

Mrs. Knapp sat behind her desk, looking busy, but she set everything aside as I took a chair facing the desk.

"Good morning, Jesse. It's been a while since you and I had a chance to talk."

"Yes, ma'am." I sat tall, head up, ready for anything.

"I'm sorry we have a difficult subject to discuss today. You are aware, I'm sure, of what someone has done to your locker."

Again, "Yes, ma'am." I was about to explain who "someone" was, but she didn't give me time.

"I can't tell you how much we disapprove of anything like that being inflicted on any of our students. I want you to know that steps will be taken immediately to remove the offensive term and restore the locker. In the meantime, I'm assigning you to a different locker."

That was about as far as she needed to go to get me really pissed. I'd been counting up responses point by point as she'd spoken.

"Mrs. Knapp, first of all, I was the one who painted the locker. Second, I don't want the word 'gay' removed, and I don't want a new locker. Third, there's nothing 'offensive' about being gay. And fourth, I'm surprised that you take this so seriously, when there are other lockers painted with truly offensive terms, and no one gets reassigned."

She sat back, her expression having gone through a few phases: surprise, confusion, and annoyance. "You do realize, Jesse, that painting a locker is considered to be vandalism, whether it's your own locker or not? So you've just confessed to vandalism."

I was sure she was going to say more, but the bell for first period rang and I took advantage of the break to prepare my next response. Struggling hard to keep my tone polite and calm, I said, "Okay, so you should probably give me the same punishment you've given to Lou and Chuck. They're always vandalizing Griffin Holyoke's locker. What action did you take against them? Just so I can be prepared."

She sucked her cheeks in, chewed on her lower lip, and stared at me. Then, "Since you've confessed, this concerns no one but you. So, first, all items from the vandalized locker have already been moved to a new locker. My secretary will give you the locker number and combination as you leave. Second, you are hereby required to stay after

118

school in Mrs. Sawicki's class each day this week, for an hour each day. You will be expected to work on your school assignments during this time, and no cell phone use will be permitted. Third—since you seem to like things itemized—if you vandalize your new locker, the punishment will be stiffer. Do you understand?"

"You didn't address one of my points."

"And that would be—?"

"You implied that there's something offensive about being gay. And I'm gay, so I found that offensive. And maybe you're not aware of what was painted by Lou and Chuck on my locker before I redecorated it. It was the word 'faggot.' Now, *that's* offensive. But being gay is not."

"Young man, that part of your life is not something we will discuss. I'm sorry about what was painted on your locker by someone else, but if what you've told me is something you're convinced of, I suggest you would be well advised not to advertise it, on your locker or anywhere else."

"So my being gay is offensive to you? And you think I should hide it, because everyone else will agree with you?"

"What I think of this issue is irrelevant. I'm suggesting that if you go out of your way to advertise it, something worse than having your locker vandalized is very likely to happen. You've already said you believe that there are other students committing vandalism, although to be truthful I wasn't aware of it. Perhaps Griffin is removing the graffiti himself before it's reported. At any rate, you should keep your head down, young man, so that we don't have anything more serious than today's subject to discuss in the near future. Now, do you understand?"

"I understand what you've said. I've understood it very well, in fact." Without waiting to be dismissed, I got up, yanked my bag off the floor, and marched out. The secretary stopped me.

"Jesse, here's your new locker number and a hall pass.

First period is already under way."

I snatched the piece of paper from her hand and nearly stomped out of the office. Rather than go to first period, I decided to find my new locker. I needed some time to cool off.

Keep my head down, she'd said. Interesting. Just yesterday I'd decided that was what I needed to do. Now it seemed like a bad idea. It seemed like a cowardly idea.

The new locker was missing a couple of items I'd left in the old one: the solvent, and the can of purple paint. Mrs. Knapp must not have known about them, or she would have known who the vandal was. I decided I'd wait a couple of days, see how I felt, and maybe go and get some more paint.

So maybe my plan was no longer "head down," but after today's episode with Mrs. Knapp I was not very pleasant to much of anyone, including Mom. Which translated into not spending any time in the kitchen voluntarily.

Mom must have got sick of my attitude, because Thursday after her four o'clock piano student left, she came to my room and interrupted my research for a history paper. My chosen topic was the usurping of Pagan traditions by Christianity. I was annoyed that she interrupted, not only because I didn't want her to confront me on anything, but also because this paper was for history, and there was a new teacher this year for that class. Mr. Duncan was around thirty, I guess, and he had a lot of really fresh ways of looking at history, ways that brought it into life like history had never done for me before. And I knew he'd be cool with my topic. He might even be really pleased with it. He might think it was original, one of his favorite words. But here was Mom, interrupting.

"Jesse, I think we need to talk."

Ominous. I sighed, shut my laptop, and leaned back in my chair, arms crossed on my chest. Mom moved over to the bed and sat down, and I had to turn my chair so I could face her; I was prepared to be only so rude. But I said nothing, just waited for her to begin.

She stared at me for a minute. Then, "I don't understand what's gotten into you lately." To which my brain responded, *OMG. What a typical parent line, to which no teenager has any acceptable response.*

She waited, but so did I, so she said, "You have nothing to say?"

I shrugged. "Don't know what *to* say. You'll need to be more specific."

She glared at me. "I have been nothing but friendly toward you. I'm doing my very best to accept what you've told us about yourself, and I think you know that. And yet you disappear for hours on end with no explanation, you're surly at the dinner table, and you're not available to help me do something I know you enjoy doing. Is that specific enough?"

"My father and brother have made it very clear to me that it makes them uncomfortable when I do things they consider unmanly. Dad practically attacked me about the cooking thing. How am I going to get them to accept me if I keep doing things they think a man shouldn't do?"

She opened her mouth to respond, but I kept going. "And as for disappearing, and not talking, how is that different from what *they* do? You don't quiz Stu when he's out for hours, and both he and Dad talk very little at any time. Dad wants me to be more like him. You want me to be—what, more like you?"

I hated myself as soon as I said that. I wanted desperately to take it back; there was no excuse for hurting my mother, and I knew damn well that's what I was doing. The look on her face confirmed it.

She stood, tears in her eyes, about to leave. Then

something flew into my brain and my mouth let it out. "Do you wish you'd had a daughter instead of me?"

As she headed for the door she threw this at me: "Not until today, no."

I wasn't the only one who could hurt people.

Brad had asked, a couple of times that week at school, if something was wrong, but I'd shrugged him off, saying I was fine. For whatever reason, he never mentioned my locker. He must have known about it, though, because I kept seeing little bunches of kids break up and move away from me as I got closer to them. But by Friday afternoon I'd had about enough isolation, so when Brad asked if I'd go rockhounding with him Sunday after church, I agreed immediately. I was ready for some companionship. It felt unnatural to be so anti-social. I decided to apologize to Mom.

Then, a few minutes later, I got a text from Griffin inviting me to walk the finished labyrinth on the following Sunday, February first, and then stay for a grove supper and the Imbolc bonfire. It probably shouldn't have surprised me how much I wanted to go. I mean, it really isn't like me to lock out everyone in my life, to stop talking, stop being myself in ways that have nothing to do with being gay. Plus, I'd be with Griffin and his people. So I agreed.

Of course I got home a little late, what with my punishment from Mrs. Knapp over the locker vandalism, but at least some of my homework was already done. As Mom's last student left, I was waiting for her. She turned back toward the room after closing the front door and saw me standing there. Her tone cold, she said, "Did you need something, Jesse?"

Hands in my pockets, shifting weight from foot to foot, I said, "I want to apologize. For being so rude. And for saying the things I said."

Her chin went into the air a little way, but I could tell I'd said what she wanted to hear. "Anything else?"

"I miss working with you in the kitchen. So if it's okay with you, I'd like to do that again."

She was trying not to smile, but she failed. "I think that could be arranged."

"There's something else, though."

I needed to prepare the ground for going into the village, which I already had more plans to do, based on Griffin's invitation. Also, I knew that having her question where I'd been, when a full answer would have included things I didn't want her to know, would get me back to the place I'd been this week. It was a place I didn't like, a place that didn't feel like the real me. If being gay was the real me, so was being truthful, and being nice to my mom.

I took a deep breath. "The thing is, I need a little more latitude when I'm not at home. If I'm out for a few hours, I need you to trust me. I mean, trust that I'm not doing anything horrible, or illegal, or anything like that. Because I won't be. I just don't want to have to account for every minute, that's all."

She thought about that for a second. "We'll need to work that out, Jesse. You're still—"

"I'm seventeen."

"And you—" She raised a hand to her hairline.

I knew what she was thinking. "I don't have a boyfriend, Mom. And I'm not having 'gay sex' all over my truck or anyplace else."

She watched my face a minute, maybe to be sure she believed me. "That could change."

"Yeah, I guess it could."

She exhaled audibly. "As I said, we'll need to work it out."

Several things occurred to me, but rather than say any of them, I asked, "So, do you need any help with dinner?"

Sunday afternoon was great weather for rockhounding, chilly but not cold. The night before I'd lain in bed for a while thinking about Brad, and about lies. I'd told him about being gay before coming out to my folks. Maybe I would test him on going into the village, too.

Brad had only one pack with him. "I won't be able to do much until this cast comes off; still a couple of weeks to go. So if you find something you want to work at, you can use my stuff."

He told me to drive to the same place we'd been when he'd pointed out the bobcat cave, and then he said, "Are we gonna talk about this locker thing, or not?"

I laughed. "If you want, sure."

"What's so funny?"

"Look, I know I've been kind of a turd this week. But— well, I painted the locker."

There was a heavy pause. Then, "Dude."

I told him about the word that had been there Friday, though I didn't mention meeting with Griffin or what was on his locker. Brad couldn't quite believe the story of my conversation with Mrs. Knapp.

"Shit, man! How the hell did you get away with that?"

"It seemed like a good idea at the time."

"And now?"

I laughed again. "It still seems like a good idea." I could feel him staring at the side of my face. "And I might just paint my new locker the same way."

"So I guess you're out for real, now. Who else knows you painted it?"

"Just Mrs. Knapp, as far as I know."

Neither of us knew what else to say about that, but the feeling I was getting from Brad was that maybe he wasn't entirely cool with my artwork. Maybe it was something about the way he grabbed the pack, broken arm notwithstanding, rather than let me carry it.

THROWING STONES

It had snowed a little since I'd hauled that limestone slab out, but when we got to where it had been, you could tell something had been removed. Brad stopped beside the spot and turned to me.

"Isn't this where that stone was? The limestone with the quartz breccia you found last time we were here?"

"Yeah. About that. I took it."

"You what?"

I inhaled deeply and looked around at the trees and the rocky ridge on my right for inspiration, or courage, or something. Then I looked at Brad again. "I took it. You'd said you didn't think it was quite worth the effort, at least for why you collect rocks. But I knew of someone else who could use it, so I hauled it out and gave it to them."

He stared at me, right hand on his hip, a scowl on his face. "You're gonna have to explain that."

I grinned. "Yeah, I know. See, this is something I've been meaning to talk with you about. There just hasn't been a great time. But—well, the thing is, I've been helping the people in the village build a labyrinth." I almost said "grove" here but caught myself in time. "It's in Mr. Ward's memory. The guy who tried to protect Mary Blaisdell?" I paused to see if I could get a read on Brad's reaction so far.

He was still scowling, but maybe more in confusion than anything else. "Why would you do that?" He sounded almost like Mom when she'd asked why I'd driven to the grove the day after Mr. Ward was killed.

I shrugged, hoping to lighten things a little, just in case this was going in a bad direction. "I felt really bad about him getting killed, and it irritated me that nobody seemed to think he'd done something good. Or, at least, tried to. I mean, if my dad had been in his place and had gotten killed, he'd have died a hero. But Mr. Ward gets hung in effigy, and his family got pestered by the police as though he'd been after Mary, himself. And every time I mention the situation, everyone acts like it isn't something he should have done. Protect Mary, I mean."

The scowl deepened. Like he knew this conversation would take a few minutes, he lowered the pack to the ground. "How do you know how the police treated the Wards?"

"Griffin told me."

"Griffin Holyoke? Since when do you talk to Griffin Holyoke?"

I felt my own scowl start; couldn't quite stop it. "Why shouldn't I talk to him? He's in our classes, for fuck's sake."

The air between us felt thick with some kind of tension, some of it left over from the locker discussion, and some from this new difference between us. Neither of us moved or spoke for maybe half a minute. Brad must have decided to avoid working through it. He went around it. "And what's this about a maze?"

"Not a maze, a labyrinth. Mazes try to get you lost. Labyrinths lead you into the center and out again."

"Why?"

I waved a hand. "I can go into that later. Right now what I need to tell you is that I've been helping them build one. And this stone," I pointed to where it wasn't any longer, "is at the very center. It's where you end up when you walk in, and where you leave from when you walk out. And I need to ask you not to say anything to anyone about my having anything to do with the village, because I'll be going there again. And I'm not supposed to. Will you do that? Will you promise?"

His scowl let up a little; I hoped he was remembering that I was keeping a promise for him already. about his dad. Finally he shrugged and his face relaxed. "Who would I tell, anyway?"

"Staci. Your sisters. Maybe someone at school. Your mom."

"I got it, okay? But I can't say I understand."

I really wanted him to. "Here's the thing. I really like

being there. I liked working on the labyrinth. I like the people, I like the way they approach things. They couldn't care less if someone's gay. They've done the dedication of the labyrinth for Mr. Ward—I wasn't there, it was on a Tuesday night—but there's a holiday coming up for their... um, tradition," I wasn't quite sure I'd call it a religion, and I made a mental note to ask Griffin about that, "when they'll walk the labyrinth and have supper and a bonfire. I've been invited to be there. It's next Sunday. I really want to go. But just a few weeks ago, Mom told me to stay away from the village."

"So you're asking me to say you're with me next Sunday?"

"Well..." That hadn't occurred to me, actually, because I'd been so focused on having enough freedom that I wouldn't need a cover. And almost immediately I saw that it would involve another lie, one I'd be dragging Brad into. "No. That's not why I'm telling you. I'm telling you because you're my best friend, and because I want you to know about something that's important to me."

He stood there, scratching near the edges of the cast on his left arm, looking around at nothing in particular. Then, "This is a lot, Jesse. First, I find out you're gay, and that you've known for a long time. I'm not saying it's a problem, just that it was a bit of a surprise, and I'm still adjusting. And now, out of the blue, you're chumming around with the freaks? *That*, I don't get."

"Don't call them that. They're people. And they—well, they have no problem at all with anyone being different."

"Yeah, well, they're all a little 'different,' aren't they?"

"Knock it off, Brad. They're just people. I'm the one who's different. And like I said before, they couldn't care less." I watched his face, hoping I'd see something like understanding, but I didn't. I thought about describing this mission I'm on—this mission to dissolve the fear that townies have for the village—with love. But best friend no,

Brad was still Brad, and I didn't think he'd know what to do with that information. So instead I fell back on the gay thing.

"Look, maybe you don't get how tough it's been for me. I've been hiding for over two years, terrified of giving away something about me I couldn't change, something that everyone around me would think was horrible. Hell, even I've had moments when I've felt ashamed of who I am. And that's bullshit. The people in the village know it's bullshit. Your reaction was great. It made me feel worlds better. But you never even asked how my folks reacted."

"Wait. You told your folks? I thought you decided not to."

"I decided not to open with all that research you saw. I opened with love. It didn't make much difference. I could have opened with anything, and Stu would still hate me, Dad would still be ashamed of me, and Mom would still be watching me like a hawk, afraid I'm dating boys. And now the same assholes who paint Griffin's locker are painting mine, and our own principal practically told me to be ashamed of who I am. So I hope you see how—God, how *free* I feel with Griffin and his people. So fucking free. So fucking great."

This was so true and so real that I was near tears, and I think Brad saw that. I turned away so he couldn't see my face, my breathing a little tight. I barely heard him speak.

"Jesse, it's okay. I'll keep both your secrets."

Without turning back, I gave a tiny nod, afraid of what would happen if I tried to say *Thanks*. We stood there like that for some huge number of seconds.

Then, obviously trying to make his voice sound normal, he said, "So this labyrinth thing. Am I going to get to see it?" This time it didn't feel like he was avoiding tension. It felt like that was behind us, and he was just moving on to the next thing.

I let out a sound that was half laugh, half bark. "I'll see

if I can get you safe passage."

"Great. So why are we still standing here? Let's get chiseling." He handed me the pack and led the way along the trail to the far side of the outcropping..

It was amazing to watch Brad work his way up the rock face. It wasn't straight up, or anything, but he had only the one hand to work with, and it was a scramble. Before too long he stood up straight on a flat outcropping and waited for me to catch up. In front of him was a cave.

"Gimme the pack." His voice was very quiet. He pulled out a cylinder of some kind, turned the head a quarter of a revolution, and handed the thing to me. "Stand over there," and he pointed toward where the rock face made a kind of wall off to the right side of the cave. "If something comes out and doesn't run away from us, stand tall and get ready to spray it with pepper spray. If it comes near either of us, you need to spray it."

WTF?

He picked up some rocks, cradling them against his chest with the cast, and threw one into the cave. He was poised like anything could happen, but nothing did. He threw another rock, and another. He moved closer and threw a couple more.

"K. Looks good."

While he dug a helmet, goggles, a headlamp, and a chisel from his pack, I asked, "So, what might have come out? Are we talking bobcats again? Or bears?"

"Cougars. They're mostly in the western part of the state, but there've been a few sightings farther east, and even into Arkansas."

Cougars. Mountain lions. He was gonna owe me *big* time after this! Bobcats avoid people whenever possible. Cougars eat them.

I struggled to keep my voice calm. "So, I'm guessing my job is to stand guard and watch for returning cats?"

"Yup. If you see something, start shouting. I'll get out

as quick as I can. The rest will be obvious. Meanwhile, if you have a few songs at your command, or if you know a poem, it would be good to keep some sound going." He crouched down as well as he could, hampered by his cast, and crawled into the cave. It didn't seem to be very deep; I could still see his boots when a light inside told me he'd switched on his headlamp.

I pulled my phone out, turned the volume up to maximum, and set it to repeat a tune that had a lot of noise to it. Then I found a good lookout position. "Can you hear me in there?"

"Yeah."

"So besides my phone, I think what I'll do for sound is talk to you about the village." While he chipped away at rocky bits in the cave, I kept up a running stream of chatter, telling him about the time I'd driven out after Mr. Ward was killed, about the Samhain celebration (though I called it Halloween for Brad's sake), about the beauty of the funeral in the woods, about the other stones I'd collected for the labyrinth, about the great food at the worksite that day, and about blacksmith and all-around superman, Todd Swazey. I didn't mention Ronan or anything he'd told me about dousing, or energy, or cold moons. I almost—but not quite—forgot to look around for cats.

When Brad scrambled out of the cave again, he was pulling a chamois cloth with rocks and stones on it, his haul from the chipping efforts. As he packed everything back up again, I asked, "Get anything good?"

"Naw. Couldn't really maneuver in there with this cast. Besides, I'd pretty much worked it dry before today. You can go in if you want, but I doubt you'll find anything worth keeping."

"Okay, so why come here?"

He sat on the stone ledge, legs out straight, the chamois between his knees. He was folding it up, awkwardly, and didn't look at me. "Actually, I thought you'd get a kick out of this spot. I love it. And anyway, I'm saving this paltry collection. Maybe someday I'll want to show it to my dad. Tell him this is all I could get with the broken arm he gave me."

Dark. And it was the only time he'd mentioned his dad without me prodding him. His tone told me he didn't want to discuss it even now. I went in a different direction. "So how likely was it, really, that there would have been a cougar here?"

"Not very. I did look for scat around the bottom of the ledge, and scratch marks as we came up, and all around the cave entrance. It was very unlikely. But with cougars, you need to be real careful."

"Have you ever actually seen one?"

"Nope. And I hope that doesn't change."

Oddly, I felt myself kind of hoping I would see one sometime, but from a safe distance.

Brad sat on the ledge, his back to the rock wall, and pulled out an insulated bag. "I packed us a snack. You hungry?"

"Great! Yeah."

He handed me a plastic bottle. "Here's water for you."

I moved over to sit beside him as we downed peanut butter sandwiches and apples. I couldn't help wondering if he'd brought something to feed us in compensation for dragging me someplace I wouldn't find any good rocks.

Food gone, we were sipping our water, and Brad said, "So this labyrinth thing. Tell me again. What's the point?"

"You're supposed to contemplate something important in your life as you walk it. Other things occur to you on your way in, and you just keep moving your thoughts back to what you wanted to think about. When you get to the center, you see how everything in your head is stacking up, kind of. And when you're ready, you walk out again and see if something else comes to you, like what to do about a problem, that sort of thing."

He stared out at the branches of trees. We were about half-way up some of them, close to the tops for others. Lots of pines in the mix meant there was a lot of green.

"So here's the thing," he said, finally. "I know I owe you, so I'm gonna keep your secret, like I said earlier. And," he took a final swig of water and crushed the plastic bottle in his hand, "I wanna see this labyrinth. Doesn't need to be on this holiday thingy, whatever that is. Could be a couple of weeks, whatever. I wanna see how they used that rock, and I wanna meet these people you're getting to know." He looked at me. "Deal?"

It's hard to describe the relief I felt after he said that. The only thing was whether I really could get him in to see the labyrinth. It isn't exactly up to me. Griffin and Ronan had both led me to believe they'd welcome an approach in good faith, but did Brad have reasons other than what he'd said? Was he prepared to change his mind about the people he'd been taught to fear, or at least to ridicule?

"I just need to ask you first if you're genuinely interested in the village. Because," he started to protest and I had to talk over him, "the thing is, they're so used to folks from the town kind of spying on them, or making fun of what they do, kind of like they're some kind of circus act, and that really makes them crazy. I don't blame them. They've opened things up to me because they know I don't go talking about them, and because I take what they do seriously. Doesn't mean I'm ready to join them, or anything, but I'm trying to understand them. Do you know what I mean?"

"What d'you take me for?"

"I just need to be sure you understand that they're skittish about opening themselves up to—you know, ridicule, gossip. Look, even today, when I mentioned Griffin, you wanted to know why I would talk to him. Remember?"

He shrugged, looking a little sheepish. "Yeah. Okay. I

get it. I'll play nice."

I grinned at him until he looked at me and grinned back. "I just need to clear it with them, but I'm pretty sure it won't be a problem."

We'd finished all the food, our water was gone, but I wasn't ready to leave, and it seemed Brad wasn't, either. He lay back, and I sat near the edge of the ledge, legs hanging over. The rock was warm where the sun had been shining on it.

After a few minutes I heard Brad snore once or twice, just a little. Maybe he woke himself up, because he sat up, yawned, and rubbed his face with his right hand. That's when I decided to take a small risk.

"So, things with your dad. Are they getting any better at all?"

Brad took a little time to pretend he was looking around, maybe for cougars or something, before he said, "He has this meeting every week with Reverend Gilman."

"I remember you'd mentioned something about that, the day we watched *Gravity*." I waited; silence. "The meetings are helping, then?"

No response right away, but I was determined to wait him out. Finally, grudgingly, he said, "I think so. I'm just not ready to forgive him."

"Yeah, well, I don't blame you for that." I didn't see any point in pushing him further. It was enough to know Brad's mom and sisters—and Brad, too, for that matter—weren't likely to be in any immediate danger of being zapped. And it was starting to feel like we needed to lighten things up.

Brad must have thought the same. "By the way, how the hell did you get that limestone slab out all by yourself?"

I grinned, remembering my struggle, and described my process. "The toughest part was that slope back up to the truck."

He laughed, and I couldn't remember the last time he'd laughed with humor. His antics after we'd

133

watched *Gravity* didn't count. He said, "Well, shit. I'm impressed."

Griffin was not altogether happy about my request for Brad to see the labyrinth, however. I asked him about it after school Monday, at our trysting spot in the cafeteria.

"Jesse, does he even know what a labyrinth is?"

"I explained it to him. See, the thing that caught his attention was that rock, the one you've put in the center. He goes rock hunting out near where it came from. He knows a lot about rocks. Not like Ronan, I mean, but—you know. What kind of rock it is, that sort of thing. He has a huge collection, and most of them are specimens he's found himself. And, actually, you kind of owe him; the only reason I knew about that rock was because we went hunting together."

"So he knows rocks from a geological point of view."

"Yeah, I guess."

"And how open is he to hearing about them from more of an energetic viewpoint?"

"You mean, like Eleanor and Ronan see them? I'm not sure. But if you don't want to go into that aspect with him, that's okay. I don't think he'd be there more than a few minutes, anyway." I was kind of hoping no one would describe rock energies, to tell the truth; I didn't know how Brad would respond to Ronan's description of that dousing stone, for example, or about the less scientific qualities of white quartz.

"Well, I'll need to talk to Eleanor. I'll have to let you know."

"Is Eleanor, like, the lead person in the grove, or something?"

"Yes."

"Is she married?"

"Widowed. Why do you ask?"

I shrugged. "Just wondering if there's a king of the grove, if she's queen, or whatever."

"She's the Elder. And not just because her husband died several years ago; he never had that role. And it has only a little to do with her age." He exhaled loudly. "Okay, well, if you don't hear otherwise, let's assume it'll be fine. So on Sunday, people will be walking the labyrinth on and off all afternoon, and then we'll all be involved in dinner prep. Why don't you come by sometime after three?"

Chapter Six

Sunday after church I tried my best to be polite during lunch without overdoing it; I was afraid that if I was too forthcoming, it might encourage Mom to ask what my plans were for the afternoon, and my plan was to say as little about that as possible. For sure, I wasn't about to say anything about going to the village.

But I needed to say something, because I'd be at the village through dinner, and even though I'd mentioned it to Mom last night, I didn't want there to be any misunderstandings. I waited until Dad had disappeared downstairs and Stu had headed out without any explanation about where he was going or for how long. I grabbed my jacket and keys, and as I headed for the door I called "See you" to Mom.

"Jesse? Where are you going?"

"Like I told you last night, I'm having dinner with a few friends from school. I'll be home in plenty of time to finish my homework for tomorrow."

"But where are you going *now*? It's not dinner time."

I stood with one hand on the open door and did my best to arrange my face into an expression of exasperation that didn't quite cross the line into impertinence, and I just looked at her as if to say, *Really? Haven't we talked about this?*

All I did say was, "I have my cell if you need me. See you later." And I escaped quickly, pretending I didn't hear her call my name again.

The afternoon was kind of warm for February, high

forties, but overcast. It was still kind of early to show up at the village, but I'd wanted to get out of the house as soon after lunch as possible so nobody (read: Mom) could involve me in anything. So I needed to drive around for a little while. I was feeling kind of anxious about today, though I couldn't have said why.

I drove over to Wister Lake and sat looking at the water, which was almost black with no sun shining on it. I stared into it as though I could see what was hiding down there. Thinking back to the day I'd worked on the labyrinth, I tried to pick individual impressions apart; maybe that would help me figure out what was making me nervous about being in the village again.

There was Griffin, of course, but when I let my mind linger on him, what I felt was something light and fun, despite the black hair and all the piercings and that tree on his back. I was surprised that I felt absolutely nothing sexual at all now. Self-preservation, maybe? Because I knew he was straight? And the impression I used to have about him, that he'd know the answers to those universal and unanswerable questions, felt like misplaced hero worship now. I genuinely liked him. But he was not my hero.

Todd Swazey was impressive, but that's all. Eleanor was Eleanor; she seemed distant, but not out of anything unfriendly. It was more like that's just who she is, and maybe as Elder of the grove she needs to maintain a feeling of remove.

Then there was Ronan.

As soon as I focused on Ronan, there was a kind of chaos happening in my brain. I couldn't get my thoughts to land on anything and stay there. Impressions such as bristly, protective, cautious, dangerous, and fascinating flew around, and I just watched that black water and let the thoughts fly. After a bit, I wasn't seeing the water. I was seeing something in the center of all those flying things. It was like two eyes looking back at me, only they seemed more like an animal's eyes. They were looking right at me, not boring into me exactly, but something about them made me think of power that lies deep. Not like Todd's strength, but something other than a physical kind of power. The eyes were frightening and also compelling, and I wasn't sure which of those things made me pull away and blink until I saw the lake again.

I shook my arms out and decided I needed to immerse myself in something familiar, something mundane. So I sat in the truck for a bit, listening to music before heading to the village.

Griffin invited me inside his house, which I'd been hoping would happen so I could see if the insides of the houses here were as normal as the outsides. They were. Though I did notice a difference in the kinds of things the Holyokes had by way of knick-knacks. Instead of something like the Hummel figurines my mom collects, the Holyokes had things made of wood, like carved animal shapes, or stone things, some carved and some more natural forms. I was really drawn to something Griffin said was an amethyst geode. It was on the floor, standing upright about two feet high, gray and oddly shaped on the back and top. It had been cut open so you could see inside to all these purple crystal teeth. It was incredibly beautiful. Griffin said it came from Brazil, I think, not from around here, so it wasn't something Brad was likely to find. Too bad.

Griffin said that I'd get to meet his father, and also Selena and Parker, at the supper later. Mrs. Holyoke seemed nice, although she also seemed a little scattered as she worked on things she was preparing for the supper later. She talked mostly about how glad she was that Selena and Parker were moving back and would live in the village, which was news to me. She offered us apples with cheddar cheese, and as soon as we'd devoured everything, Griffin suggested going to the labyrinth.

THROWING STONES

"Most people have already walked it at least once, and although they might do it again later because of Imbolc, it's probably pretty empty right now."

On the way out of the house I noticed something beside the door. Two somethings, actually. They looked like crude dolls, made out of what must be corn husks. One was obviously newer than the other.

"What are those?" I asked Griffin.

"Imbolc dolls. They symbolize the old year, the crone, and the new year, the maiden. The crone was last year's doll, and the maiden will be the crone next year. Mom always has me make them, though she can't explain why. It's just a tradition that someone in the house who's male is supposed to make them."

"Do they live here near the door for a reason?"

Griffin laughed. "No. We'll give the crone to the fire later. The maiden doll will get put away until Imbolc next year. Come on."

The sun began to peek out from behind the clouds as Griffin and I walked over to the labyrinth. I could see there were a couple of other people walking it now. There was a bench off to the left, to the north of the shape and looking toward the woods that led to the funeral site.

I asked, "Is there one path in and another path out?" I was wondering what happened if two people met going opposite directions. I knew the path was single-file wide.

"In this particular design, you enter on the left, and it leads you all the way around. You'll probably want to stop for a minute, to contemplate or whatever, when you get to the limestone with the quartz. Then keep going, and it will lead you out."

By the time we got to the labyrinth, there was no one on it anymore. Griffin said, "Why don't we just walk around the outside first? It will give you a sense of the thing, and you can see all the work that was done, maybe pick out the standing stones you brought."

As we started around, clockwise, he asked, "Have you decided what you'll bring into the walk?"

OMG, was I supposed to bring more stones, or something? An offering of some kind? "Like what?"

"A question, maybe. Or a feeling. A problem. Something you want to offer, like gratitude, or something you want to know, like what you should do about something bothering you. That kind of thing."

Right. I'd forgotten to come up with something. "Can I think about that while we're walking around the outside?"

"Sure. Or you can just walk the pattern and see what comes to you. Up to you."

"If I think of something, do I need to tell you what it is? Or is that bad luck?"

He chuckled. "No need to tell anyone. Do you see your standing stones?"

As I recalled, I'd brought four, all thin, taller than they were wide. There were quite a few like that, but then I saw the one I'd found first, with the irregular points on top. "That's one of them, I think."

As we approached the entrance again, I asked, "Are you going to walk now, too?"

"I'm gonna sit in the sun, just over there," and he pointed to the bench facing the path into the woods. "I've already walked it today."

"Are you supposed to walk it every day?"

"See, Jesse, the thing about labyrinths is there are no rules. You could walk it every day, but for most people that's probably too often. I think folks here have walked it a lot, because they probably walked it once or twice for Allen, and then they walked it again for their own reasons. The novelty will wear off, and I think everyone will find their own routine. It's whatever feels right, that's all."

We stood together at the opening. The path in led between two metal posts that stood like gate keepers, about seven feet tall, square columns that were hollow and had images cut out of them in various places. On the top of each was a different three-dimensional shape I couldn't make sense out of, but I'd already asked so many questions I decided not to ask about those. I couldn't help wondering, though, if it was Todd the blacksmith who made those columns, who did all the cutouts, who created those mystical shapes.

"Whenever you're ready, just walk in. When you get to your limestone slab, see if you have any clarity on whatever you were thinking about on your way in."

Walking around the outside, nothing much had come to me. I considered contemplating what those eyes had been, staring up at me from the lake, but I wasn't sure I wanted to know, and I figured that was enough metaphysics for one day, anyway. So I just stepped forward, slowly, like Griffin had said.

The brick path was set level with the dirt, and in between one curved brick path and the next were flat stones set so they were slightly higher than the bricks, probably to help keep you on the path. At first I tried to remember where I'd been digging so I'd know when I got to the bricks in my section, but I couldn't figure it out. So I just walked.

My mind kept going back to the lake, but it wasn't focusing on the water. Instead, it was all about being there with Stu, with what I'd felt about our relationship and about what I couldn't tell him. Without any conscious effort, I realized my thoughts for the walk would be about being gay. It would be about what it meant to tell the people I love, the people who love me, this really important thing about who I am. And about what had happened once they knew.

Thinking into the future, I wondered whether my family would ever get to the point where they'd want to meet my boyfriend, if I ever had one. And someday, maybe a fiancé. I just couldn't wrap my mind around that. And if my own family couldn't accept me, couldn't accept the way I need to live my life, what could I expect from the rest of the town? It had occurred to me already that I wouldn't be able to stay in Himlen, but I hadn't allowed myself to dwell on it. But now, with nothing else to do but think about it, it hit me. It hit me hard.

By the time I got to the limestone slab with the quartz breccia, I was kind of emotional. All these questions were tumbling over each other with no clear way for me to move forward, nothing to help me decide what I should do. I stared at the quartz pieces, and that spiral that Eleanor said represents eternal life was more obvious to me now. But it wasn't comforting. If I had to live my life as a lie, I didn't want any part of "eternal."

I stood right on the spiral and closed my eyes. The deep breath I took was shaky, so I took a few more until they were smooth, and until I felt calmer. The sun was fully out now, and I could feel its warmth on my face.

When I opened my eyes, I was facing the path that led into the woods. I knew the bench where Griffin went to sit was behind me, and as I was about to turn toward it I already knew there would be someone else there, too. Maybe I hadn't been as unaware of the bench as it had felt while I was walking, so maybe I'd already seen him—but before I turned around I knew Ronan was there.

He looked quite small next to Griffin, but somehow his presence was larger. He was looking right at me, that level gaze that made me feel like he was seeing right into me. I walked over and sat on the other side of Griffin from Ronan, and we all gazed toward the woods without speaking for a few minutes.

Griffin broke the silence. "I have to go help get stuff ready for supper. Not cooking, of course," and he grinned at me, "though maybe another time you'd like to bring something you've made." He turned to Ronan. "Jesse's quite the chef, it seems."

"I—well, that's overstating things, really. I just like to

cook." I kept my eyes on the woods.

"And create things," Griffin said. "Don't be too modest. I know you make up your own recipes. Anyway, Ronan has something he'd like to talk to you about, so I'll head off. See you in a bit." As he got up, the space where he'd been felt electric, or pulsing, or something. I couldn't tell whether it was coming from him or Ronan or what. I wanted to turn to look at Ronan, and I didn't want to do that. I looked down at my hands instead, open flat on my thighs.

Ronan said, "I have something I'd like to show you. But you'd need to keep it a strict secret. Very strict. From anyone outside the grove. Can you accept that?"

My impulse was to say Sure, but that felt way too casual. Turning to look at him, I asked, "It's not anything too weird, is it?"

He smiled. It changed his face so it was less intense, less guarded. "Not at all. It's something fun. Feel up to a short walk?"

Now I could say it: "Sure."

I followed him toward that path into the woods. He knew I'd seen the clearing where they'd had the funeral ceremony, so it seemed unlikely that was where he was headed. And in fact, just after the path headed south into the trees, he turned left on a narrow trail I hadn't noticed in the dark the last time I'd been here. We walked single file as the land started to rise through the woods, and then the trail led steeply uphill for maybe a hundred yards. Ahead of me and above me, the trees and Ronan blocked the view or I'd have been less surprised by what was in front of us suddenly. When I saw it, I stopped short, next to a pile of split logs.

The path we'd been following had led us to the top of a cliff. Right in front of us was a short swinging bridge, ropes along the sides to hold onto, and it led to the door of a small house that looked like it was perched in the branches of a huge tree growing from below the cliff. When I got over my initial shock, I saw it was really built around the tree trunk, on some kind of platform that was bigger than the house part. Around the outside of the door was a wooden frame with ornate carvings that looked like branches or vines wrapping around different kinds of animals. The windows had shutters that actually worked— that is, they were pulled closed over the windows.

Ronan had turned, no doubt to see my reaction. I was completely stunned and didn't know what to say. So I went with, "Words fail me."

He grinned and said, "Let's go in."

The footbridge swayed gently as we crossed. There was a kind of small porch, or deck, in front of the door, which wasn't locked. Inside was dark and cold. There was only one room, though the tree came right up through the middle.

Around to the right, I could see a mattress on the floor, covered by a quilt and several colorful pillows. On my near left was a small table with short legs that looked like wooden balls, and there were pillows on the floor to sit on. Past the table, against the back wall, was a very small wood stove with several tiles on the floor around it, the pipe over it going straight up for a bit before bending at a right angle and pointing through the wall. There was a small pile of split logs to the right of the stove, and from there a screen blocked the view of the bed. Two wooden rocking chairs stood on either side of the stove, not quite facing each other. There were small braided rugs in various places on the wooden floor.

Ronan moved around to the windows—a few near the stove, and then two near the mattress—and opened them so he could open the shutters. He left one window open a few inches, and I could hear the sounds of water; must have been a stream below the cliff. Ronan gestured toward the chairs at the stove.

THROWING STONES

Our rockers made soft creaking sounds against the floor for a few minutes before Ronan said, "This is my home away from home. I can even get water from the stream if I lower a rope ladder through the window over the bed, and I can purify it, or boil it."

"Who built this place?"

"My grandfather started it, and my father and my aunt worked on it after that. When I was younger, I always came here when I wanted to be someplace fun, but most of the village kids used to go play in that barn on the side of the highway. I think the younger kids do that now, too. You know the one?"

"I think so. It's just south of the Woods Way entrance. Why don't you all take it down? It's a wreck."

"It's not on grove land, actually. It's on a single acre of land—I don't remember how that happened—that belongs to someone in town, and it's surrounded by woods that we do own. We've asked them to take it down, but they keep refusing. And village kids love to play in it. Someday someone will get hurt." He chuckled. "Then we can sue them."

"Does anyone else use this treehouse? Anyone but you, I mean?"

"Not any more."

I noticed some lamps mounted on the walls. "Electricity?"

He shook his head. "LEDs. Battery-powered." I looked around, taking it all in, thinking how amazing it would be to have a place like this. He added, "If we were going to be here longer, I'd light the stove. But it takes a while to warm the place, and then I'd have to bring in more wood."

"That's okay. This is—I don't know what to say. You must love this so much."

"I do."

I glanced at him; he was watching me. "And is there any particular reason you wanted me to see it?"

"It's a gesture of good faith. I want you to know I trust you. And I wanted to tell you a few things about the grove you might not hear from anyone else."

"Like what?"

"Have you ever heard of porphyria?"

"No. What is it?"

"It's a disease of the blood. Some historians think King George III of England might have had it. I don't remember all the details, but I do know that the medicines they have to treat it today have really bad side effects. They usually try to manage it with blood-letting. Transfusions can help, sometimes. People who have it tend to be extremely light-sensitive, and some of them can't stand sunlight at all. Garlic makes their symptoms worse. And sometimes the skin shrinks in places, like when gums pull away from the teeth, making them appear larger." He waited a few beats and asked, "Does this remind you of anything?"

I didn't want to say what had come to mind, which was an image of Griffin's locker before he'd removed the red paint. I shook my head.

He said, "Vampires, perhaps?"

I shrugged. "Yeah, I guess." That was it; he'd nailed it.

"It's okay. You can admit it without offending me. I think you know Pagans aren't vampires. But there used to be someone in the grove who had porphyria, and they had a really hard time treating him for it. He used to take walks at night to avoid the sun, and some folks say he also went a little crazy, or unpredictable, which isn't uncommon when the disease isn't treated effectively. Of course, part of his oddness might have come from the fact that troublemakers in the area would sometimes watch for him and throw stones and garlic cloves at him, shouting 'Vampire!' at him the whole time."

Ronan took a breath, and I didn't know what to say, so I waited for him to go on.

"Anyway, people outside the grove blamed him for

things like drinking animal blood every time someone's pet went missing. Then there was a teenage girl in the town who got pregnant. Rumor had it that she tried everything she could think of to create a spontaneous abortion. Finally the poor baby was delivered prematurely, with a deformed leg. Then it went missing."

He rocked for a minute, maybe gathering his thoughts, and I said, "I suppose she denied doing anything to it."

"Correct. And the town blamed the Pagan with porphyria for stealing it and eating it, or at least drinking its blood. Totally ridiculous, and of course they couldn't prove anything, but there it is. You can imagine how horrible things got after that, though." If the picture in my mind wasn't enough, his tone of voice said worlds.

"And the guy with—whatever it's called?"

"Porphyria. He died when I was three, childless. I never knew him. So, now we're all vampires, even though no one's complained of missing babies. Some pets have gone missing, but that's coyotes. And delinquents."

And, maybe, cougars. An image flashed into my brain of the way Mom had looked at me the time I'd told her about driving to the village. Now that I knew this history, I knew it was where the fear came from. But I also saw that the fear itself was because they didn't understand what was really going on.

I said, "Has anyone ever tried to explain about this? About the disease, and how it has nothing to do with vampires?"

"How would we do that, Jesse? We can't exactly get on a soap box on the town green. We'd be stoned to death before we could explain anything. And anyway, Eleanor has tried. She's met with the last two mayors. But both times, when she showed up, there were, like, seven other people in the room. She'd get about five words out, and they'd start shouting her down."

"Shouting her down?"

His voice rose, and if possible his eyes got even more intense; he was really angry, now. "They wouldn't let her speak long enough to explain anything before they'd bring up stories about missing pets, or they'd ask her to admit we'd done unspeakable things to Sherrie Williams. It was eight years ago, and she must have run away or maybe was taken by a predator. She was twelve at the time. Never found, never heard from again. And we got blamed."

Eight and twelve would mean she'd be how old now? Twenty? Stu's age. There was something in the back of my mind, some memory about it. I could hear my heartbeats. "Anyone in particular blamed?"

He shook his head, looked at the floor. His tone some odd combination of disgust and despair, he said, "They didn't have a clue which way to point, other than toward the village. And that teenage girl who got pregnant wouldn't say who the father was. Of course the fact that the leg was deformed was our fault. Evidently, we'd cast some spell on her, first to get her pregnant, and then to make the child hideous, and finally we stole it for our own nefarious purposes."

We watched each other's faces, and then he said, "And it's not just these disappearances. People of the town seem to think we do horrible things in secret, out here in the woods. They don't understand our relationship to nature, to the earth, and they think there's something satanic about it. If they wouldn't even let Eleanor explain about the porphyria, you can imagine how much time they gave her to talk about our 'heathen' practices."

I had to ask something that had been rising into my brain for a few minutes now. "Don't take this the wrong way, but why do you all stay here?"

Ronan heaved a long breath, closed his eyes like he was trying to calm himself down, opened his eyes, and stared across the room. "I suppose we could leave. It would be a huge deal, though. Todd Swazey's grandfather inherited the land you refer to as the village, along with a massive amount of farmland across the road, and a few hundred wooded acres on this side of the road, in the direction of where you saw Allen Ward's funeral. There are a number of... well, maybe artifacts is the best term. Or maybe features. Many features about this land that contain magic. We all feel it, everyone in their own way."

He rocked back and forth a few more times. "And even if we could find someone else willing to risk exposing themselves to all the 'evil' we've done here and buy this land, the chances of finding another place as rich in spirit as this are very slight."

"Magic." That was the word my mind had stuck on. "What does that mean?"

"Well... like Talise dousing for where to build the labyrinth. And that place in the woods where we had the funeral. It probably looks like just a clearing in the woods to you, but to us it's a place where the physical and spiritual worlds come very close together." He looked at me. "I'm not sure I can explain it any better than that."

I wracked my brain for some way to respond and came up with rockhounding, and the reaction in the village to my limestone slab, which might be considered a kind of artifact. Did they see magic in that? "I think I told you I found that limestone slab in a place where my friend Brad and I look for rocks. He has some really gorgeous crystals he found when he was younger."

Ronan smiled, almost like an adult might smile at a child who's learned something important. It annoyed me. Then he nodded. "Different crystals and minerals possess different qualities. It's true this entire area of the country is riddled with this energy. And when we use the word 'magic' here, we're referring to the way different energies play out in our lives. These are all things you can't see, but they can be sensed. So I think what you said is a good connection to make."

That was a friendly enough response; maybe he couldn't help looking arrogant. I decided to cut him a break. "Thanks for telling me all this."

I think he was about to say something else, but I'd just noticed an object in the middle of the table for the first time, between two lanterns. I stood and walked over to look more closely. It was a carving in wood, maybe four inches long. A cougar. One rear leg reached far back, the opposite front leg stretched forward, and the was mouth wide open with teeth exposed. I picked it up, testing the smoothness of the wood, feeling the power implied in the haunches. Then I looked at directly at the face.

The lake. It had been a cougar staring back at me. I started, nearly dropping the carving. Setting it gently back on the table I risked a glance at Ronan. He was watching me closely, head a little lowered, eyes trained on me from under his eyebrows. And it hit me: He was a cougar. I didn't know what this meant, or why it made sense, but I knew it was true on some level I couldn't understand.

Neither of us spoke right away while I debated whether to say anything directly related to what I was feeling. I decided on something different that fell in the same general category. "Am I ready to hear what you meant by sensing my energy?"

Several heartbeats later he said, "I'll try." I turned my chair so I could see him better and sat in it. "It's not something that's easy to explain, and it will be difficult to understand if you've never felt it. Everything has energy in one way or another. Each person has a unique energy signature all their own. With people I know well, if I want to I can usually sense when they're nearby. Or if they're far away and I really concentrate, I can sense them even then. It's not like hearing their voice or seeing their face. It's a different kind of sensing. Maybe more of an awareness. But it's definite."

Once again, so many questions… "So you have to try to

sense someone?"

"I do if there are lots of people around, or if I'm feeling distracted by something. And even then, even if I don't try, if there's something happening that makes a person's energy especially vivid, it might just hit me."

And the more important question: "So, what was it about my energy that made you sense it at Samhain, and at the funeral? There were lots of people around. Lots of distractions."

"It just hit me." He stopped; I expected him to say more, but he didn't.

"But, why?"

"I don't know yet. Not for sure."

"Yet?"

"I'm still getting to know you."

That made a certain amount of sense. I thought back to Samhain: seeing Griffin as a girl, letting my feelings about that go a little crazy, hiding on the edge of the woods and remembering the dream where I climbed Griffin's back, following the bonfire smoke up into the glittering sky…

Suddenly I was feeling uncomfortable. I was about to suggest going back to the village, and I stood, but then something else caught my attention. On shelves all around were different stones, crystals, rocks, all over the place. It was like Brad's room, but on steroids, and yet it was totally different. Why hadn't I noticed this earlier? I turned toward Ronan.

"You and Eleanor. You both get feelings from rocks, don't you?"

"Yes. She saw that I had that sensitivity, and she's taught me a lot." He got up and reached to a shelf near the door for a bright green rock. He held his hand out, palm up, and I took the stone in my left hand. It was completely smooth, not quite a rectangle, not quite an egg shape, maybe two inches long, and there were dark green swirly lines all over it with slightly lighter green color between them. "That's malachite."

As I was wondering why my hand felt like the stone was buzzing, Ronan reached for another stone on the other side of the door, a deep blue one. When he handed it to me, I could see tiny gold flecks in it. "Hold one in each hand, and close your eyes."

When I did this, I felt myself sway, and then Ronan's hand caught my arm. Eyes open again, I asked, "What happened?"

"It seems you have some sensitivity, yourself. Malachite absorbs negative energy, but it tends to leave emptiness behind. The lapis, the blue stone, gathers positive energy. You probably sensed the imbalance of one pulling out and another pulling in from the other side. I should have had you sit down first, but I didn't really think you'd react." He smiled. "I'm glad you did."

"The green one was buzzing."

"Exactly right."

I wasn't sure what to make of this, or what I even wanted to make of this. Negative energy, positive energy—it was more than I wanted to think about, and it was entirely possible that just closing my eyes in a house in the treetops would make me a little dizzy. I handed the stones back to him, and he replaced them on their shelves.

"Too much energy talk, perhaps," he said like he knew what I was thinking. "Ready to head back?"

"Yeah. What time is it, anyway?" I glanced at my watch: four-thirty already?

"Would you close the shutters near the stove? I'll get the others. They keep falling branches from breaking the windows."

On the walk back through the woods, Ronan told me about a couple of stormy nights he spent in the treehouse just for the fun of it, and how furious his mother was, sure he would crash to the forest floor. He described the columns of energy he sent up the tree trunk to help keep it upright. I had no idea what to make of that.

"So, Jesse, I'm glad your folks are okay with you visiting. I guess they're friendlier toward us than most."

I chuckled. "They don't exactly know where I am."

Ronan, a few steps ahead of me, stopped and turned. "Where do they think you are?"

"Dad doesn't really care. As for Mom... well, I was pretty vague."

He stood there staring at me for several seconds. Then, "What would happen if they found out where you are?"

"I have no idea," I lied. "Why do you care? It's not your problem."

He shook his head. "You're wrong. It *is* my problem. The grove's problem. All we need—" He turned quickly, saying, "We have to talk with Eleanor about this." He marched forward, assuming I'd follow.

I wasn't any too happy with Ronan right then. He was treating me like some naughty child. And there was Eleanor, again. Always, Eleanor. What business was it of hers, or Ronan's? I was tempted to go directly to my truck and leave the village, but I really wanted to be at the bonfire later. I'd been picturing myself locking arms with everyone and swaying like I'd seen them do twice, now, and I didn't want to be left out again.

Eleanor's house was a simple ranch style, with the obligatory garden of dead plants in front. A path of flat slate stones meandered through it, and it looked as though some steps had been taken to get ready for this year's growing season.

A man I didn't know answered the door, and Ronan's tone had an intensity when he said, "Parker, we need to speak with Eleanor." So this person with spiky, dyed-blond hair was Selena's partner. No one introduced me; I had no idea whether he had a clue who I was.

The kitchen was probably the biggest room in the house. It even had its own fireplace and a big island with a sink, in addition to the sink on the side under the window. There didn't seem to be a dining room, but the kitchen table, on the far side of the room and surrounded by a large number of wooden chairs, was huge. There was food preparation going on all over the counters, but I didn't see anyone other than Parker and Eleanor.

Eleanor glanced at me, put down what she was working on, and wiped her hands on a towel as she approached us. There was no preamble, no small talk.

Ronan told her, "I've just found out that Jesse's parents don't know he's here."

Her steely blue eyes bored into me. "Where do they think you are, Jesse?"

"No place special."

"If they found out you were here, would they be angry?"

WTF? Why does she care? "I—I guess, yeah."

She turned toward the table, gesturing for me to follow, and sat in a chair at one end. I sat also, leaving a chair between us along the side of the table. She said, "Ronan, would you find Griffin and ask him to come see me?" Ronan left, and before Eleanor could say anything else, I decided to speak up.

"Look, I didn't exactly have a lot of options, here. Griffin and Ronan made it very clear that you don't want to call a lot of attention to yourselves." I didn't want to admit that my mom had already told me to stay clear of the village.

"Jesse, it's not my place to tell you what your relationship with your family should be like. However, here in the grove, we do not tolerate lies or deliberate deception. I encouraged Griffin to—well, to encourage you, because I want to think that we can improve the relationship between the communities by increasing the number of good relationships between people, and it seemed as though you could be one of those connections. But if you deceive your family in order to be with us, the chances are very great that the opposite will happen."

Griffin must have been very close; he entered the house without knocking and sat quietly across from me. Ronan was not with him.

Eleanor glanced briefly at him and back to me. "There are many things said in the town about us that are not true. No doubt you've heard some of these rumors. Are you aware that one of them has to do with stealing children?"

"I remember Sherrie Williams."

"Sherrie is not the only child we're accused of taking from her family. All the accusations are groundless, but there's no way we can prove a negative. And what I want is for the accusations themselves to stop. If you come here without your parents' consent, and—as it turns out—without even their knowledge, what rumors do you think that might start once it's known?"

I was getting the feeling I was about to get kicked out of the grove. I looked at Griffin as though he'd be able to help me, but his expression was unreadable. My brain was jumping around all over the place, like static electricity caught in a small space, trying to come up with something to say that would make Eleanor let me stay. So maybe it was just desperation, but what came out finally was, "I can't be myself at home. They hate who I am. And they make me ashamed of it."

"What is it about yourself that's different here?"

I looked right at her. "I'm gay. And I'm not ashamed here."

She nodded. "I can understand how difficult that would be for you. But it doesn't change the situation I've described. If anything, it could make it worse. If your parents aren't accepting of your true nature, they're very likely to lump other things they don't understand together with their lack of understanding of that. This means that if you know they don't want you to be here, and you come here anyway, then when they find out—and that's pretty inevitable—we'll be blamed not only for seducing you into our ways, but also, very likely, for having something to do with your orientation. I realize this is completely illogical, but when people are afraid, they tend not to bother with logic. And we have a lot of experience with how that plays out."

She sat back and heaved a deep sigh, eyes on mine, but more thoughtful than anything else. She turned to Griffin. "Any suggestions?" Something in her tone made me think she expected Griffin to know what he was supposed to say.

"It's at least partly my fault," he said. "I didn't make it clear to Jesse that he shouldn't keep his time here a secret from his parents. I might even have given him the opposite impression, because we've decided to be so careful about what we tell people of the town about us." He looked down at his hands, then back at Eleanor. "As for suggestions? I can't think of anything other than Jesse not visiting again unless he has permission."

Suddenly I was Sandra Bullock, floating out of control in space, helpless to establish a firm connection, likely to die isolated and alone. "That's not fair!" My tone was frantic; even I could hear that.

Eleanor's tone didn't change; she still sounded calm, sane. "Jesse, as I said, I can't tell you how to manage your relationship with your family. And although I understand how isolated your situation can make you feel, I can't be a party to secrecy concerning us, here in the grove. I think you need to decide whether to tell your parents about your visit here today. But whatever you decide about that, as Griffin says, any future visits must be with permission. Otherwise I would be bringing the wrath of the town down on us for something justified. There is already more than enough unjustified ill will. Do you understand?"

My throat was so tight, struggling against a battle between tears and screaming, that I wasn't sure I could speak. All I could manage was, "What about tonight? The bonfire?"

She shook her head. "I'm sorry, Jesse."

I stared at her in disbelief. She had just uninvited me to the very thing I knew I needed. She had sent me back into my hiding place in the trees. And as the spokesperson for the grove, she had rejected me.

I stood so fast that my chair went over backward. I needed to get out of there, now. Eleanor called my name twice, but I ignored her. I ran to where I'd left my truck, got in and slammed the door hard, revved the engine, and that time I did leave black rubber on the road. I wanted those marks there. I wanted Eleanor and everyone else to remember what they'd done to me today.

I had no idea where I was going. I could go home and hide away in my room, but there was always the chance that Mom would want me for something. Besides, I needed to be someplace where I'd be completely alone. So I headed for my spot at Wister Lake. I was half-way there when my phone played the constellation chime, Griffin's text sound. I ignored it.

God damn them anyway! Here I was trying to help them, trying to build some kind of bridge of love between them and my people, and they treat me like this? They reject me?

At the lake, I left my phone in the truck and went right back to the same spot Stu and I had sat, where I'd seen the cougar in the water. Somehow this spot represented a place where both my worlds met, but also where they collided. At home, my family didn't want to know who I was. They actually hated what I was. And they hated the village and everything about it. The grove welcomed me and gave me a place where the part of me my family hates can belong, but I can be there only if I can convince my family to stop hating the place that would accept me in a way they can't.

I didn't sit on the rocks. I went down near the shore and

157

threw stone after stone after stone, hard, one after the other. No one else was around, and I screamed with every stone. Wordless, howling screams. And then I was on the ground, on my knees, sobbing. The tears melted into the wet sand and disappeared, and it felt like they were pulling me in with them.

My family, who were supposed to love me, were ashamed of me. And they hated and feared people of the grove, who laughed at the shame, but who sent me away because of my family's fear of them.

This is what I was screaming about. This is what made me feel like I really was disappearing, falling fast into a gulf of hatred and fear. Maybe I'd seen myself on a mission to build a bridge across this gulf for the sake of the village, but even more, I'd been doing it for myself. And if they'd just caused it to fail, it wasn't my fault. But I would still fall.

No one seemed willing to help me. No one.

Maybe an hour later, sitting in my truck and staring sightlessly over the lake, I realized I was really hungry. But I'd told Mom not to expect me for dinner, and I wasn't up to facing any questioning if I showed up earlier. She might not even have made enough for me. I decided to head to The Flying Pig on my own.

I settled into a booth toward the back of the restaurant and ordered a hamburger with fries and a drink called "Beeer" that I knew would be a tall beer mug full of root beer with something extra in it to maintain a thin, foamy head and also something—yeast? hops?—to make it taste a little like beer.

While I waited for my food to arrive, I checked the two text messages that had come in right after I'd left the village. I knew one was from Griffin. His said:

We'll figure this out pls don't be mad

THROWING STONES

If I'd been on the phone with him, here's what I would have said: "Yeah, right. Like it's not eating at me right now that you're all there, one big, happy family, arm in arm around a big fire that's meant to symbolize new beginnings. And as for my new beginning? You don't give a fuck about mine."

The other one was from Ronan.

I'm so sorry I had to do that. So very sorry. I wanted you to stay. I wanted to stand with you at the bonfire. Know this: you will be here again. I'm certain of it.

I don't know whether I was more surprised that he'd texted me or that his apology was so heart-felt. On one hand, it was a little like when Griffin had texted me to ask me to forgive him. On the other though, I'd told Griffin I thought we were friends. Who was I to Ronan? I mean, okay, he showed me his treehouse and revealed some information about the grove, but it wasn't like we'd been all friendly; he'd still been at least a little prickly. Or maybe it was just that he was so intense? I don't know.

It wasn't until I'd read this message three times that it hit me how careful he'd been with his construction. No abbreviations, no omitted punctuation. It was more like a written note than a text message. I decided to answer this one. He wouldn't get it right away; he was probably at that bonfire right now. So I didn't expect an answer.

I'm certain of absolutely nothing.

I decided to keep Ronan's message. No idea why.

I sat back and closed my eyes, trying to calm down; it was all hitting me again what had happened, what I was missing, and how very much I wanted it. *Needed* it. A few breaths later I opened my eyes as the waiter set my drink in front of me, and almost immediately I noticed a girl sitting alone at the counter. Her side was toward me. In front of her was something dark in a tall, thin glass with a twisty straw, and she was picking at a blooming onion like she cherished it and wanted to make it last forever. The girl was

Ivy Gilman, the reverend's daughter. She was in my classes at school.

She must have felt me looking at her, because she started to gaze around the room. There weren't many other people there, so she spotted me pretty quickly. I nodded, which was all the acknowledgement I thought she'd expect or even want, but she smiled, and the next thing I knew she'd picked up her plate and drink and was headed my way. She stopped at the edge of the table.

"Hi, Jesse. Mind if I join you?"

I didn't know Ivy very well, and I had no reason to think that her opinion of gay people was any more enlightened than her father's. Even so, what choice did I have?

"Sure." As she settled into the booth across from me I added, "Fried onion for dinner?"

"I already had dinner. And I didn't have dessert so I could have this. It's one of my vices."

The idea of the reverend's daughter having vices made it impossible for me to respond before she said, "I've been hoping for a chance to talk to you."

"Oh? Why is that?" I didn't want to be unfriendly, but I half expected her to lecture me on the perils of choosing to be homosexual.

"Have you been wondering who it was who moved the contents of your old locker?" She drew a curly line of her drink up through the straw, her eyes on my face.

I was thinking, *Uh oh. Here it comes.* "Maybe a little."

"It was me." She pulled a couple of fried fingers with flaking batter off of her onion and grinned at me before starting to nibble.

Thoughts fought for attention in my head: *And you're telling me this why?* and *At what point are you going to start lecturing me?* and *Are you gonna tell me your father insists on a friendly consult with me and my folks?* I chose as neutral a reply as possible. "I didn't know you were an office assistant."

"Yup. Daddy insisted. It's kind of fun, though, because I hear and see lots of things that go on in the school that most kids have no idea about."

I decided to get it over with, stop beating around the proverbial bush. "Like when someone paints their own locker."

Her laugh was musical. I would have liked it if I hadn't been determined not to like her. "Yes. Exactly like that."

"So you've been holding onto this information, I take it, or else lots of other kids would know. And it doesn't seem like anybody does. You've been saving all the castigation for yourself?"

She blinked twice and scowled. "Castigation?" Then she shook her head. "No, that's not—Jesse, I wanted to talk to you about it because I wanted you to know how wonderfully brave I think you are. You could have just kept quiet about it, but you told Mrs. Knapp outright that you did it. Obviously you expected word to get around. That took some guts, mister. No, I'm not into castigation. I'm into approbation."

It took me a minute to remember that approbation would be a good thing. "Really? Are you serious? But your father—"

"Oh, Daddy. Yes, I know. He's really a great guy, Jesse. He just needs to let go of that prejudice. I'm working on him."

"Why?"

"Because he's wrong. About that. He's holding onto that prejudice for all the wrong reasons. Oh, believe me, I've warned him that if he tries to sell me as a slave to a distant tribe, or if he wants to offer me as a plaything to a violent crowd as though I were merely his concubine, or if he thinks he can beget sons off of me, he's got another think coming. That's all scripture, too; I'm not making it up. I'm trying to get him to bring all of his thinking into the twenty-first century, not just the parts that he's more comfortable with."

The waiter arrived and set my burger in front of me. I was barely aware of it, a little in shock at what Ivy was saying to me. And I had no idea how to reply. I just stared at her until she laughed again, and it sounded even better to me this time. It broke the tension, and I reached for the ketchup.

She downed another onion finger and then said, "I've been trying to think of what to do about the other lockers that keep getting painted. One in particular. I think you know which one I mean."

"How would I know that?"

"Well... you mean, Griffin didn't tell you?"

"Griffin? *Griffin Holyoke?*" She nodded, and I sputtered, "I—I mean, I did see him this afternoon, but I, uh, I had to leave sooner than expected. What was he going to tell me?"

She took another sip of her drink, then another, obviously enjoying creating this suspense. "Griffin and I are dating. Sort of."

I think my jaw dropped, I'm not sure. "What?"

"It has to be 'sort of' because I haven't told my father. And, of course, I can't go into the village. We meet someplace, and then we go to some restaurant far out of town, or just drive around and—well, you know. Anyway, he was going to tell you. Um, why did you have to leave? You were there for Imbolc, right?"

So she knew that term. She knew about that sabbat. I nodded and took a bite of burger; let her wait this time. Then, "I guess they all thought I had my folks' permission to be there. They found out I didn't, and I had to leave before dinner started. At least I got to walk the labyrinth." Let's see if she knows about*that.*

"Oh, I wish I could do that! Griffin says you were a big help with that, and even gave them, like, the most important stone."

She was passing test after test. "Yeah. So, how long has this been going on, with you and Griffin?"

"He asked me out on the Presidents Day holiday. He said Ronan told him to, because Ronan had figured out that I liked Griffin. Ronan also told him where I was at that moment, and he came to find me."

"Where was that?"

"I like to drive out to Wister Lake to be alone, and—"

"No way! *I* drive out there all the time!"

She grinned. "I know. Ronan told Griffin that, too."

"How—how the hell does Ronan know any of this stuff?" He'd told me that he could sense my energy, but this was too much.

"I don't understand Ronan very well. He has powers of some kind that let him see things." She laughed nervously. "Maybe he has a crystal ball or something."

Yeah, maybe. I didn't see a crystal ball in the treehouse, but there was a lot of stuff there I didn't take in. "So Ronan told Griffin to ask you out?"

Ivy nodded. "And Griffin and I both thought you'd like to know about us. Because, you now, you and I both have connections with the grove, and that's something really important to have in common."

I had to ask: "Have you ever been to a bonfire there?"

She shook her head and then looked at me intently. "Wouldn't that just be the best? I would *so* love to do that!"

Griffin had been right; Ivy and I had a lot in common.

"Well, anyway," she went on, "about the locker, I wanted you to know that I haven't said anything to anyone. And I won't, unless you decide to, you know, come out in a big way. You know, I was looking into a GSA at school. Do you know any other kids who are gay?"

"Whoa. First, what's a GSA?"

"Gay Straight Alliance. It's like a club, in a way, at school. Gay and straight kids get together and talk. It's really great support for the gay kids, and the straight kids learn a lot about what it means to be gay."

"Great support, huh? But any gay kid who attended would automatically be outed. And, no, I don't know any other gay kids. If I did, I'm pretty certain they wouldn't join something like that. Are you, uh, looking for a cause, or something?"

"I have a cause. It's called love. And it doesn't work when we judge each other and condemn each other. I'm all about getting to understand each other."

I chewed a mouthful of burger, thinking, and came out with this: "So, being with Griffin and all, are you still Christian?"

"Of course. Aren't you?"

"I guess, yeah. No one's asked me to be anything else."

"If you mean no one from the grove, I don't think they'd ever do that."

We spent several minutes comparing notes on Paganism, and—no surprise, considering each of us had started by asking questions of Griffin—came up with the same understanding.

Ivy topped me, though. "Their credo is 'An it harm none, do as ye will.' That might sound permissive, but it isn't at all. Because harming no one is a pretty tough thing to be sure of. And it includes yourself."

She was right. I was gonna have to think about it.

"Sigh. Well, I'm done with my onion, and I see your plate's about empty. Wanna order some ice cream?"

"I thought the onion was *instead* of dessert."

"Well, I'm sure you'll have something sweet. And I can't let you eat alone, can I?" She laughed again, and by this time I was starting to see why Griffin liked her.

Over sundaes (hot fudge for me, butterscotch for Ivy), I was turning something over in my mind. Something in my brain had stuck on Ivy's GSA idea, and I was trying to work out how many kids there were in the village who might be gay. I figured, you know, they'd be already out at home. They'd risk having yet another reason for town kids to terrorize them if they came out at school, though. And then inside my head, this bright light happened. It just happened, that's the only word for it.

"Ivy, that GSA thing. Would it work for something else?"

"Like what?"

"Like instead of gay-straight, what if it were town-village? What if we had, I don't know, a TVA?"

Her spoon clanked against the inside of her ice cream bowl as she let go of it. She stared at me, looking more excited by the second. "Oh, my God! Do you think it would work?"

"If you think about it, a GSA would make kids come out when they're going to get terrorized, and they know it. But everybody already knows which kids are from the village, so maybe being in a TVA would increase the risk a little, but if this worked, it should help things."

"And if we really get some traction, we increase our chances of getting permission to visit each other!" She bounced in her seat a couple of times. "I think Griffin would join."

"I might be able to get Brad to join."

We stared at each other, kind of in shock. Then I pulled out my phone and did a search on "GSA" to see what came up. I read out loud some of the requirements, like you'd need a teacher or someone from the school to be a sponsor. I found some starter documents that were hard to read on the screen.

Ivy said, "Who could we get as a sponsor?"

I laughed. "Mrs. Knapp?" Ivy glared at me. "Wait, though, what about Mr. Duncan? I wrote a paper on how Pagan traditions had been taken over by Christianity, and he really liked that."

"Great idea! So, here's what I think we should do.

When we get home, let's each look up what we'd need to do."

"We can Skype while we do it."

"Great! We'll probably need to rework that starter stuff—we can each take some of it—and then when we have our ducks in a row, we can talk to Mr. Duncan. Oh, Jesse! This is so exciting!"

I grinned at her, feeling almost as excited as she sounded. "And it's in keeping with your Christian goal of love and understanding."

"Yours, too!"

I laughed. "Yeah, okay. Mine, too."

We exchanged phone numbers and left pretty soon after that; Ivy wanted to get started with the TVA project. I walked her to her car, which was parked a few spaces farther away than mine, and I was watching her tail lights disappear when Brad called.

"Hey," he said. "What happened to your plans? Weren't you supposed to be you-know-where for some group dinner?"

A fresh pain shot through my gut. Ivy and the TVA had almost made me forget. "Yeah, that didn't work out. Seems they didn't know my folks hadn't given me permission to be there." I gave him an abridged version of what Eleanor had said. And then something occurred to me. "How did you know?"

"Your buddy Griffin called me. Said you could maybe use some cheering up. And now that I know why he said that, I have to ask: Does this mean you're, like, shut out? Or are you gonna talk to your folks?"

I let out a sarcastic bark. "Yeah, that ain't happ'nin'."

"I guess this means I won't get to see the labyrinth. No way my folks are gonna give *me* permission."

"Sorry about that. Anyway, I went to the Pig for dinner; I knew my mom wasn't expecting me." I debated telling him about meeting Ivy, but there was so much going on with that—some of it still outstanding, like whether we'd ever really go forward with a TVA—that I decided it could wait for another time.

We chatted for minute, and then I headed home, my brain so full of conflicting feelings that I was glad I didn't have much homework left to do. No one at home asked where I'd been, and if it's possible to not ask something pointedly, that's what Mom did. She was reading in the living room, and she glanced up at me and back down to her book. So I just headed upstairs; I was anxious to get started on this idea Ivy and I'd had, because it seemed like a way—maybe the only way—to make any progress toward my goal of being able to be with people I didn't have to hide myself from, to get to that sense of belonging that pulled me toward those bonfires.

Chapter Seven

Ivy was as good as her word, and it felt so great to be working together with someone toward this common goal. We went through the online material that evening, dividing up the work of modifying it to suit our purpose, and we met in the library after school Monday to compare notes and lay out a plan of attack. We agreed that we'd Skype again Tuesday evening to work out what we'd say, because we figured by Wednesday we'd be ready to meet with Mr. Duncan. It was my job to set that up.

As we were packing up to leave the library on Monday, Ivy gave me a sly, sideways glance. "Other than being there for a bonfire, why are you so interested in being able to visit the grove?"

This was not the first time she'd said "the grove" even though I kept saying "the village." I knew the difference, and I'd sort of been staying with a term non-villagers would understand. But I liked "the grove." I decided to use it around Ivy.

I said, "When I'm with the Pagans, and especially in the grove, it's like that's the only place I can be myself. I don't have to hide or pretend or lie or worry that someone will yell 'faggot' at me. They couldn't care less about that, and it feels *so great!* It feels like freedom."

She nodded. "So you're not interested in anyone there?" I shook my head, but she looked at me like she didn't believe me.

I had to force myself not to smile at what she might say if I told her about the crush I'd had on Griffin. "It's true. I just want to be able to be myself someplace. And if we can get this TVA thing off the ground—well, maybe we can't visit Eleanor's grove yet, but we can make our own."

During classes that week I found myself following three people with my eyes: Ivy, Griffin, and Ronan. Ivy intrigued me because I'd had a completely different picture of her from what turned out to be the case, and I was getting to like her a lot. I wasn't terribly happy with Griffin after his part in getting me kicked out of the grove, but I wasn't actually mad at him or anything, and I thought it was pretty cool that he and Ivy were an item. And I was oddly aware of Ronan, maybe because it had been Ronan who had helped me understand about the fear my people felt about his, and then he'd caused me to get tossed out because the village feared *me*. Or at least they feared the consequences of the town's fear because of me. God, this was so convoluted.

Another reason I was aware of Ronan was that he seemed to be very aware of me. I caught him looking in my direction too many times to dismiss it as coincidence.

Everything about my life was totally fucked up. And here I was again, trapped in that chasm, that gulf of fear between the two worlds. I had my fears, too, damn it! And mine were real! This TVA thing *had* to work. I debated whether to tell Brad about it, but I wasn't entirely sure of his reaction, and I didn't want to risk stirring him up unless we actually went forward. So I waited.

At the end of history class Wednesday, I approached Mr. Duncan to ask if Ivy and I could meet with him after school, and he said sure.

After classes were over, Ivy and I met at the library first to make sure we both had copies of everything. When we walked into the history classroom, Mr. Duncan was at his desk, correcting papers or something, and there were two classroom chairs beside the desk that hadn't been there earlier.

He looked up and smiled. "Ivy. Jesse. Please, take a seat and tell me what I can do for you."

I slid in behind that half-desk piece attached to the right side of one chair and pulled a blue paper folder out of my book bag, and Ivy did the same. My hand was shaking a little, and the folder gave that away, so I set it down firmly on the desk part of the chair. Ever since Ivy and I had agreed that I'd open, I'd been practicing. And we'd decided on "village" for Mr. Duncan; he wouldn't know what "grove" meant.

Deep breath, Jesse. Relax. Here goes. "I've noticed that we have a problem that's been causing bad feelings between some people who live in the town and the people who live in the village. One kid in my class gets 'Vampire' painted on his locker, and he gets beat up sometimes. The town kids mostly don't talk to the village kids, and vice versa. And I know that Eleanor Darling, from the village, tried to help get things on better footing by talking to the mayor, but he and a few other people who were there wouldn't listen to her. So Ivy and I were thinking, you know, if we could all learn more about each other, that would help. Kind of like a Gay Straight Alliance, only this would be a Town Village Alliance."

"What's causing the trouble, do you think?"

Right; he's new. He wouldn't know the history. (History. Heh.) So I told him about Sherrie as Ronan had described it. I reminded him about the dead cat at Halloween and told him what "GH" was meant to stand for and why I knew the truth about it. I told him I knew townie kids who were afraid of having hexes put on them. I mentioned Eleanor's mayoral rejection again. And finally, without telling him all the details, I repeated some of what

Eleanor had told me when she'd kicked me out of the village.

When I'd told him everything I could think of that ought to give him the picture he needed to see, he asked, "Given the mayor's reaction to Ms. Darling, what makes you think any students would join this TVA?"

Ivy had anticipated this question, and it was her turn to talk. "Our parents didn't go to school with people from the village. The villagers moved here more recently than that. So the only things my parents know about them is rumors and misunderstanding. And change usually starts with younger generations. If enough students join and learn the truth, we'll be able to help our parents understand. We'll be able to show them there's nothing to be afraid of."

He looked from one of us to the next. Then he asked Ivy, "What makes the two of you different? Why aren't you afraid of them, if everyone else is?"

Ivy and I exchanged a glance; we hadn't thought of this one, and it seemed to me that she wasn't ready to confess about dating a Pagan. So I took over again.

"We've made friends with a couple of kids from the village, and we've learned a lot about them. We've talked with them about why they're here, what their religion is like, that sort of thing. Like, they don't even believe in a devil, so they certainly don't worship one." I stopped just short of telling him I'd been in the grove alone at Halloween with no ill effects.

I watched his face carefully, and it looked to me like he was thinking hard. Ivy took advantage of the silence and said, "We've got some material prepared. It's all based on how a GSA would be set up, and we've changed the wording so it fits this idea. We'd need a sponsor."

Several seconds went by. "And you want me to be that sponsor?"

"Yes, sir. Please."

She handed him her folder, and he opened it, scanning

quickly here, reading carefully there, then he set it down, and sat back in his chair, staring down at the folder like he wasn't really seeing it. Then, "Tell you what. I'll take a look at the work you've done, and I'll do a little research myself. And I need to speak to the administration about this idea. Give me a few days, maybe a week. Meanwhile, I'm going to ask you not to talk to any of your classmates about this. Let's find out whether it's something we'd be allowed to move forward with, and if it is, we can decide on the next steps. How does that sound?"

My face must have let on that this wasn't entirely what I'd hoped for, because he said, "What did you think would happen this afternoon, Jesse?"

"I thought you'd agree to be the sponsor. Or, I'd hoped you would. And then Ivy and I were going to talk to a bunch of other students to get them to join, and they'd get others to join. I guess I was hoping we'd get started right away."

He nodded. "So you did your homework, as it were, in finding out about how to get an alliance like this started. But you didn't check the school's policies about clubs. We can't go forward without administrative approval. I'll work on that. Also understand that while I will admit I've noticed this animosity you talk about, I haven't seen or even heard about as much of it as you have—maybe because I haven't been here very long. If the situation is as challenging as you've described, there might even be some blowback from an effort like this. So I'll be asking some questions, myself. Discreetly."

He closed the folder he'd taken from Ivy and pulled it toward him as he leaned back. "I really like that you've taken this initiative, both of you. And I like how you've gone about it. Moving forward thoughtfully, making sure we're doing it in the most responsible manner, will be the best way to get it to work. Do you see that?"

I did. He was right, even if it was frustrating. Almost in

unison, Ivy and I said, "Yes, sir."

"So we have a plan? And you won't talk about this until you hear from me, so we don't get anyone else excited in case we can't do it?"

I wanted him to know he had a part in this bargain. "And if it works, you'll be the sponsor?"

"I will."

"Deal."

Ivy and I started to get up, but then Mr. Duncan said, "Jesse, can you and I have a minute before you go home?"

I just stared at him; what was this about? I barely heard Ivy say, "I'll wait for you in the library, Jesse." I sat down again.

Mr. Duncan leaned a little toward me, arms on his desk. "When you asked earlier today about meeting, I thought there was something else you wanted to talk about. I thought it had to do with your locker."

I blinked, shook my head. "Why?"

"I understand you're the one who wrote 'GAY' on it. That was as pretty bold statement to make."

"It was better than 'Faggot,' which is what Lou Dwyer and Chuck Armstedt had written on it. Right after they wrote 'Vampire' on Griffin Holyoke's locker."

"You know it was those two?"

"Did I see them? No. Griffin did, though, and they beat him up for it. And I didn't need to. Anyone who doesn't know what they're like, and what they're likely to do, isn't paying attention."

He watched my face for a few seconds, maybe trying to figure out if I thought *he* wasn't paying attention. And I watched his face, ready to see any sign that he thought "gay" was offensive. I didn't see one. Could he really be totally cool with this? But he didn't dwell on it.

His tone heavy, he said, "There's something you need to give some serious thought to about this alliance. It's something that history demonstrates over and over.

Something we're seeing right now, around the issue of marriage equality. I'm sure you know that in April, the US Supreme Court is due to hear arguments that will determine the constitutionality concerning states' rights over marriage, and I'm also sure you know that most of the speculation about it says the decision will go in the direction of equality. What I find fascinating, although predictable, is that the closer we get to April twenty-eight, the more ferocious, and desperate, and irrational, and downright vituperative the resistance is getting. If the antipathy between village and town is as bad as you say, this pattern is going to repeat itself yet again if we go forward with a TVA. It's—"

"It's fear."

"What?"

"Fear. They're afraid of the village. Just like they're afraid of me."

He nodded. "People are usually afraid of what they don't understand. And that fear gets more intense, pushing people to fight harder and harder, if they feel their backs are up against the wall with the thing they fear getting closer. What I'm telling you is that we would need to be prepared for both kinds of fear. That is, fear of the village, and—if word gets around about your orientation—fear of non-conventional sexuality."

Wow. "That would make a great paper."

He laughed. "It would, indeed. Maybe I'll make sure you have a chance to work on it."

"You'll still do it, though, right? Even though things might happen?"

He grinned. "I love a good fight. You?"

I grinned back. "For sure."

He stood, and I stood, and he walked me to the door. "Jesse, also, please know that if you need to talk to anyone about any difficulties you're having because of your orientation, I'm here. I'm not afraid of that fight, either."

"Thanks."

He held his hand out, and I shook it. It felt great. It felt really great. Maybe not all acceptance would come from the grove after all.

The rest of the week, I felt like I was walking on coals, or like there were bugs under my skin again. This excitement was running through me, coming from a place even I didn't really understand. I was dying to talk to Brad about both issues—the TVA, and what Mr. Duncan had said about me—and I couldn't mention even the second one without telling Brad why I'd talked to Mr. Duncan at all.

Meanwhile I was still in limbo. The TVA wasn't exactly a sure thing. I had to stay away from the village until something shifted. There was a gulf between Mr. Duncan's support and what it felt like at home. So maybe all this combined together was what put me over the edge, but by Friday evening I'd hit some kind of wall. Over dinner at home, I was rude to Mom when she asked about my weekend plans, when it was just a casual question. I knew she wasn't prying. Then I snapped at Stu when all he did was talk about someplace he and Patty are going next weekend, over Valentine's Day. I mean, what in God's name would anyone have said to me if I said I was in love with another guy, and we were going off to fornicate like that? And it wouldn't have been any better if I'd been three years older, either. As long as it would have been a guy, the shit would have hit the fan.

I didn't wait for dessert, which wasn't like me. I announced rather than requested that they excuse me from the table and I stormed up the stairs. Behind me I heard Dad say, "He's just being a teenager, mad at everyone."

I nearly screamed in frustration. I nearly shouted, "I'm *not* just being a teenager! I'm just being *gay*!" That made no sense, of course, in addition to being a stupid idea, so I slammed my door instead.

Sometime around midnight, after everyone had gone to bed, I admitted to myself that not only could I not sleep, but also I couldn't lie still. I tiptoed downstairs, grabbed a couple of cookies and a glass of milk, and sat at the kitchen table not eating, not drinking. Maybe twenty minutes later, I threw all of it out, nearly breaking the glass as I dropped it in the sink, and tiptoed back upstairs. I threw on some clothes, grabbed my jacket, tossed a couple of flashlights into a backpack, and dug my bicycle out from where it had been neglected since I got the truck. Starting the truck would have waked people up. So I made sure my bike tires were okay, gave one of them a little more air, and headed south. I was going to confront Ronan. Why? I didn't allow my mind to work on that; it was just something I had to do. And *how* it would happen was pretty vague, but I had at least the outline of a plan.

I rode as far in toward the village as I dared and stashed the bike behind a tree I was sure of finding in the dark. Then I wormed my way around the perimeter of the village, close to the edge of the woods, until I got to that path Ronan had taken.

When I'd followed the villagers for Mr. Ward's funeral, I'd been too focused on them, and on not being seen, to worry about anything that might be coming at me from behind. Tonight it was different. The only sounds I could hear were my own breathing, my heartbeat, and the occasional odd noise from somewhere nearby that I couldn't see or identify. I almost missed the path to the left, and I kept that cliff in mind so I wouldn't go over it in the dark if I missed the swinging bridge.

The worst part was the treehouse itself. I stood at the edge of the cliff, staring across the bridge at the door, painfully aware that I couldn't see anything at the foot of the cliff. I had to navigate maybe fifteen feet of swaying above that chasm, with only one hand to hold onto the rope so I could keep hold of the flashlight, with no idea what might be watching from below. I strained my ears, but there was no telltale sound of trolls or vampires or werewolves. So I started across.

About half-way I was thinking I should really turn around and go home. Why the fuck had I thought this was such a great idea?

But the truth was that I didn't quite have the guts to go back through those woods right now. So I kept going and finally made it to the door. I slammed it behind me as quickly as possible in case something was following me, and then I shone my light around to be sure I was alone in here.

Moving fast, I went from LED lamp to LED lamp, turning all of them on so I could see into every shadow. I stood with my back up against the tree, my guts in knots, feeling like I had to crap, until I calmed down enough to snap my flashlight off. I moved from one shuttered window to the next, listening hard to make sure nothing was moving out there. Then I wandered around, looking at the crystals and the wood stove and the carved cougar, shivering like mad the whole time, partly from leftover fear and partly from the cold.

A deep breath that was supposed to calm me only made things worse, it was that shaky. So I took a few more, and gradually I felt calm enough to think about how to execute the first part of my plan, which was to get Ronan to come to the treehouse.

Wishing I'd done some research about what kinds of rocks might enhance whatever it is about my energy that Ronan would sense, I took another look around at the various crystals and stones, finally selecting one that reminded me of the one of Brad's that I liked so much: a three-inch long, multi-sided, pointed spear of clear crystal with just a few streaks of white deep inside it.

I sat in one of the rocking chairs, and even though my

rocking was a little crazed it had a calming effect. Oddly, I started to chuckle; maybe Eleanor could keep me away from Imbolc bonfires, but she couldn't keep me out of Ronan's treehouse. Maybe he'd tell me to get out and stay out, but at least this once, I'd pulled something over on Eleanor.

So I rocked, and smiled, and wondered what to do next. Christ, but it was cold! I got up and moved toward the bed. There were blankets there, and that quilt. I could curl up and get warm, but that felt just too odd. So I pulled the quilt from the bed and hauled one of the blankets off. I wrapped it around myself and went back to my rocking chair.

Much better. I rocked more slowly, getting used to the odd light from the LEDs, feeling more comfortable generally. My fingers around the tooth-shaped crystal, I almost giggled as I held it like it was my dick, pointing it toward the door. I closed my eyes.

"Shit!" It was my own voice. I was standing, my heart pounding.

"Sorry I woke you."

It was Ronan, in the other chair. At first everything felt surreal, and I wasn't altogether sure he was really there. I thought I might be still asleep, dreaming. Had this crazy plan actually worked?

Carefully I adjusted my hold on the crystal—which, miraculously, I hadn't dropped—and then on the blanket. I bit my lip; that seemed real. I curled my toes inside my shoes; that seemed real. I scratched my cheek. Still real. And then there was a fragrance. You don't smell things in dreams, do you?

Glancing around, I saw a little pot on the table, a ceramic tile under it, with twirls of smoke rising into the air. Incense? Whatever it was, it smelled nice.

Ronan was watching me, but it wasn't that intense look

I was used to. He seemed relaxed, totally comfortable, completely in his element. I started to speak, but there was no sound. I cleared my throat and managed to say, "You sensed my energy?"

Ronan smiled, like he'd heard a joke that was only slightly amusing. "I did. Yes." Nothing else. Calm as you please.

"And are you going to chase me out?"

"Why would I do that?"

"In case you've forgotten, I've been kicked out of the grove. I'm persona non grata."

He shook his head. "Oh, Jesse, no. That's not it at all. You'd be welcome in the grove."

This made no sense, and it reminded me how furious I'd been with Eleanor the day she'd exiled me. "What the fuck are you talking about?"

He stood, and in this small space there wasn't much more than a foot of air between us. "You didn't understand? It's just that we can't afford to have your family think we've lured you out here against your will. Or theirs. It's like Eleanor said: There's already too much bad feeling about us in the town. Can't you see that?"

"And can't you see that's crazy? My folks are never gonna say, 'You go ahead, Jesse. Go right ahead and play with the freaks.' Can't you see that it's the same thing as exile?"

Now he looked angry, too, and his tone confirmed it. "I never thought I'd hear that word from you."

I knew he meant "freaks." "Oh, yes, you did. You thought I was just like the other townies. You didn't trust me at all, that day I showed up with all those rocks for your precious labyrinth. So here we are. I worked really hard to collect those rocks and bring them to you, and then I worked all afternoon, digging part of the bed for the path, and last Sunday I walked it in good faith, and now you won't let me near it! There's some Greek myth that goes

179

something like this."

"Tantalus. He sees what he needs—what he desperately wants—and he keeps reaching for it, but it keeps withdrawing. Well, I feel kind of like that, too." My mind was a blank, and I just stared at him. His voice softer now, he added, "You still don't see it, do you, Jesse?"

I scowled in confusion; what was he talking about?

He stepped closer, his face turned up a little to see into mine, those gray animal's eyes staring into my human ones. I felt my ass start to tingle, and it spread to my thighs. I couldn't breathe.

Suddenly his hands were in my hair, and his mouth covered mine just for a second. He pulled his face away, but then he kissed me again, light and teasing. Away, and back again, harder. By the time he reached for me a fourth time, I was reaching for him as well. I grabbed the sides of his face to keep him from pulling away again. I couldn't get my tongue deep enough into his mouth. I couldn't get myself deep enough into him at all, no matter how far I wrapped my arms around him. But I loved the fierceness of what I felt.

We were on the floor, the blanket twisting around our legs. Ronan managed to undo my jeans, and before I knew it I'd come in his hand. He laughed and rubbed my balls with it, and I laughed, too, between panting breaths. He fell onto his back beside me on the floor, smiling at me, his breathing not quite as hard as mine.

Was he waiting for me to do the same thing he'd just done for me? I rose up on one elbow, our eyes locked. I couldn't believe how sexy he looked, and I really fucking couldn't believe why I hadn't seen that before. I felt my way to his waistband, wanting more than anything else to feel him in my hand, to know what it was like to have another guy's dick at my mercy.

I watched his face as I wrapped my fingers around him and teased the end with my thumb. I'd done this to myself

180

enough to know how great it felt. His eyes closed, his jaw dropped a little, and his breathing came in short little gasps. That's when I started to pull. And it's when he started to laugh. It threw me at first, but I kept pulling. As he came he made this sighing sound that started someplace deep inside him, and then he relaxed against me, completely vulnerable, looking like he was in some kind of trance. Maybe he was. And I'd put him in it. Me. The townie. The Christian.

I wasn't sure what to do next. All I knew was that I couldn't take my eyes from his face. He looked—I don't know, almost pretty. But that wasn't quite it. Because he was definitely male. Wasn't there a Greek word for this, too? And then it came to me: He looked androgynous. Finally he opened his eyes, smiled, and with his hand he pulled my face down to his. We kissed for the longest time, deep and intense, but quiet, and like nothing else existed in the world.

Ronan fell into a dose, and I watched him, totally not able to believe what had just happened, totally confused that my feelings about him could change so quickly. I mean, I'd seen TV shows and movies, and I'd read books, where two people seem to have this intense relationship that looks like they hate each other's guts, and suddenly they're in some passionate embrace. But I never really believed it.

I watched Ronan's chest rise and fall, noticed the shadow his eyelashes make on his face, followed the dark lines of his eyebrows with my eyes. What was I feeling, now that the tension was gone, now that I was kind of alone with my own thoughts? Were we in love? I didn't think that was it. Somehow, I didn't believe love would happen that quickly. But it was not a crush. It was so much more than that.

As great as I felt, there was also a pull in another direction. It was that horrible sense of shame that I knew

181

my family felt on my behalf, that I felt more than I wanted to admit. Grinding my jaw, I repeated in my head: *There is nothing wrong with me. There is nothing wrong with me.* This helped only so much, but it did help.

Lying on the floor there, watching Ronan sleep, I thought, "I've just had sex with a cougar." I had to stop myself laughing out loud; hadn't I thought, that day with Brad on that stone ledge, that I'd like to encounter one of those man-eating cats? Well, here was one beside me. And somehow this one felt even more dangerous in his own way than the kind that would live in a cave.

The cougar beside me took an audible breath in and stretched luxuriously, cat-like. The gray eyes opened, a softness in them I'd never seen. He smiled and said, "Then it wasn't just a beautiful dream." I shook my head. "And how do you feel now? Are you okay?"

"You mean, you can't tell? You can't read my energy?"

He laughed. "I can't read your mind. I can tell you *seem* to be okay with things, but I want to be sure. You weren't expecting this. Not in a million years. So I want to hear what you have to say."

I sat up and wrapped my arms around my knees, determined not to let on about the shame that was still hanging out someplace just out of reach. "I'm not sure."

Ronan stood and grabbed a corner of the blanket. I took the hand he held out to me and followed him over to the bed, and we sat with our backs against the wall and the blanket over both of us together. He waited until I was ready to say something.

"I don't really know what I feel," I told him, finally, forcing myself to focus only on what was going on right then, right there. No shame. "I mean, I can't tell you I love you, or anything."

He chuckled. "That's good. I can't tell you I love you, either. Not the way I think you mean."

"But you said—"

"I've wanted you for a long time. I still do."

I thought back to the conversation I'd had with Griffin behind the bleachers. "Isn't love supposed to be a part of this, though? It isn't just about sex, is it?"

"Stop me if this makes you feel weird, but there's some kind of spiritual connection between us. It's not the same as romantic love, at least not yet, but it's real, and it's a lot more than sex."

"I don't know how to respond to that."

"That's fair. I just want to make sure you're not freaked out. Have you ever been with a boy before?"

"I've never been with anyone before."

"But you knew you were attracted to guys, right? This whole thing hasn't come as a complete surprise in that way, has it?"

I shook my head. "Just you. You're the surprise."

"I like that."

"I don't know how to respond to that, either."

"Does anyone else know about you?"

"My family. My friend Brad. I told Griffin last November. And I said it to Eleanor Sunday." I didn't mention Mr. Duncan for fear of spilling the beans about the TVA.

He looked at me, thinking. Then, "What is it about the grove that's been drawing you to us?"

I shrugged. "I wish I knew. At first I think it was just that I found out in November about Selena and Parker, and how you all circled the wagons for them when the Harrisons kicked Parker out. So it was like this was a place where I could be myself."

"Selena." His tone was odd.

"You don't like her?"

"She's okay. She's a scatterbrain, like her mother. I like Parker, though."

"I was supposed to meet Selena, before Eleanor sent me packing."

He shrugged. "She's Griffin's sister, for sure."

"What does that mean?"

"Don't get me wrong. I like Griffin a lot; he's a great guy, and he has his shit together better than his sister. But he's a bit of a goof."

I couldn't believe my ears. "A goof? Griffin?" Were we talking about the same guy? The one I used to think had the answers to cosmic questions?

"Maybe that's too harsh. I know people think I'm too intense."

A whiff of that smoke reached me, and I pointed toward the table. "Is that an aphrodisiac, or something?"

"No. I'd have used patchouli, or possibly dragon's blood for that. No, that's frankincense. It wards off evil and spirits of the night. It slows down and deepens your breathing, so it's good for meditation. And it can lessen depression and confusion. I used it tonight because you seem so unsettled."

"You got that from my energy?"

"Yes."

I threw myself back against the wall. "Do you think Eleanor has any idea what it's like for me at home? How much I have to deal with because I'm gay?"

"I'm sure she does. And she was very sorry to have to send you away. I know she's trying to think of some way to help you. So, was that what brought you to the grove? Being gay, and not feeling at home in your home? Your world? Or is there something else pulling you in our direction?"

"Well... part of it is the bonfires."

"The bonfires?"

"Yeah. I've seen two of them, now, and both times I wanted to be right there in the circle with all of you. I wanted that feeling of being where I belonged. You know what I mean. I know you do. It's like this bubble of love or something. I don't know how else to describe it."

THROWING STONES

He got up and brought a messenger bag back with him. As he pulled out his phone and some earbuds, he said, "Just so you know, this treehouse is outside the village. You're not barred from it." He grinned at me. "Not by a long shot."

He browsed through the phone for a minute. Then, "There's something I'd like you to hear." He dug into the bag again and pulled out a CD jewel case. "The words to the song are in there. It's called *The Stolen Child.* " He handed me the ear buds, waited for me to open to the lyrics, and then played the song.

The woman's voice was kind of mysterious, even haunting. I glanced at the cover: Loreena McKennitt. The song was about faery people who live in the woods, and about the human child they're luring away from a life where "the world's more full of weeping than you can understand," away from troubled people whose sleep is anxious. I listened all the way through and then pulled the ear buds out. I leaned my head against the wall behind me, closed my eyes, and tried to make sense out of what I was feeling. Ronan didn't say anything, just let me think. Feel.

There was a pull; that was undeniable. Something about this song made me want to let the faery in it take me by the hand and lead me from the troubled world. Finally I said, "Why did you want me to hear this?"

"To see how it makes you feel. To see if what you see here, in the grove, seems to you like what you hear in that song."

"So you don't steal children, but the title of the song is *The Stolen Child*."

"Exactly."

"What's that supposed to mean? Isn't that song supposed to remind me of the grove?"

"No. Well, not really. And that's the point. That's not us. Maybe that song makes you think about the way we live because we're so tied to the natural world here, but it's also about faeries who steal human babies. So it kind of points in our general direction, but it's not the same at all. That's one point I wanted to make. The other is that if what attracts you to the grove is what you hear in this song, then you're in for a disappointment. If your attraction to me has to do with something I'm not, you'll be disappointed. And I—well, I don't want you to be disappointed."

It seemed like this might be a good time to get a few more questions answered. Maybe that would help me avoid disappointment. "I need to ask about a few things."

"Okay. I'll answer as well as I can."

"Can everyone here sense energies the way you can?"

"No. And there's nothing about sensing energy that means you have to be Pagan, anyway. There are people all over the place who can do it. If it has anything to do with being in the grove, it's just that everyone here gets it. They accept it."

"So, is Paganism a religion?"

"It's more of a spiritual belief system. But I guess that's sort of the definition of religion, isn't it? It's definitely a spiritual way of life."

"And… the Goddess?"

He chuckled. "Yes. Well, let's just say she means different things to different people. To me, the idea of the Goddess is more like a way of thinking, a way of being. She creates a kind of centerpiece for the belief system, one that's gentler and more—I don't know, maybe more connected, more integrated with everything than a more masculine centerpiece. For sure, she makes a better bridge between the physical and the spiritual. For others in the grove?" He shrugged. "There are some here who take her very seriously."

"Okay, that's just weird. You mean you don't all worship the same way?"

He looked at me intently for a few seconds. "Jesse, I don't believe there are any two people anywhere, in any religion, who worship the same way. Are you Christian?" I

186

nodded. "And your family, too? I'll bet if you were in one room, and your father or someone else in your family was in another room, and someone asked each of you the same set of twenty questions about how you see Jesus and God, the answers would be as different as they'd be the same."

I wasn't sure I agreed with that, but there were other questions I wanted answered. "And how do you worship generally, in the grove?"

"You missed Imbolc, I know, but you saw us at Samhain. And you saw Allen's funeral. So we have rituals we follow that coincide with the natural world. We don't have a church; our church is wherever we are. And so is the Goddess. Everything we do is part of worshipping."

"Griffin said something like that once, like everything you do in the grove is a sacred task. But—everything? What about sex? Were we worshipping, earlier?"

I half expected him to laugh, but he didn't even smile. "Most definitely." He got up onto his knees in front of me and planted his hands on the wall behind my head. "And so is this. Sacred."

He kissed my eyes, my cheeks, my chin, my nose, my neck until I couldn't stand not having his mouth on mine. I grabbed his face and kissed him. We fell sideways on the mattress and did everything we'd already done all over again.

When I woke up, it was almost dawn. And I was alone. An unfamiliar sound hammered at me. I scrambled up and found Ronan's phone on the table. He'd left it here with the timer on for me.

I nearly fell two or three times running through the woods to where I'd left my bike, and by the time I got home the sun was definitely beginning to make an appearance. No one was up yet; thank the Goddess! I was out of my clothes and into my pajamas like lightening. And I fell asleep again almost as fast.

That morning, I lay in bed a long time after I woke up. Well... lay in bed, dozing on and off, and jerking off with Ronan's face in my mind's eye.

Ronan. I really, *really* loved the sound of his name, even if that made me sound silly and romantic. And to think I believed he didn't like me! I'd have to ask him about that sometime.

Chapter Eight

School the next week was totally weird. I kept looking for Ronan, and either we were really in sync somehow or he was really good at sensing my energy, because usually he was looking at me, too. I was so preoccupied with Ronan I almost didn't notice that Brad's cast was gone.

I really wanted some word from Mr. Duncan, but all was quiet on the TVA front, right through Friday afternoon. Add to that the fact there was a long weekend coming up, with Presidents Day on Monday, and that I knew Brad and Staci were planning on the Skyline scenic drive in Arkansas, and I was feeling rather at large. I wasn't at all sure enough of myself to see what Ronan was doing. Was it too soon to get together again? Would it look like I was needy or anxious or unsure or any of those things that I'd never bothered myself about with a girl? Those things I knew Brad had felt when he'd started going out with Staci? Those things I thought I'd never feel about anyone?

I was packing up things at my new locker, still paint-free, when I got a text from Ronan.

Do you have plans for tomorrow that would get in the way of a visit to the trees?

My heart sang, my dick jumped; life was good. *If you'll be there so will I*

Excellent. I'll feed you. Say, one?

Saying yes CU

All of me.

That made my breath catch very pleasantly. Take that, Stu of the Valentine's weekend away! You won't be the

189

only one fornicating.

Evidently Ronan didn't trouble himself with worries about whether he'd seem needy. And I have to say, nothing about what I'd seen from him made him appear needy at all. I gave about two seconds of thought to whether I should do or expect anything special, seeing as how we were getting together on Valentines Day itself, but I decided not.

I would *so* loved to have let Brad know what I'd be doing on Valentine's Day. But—no. Not yet, anyway. And I knew I should ask Ronan first.

As I was about to head out of the house Saturday, Mom stopped me.

"Jesse, I'm not asking you where you're going, but I do think it's reasonable for me to know if you'll be back for dinner."

"I will, yes." As far as I knew...

"And tomorrow, would you be able to pick some things up for Monday dinner? Patty and Stu will be back, and they'll have dinner with us."

I was feeling much more generous about my brother's romantic weekend than I had the night I'd learned about it. "Sure. Do you want me to help with the dinner?"

"Well... would you mind doing a roast chicken? The way you make it with the onions and carrots that get all caramelized? I'll make dessert."

I gave her a big grin. "You're expecting an announcement from them, aren't you?"

"I think so, yes." She grinned back.

I turned toward the door. "Roast chicken it is, then. See you later."

"Jesse?" I turned just my head toward her. "You seem happier lately." She paused, and I just kept looking at her, unsure whether to say anything. Then she added, "I'm glad."

THROWING STONES

The look on her face told me she had at least some idea why my mood had changed. So I smiled at her again and left.

It was pouring rain, and I was very glad I didn't have to ride my bicycle this time. I would, however, need to leave my truck in that pullout across from Woods Way and skirt around the edges of the village itself, on foot, through trees and underbrush. By the time I got close to the treehouse, I was cold and partly drenched despite my hooded rain parka. The smell of wood burning got my attention, and smoke rose from behind the treehouse. Ronan had the wood stove going! Thank the Goddess.

I knocked just to let him know I was there, in case he couldn't follow my energy that closely, and then opened it. He was in a rocker, watching the door, a relaxed smile on his face. I shed my rain parka at the door, and the next thing I knew Ronan's arms were around me.

God! It was the most amazing thing, to just stand there and kiss him. Something pulsed between us, something other than the blood racing around my body. Eventually he pulled away, taking my hand in his, and he led me to the table, where there was incense burning again. It smelled different, but I didn't know what else it would be. So I said, "Frankincense?"

"I'll tell you later. Sit here." Ronan pointed to the pillow closer to the stove. "You'll warm up quicker." He fetched a pan from the stove and poured hot cider into two beautiful, deep blue mugs on the table. There were forks, too, and glass plates. Beside my plate was something wrapped in thin green paper and tied with brown raffia.

"What's this?"

He smiled. "Valentine's Day present. Don't worry; I didn't want you to get me anything. I'd bought this a while ago and didn't use it, but I think you might."

I waited until he sat across from me and then pulled the raffia and paper off. It was a cookbook about using

191

ingredients you can find in the forests of the US, organized by geography. He'd written on the first page: "To a courageous chef. –R."

"Courageous?"

"Aren't you? I think you are. Griffin says you create your own recipes. You wander into the woods late at night, alone. You defy the conventional wisdom of your family and friends to come to this den of heathens so you can explore something that calls to you, something they aren't likely to understand." He laughed. "And you let a Pagan kiss you, and more." He held his mug toward mine, and we clinked before taking a sip.

"These are gorgeous. These mugs."

"My mom made them. She throws pots."

"'Throws pots?'"

"Makes ceramic things."

"And what have you got in here? It's really good."

"Spices only. Nothing alcoholic." He got up and fetched a straw picnic basket, pulling out sandwiches with lettuce and cold cuts on that terrific bread I'd had at the labyrinth build, as well as tiny tomatoes and cucumber slices.

"Who makes this bread?"

"It's my mom's secret recipe." As he sat down again, he asked, "Isn't Patty Arnold your brother's girlfriend?"

I'd picked up half my sandwich, but his question made me hold it in midair. "Yeah. Actually, he's very likely proposing to her tonight. They're away for a romantic weekend. Why?" And I allowed myself the luxury of a large bite of sandwich. The mustard was unusual, and I held it up to get a good look at a tiny blob that was trying to escape from the bread, almost missing Ronan's answer.

"Patty came to visit my mother about a month ago. My mom knows wortcunning. Do you know what that is?" I nodded, and he looked like he wasn't sure he believed me, but he went on. "Patty wanted a potion. I don't know what it was for." And he took a huge bite from his own sandwich.

I let this information sink into my brain. What kind of potion might Patty have wanted? Maybe a love potion? Something to make Stu propose? Whatever. "Is there anything your mom *can't* do?"

Ronan chuckled. "Not much." He took a sip of cider and asked, "How did you end up coming out? To the people who know, that is."

"I told Brad first. He was pretty cool, actually. Told my folks next, and then my dad told my brother. Kind of ugly. Mom's doing her best. And then, well... I kept expecting more kids at school to know. After my locker got painted. You heard about that?"

"Griffin told me."

"I scrubbed off what those assholes had painted and sprayed 'GAY' in purple, instead."

He held onto the cucumber slice he'd picked up, but his hand landed on the table edge. "Wait—you did that? You painted 'gay' on your own locker?"

I teased, "You mean, you didn't just know that?"

"Very funny. No, I didn't. That was—I don't know what that was. Brave? Stupid?"

"Whatever. In any case, it seems Ivy Gilman, in her office assistant role, was the one who moved my stuff to a new locker. She saw the can of paint I'd left there, but she didn't tell anyone. So at this point, I'm not sure who at school knows about me and who doesn't. Though Brad tells me the football team knows. Oh, by the way, Ivy tells me she's seeing Griffin. You did that?"

He just grinned and popped a baby tomato into his mouth.

I sent the last of my sandwich on its way to my stomach. Then, "Listen, um, I'm not sure whether it would be appropriate to tell Brad anything about—well, about being with you. I don't really know that I would, but if I did, would that be okay with you?"

"You said he was okay with your being gay. But I'm more than just some guy you've had sex with. I'm a 'freak.'"

"Don't say that. And anyway, I've also told Brad about working on the labyrinth, and about how I can't go into the village again. He was interested. Wanted to see the labyrinth himself, though that seems unlikely now. But anyway, I think he could handle that I like a guy from the village. If it's a problem, though, I won't. Absolutely."

"Let me give that some thought." Ronan rubbed his hands over his face. "Jesse, I want so much for the day to come when you don't have to worry about anyone keeping things to themselves. I want you to have the freedom in your life that I have in mine."

So he was out at home, anyway; no surprise there. "Well, hell, Ronan. I want both of us to have that freedom in each other's world."

I stood, and he did, too, and then we we're hugging, then we we're kissing, and before long we were on that mattress on the other side of the tree, naked and under the covers this time. After the first... well, the first excitement was over for each of us, he got up and went over to the same messenger bag he'd brought last time. I watched his body, the smooth, supple movements, the way his ass moved, and on the way back the way his dick moved, how the dark hair stood out against his pale skin. He had a long feather with him, peacock, I think. How appropriate. And a towel. He spread that on the bed and then told me to lie face down on it.

"Close your eyes," he said.

Man, the shivers he gave me! He used the feather, he used his mouth and his teeth, and I swear he used his own hard dick a few times. I never knew where he'd touch me or with what, and then he flipped me over and did it some more until I couldn't stand it. Then we were on our sides, facing each other, kissing, each of us with our hands on the other's dick. Then his laughing started, and we made this rich cum soup, contributing almost at the same instant.

Ronan balled up the towel, dropped it on the floor, and then pulled the covers over us. He curled against me, under my arm, and as I was dozing off it occurred to me that Ronan had done this before. Even last time, it had seemed as though he knew what to expect, he knew what he wanted, he was familiar with what was going on. I was tempted to ask him about this, but I was too sleepy. And I wasn't really sure I wanted to know.

He woke me up by pinching my tits. "Haven't you had enough sex for one day?" I teased.

"There's no such thing."

We kissed for a while, but then things calmed down. The wind had picked up, and I could feel the treehouse swaying a little. Ronan got up to put another log into the stove, and again I watched him move. He was so sultry, just like a cat. Just like a cougar.

When he climbed in beside me again he said, "My alarm is set for four. If we really fall asleep, that should leave us enough time for a little more activity."

"You're oversexed, you know."

"Mmmm. And you love it. By the way, the incense today is patchouli."

The aphrodisiac scent. This gave me an odd rush. I mean, we didn't really know much of anything about each other, but here we were in bed. Kissing, fucking, you name it. This person was a total mystery to me, and I felt the need to solve at least a little of it. But where to start? I didn't exactly want to ask his favorite color or what movies he'd seen lately. This is Ronan, the Pagan, the sexy heathen. I said, "Can I ask you something?"

His eyes were closed, his words muffled and slow. "I've just had my tongue in your mouth and you want to know if you can ask me something."

I took that as permission. "That cougar on the table over there. Somehow that's about you, isn't it?"

That got his attention. He looked closely at my face. "What makes you ask that?"

I'd been thinking I wouldn't talk about what I'd seen in the lake that day, but maybe it was the only way to explain. So I did, but with no details—only that I'd been thinking about the village when I saw the eyes.

He sat up. "Have you ever heard of scrying?"

I gave a little snort. "Is this another way to have sex, or something?" I was thinking that would make him laugh, but it didn't.

"Scrying is when you use some object or pattern to open a door for the spirit world to speak to you. To tell you something, or guide you in some way. Some folks see it more as your own subconscious rising to the surface and telling you something you already know but can't put your finger on. Usually you'd start with a question. What were you thinking about, specifically, when you saw the cougar in the water?"

There was no use beating about the bush at this point. "You."

We stared into each other's eyes for several seconds. Then something heavy landed on the roof and rolled, and we both jumped. Ronan laughed nervously. "It's just a falling branch." Then, "What were you thinking about me?"

"I was trying to figure out why I'm so interested in this place, and I was thinking about the people I knew best. When I thought of you, that's when I saw the eyes. Then later, when you brought me here, I saw the cougar on the table, and when I turned toward you there was this—this weird look in your eyes, like you were a big cat, and you were trying to decide whether to rip my throat out or turn and leave."

Ronan was quiet for a bit, and then he said, "You would have to do something really awful at this point for me to rip your throat out."

"Okay, but I'd kinda hoped you were gonna say that you

196

would never do it." Again, when I expected him to laugh, or at least smile, he didn't.

"Maybe we'll get there. Not yet."

I had to set that aside. "So... the cougar?"

He pulled a blanket around himself and sat with his back to the wall, knees up, arms around them, and watched my face. "If you've never heard of scrying, have you ever heard of power animals?"

"No. And—see, this is the sort of stuff that makes me feel like that stolen child song isn't so far away from what you are."

He shook his head. "No. There's a huge middle ground, and working with the connection between the physical and spiritual worlds is in it. For us it's a believe system, Jesse, not some kind of alternate universe. And you don't even have to be a Pagan to know about power animals, or to scry, or to sense someone's energy. There are Christian people who work with power animals, and do all the same things we do here."

This blew my mind, but it wasn't what I wanted to focus on at the moment. "So, about the cougar. Is that, like, your power animal? It's powerful, that's for sure."

"The power of a power animal has nothing to do with physical size or strength. Someone could have Mouse for a power animal. Its power is to pay attention to every detail of life and be able to figure out very quickly which things are important, which are necessary, and which are dangerous. Sometimes you might have more than one power animal. But usually you have a primary one. And— well, it's a very personal thing, to talk about your power animal."

He stopped; I thought he'd go on. I wanted him to go on. So I said, "You've just had your tongue in my mouth, and you don't want me to know what your power animal is?"

This time he laughed. "Think of it this way. Sex is

something that's possible to do with someone else and keep the intimacy purely on a physical level. That's important, but the inner levels of who we are? They're more intimate. Much more."

This hurt, actually, and I remembered that he'd referred to himself as some guy I was having sex with. "Are you saying that what we have is only physical? Because it's not for me."

He smiled. "No. It's not for me, either. I'm falling in love with you, Jesse Bryce. I'm not there yet, but I can feel it getting closer."

This hit me hard, in a good way. "So when you finally love me you won't ever rip my throat out, and you'll tell me what your power animal is?"

He laughed, but he still didn't say anything. We lay side by side, holding hands, and just before I fell asleep I heard him say, "Cougar is my power animal."

So of course, back at home in the evening, I spent some time researching power animals in general and Cougar in particular (it appears each animal is referred to as though the kind of animal is also it's name, and it's capitalized). And what I read about Cougar was spot-on with what I knew about Ronan.

Cougar people's boundaries are very clear, and if you cross one you'll know immediately. They're great at camouflage, and they tend to watch things from a distance, even under cover, before they decide whether to take action. Cougar's roar is blood-curdling, and non-Cougar people tend to avoid making Cougar people roar. Cougar people need space—emotional and otherwise—and they'll choose to be with someone who respects that. Once they find this person, they tend to stay with them. And this point I really liked: When Cougar is happy, the purr is wonderful.

There was no way Ronan wouldn't have Cougar for his

power animal. It made me even more fascinated by him. And a little afraid.

My roast chicken dinner was well on its way to being ready when Stu and Patty showed up around five on Monday. I was really looking forward to this dinner; I wanted Patty to be officially on her way to becoming my sister-in-law.

I wasn't disappointed. Stu had even bought an engagement ring, with a diamond—a small one, but still—in what Stu called a channel setting, which left room for more diamonds in the future. Patty was over the moon, and so was Mom. Dad was grinning a lot, not saying much, patting Stu on the back every now and again. Stu and Patty had already stopped by to tell her folks.

Patty raved about my roast chicken and even asked for the recipe, joking that she'd need to take cooking more seriously now that she was going to be a married lady.

Mom couldn't resist getting a plug in for grandchildren: "And a mother soon after, I hope!"

Once the engagement conversation was exhausted, there was a lull. Maybe it was my new-found romance, or maybe it was this TVA idea hanging over my head and waiting to drop, maybe it was both. Whatever the source, almost without knowing what I was going to say I blurted this out: "Say, has anyone heard of porphyria?"

I saw a bunch of blank stares, and then Dad said, "Wait... I saw that. On CSI. Crime Scene Investigation. The one in Las Vegas. It was an old episode, and this girl had it. She sicced her dog on joggers, and when they were dead she drained their blood so she could drink it."

Leave it to Dad to come up with something criminal. But at least he'd replied to me, which made a break from the near-silence between us since I'd come out.

"Oh, for heaven's sake!" Mom said. "We're at the table!

Jesse, why would you bring that up now? Or at all?"

I shrugged. "Schoolwork. Something about how King George might have had it."

Patty said, "That's right! I remember that. Though I think they decided he didn't, after all."

I didn't want to get too far away from my agenda. "There was someone in the village who had it. That's how all the vampire stories got started. But he never really drank anyone's blood. He got medical treatment, not truly-bloody Mary cocktails."

Suddenly I had everyone's attention. Everyone's silent attention. I looked from face to face, wondering where I should go from here, or if I should just shut up. Then Dad said, "How would you know that, Jesse?" His tone was heavy, like there was a lot riding on my answer.

I hadn't thought this far ahead, but somehow I landed on something that was at least reasonable. "I do go to school with kids from the village, you know. And it came up when we were discussing King George." Lies and more lies. Someday this would have to work itself out.

"Anyway," I added to try and get back on track, "that man died a while ago, and no one else in the village has it. So it makes them kind of mad when people call them vampires. And it makes them mad when they get blamed for killing animals, too, because even if someone had porphyria, they couldn't drink animal blood."

Stu said, "How do you know no one else there has it?"

Good question. How did I know? Then I remembered the sunlight issue, and I called on the research I'd done. "People who have porphyria can't stand sunlight. It's an inherited condition, and that man had no children. All the kids at school from the village are there in the daylight, and I don't know of anyone who doesn't go outside." They seemed unconvinced. So I tried again. "And anyway, that lady on CSI was fiction. People with porphyria don't go around harvesting blood. They can get medicines, and they can get transfusions." And one last shot: "There's no such thing as vampires, anyway."

"I should hope not," Mom said. "Now, can we talk about something else, please?"

Stu was not quite ready to let it go, though. "They could have other reasons for killing animals, you know. What about that cat last Halloween?"

I couldn't let that go by. "That was almost certainly done by Chuck Armstedt, or Lou Dwyer, or both. I saw them cornering a black cat just before Halloween. Griffin Holyoke stopped them. He took the cat."

"That proves it!" Stu was almost shouting. "His initials were written in the cat's blood."

"That's stupid! He'd have to be an idiot to sign his initials to that. Besides, I know Griffin still has that cat. He named it New Moon."

Now Mom got into the act. "And you know this how?"

I didn't have to lie about this one. "Remember I told you I'd gone to the village after Mr. Ward was killed? I saw Griffin, and that cat."

Dad's voice rose above those of Mom and Stu, who both tried to respond to that. "I think we've had enough talk about those people. Let's not derail our celebration."

When it was time to clear the table, which Mom and I usually did, Patty said, "Mrs. Bryce—"

Mom interrupted her. "Oh, Patty, it's 'Diane' to you, please."

Patty actually blushed. "Diane, then, please stay where you are. Jesse and I will clear tonight."

"But the dinner was in your honor!"

"And I'm honored. So if it's my dinner, this is what I choose. Come, Jesse." She smiled at me and jerked her head a little toward the sink. To everyone else, she said, "Talk amongst yourselves."

As soon as conversation at the table picked up a little, Patty turned to me and, very quietly, said, "Jesse, how are things going with you? Are you okay at home?"

I knew she meant about coming out. I shrugged. "About like you'd expect."

"Would you like to talk sometime, just the two of us?"

I almost answered no, thanks anyway, but something stopped me. "Sure. Nothing urgent, though. I'm fine. Really." Maybe we'd connect, maybe we wouldn't. But if she could give me any more indication of what Stu was thinking about my situation, that might be good to know.

Per Mom's policy for dinner, I'd left my phone in my room. When I got upstairs after the meal, I saw Ronan had texted me about an hour earlier.

It's fine to tell Brad if you're sure he'll be cool about it.

I knew this was a response to my question of letting Brad know I had a boyfriend from the village. I replied, *Thanks I'll let you know if I do.*

I sat in front of my PC, knowing I had homework to finish but unable to think of anything other than telling Brad about Ronan. It was more than just "I can't wait to tell someone." It was a lot more than that. It was about being honest with Brad, and it was a test for him. Would he, in fact, still be cool with my being gay if it meant there was actually someone in the picture for me? Or was he one of those "Just don't make me see the reality of it" people?

Also, I still felt like I was holding things back from Brad, not telling him about the TVA yet. And telling him about Ronan was telling him something important. So I texted him an invite to meet me at The Pig for some fun news.

Never mind that I'd had dessert at home; each of us ordered a sundae. Then Brad asked, "So what's this news, anyway?"

I didn't start with my own news. "Just had Patty over for dinner. She and Stu were away for the weekend, and when they got back she had a ring."

"They're engaged?"

"Sure are."

"You like Patty, right? I mean, as a sister-in-law?"

"Yeah. She's great."

Our ice cream arrived, and of course we had to get started on that before anything else was said. Before I could go on with my other news, Brad scooped me.

"I have some news of my own, actually. I've made a decision. Just today, really. Been thinking about it a long time. I haven't told my folks this yet, so don't go blabbing to anyone. But I don't think I want to go to college."

I was surprised, and I wasn't. I'd kind of hoped we could go to the same school, but I'd known better than to hope very hard. "You have something else in mind, or you just don't want to go to college?"

"Truth? I wanna take the courses Stu took. I wanna work on engines."

His eyes were on his spoon as he poked at the melting ice cream, but this was heavy stuff, for both of us. Not for the first time, it occurred to me that my father would have preferred Brad over me as his son.

I sat back, hands on the table, and gave him the best smile I could muster. "Then that's what you should do."

I waited to see if he had anything else to say about that, but he just said, "I might. I just might. Yeah. Mum's the word for now, though." And he dug into what was left in his dish.

"I'll keep your secret if you'll keep the one I'm about to tell you. Don't you owe me about now, anyway? Or were we already even?"

He looked right at me and grinned. "Best friends are never even."

"Agreed. So my news is—God, I'm not sure I can say this out loud. But—I have a boyfriend."

His spoon dropped. "You what?"

I let a few beats go by; did I hear negativity in his tone? I couldn't be sure one way or the other. "It's a guy from the village, actually." I paused to see if he had anything to say.

"Don't keep me in suspense. What are you waiting for? Who is it?"

All good. I heaved a sigh of relief. "Ronan Coulter."

And there was more silence. Then, "Dude... Ronan Coulter? Really?"

I was pissed. "Don't bowl me over with your enthusiastic support."

He breathed out through his nose. "Sorry. Are you gonna tell me you have to get to know him before you like him?"

"Yeah. It's true. He's edgy, and a little intense. But Brad, I really like him. And he really likes me."

Another pause. "You're sure? I mean, that he likes you the way you like him?"

What the... I didn't want there to be any doubt. "Oh, yeah. We've been down that road. More than once. And we'll go down it again."

"Really."

"Um, what the hell, Brad?"

"It's just—don't you remember that he used to be with that girl Adara? What was her name... Farrow. From the village. A year older than us."

My entire world went blank, and it felt like my brain was trying to pass a stone. "He had a girlfriend?"

"Sure did. She died in that tornado a year ago April."

I scrambled to push this information aside. "Well, whoever he was with last year, he's with me, now."

"Maybe he's bi. Not gay."

"Maybe. Anyway, we're together." Even I could sense the anticlimax.

"Jesse, I—well, sorry if I seemed unimpressed, or something. I'm real happy for you. I can't imagine what it must be like not to be able to talk about something like this.

THROWING STONES

I mean, when I decided I liked Staci and she agreed to go out with me? It's like I wanted everyone to know. I wanted to shout it from the rooftops: 'Staci Thompson likes Brad Everett!' And *you* can't say a fucking thing to anyone you can't trust to keep it under wraps. Fuck that shit, man! I just can't get there in my head. It must piss you off royally."

Suddenly it struck me hard how much I had bought into the need to hide. I'd accepted it so thoroughly that it hadn't even occurred to me to be pissed. Brad was right. "One of these days, in a galaxy far, far away, people will be cool with who I am."

"I know you'll go to college. I bet you'll be able to branch out, there."

"God, I hope so."

I didn't remember anything about the drive home. *Ronan had a girlfriend.* It kept repeating in my brain. Back in my room, I sat there staring at my phone. And staring at it. And staring at it. I was trying so, so hard not to feel pain. Telling your best friend you have a boyfriend and then having him say, *Well what about that girl last year?* How the fuck was I going to recover from that?

When Griffin had told me about his sister being bi, it had made sense that she was with Parker, because Parker was kind of both male and female in an odd sort of way. But if bi people want everything, how would I ever mean as much to Ronan as he means to me? And was I in love with the guy yet? He'd told me he was falling for me. And, yeah, okay, I've fallen for him. But how can that mean much to him? I can't give him what he wants. Not all of it.

And if I can't, then Adara couldn't have, either. So what did that mean?

I couldn't stand it. I had to know more.

Ronan answered on the second ring. "Jesse." His tone

205

was low and sexy.

"Hey. Um, I heard something I gotta ask you about, 'cause it's confusing me."

"All right." The tone was flat, now; he was on guard.

"Didn't you have a girlfriend last year?"

Slowly, he said, "Yes."

"But—"

"Are you asking me if I'm bisexual?"

"Yeah. That's what I'm asking."

"I am."

That took my breath away. I needed a few seconds to recover before I said, "What does that mean for us?"

"I don't understand the question."

My voice wanted to get louder, but I was afraid of being overheard. So instead, I nearly hissed. "Look, Ronan, I'm gay. That means when I love a guy, he's exactly what I want. But when *you're* with a guy, he's only half of what you want."

Ronan's laughter took me completely by surprise. "I'm sorry, Jesse, I didn't mean to laugh. But that's not what it means to be bi. See, it's just—Okay, here's the thing. I can be fully and passionately in love with a girl, or I can be fully and passionately in love with a guy. I'm not the sort of person who wants more than one 'significant other,' so for me—and, I'm going to venture to say, for all bi people—a relationship with a girl *or* a guy could be the same for me as your relationship with a guy could be, for you. I don't need both, I just need the right person. Do you understand?"

"Well... that's not what I thought."

"Yeah, I think a lot of people have the wrong idea. But, Jesse, I want just one person. Adara was great. Really great. I'll never know how far we might have gotten. Maybe we'd already be broken up by now. And maybe you and I won't be together in a year. But if that's true, it won't be because I'm bi. Unless you make it about that."

THROWING STONES

Even though I knew I'd need to spend some time thinking about this, I'd started to breathe normally again by this point. So I was able to say, "I won't. I'm not sure I get it, exactly, but I believe you."

"That's good enough for now. Um, what brought it to your attention?"

"You said I could tell Brad about you, so I did. And he remembered about Adara."

"How was he? I mean, about us?"

"He was pretty cool, actually. He has a lot of sympathy for how we need secrecy when he doesn't."

"I don't need secrecy. And—*you* need secrecy? You're the one who painted 'Gay' on your own locker.'"

"Yeah, but no one knows about that except Mrs. Knapp. And anyway, even if the other kids know I'm gay, that's different from seeing us walking down the hall holding hands."

"Which we couldn't do anyway, because of the town hating the grove."

I came so close—so close!—to telling Ronan about the TVA. But I didn't. "Ronan, you know what I mean. What Brad means. If we were both from the grove *or* the town, we still couldn't do it without getting murdered."

"True. All right, I give Brad a gold star for his empathy. I really do appreciate it, especially for your sake."

We spent another couple of minutes planning our next meeting, and Ronan suggested another treetop tryst. But Brad's comment had got me thinking about what dating relationships look like out there in the real world.

I said, "Here's an idea. Now, don't get me wrong, I'd love to be alone with you in the trees. But what if, before that, we do something like a double date with Griffin and Ivy? A movie, or dinner, or something. We'd have to go out of town, for sure, but *they're* already doing that. What do you think?"

"Wow. That sounds... Are you trying to be normal,

Jesse?"

All I could do was echo the word, "Normal?"

"Which one of us should ask the other out? Which one should pay for dinner? Who drives? Who makes the first move?"

"Hey, I think *I* just asked *you* out. Look, I don't have everything all figured out, okay? I just feel like—well, all right, I feel like maybe I'd like to at least nod in the direction of normal. What's wrong with that?"

"Well, okay, let me think about that." He seemed reluctant, and I couldn't figure why.

"You don't sound enthusiastic."

"It's just that I've never done that before."

"What, double date?"

"Yeah."

"Aha! Something I've done that you haven't."

Ronan laughed, and I felt better immediately. He said, "I'll talk to Griffin, okay?"

"Great. And even if that doesn't work out, we always have the trees."

"We do."

Ivy approached me at my locker Tuesday after school. "Got a sec for me?"

"Sure."

She looked around to be sure we wouldn't be overheard. "I understand we're double dating on Saturday."

OMG. Ronan did it! He asked Griffin! And he never said a word. Maybe he was going to call me later. I grinned at Ivy. "Had you guessed? About us?"

She laughed. "No way! But I love it. We'll have a blast." And she nearly bounced off.

Ronan did call me after dinner. I told him, "Yeah, Ivy surprised me with the news. I, uh... thanks, Ronan. I know this wasn't what you had in mind."

THROWING STONES

His tone teasing, he said, "For you, Jesse, anything. To quote Elwood P. Dowd in *Harvey*, 'I'd almost be willing to live my live over again.' I'll expect appropriate compensation when I get you alone afterward."

Which, of course, made me want him even more than I already did. It also made it that much harder to pay no attention to him at school. This secrecy was maddening. But it didn't stop me from following him with my eyes. It wasn't until I looked back on this week later that it struck me, but never once after Tuesday was he looking back at me.

Chapter Nine

Twice that week I stayed after class to ask Mr. Duncan about the TVA, and twice he smiled and said, "Patience. I promise I'll let you know." Then on Friday, he asked Ivy and me to come to the history classroom before leaving for the day.

"The school board is intrigued," he opened. "They've seen this divide between village and town that you described, and they'd love to be able to diminish it. But they're also wary. They're not happy about painted lockers or about students fighting, and they're a little worried that this TVA would make matters even worse, at least initially. They're probably right. But they agreed to let us go forward with a few conditions."

He looked from one of us to the other, and I prodded him. "And these are?"

"Because school board is concerned about escalation, they don't want the meetings to take place on school grounds." I opened my mouth to protest, but he held a hand up. "So Mrs. Knapp and I spoke to your father, Ivy. He probably hasn't said anything to you yet."

She shook her head. "Not a word."

I asked, "Does Mrs. Knapp know I'm involved?"

Mr. Duncan grinned at me. "She does. And before you ask, no, we didn't discuss you in any detail, though she did tell me you'd confessed to painting your old locker. She thought that was a pretty gutsy move, but please keep in mind that she doesn't condone it. Another episode would bring consequences. Anyway," and he sat back, "Ivy, your father wants to partner with me as co-sponsors, and I think it's a terrific idea. We both feel as though violence is less likely at the church, and his influence in the town is far greater than mine. I see this as a big win."

"What about the village kids?" I asked.

"What about them?"

"They're not Christian. They're Pagan."

"I've gathered that, yes. But not all the townie kids are Christian. These meetings won't be worship services, and they'll be in the function room, not the nave."

Ivy said, "What if someone wants to open with a prayer?"

"Do you mean a Pagan prayer or a Christian prayer?"

Ivy and I looked at each other for a second, surprised, and then I laughed and said, "Touché! Why don't we say no prayers for now?"

Mr. Duncan picked up his description. "Good plan. Now, we were thinking of meeting after school on Mondays, which tend to have fewer other extra curricular events planned. Thoughts?"

"Sounds good," I said, and Ivy agreed.

"So the first meeting will be this coming Monday, even if we don't have any other members yet. We can write a mission statement, and talk about ground rules and what our agenda items should be. Now, I assume you kept your word and didn't talk about this yet?" He waited for us to agree. "I think we're ready. Do you have specific students in mind?"

Ivy spoke first. "My first invitation will be to Griffin Holyoke. He's suffered the most, and I think he'd be a great person to have."

"And I'll ask my best friend, Brad Everett. And I'll probably ask Ronan Coulter. He's Griffin's best friend."

"Then, Ivy, why don't you ask both Griffin and Ronan?"

"I can do that," she said, glancing at me. I knew she was letting me know we'd work this out between us.

211

"Others?"

"I think maybe Wren Ward," I offered, and Ivy mentioned one of her townie friends.

"All good," Mr. Duncan said. "Let's not go for more just yet; let's get our feet under us." He handed us each a piece of paper. "Here's my cell phone number and email address. If anyone you ask decides to join, please let me know as soon as possible." Ivy and I gave him our contact information, and then he smiled at us and said, "Go forth and multiply."

At our usual table in the library, Ivy and I decided we'd both speak to Griffin and Ronan over dinner the next evening. Meanwhile, she would ask one of her friends, and I would talk to Brad, and then we'd connect and see where we were. It was happening!

With no Friday night date this week, Brad was willing to meet me at The Flying Pig after dinner for ice cream floats. For some reason, Brad asked our waitress if she knew where the restaurant's name came from. She shook her head, but in a few minutes the night manager came over to our table.

The manager was a hefty woman, probably in her twenties, who introduced herself as Bonnie Harrison. "Mind if I sit down?" And she pulled out a chair and sat. Her voice even and low, she asked, "How much do you boys know about the village?"

Brad said nothing, and even though I wasn't sure where the question was coming from, I said, "Quite a bit, actually. Are you related to Parker?"

She grinned and nodded. He's my brother. Used to be my sister."

I told her, "I'm friends with Selena's brother, Griffin."

"Then I'll tell you I hate what my family did to Parker. We're still in touch. Now, about The Pig. It's owned by two partners, one from the village and one from the town. The village partner is what's known as 'silent.' I'm not saying

212

who that is, though if you really wanted to find out, I suppose you could. Anyway, you've heard the expression, 'When pigs fly,' meaning something's probably never gonna happen?"

Brad and I both nodded. Bonnie said, "In this case, that 'something' is the town and the village getting along like good neighbors. Both partners want that, but it seems unlikely. You know?"

I wondered if it was within the parameters of the TVA to involve adults, but I decided to ask about that before blabbing to Bonnie. "I hope we can get more pigs in the air, though," was all I said.

"Me, too. Meanwhile, at least these two partners have made a start, so maybe there's a one-winged pig trying to get off the ground, anyway. But boys... not too many people know, so keep it under your hats, eh?" Then she shrugged and got up. "You boys enjoy your floats on the house tonight."

Now Brad spoke. "Thanks!"

Bonnie couldn't have provided me with a better segue. "So, Brad, I'm sure you're wondering why I asked you here." He laughed at my clichéd opening. "I've wanted to talk to you about this for a couple of weeks, but they told me to keep quiet until we were sure things would go forward. It's the same thing Bonnie was just talking about. And you already know how important this is to me. There's going to be a kind of club, called the Town Village Alliance. It will have some kids from each area, and the idea is that we'll learn about each other so we can all get along better. And—well, Ivy Gilman and I started it. And I really want you to be in it, too."

"Ivy Gilman?"

I wasn't sure whether he was stalling for time or genuinely surprised at the mention of Ivy. Probably both. "She and I both have friends in the village. And her father's involved, too. The school liked the idea, and Mr. Duncan

213

will be the school sponsor, but they were worried about how some kids will react. You know what our 'friends' Lou and Chuck are like. So the meetings will be Mondays after school in the church function hall." I paused to get a read on Brad's reaction so far. I wasn't sure I liked what I was seeing, which was nervousness bordering on anxiety.

"See, Jesse, the thing is, I got a reputation to uphold."

I shook my head. "I have no idea what that means. You don't go around making snarky comments about the village kids, do you?"

"No. But I do have my place on the team to maintain."

"And they make snarky comments?"

He shrugged. "Sometimes."

My back was up a little by this point, and I threw a challenge at him. "All of them? Because maybe there's someone else on the team who'd actually be interested in joining."

He sat back against the booth hard enough to jostle the salt shaker. "Jesse, look, dude, I'm cool with you being gay. I don't mind that you're seeing—you know." He looked around nervously. "But I don't really wanna be dragged into this mess."

"Are you okay with Griffin getting beat up? Are you okay with tortured cats and effigies of a man who should be a hero and seeing 'Vampire' scribbled all over the place?"

He literally squirmed in his seat. "Of course not."

"What are you afraid of?"

He stared at me as the waitress set our floats on the table and disappeared, but he didn't say anything. And then it hit me.

"It's Staci, isn't it? She and her folks all hate the village, don't they?"

He grabbed his glass and slurped, staring into the root beer, still not talking. And I knew it would do me no good to push him. He adored Staci. So I changed tactics.

"All right, so is there anyone you know of who might

be interested in joining, if you won't?"

He drained half the glass before he spoke. "There's one guy on the team who might. Phil Ahearn. He said he wished he'd written that paper you wrote, the one about Pagan traditions."

I nodded, doing my best to relieve the prickly tension between us. "Okay with you if I lead with that paper? I'll have to say you told me what he said."

"Just don't tell him I gave you his name because of this club thing."

"TVA."

"Whatever."

We finished our floats in silence, and then Brad set some money on the table and stood up. "Look, Jesse, I'm real sorry. I just can't do it."

"I get it. Maybe at some point. Thanks for Phil's name. I'll be discreet."

"You bet." And he was gone.

I was doing homework after supper, or least making a stab at it while watching Iron Chef Bobby Flay beat the pants off some wannabe on my PC, when I heard a door slam, hard, and someone came stomping up the stairs. I cracked my door open in time to see Stu go into his room and slam that door, too. Next, Mom came up the stairs and knocked quietly on his door. She looked more worried than pissed about the noise.

"Stu? What is it, sweetie? I'm coming in."

I heard him shout, "Go away!" But she opened the door and closed it behind her. I got up and tiptoed into the hall. I wanted to know if this storm had anything to do with me.

"I don't want to talk about it!"

"Is there something wrong between you and Patty?"

Silence, and I pictured Stu a little stunned, because he said, "How did you know?"

215

"I'm your mother, Stu. Now, tell me what's happened. Sometimes these things have a way of starting to work themselves out when we put them into words."

More silence, in which I pictured the two of them getting comfortable. In my mind Stu was on the edge of his bed, with Mom in his desk chair.

"It's actually Jesse's fault." He sounded sulky. And I'd been right after all.

"How could Jesse cause a problem—"

"It's because he's gay, don't you get it?"

"What? She's mad at you because—"

His voice turned sarcastic. "Oh, no. *That's* not the problem."

"Stu—"

"Do I have to spell it out? Fine. She's mad at me because I'm mad at Jesse, and because I'm mad at Dad and you for not taking any steps." He stopped.

"So she agrees there are no steps to be taken?"

His laugh was ugly. "Oh, she didn't stop there. She accused me of not being able to be a good father. Me!"

"Did she say why?"

"What if one of our kids is gay, that's what she said to me. She'd be even less upset than you are! And she says I'm all wrong when it comes to this problem. Because I see it as a problem. And she doesn't."

There was quiet for a few seconds, and then Mom asked, "How did you leave things?"

Yet more silence, and then I heard something small and metallic bounce off the wooden floor. It had to be Patty's engagement ring. She'd given it back to Stu.

Oh my god. What if this *was* my fault? I loved Patty! I wanted her as a sister-in-law. But—what if she was right? Would Stu hate his own gay child? Even my dad didn't *hate* me.

I heard movement, probably Mom retrieving the ring. She said, "I'll hold onto this for you."

216

"Oh, there's more. We hadn't told anyone yet, but—oh hell. Patty's pregnant."

"Oh, Stuart! Oh, my goodness. Well—I have to believe we can work this out. Maybe you just need more time. Maybe—"

"There is no 'maybe,' Mom. I hate this whole thing. It's all wrong. It goes against every fiber in my body."

"That's because you're not gay. Keep in mind that the opposite goes against every fiber in Jesse's."

"I can't believe that! I can't!"

"You need to find a way, sweetie. Because the truth is that the idea of being gay will always feel wrong to you, because it *should* feel wrong to you. It *is* wrong. For *you*. But not for Jesse."

Wow. This floored me. I mean, sure, Mom had been treating me better than anyone else at home, but it sounded like she really got it now, like she was actually on my side.

I expected Stu to raise his voice, to get angrier still, to protest even more. But he said nothing. So Mom said, "Maybe it would help if you knew more about it. I have some research I gave your father to read. I suggest you read it as well."

I pictured Stu's head bent over, hands grasping his hair.

Mom spoke again. "Let me just be sure of something, though. You do still want to marry Patty, don't you?"

Stu's breath caught in a loud gasp, like he was trying very hard not to cry. I heard a strangled, "Yes." That seemed to be all he could manage. And it's all I dared hang around for. I snuck back into my room and closed the door as quietly as possible.

Did I do this? Should I have waited until I was ready to leave home before coming out? Or would it have been worse if Patty and Stu had had this argument after they got married?

We hadn't yet had that conversation she'd suggested the night she and Stu announced their engagement, so it felt a little odd to call her now, but I wanted to hear her side of things. I reached for my phone. "Are you all right?"

I could tell she'd been crying. "I will be."

"He still loves you, you know. He still wants to marry you."

"Oh, Jessc! I wish I could say thc samc. Did hc mention the baby?"

"Yeah."

"I just told him about it. And when I did, it suddenly occurred to me that if we had a child who was gay, Stu was going to have to be fine with that. So I asked him about it." She stopped, and it sounded like she blew her nose. "He was *not* fine. And he was so awful about it! So I told him I don't want a husband who yells at me, and I won't marry someone who could hate his own child." She started crying again. "I have to go."

"Okay, but please, let me know if there's anything I can do. Anything at all."

"Sure." And she was gone. And as far as Stu was concerned, not only had I bought a ticket to hell for myself, I'd now bought two.

Three. Patty was pregnant.

Saturday night I picked Ivy up, and we met Griffin and Ronan at the pullout. Ronan got into the truck and Ivy slid in beside Griffin in his car, and we were off, with me following Griffin to a restaurant he and Ivy were convinced was safe for a mixed crowd like ours. On the way, it was everything I could do not to launch into news about my TVA with Ronan, but Ivy and I had agreed we'd describe it together. So I tried to engage him in other conversation, but he seemed oddly quiet. I wondered if he might not be as happy to do this "date" thing as it had seemed.

Things were better once we were in a booth toward the back of a restaurant about half-way to McAlester, Ronan beside me. Ivy had told me she was going to warm up the room, as it were, by talking about her parents a little, so her dad wouldn't seem intimidating.

"I don't really know where they got the name Ivy from," she said, "but what with my mom's obsession for historical romance novels I almost got Tangwystl. Daddy put his foot down."

Griffin laughed and said, "How do you even spell that?"

"No idea. And get this. Last year, Mom went on a mission to get e-copies of her favorite books from the dark ages. You know, when everything had to be printed? Daddy found the software program for her."

Ronan said, "He supports this habit?"

"Oh, you know, he loves her, and it's mostly harmless. But he did come to a little grief with this program, because there was this software glitch in the original conversion process that turned the word 'arms' into something else. You know how your phone autocorrects, and sometimes it's not what you want? Well, this autocorrect changed the word arms to... well, something else that begins with 'a.' Also four letters. Also ending in 's.' Also a body part. Can you guess?"

I wracked my brain and came up with nothing. I shook my head.

Ivy leaned a little forward over the table, and in a near-whisper she said, "Anus."

Practically in unison, Griffin and I said, "Oh my God!"

"Can you imagine?" Ivy put on a breathy voice like she was narrating one of those novels, acting out the parts. She spoke quietly but clearly. "Lance gazed deep into her eyes, the fire in his mirrored in hers. 'Darling!' Tangwystl cried. 'Take me in your anus!' The muscles in his anus bulged as he held her, leaned over her, and pressed his mouth over throat. Her anus wrapped around him as her neck arched back, her bosom heaving."

Even Ronan cracked up, and I realized that I'd never

seen him really laugh. Of course, he'd probably never seen me really laugh, either. So much of our relationship had been spent in antagonism in the beginning, and in passion after that, and that's why this "normal" date felt so good to me. I laughed and laughed, partly at Ivy's act, and partly because I felt like a teenager on a date. And that felt great.

When we'd all quieted into chuckles, Ivy said, "Anyway, you should have seen Daddy laugh about that. My mom was mortified, but he thought it was hysterical."

Our food arrived, and after everyone had examined everyone else's dish and settled down to eat, I glanced at Ivy, who nodded. My turn.

"So Ivy and I have something we want to talk to both of you about." Suddenly the attention wasn't on the food any more. Fine. "We both really hate that there's so much bad blood between the town and the village, and we really hate that we can't spend any time in the grove because of that. So we thought we'd do something about it."

Between us, Ivy and I described pretty thoroughly what we wanted to accomplish and what the first steps would be. I got so into this presentation that I hadn't noticed Ronan's reaction until after the part about when and where we'd meet. His whole body was kind of stiff, and he'd stopped eating. I was looking at him, surprised and maybe a little hurt, when Ivy picked up the thread.

"Anyway, Jesse and I were hoping that you'd both be willing to join us."

After several silent seconds Griffin said, "You two have been busy, haven't you?" He set down his fork and leaned back. "Wow. Well, I mean, you know, it's a lot to ask."

I looked from him to Ronan and back again. "Why? What do you mean?"

"Jesse, um, look. I think it's a great idea, in concept. But you have to remember how nasty the town has been to us. You probably don't even know the worst of it."

"Ronan has told me some things." I glanced at Ronan,

but his eyes were on his plate. The one he wasn't eating from.

Griffin said, "There are things you don't know. Believe me. And, now, all of sudden we're supposed to be all sweetness and light?"

Ivy tried next. "Isn't it true that most of the bad feelings are coming from the town itself? I mean, the adults? There aren't very many kids in school who've been mean, are there?"

"Enough," Griffin said. "Enough of them. But—let's leave it like this. I'll think about it. And we'd have to talk to Eleanor, anyway."

"Why?" I demanded, annoyed at Ronan and taking it out on Griffin. "I happen to know she wants exactly this kind of thing to happen. She wants reconciliation."

"Well, she is the elder, and—"

"Ivy's dad is in on this because he's helping, but I haven't mentioned it to my folks. Why does Eleanor need to know?"

Ronan threw his napkin onto the table between us. It landed almost like it had something heavy in it. He turned his head to glare at me. "You don't understand us at all, do you?"

I blinked at him. How could he say that?

But he wasn't finished. "You want to be at our bonfires so badly. Or so you've said. You want that sense of belonging. But that belonging comes from something real, something alive that keeps us together. No one in the grove would *ever* take a step like the one you're asking for without discussing it. Something like that affects all of us."

"So you're saying you won't do it unless the entire grove approves?" My tone was acid; I couldn't help it.

"That's not what I'm saying, no. Maybe we'll all talk about it and reach a consensus that we don't really like the idea, but maybe Griffin will disagree with the rest of us and go ahead and join. He has that right. But he wouldn't do it in some kind of unilateral way. And he wouldn't do it without our knowledge."

I turned to Ivy, wondering if I looked as angry as she looked worried.

Griffin did his best to throw oil on the waters. "So, like I said, we'll talk about this. I'm not saying it isn't a good idea. And I'm not saying we won't do it. But it feels kind of out-of-the-blue, you know?"

Ivy had another idea. "What if Eleanor and my father get together to talk about it?"

"Now that, I like!" Griffin kissed the side of Ivy's head. "Ronan, let's you and I talk with Eleanor tomorrow and see where we might go from here."

Ronan didn't respond one way or the other. Ivy and Griffin did their best to bring conversation back around to non-confrontational topics, but there was a barrier between Ronan and me that couldn't be denied.

I'm not sure where Griffin and Ivy were going after dinner was over. They might have said, but I was a little preoccupied. I drove kind of fast back to the pullout. Neither Ronan nor I said anything until I was off the road. I pulled on the parking brake and killed the engine.

"Am I still invited to the treehouse?"

Ronan shifted in his seat to face me. "You know, one reason I took you there the first time was that I believed you wanted to understand the grove. But this expectation you had, that Griffin and I would jump for joy right into this alliance, shows me you don't."

"Okay, stop right there. It wasn't my idea to stop coming to the village. If I'd been able to see more of what you all do there, maybe I would understand a lot of things better than I do. But I've gone out of my way to understand as much as I can, given my exile. And what do you think this TVA is all about, anyway? It's to let me in so I *can* understand it better. I'm doing *my* part."

"And I'm not doing mine, is that what you're saying?"

I let out a loud exhale. "I'm saying you're expecting me to understand things that I can't, because you—Eleanor— won't let me close enough to even see them. And I'm saying I'm trying to fix what it is that makes her tell me to stay away. And you're not giving me any credit for that."

We sat there in the darkness, staring at each other, for several seconds. Then I said, "So tell me this. If Eleanor and whoever discusses this idea think it's a good one, will you join?"

I heard Ronan take a few breaths before he said, "I don't think so."

"And why not?"

"Jesse, you can't know what it's like to be treated like something other than human. To be called unnatural, and freakish, and heathen, and perverted, and—"

"Are you fucking *kidding* me?" I was nearly shouting. "I know *exactly* what that feels like! My own father barely speaks to me. My brother says I should be forced to be 'normal,' and he thinks a good talking to by Ivy's father would do that. Griffin's locker says 'Vampire,' but mine said 'Faggot.' Your close friends all know you're Pagan, and they don't look at you oddly when you talk about sensing energy. My family thinks I'm a changeling, and only a few kids know I'm gay. And *they* don't understand it. You tell me which is worse, your situation or mine."

"And would you be willing to join a Gay Straight Alliance if I started one?"

"Yes! Don't you get it? The members would want to *help* me! I'm starting to think you don't understand me very well, either. And I'm not convinced you're trying."

He sat back hard, facing the windshield. "I just don't think I could put aside everything that's happened to us."

There was something in his voice, like something hidden. Something secret. "Ronan, is there something you're not telling me?"

His silence told me there was. I waited, and finally he

said, "There's a sacred place on the grove's land, a hilltop almost surrounded by trees. The energy there is deeper and richer than anywhere else anyone in the village has ever been. It's the real reason we stay here, the reason we put up with all the shit the town throws at us. And we thought no one there knew about it."

He stopped long enough to take a few shaky breaths before going on. "It's a stone circle. The stones are large, some twice the height of Eleanor. We don't know how long they've been there, but they were deep enough in the earth to make them seem immovable."

Suddenly he opened his door and stepped out of the truck, so I did, too. He walked a little farther away from the road into the trees, arms hugging his ribcage. I followed until I was close behind him. "What happened?"

An owl hooted. A car drove by on the highway. I shifted my weight, and a twig snapped.

"Someone pulled three of them over. There were tire tracks from some kind of truck, and scrapes on the stones where a chain had been wrapped around them. The other four, the ones they didn't knock over, now have 'Fucking Vampires' written on them in bright, red letters."

"Oh my God, Ronan, I'm so sorry. When did this happen?"

"Late Tuesday night." He wheeled around to face me. "We don't know what we're going to do. What if we clean off the paint and pull the others back into place, which would be a massive effort, and the same people come and pull them over again? It's much easier to pull them over than to set them upright. And every time that happened again, the magic would be disturbed. Every time, the energy would grow weaker and more diffuse. Every time, there would be less and less reason for us to stay here, where there's so much hatred and so much—" His breath caught, and I knew he was on the verge of tears.

My arms went around him, and he leaned against me

and wept. When he could speak, he said, "I can't tell you how important that circle is to us." He pulled away and half turned, so his side was toward me.

"Why didn't you try?"

"What?" He still didn't look at me, like the question was meaningless.

"You never mentioned that circle to me. You talked about the energy of the one in the woods, but not about this really important one."

"I couldn't. No one of the town was supposed to know. You and I were still getting to know each other. And when it happened, the first person they looked at was me. 'Did you tell Jesse?' they wanted to know. It was so, *so* much better that I was able to tell them I had not."

I wracked my brain. All I could come up with was, "Did you tell the police? Did you report it?"

He turned just his face toward me. "And tell them what?" He waited, but I didn't know what to say. "Not only would they not take it seriously, not only would they spend no time finding—let alone prosecuting—anyone, but also it would mean telling the town the circle even exists. How long would it be before other assholes pushed stones over and painted obscenities on them?"

He was right. I knew he was right, but I sure as hell didn't want him to be right. I played the only card I had. "And it's precisely this kind of thing Ivy and I want to stop. And we're not the only ones, Ronan. We already know of a few town kids who'll almost certainly join, and Ivy's father wants to help, and Mr. Duncan, and even Mrs. Knapp, who thinks the word 'gay' is offensive."

"It's hopeless, Jesse. The whole thing. The club, the labyrinth you helped build, none of it will make any difference." He turned to face me. "And I think we both know that this is hopeless, too. Us."

I felt my head shaking. "No! Ronan, don't say that. What we have is—well, it's really special. I don't

225

understand it, but—shit, I want to. And I want to understand you better, and I want you to understand me better."

"You want us to be some kind of beacon, to lead the way, don't you? It won't work, Jesse. We're not going to be able to bring our two worlds together. We're more like Romeo and Juliet. And the hopelessness might just kill us both."

My jaw was practically flapping with desperation to say something that would change his mind, that would make him stop walking past me toward the village. I reached for his hand as he came close, and he turned toward me. When I put my other hand on the side of his face, I felt tears.

We stood there, trying to see through the darkness into each other's eyes, and then he stepped closer and kissed me. "I love you, Jesse. And I'm sorry for both of us."

Words caught in my throat. So many words. *I love you, too!* and *Don't do this!* and *We'll make it work, I promise!* I said none of them as he walked away from me and disappeared.

Back in my truck, I revved the engine and nearly threw the vehicle onto the highway, headed south. I tore down the road, passing the few other cars in front of me, not knowing where I was going until I found myself bouncing down that track that led to the trail to the bobcat cave, to the place I'd found that stone with the symbol for eternal life embedded in it. Outside the truck everything was pitch black, I had no idea where I was, and as I pushed farther into the unknown I heard stones and who-knows-what scraping against the wheel covers. After maybe twenty minutes my front right wheel landed in some kind of ditch, and I knew I was stuck. Or, I would be until I went into four-wheel-drive. I sat there, feeling alternately murderous and wretched, pounding on the steering wheel from time to time, and finally the tears came. I leaned my hands on the wheel and my head on my hands and cried like a baby. I cried like a cougar had ripped my heart out.

As my sobbing grew quieter, it occurred to me that all evening, Ronan had been aloof at best and antagonistic at worst, and I realized now that he'd been laying the foundation for a fight once we were alone. It was reasonable that he might be skeptical that this TVA thing would have worked, but he'd seemed a hell of a lot more than skeptical.

Ronan had already decided to end things. With this damage to the stone circle, he'd reached some kind of critical mass, and he saw that same gulf between us that I'd seen. Only to him, it was too wide to bridge. But he'd underestimated my feelings. So had I. Until he'd walked away from me, I'd had no idea how much of my chest would be ripped away at the same time.

I pulled my phone out and texted him.

I blamed the town for standing on one side of this gulf and throwing stones at you. Now you're throwing them at me.

I turned my phone off.

It took less than a minute to get myself out of the ditch and maybe forty minutes to drive backward over that track, with no way to find a place to turn around in the darkness. Plenty of time to think about what it would mean to go backward in my life, back to before I knew who I was or what I wanted or who I loved. By the time I got back to the paved road, I knew backward was not for me. I was determined to do something—whatever it took—to get Ronan to see that this *could* work. That we *could* be a beacon of love and hope and reconciliation. That we *could* lead the way.

Sunday's sermon was interesting. I could tell by the

readings Reverend Gilman chose that he was already planting seeds for us by talking about extending good will toward "all nations." Even so, after school Monday, as Ivy and I walked together to the church, we weren't nearly as excited as we'd been last week. Both of us were pretty discouraged about the reaction we'd gotten Saturday night.

In the function hall, our little group made a pathetic showing, huddled together at one end of a long table. Reverend Gilman was already there, and Mr. Duncan and Mrs. Knapp arrived soon after Ivy and I sat down.

Reverend Gilman set up a standing easel with a huge pad of paper on it. Then Mr. Duncan took over and wasted no time getting down to business.

"First, I hope there won't be many more meetings where the adults outnumber the students." He grinned at us, and I tried to smile back, but I was feeling pretty grim. Determined, but grim. "The best way to bring in new members who are interested in what we're doing is to be really clear about what we want to accomplish. So let's work on that."

He talked for a minute about the difference between a mission statement, which he said was a descriptive phrase, and an objective, which ideally should be one or two words with no verbs. That didn't make any sense to me until he started writing stuff down on that huge pad.

"What's our end game?" he asked, and looked around at blank faces. "What state or condition do we want to be in when we're done? In one or two words, what is it that must not fail?"

Ivy piped up, "Love." I glanced at her and saw she was looking at her father, smiling, and he smiled back.

Mr. Duncan said, "No argument, Ivy. But let's sharpen our focus on the specifics we want to address. Jesse? Any suggestions?"

The specific I was focused on was Ronan. My voice quieter than I expected, I said, "Reconciliation."

THROWING STONES

He wrote that down. "Good. And why? What would that look like?"

Mrs. Knapp and Reverend Gilman stayed pretty quiet. They listened as the other three of us went round and round, finally agreeing that if there was reconciliation, there would be at least a partial integration of the two communities. There would be friendships that crossed the town-village boundary. Ivy said the village kids might participate in school activities outside of classes, and I said the town kids might attend an outdoor festival and bonfire at the village.

Then Mrs. Knapp said, "As things are now, when a town student mistreats a village student and I don't know who it was, there's no consequence. If this group succeeds, that town student will face negative peer pressure more meaningful than anything I could do."

So "Reconciliation" became our official objective, and our mission statement described what that would look like: An environment in which town and village students feel comfortable with each other and welcome in each other's communities. We also agreed that, ideally, the good will would spread outside the school and convince our parents and other adults that this was a better way to live.

Then we talked about what would happen at the meetings, and Mr. Duncan suggested that one thing might be for a student from each area to get together ahead of a meeting, talk about some aspects of their lives and draw comparisons, and then at the meeting, the town student would say what he'd learned about the village, and vice versa.

Then he said, "Probably at the first meeting where we have a few new members, Jesse and Ivy should each talk for a few minutes about why they decided to start this effort. Then each new member can say why he or she is interested in the club. This might be a good way to start meetings generally until you really get going."

229

And in terms of getting more members, we knew we needed to get the word out. Mr. Duncan suggested Ivy and I work on a flyer and a distribution plan by next week's meeting. Ivy volunteered to write an article about the club for the school paper, and her father said they'd work together on one for the town newspaper. Mr. Duncan and Mrs. Knapp said they would talk to teachers and the school counselor about the alliance. And Reverend Gilman said he was planning a series of Sunday sermons designed to promote understanding and empathy.

By the end of the meeting, although I agreed with everything we did, I still felt heavy and discouraged. I didn't see how this was going to help enough to convince Ronan that we should still be together, at least not in the near future—especially if he wouldn't join. The image of those toppled and defiled stones blocked any image I tried to create of a kinder, gentler world.

As everyone was packing up to leave, I told Ivy I had something else to do, that we could connect later. Probably because we were in the church function hall, Reverend Gilman was waiting for everyone else to leave. But I wanted to talk with him. Alone.

"Jesse? Something I can help with?"

I had no idea whether Mrs. Knapp had spilled the beans about me—either the vandalism of my locker or why I had done it—so I proceeded as though he didn't know, or that it didn't matter.

"If I tell you something in confidence, are you required to keep it secret?"

He moved to the end of the table we'd sat around for the meeting. "Please. Sit. Before you say anything, let me ask you some questions." He wanted to know if a law had been broken, and I said yes, but not by me. He asked if anyone's life or safety was in danger, and I said I didn't think so. After another couple of questions like that, he said, "Tell me what's troubling you. I will keep your confidence."

THROWING STONES

So far, so good. "It relates to the TVA, actually." I told him about Griffin's locker, about the fight, about the cat. I told him about the reaction I'd seen to Mr. Ward's sacrifice. I told him what happened to the standing stones, about how sacred the place was to the village, about how they had been really careful not to tell anyone outside the village where the stones were for fear of exactly something like this. And I told him I was pretty certain I knew who was doing the damage.

He listened to everything I said, which impressed me; he never interrupted. Then, "What is it you'd like me to do, Jesse?"

"Well, for one thing, I want to fix the stones. You know, clean off the ones that were painted, and put the ones that got tipped over back in place, which I can't do by myself. I think it would be a huge win if people from the town repaired this site. Plus, with the farming season just starting, the villagers don't have a lot of time and energy to go up there and do all that work right now."

"So you're asking my help in fixing the sacred site of a non-Christian religion. Have I got that right?"

My first reaction was a balancing act between anger and intimidation. But then I looked closely at his face. He was teasing me! I grinned. "Yeah. I guess that about covers it."

He took a deep breath in, exhaled slowly, and said, "Earlier, Ivy said love was the objective. It's my objective for what I do with my life. And as you know, Christianity is supposed to be about love. Jesus knew the best way to get someone to listen to you is not to shout at them, but to love them, and love can take many different forms. So in principle, Jesse, I support this effort. But I can see a few challenges."

He counted on his fingers what I'd just told him: I didn't know where the stones were; no village person was supposed to even know *about* the stones, let alone know where they were; in order to get enough help to fix the stones, we'd have to find them *and* tell a number of townsfolk where they were; doing this at all could get a villager in trouble for telling me about the stones in the first place; and the chances that the vandalism would be repeated were not small.

"In short, Jesse, this would need to be handled with a good deal of discretion. Now, it might surprise you to know that I'm already aware of where these stones are. So that removes the problems of your not knowing where they are and of having you be the one to reveal the location. But the other challenges remain. Let me do some thinking about this."

Surprise doesn't cover how I felt about his reaction to my idea. I was so encouraged that as I stood up, and he held out his hand to shake, I came so close to telling him about me. But—no. And I couldn't help wondering how he knew where the circle was, though I decided against asking; there was probably a confidence involved.

When I got home, Mom was just seeing a piano student out the door at the end of a lesson. The little girl—maybe ten—stood in front of Mom's case of Hummels.

In a soft, shy voice, the girl said, "I love Hummels. You have my favorite. 'Just Reading.'"

"It's one of my favorites, too. Do you have any?"

The girl nodded. "My daddy bought 'Tuck Me In' for me when I was born. And I got 'School Girl' when I started first grade. Someday I'll have enough money to buy one for myself."

I didn't remember seeing this student before, so while I helped get dinner ready I asked about her.

"Yes, she's new. I almost didn't take her on, though. She's from the village."

I nearly dropped the vegetable peeler on the floor. Doing my very, very best to seem nonchalant, I said, "Oh? What's her name?"

"Violet Fisher. Her family just bought a piano recently."

Ha! Must be the one I'd seen being delivered the day I'd worked on the labyrinth. "I gather she likes Hummels." I wanted Mom to say out loud that she had something in common with this village girl beyond playing piano. But Mom just made a humming sound—in agreement, but not very enthusiastic. So I asked, "How did Violet find you?"

Mom kept busy with dinner prep while she talked. "A woman named Eleanor Darling called me last Wednesday. She said she couldn't remember where she'd heard that I teach."

OMG! *Eleanor?!?* So maybe Ronan didn't think this bridge could be built, but it seemed Eleanor did. And she'd called on Wednesday, which was after the stones had been damaged. Mom had stopped talking, but I wanted more. "And the reason you almost didn't take her on is because she's from the village?"

"Yes, Jesse. I didn't think that needed explanation."

Deep breath; don't try to fight this battle just yet. "She looked pretty normal to me." And she had; nothing about her had reminded me of Silver Shaw. "Are you gonna keep teaching her?"

Mom let a few beats go by. "Unless some reason to stop presents itself, yes, I suppose so."

One step at a time.

After dinner I texted Griffin. *Did u know E called my mom about violet*

Maybe thirty seconds later: *Y great huh*
So far so good

Chapter Ten

The next two weeks went by super fast and really slowly. I thought about Ronan all the time, which made time slow way, way down. Whenever I glanced his way at school, he was never looking at me.

But Ivy and I were hard at work on the TVA, and that helped. We got an article into the school paper, and a few kids asked us why were doing it, even though our article had spelled that all out. Sometimes the questions were obviously antagonistic. But I was surprised that some were not.

Ivy told me that Eleanor and her father got together a few days after that first meeting, and Eleanor agreed to encourage village kids to join. Griffin joined right away, which of course made me sad, because I knew Ronan wouldn't. But then Wren Ward joined, too. Considering the town's reaction to her father's heroism, I was thinking Ronan should be ashamed of himself.

Reverend Gilman's letter to the editor was published in two local papers, and after his second sermon about opening our hearts to people whose lives seem different from ours, a couple of Ivy's town friends, Meg and Janice, joined. I finally got up the guts to talk to Phil, who said, "I'd been thinking about it. So, yeah. Sure."

By the third meeting, Ivy and I were pretty good with our opening statements, and we got Griffin and Phil to agree to meet and then present what they learned about each other at the fourth meeting. The only bad thing about the meetings was that Ronan was conspicuously absent.

THROWING STONES

Then, when I got to school on Tuesday morning, my locker had been painted again. "Faggot" again. No imagination. But this time, during home room on Tuesday, there was a PA announcement about how the culprits were known, and one more act of vandalism would result in serious consequences. Ivy told me that Lou and Chuck had been given detention for a week, and that they'd be forced to clean my locker. I wondered whether someone had really caught them at it, or if Mrs. Knapp had believed me. I wondered what "serious consequences" might mean. I also wondered whether my efforts on the TVA, which by now everybody knew about, had inspired Lou and Chuck to attack my locker again.

By this time I was feeling pretty flush with success: Our little group had grown, we had members from town and village, there was some push-back and the occasional snarky comment from some kids at school but not as much as I had expected, and Lou and Chuck had been identified and punished (at least a little). But besides Ronan's absence, there was something else that seemed directly related to the TVA that was bothering me. It seemed like Brad was pulling away from me.

On the phone, there was some awkwardness that seemed to come from nowhere. Sometimes he wouldn't answer at all, and when I texted him he'd say something about being busy with homework, or he'd say he'd been on the phone with Staci. At school, she was always with him, even at lunch, so I ended up having lunch with my TVA crowd. I texted him a couple of times to see if he wanted to go rockhounding, but he always replied, *Rain check*.

God knows I spent a lot of time, lost lots of sleep, thinking about Ronan. Wanting Ronan. Jerking off to images of Ronan, feeling the cougar's gaze almost like electric energy, imagining his hand on me, hearing that laugh of his when he came. Seeing him in school every day was like torture. Sending scads of energetic intention in his

235

direction wasn't making him turn toward me with those haunting gray eyes. I was still determined to get him back, but I couldn't be sure that would happen. And now Brad was fading into the distance? No way.

By Thursday, that second week of March, I'd had enough. After dinner I waited for maybe an hour, and then I drove to his house, unannounced. I went to the front door; this was kind of a formal visit. Mrs. Everett answered, and I couldn't help thinking she looked maybe a thousand percent better than when I'd stopped by that day in December. Reverend Gilman came to mind.

She smiled at me. "Hello, Jesse. Brad's upstairs. Do you want to go on up?"

"Sure. Thanks." Good; no warning.

The door was shut, so I knocked and heard, "Come." Brad was at his desk, and he didn't look up from his laptop. No doubt he'd thought the knock was his mom. I shut the door and stood there until he looked up.

"Jesse!" He was startled, I could tell, but he tried to cover. "What's up?"

I moved over to sit on the bed, forcing him to turn or sit with his back toward me. "What's up is what I was going to ask you."

"Meaning...?"

"Meaning it feels like something's not right between us." He shrugged but didn't speak, which pissed me off. "You're gonna pretend everything's normal?"

He shrugged again. "Not sure what to tell you, bro. What's your problem?"

I stood. "My problem, 'bro,' is that I mostly can't get on you the phone anymore, and when I do you don't have time to talk. You barely respond to texts. I've suggested rockhounding, but you don't even want to do that. You've got no time for me at school; we haven't lunch together in a couple of weeks. I get that you're with Staci a lot, okay? That's fine. That's not the problem. But you've been together for months, and all of a sudden I'm out of the picture? You don't have any time for friends anymore?"

He leaned a little sideways in his chair, I'm sure to try and look casual, like I was overreacting. "Whine much? You know you sound like a girl, right?"

It was everything I could do not to say that I didn't care if he was twice my size, I was about to slug him anyway. Instead, after clenching my fists a few times, I said, "I can't wait to tell Staci you think girls are whiny and demanding. That should free up some of your time."

That got him to his feet. "Look, if you're not happy with the new order, remember that you brought it on yourself."

"What the fuck does that mean?"

"You're the one who decided it wasn't enough to start making friends with people from the village. It wasn't enough to help them build a maze."

"Labyrinth."

He ignored me. "It wasn't even enough that your new boyfriend lives there. No; you had to get the whole school involved in your obsession. You're the one who put something between us, not me."

I was shaking my head, more in disbelief than denial. "That makes no sense! *I* didn't change. *I* didn't stop calling *you*. You stopped answering. And you might not want to admit this, but your girlfriend is the one getting in the way. Your girlfriend and her fear of things she doesn't understand."

"You think she's afraid of you?"

"I think she's *terrified* of me. Because I'm about to change her world. I'm about to expose her for the frightened child she is."

We stood there, noses practically touching, fists clenching. He was a good half-head taller, but I wasn't backing down. I wasn't actually afraid he'd hit me until he said, "You take that back or I'll flatten you."

"And won't that make you feel like a big, strong man."

237

He wheeled away from me and moved to the window, leaning heavily on the sill.

"Brad, look, I came over here because I don't want to lose you as a friend. As my *best* friend." He didn't budge. "You know, when I started this TVA thing, I expected a lot of grief. I expected to get ridiculed, tormented, maybe even punched out. But not by you, man!"

He turned so fast I almost felt a breeze. "And you haven't been punched out, have you? Do you know why not? Do you know why you don't know how many kids you've pissed off doing this stupid club?"

"I give up. Why not?"

"Because Phil and I told them there'd be consequences."

I felt almost like he'd hit me after all. "So—you're protecting me?"

We stared at each other, and then I asked, "Does Staci know?" He crossed his arms over his broad chest and looked down at nothing. Quietly, I said, "She found out, didn't she? And she told you to back away from protecting someone who protects heathens."

He said nothing. So I told him, "You can stop. Protecting me. It's great that you did that, but it's getting you into trouble. I don't want that to happen."

"This is so fucked up."

Wracking my brain, trying to think of something that might help, I asked, "What is her take on the village, anyway? How bad does she think they are?"

"She thinks they cast some kind of spell on her aunt."

"She—what? Why?"

"Her mother's younger sister, Donna, ran off with some guy from the village. Donna was supposed to get married— I forget who to, someone from the town—and then all of a sudden she disappears, along with the village guy. They must have left the area altogether, because it seems like if Donna were in the village, we'd know. But her family hasn't heard from her since."

"How long ago was this?"

"We were maybe six. Something like that."

"I don't remember hearing anything about it."

"Well, no, it was all hushed up. But Staci's convinced there was a potion involved, or maybe an amulet, something like that."

Potion. Ronan's mother made love potions. I made a mental note to ask Griffin about this. "What would it take to convince her it was just what her aunt wanted to do?"

"Dunno. Kinda doubt that's possible at this stage."

"Well, so, if you stop protecting me, can we be friends again? Or is that more than Staci can handle?"

He waved a hand in front of his face, annoyed or frustrated or something. "I'll figure this out somehow, Jesse. I didn't like what was happening with us, either. Give me a little time."

"K." I stood and held out my right hand, and we shook on it. On my way out of the room, I said, "I'll wait to hear from you."

Back in my truck, I called Griffin. "Question for you. Do you know anything about a woman named Donna who ran off with some guy from the village maybe ten years ago?"

"A little. Why?"

"Trying to figure something out. What can you tell me?"

"From what I know, it's not that much of a story. This Donna person was about to get married, and one day she had a flat tire. Zayne Downey from the village came by and stopped to help. Rumor has it Donna was getting cold feet about the wedding, but in any case she called it off, and she and Zayne were gone in, like, six weeks. They went to Canada, I think. British Columbia."

"Did he stay in touch with the village?"

"To some extent, sure. And she wrote to her family, but letters kept getting returned. I know, because Zayne asked

Eleanor to take them over to the family herself, but I doubt she'd do that. I don't really know any more than that."

"Do you know if Ronan's mother gave anyone a potion?"

"For that? No way. She wouldn't interfere with people of the town like that. She'd have to be crazy."

"But—Patty—" But Griffin wouldn't know about that. "Never mind. Um, thanks. That helps." And then I had a brainstorm. "Would you, um, would you mind giving me their address or email or something?"

"Well... I'd want to ask to be sure it's okay. Can you tell me why?"

"Staci, Donna's niece, seems to think Donna never tried to stay in touch, and Staci thinks you guys in the village did something to her. Like a potion. I'm thinking if Donna would send me something I could give directly to Staci, she'd at least have a chance to believe the truth. See, this is the reason Brad won't join the TVA. But if I can change Staci's mind about her aunt, maybe there's hope. Maybe she'd join, even."

"That's kind of a cool idea. Let me look into it."

More waiting, then. Every time I got an idea—the TVA, fixing the stone circle, this letter—I had to wait for someone else to do something. I hated that. But at least I could write the message in case this idea panned out.

The fourth TVA meeting was a lot of fun. I'd never known Phil very well, so I was surprised when he turned out to be a great counterpart to Griffin. I think "foil" is the right word. Phil was kind of the straight man to Griffin's goof. The two guys had actually worked out a routine together, which was that when Griffin described what he'd learned about Phil he got everything wrong, and Phil kept correcting him in this long-suffering, eye-rolling sort of way that was hilarious. But what was even funnier was that when Phil described Griffin, he threw in all those ridiculous things towns people tend to assume about the village, and Griffin pretended they were real and acted a couple of them out.

At one point, Griffin brought out this lamp with a clamp on it, fastened it to the back of a folding chair, and turned it on. The red bulb in it cast a bloody pool of light on the floor, where Griffin placed a straw mat and then disappeared. From someplace out of sight, eerie music began to play.

Phil said, "Like most people who live in that mysterious place, Griffin takes part in infant sacrifice." As Phil talked about all the families in town who'd had a baby disappear (not true for any of them, actually), Griffin reappeared, hunched over and walking oddly, leering at everyone, clutching something against his chest. When he got to the mat, he put a doll down on it, took out a knife made of cardboard, and stabbed at the doll.

"But because the townsfolk are good Christians," Phil went on, "the village people are foiled in their attempts to slaughter the child. The knife becomes harmless, and the baby's life is spared."

Griffin sat down on the floor and pretended to weep and pull his hair, reaching his arms up in anger and frustration.

When the laughter in the room died down, Phil spoke again, this time in earnest. As Griffin cleared away the props and stopped the music, Phil told the group much of what Griffin and Ronan had told me. He talked about the Pagan credo Ivy had repeated to me: An it harm none, do as ye will. He pointed out that harm to others is not something we can predict or avoid unless we do our best to put ourselves in their place first. He said that even good intentions can have harmful results on someone else if we don't understand the other person well enough.

Then Griffin said, "What Phil and I learned about each other's culture is that everything works best, and everyone is happiest, when we approach each other with a sincere desire for understanding." He turned to Ivy and nodded, and then to me. "Many thanks to Ivy and Jesse for getting this work underway."

Everyone applauded loudly as Griffin and Phil bowed, and bowed again, grinning and obviously pleased with themselves.

At the end of the meeting, Griffin stayed behind. Outside, Ivy grabbed my arm and said, "I need to wait a few minutes. Will you wait with me?"

"Sure. For what?"

She took a deep breath. "Griffin is asking my father if he can have permission to go out with me."

OMG. I gaped at her. "For real? What if he says no?"

She actually giggled. "How can he, after that performance? And he's mentioned Griffin a couple of times at home when he's talked about the club. Mom even said she'd like to meet him."

She looked so happy and so excited that I couldn't help myself. I hugged her. It made me miss Ronan more than ever, though.

We leaned against a tree and waited, but only for a couple of minutes. We turned toward the door when it opened, and both Reverend Gilman and Griffin came out. Griffin was smiling. The reverend nodded to me and went off in another direction, and Ivy skipped over to her boyfriend. I heard Griffin tell her that the reverend wanted to meet the Holyokes. I felt my eyes water, both with pleasure for them and with pain for me.

It wasn't until the end of that week that Griffin got back to me about contacting Donna. He called me Friday after dinner while I was up in my room, sulking that I couldn't be with Ronan.

"We talked about it on and off all week, Jesse," Griffin

told me. "Most of us like the idea, so let's do it. But—well, I think you can understand that with things starting to happen, like the TVA, we want to be sure of what's said about us. So if you'll agree, what we'll do is have you send your message to me, and a few of us here will read it. If we think something should be changed, we'll let you do that; we won't change your message. Once it seems fine, we'll send it on to Donna, and then I guess we wait. If she replies to us, we'll forward that on to you. At that point, you'd be included in a discussion of what happens next, which might or might not include you giving it to Staci. Sort of depends on what it says. Does that make sense?"

This was a lot more convoluted than anything I had imagined, and again that frustration hit me, the one where my ideas are never quite good enough to just act on. But I decided I couldn't blame the village for wanting to make sure they didn't get misrepresented. That last thing I wanted this exchange to do was make things worse between town and village.

"Sure. That works," I said, trying to keep the grudging reluctance I felt out of my voice. "I've already got the email written. I'll send it to you tonight. Um, can you tell me who didn't like the idea?"

There was a pause, and then, "You'd probably rather not know." Which meant I already knew.

"Griffin, what can you tell me? Why is he so determined to keep this wall up? Why doesn't he want the village and the town to be friends?"

"Has he told you anything about power animals?"

"I know his is Cougar. I looked it up once."

"Ronan takes the concept very seriously. And I have to say, he's Cougar, through and through. You probably found out that Cougar watches from a distance before making a move that commits it to action. Because once Cougar commits, it commits for real. And that makes it vulnerable. Ronan doesn't believe anything good will come of what we're trying to do. So he's keeping his distance. Self-preservation, I guess."

"And that includes me?"

"Of course. I mean, look what you've done! You came to the grove twice to see how we do things. You asked me all kinds of questions, and you didn't flinch at any of the answers. You came right into the village to talk to me about Allen, even though someone in the town hung him in effigy. You brought us the perfect stone for our labyrinth, and you stayed to work with us. And then, even after we practically kicked you out—at least, I think that's how it felt to you—you turn around and start this TVA club! Jesse, you're doing everything Ronan can't trust. And he loves you. So if just participating in these efforts would make him commit, imagine how vulnerable he makes himself by being with the guy who keeps starting them."

I was ready to scream by this point. Here I'd been trying to win Ronan back by diving ever deeper into this work of building bridges, and that was the very thing pushing him away. "Should I stop?"

"*Can* you?" That stunned me into several seconds of silence. Then he asked, "Ever hear the fable of the scorpion and the frog?"

I shook my head, realized he couldn't see me, and said, "Don't think so."

"There's this scorpion on the side of a river. He needs to get across, but he can't swim. Along comes a frog, and the scorpion says, 'Can I ride on your back across the river?' The frog says, 'Are you kidding? You're a scorpion! How do I know you won't sting me?' 'If I do, I'll die, too,' the scorpion says. So the frog agrees. But half-way across, the scorpion stings the frog. As he starts to sink, the frog says, 'Why did you do that? Now we'll both die!' And the scorpion says, 'It's my nature. It's what I do.'"

"And the moral is?"

"You have to be true to yourself, Jesse. And the better I

know you, the more I see who you are. You've got more courage than anyone else I know, and Eleanor says your nature is to use it to make the world better. I agree. Sorry if that sounds corny, but it's what we see."

"Eleanor talks about me?"

He laughed. "Jesse, you make it impossible for her not to."

"Yeah, well... Anyway, I'll send that email over now."

Here's what I sent to Griffin:

Donna --

You don't know me, but I'm in Staci Thompson's classes at school, and I'm best friends with her boyfriend (Brad). Brad told me that Staci thinks something happened to make you call off your wedding here and move away with Zayne, and she's been told the people of the grove are to blame. I'm sure that's wrong. She thinks you never contacted your family after you left, but I know that's wrong, too.

I'm of the town, but I want things to be friendly between townspeople and people of the grove. So if you would be willing to send me something I could give directly to Staci, that would be great. I hope you can convince her that you did what you wanted to do, and that you didn't do it because of any interference from the grove.

Sincerely, Jesse Bryce

As soon as Griffin had time to read it, I got a reply that he'd show it to Eleanor right away.

And once again, I waited. And, once again, I felt determined to prove Ronan wrong and get him back. If I could get everything to a place where he wasn't vulnerable, there was hope. And I could do that. I was sure of it.

Eleanor decided not to change anything, so she sent my message off to Donna. And then there was more waiting.

Meanwhile, Ivy told me her father and Eleanor were in the process of organizing an open-attendance town meeting, and the reverend had even managed to get the mayor to agree to help plan it. Before they could get it set up, though, we had a bit of a crisis in the TVA. At our fifth meeting, Meg Parry, Ivy's friend who joined, had to resign when her parents realized what we were doing. Meg said she hadn't exactly hidden things from them, she'd just played down the involvement of the village kids. That is, she didn't mention it at all. But she let something slip in a conversation over dinner one night, and the shit hit the fan. Mr. Duncan offered to speak with her folks, but she said it wouldn't do any good.

Then Wren found that some strange-smelling substance had been forced through the vents in her locker, and when she reported the incident as vandalism, the stuff turned out to be marijuana. This, of course, was a crisis that went beyond the TVA. Wren was immediately taken home, and the police got a warrant to go searching through the Wards' house for anything illicit. To her credit, Mrs. Knapp initiated a school-wide search, of town kids' lockers as well as village kids'. Of course, they found nothing anywhere, and I still don't know who did that to Wren, but it sure didn't help anything to have that happen. Ronan looked at me a few times, but the looks were more glares than anything else, like, "See what you've caused?" and "I told you so."

I half expected Wren to leave the club after that, but instead, she made a little speech at our March thirtieth meeting about how she knows this kind of thing will continue to happen until we reach our objective. She said her commitment to our mission had not changed. She got a huge round of applause.

Mom heard about the marijuana episode and asked me about it over dinner preparation on Tuesday. "What do you know about this girl, Jesse?"

"She's as sweet as pie. It was her father who died trying to help Mary Blaisdell, remember? And then someone does this to her."

"How do you know whether she's sweet or not?"

I decided this was as good a time as any to tell her about the TVA, which until now I'd been reluctant to mention. But I had so many strikes against me at home, what was one more? Though maybe she didn't need to know what my role had been. My role as the architect of bridges, that is. So I said, "She's in this club I go to on Mondays after school. The Town Village Alliance. We have school sponsorship, and we meet at the church function hall. Reverend Gilman is involved, too. The idea is to get to understand each other more so we get along better."

Mom's hands came to rest on the edge of the counter, one with a vegetable peeler, one with a carrot. "Village? As in the... the—"

I could tell she was trying hard to avoid the word "freaks." I prompted, "Village. As in the group of people who live there, south of town. Yes."

"How long has this been going on?"

"Our first meeting was February twenty-third. There are some kids from the village, and some from the town, and Mr. Duncan, the science teacher, and the principal, Mrs. Knapp, and Reverend Gilman come to it. His daughter's in it, too."

"Ivy Gilman? Reverend Gilman lets his daughter go?"

I almost didn't say it, but it wasn't a secret, and it might help my case. "Not only that, but she's going out with Griffin Holyoke. He's from the village." I almost added something about how that proves the club is working, but I didn't want to push too hard.

"Why am I just hearing about this now?"

It didn't seem right to point out that I hadn't needed parental permission to join a school club, so I just said, "Didn't seem to be any reason to bring it up before."

Mom went back to peeling her carrot, but I could hear

the wheels turning in her head. I prayed I wasn't going too far when I said, "Reverend Gilman is working with the village elder—Eleanor Darling, who sent Violet to you—to organize a town meeting with the same idea. I mean, getting to know each other better. I'm sure you'll hear about that as soon as everyone else does."

Silence.

I needed to know: "Once they get it set up, will you go to it?"

A few heartbeats later, she said, "If only to find out more about this club you're in. I'm not sure I like this, Jesse." She turned to look at me. "You're not going in there, are you?"

I shook my head. "No, but at some point it probably makes sense. Once you know more about them. Once you can be sure they aren't up to anything."

I didn't keep the subject going, and Mom let it drop, too; more waiting, I figured. But I'd planted a seed.

Thursday evening I got a Skype invite from Ivy. "Jesse?" Just the tone of her voice told me she wanted a favor. "How do you feel about mushrooms?"

Not what I'd expected. "What kind of mushrooms?"

She laughed. "The kind you eat, not the kind that takes you on weird trips. It's morel season, and Griffin invited me to go morel hunting with him Saturday afternoon. He does it every year, and he knows how to tell what's safe. Daddy said I could go, except that he hasn't met Griffin's parents yet. That'll happen Sunday afternoon. So I can go if someone else goes with us, someone Daddy knows. I said would you do, and he said absolutely. So—will you come with us?"

Immediately it sounded like the sort of thing I'd like to do with Ronan. Not much chance of that. So the next question was whether I wanted to chaperone. "You guys won't be making things difficult for me by disappearing into the woods or anything, will you?"

She laughed in a way that made me suspect her answer wasn't entirely truthful: "Of course not, silly!" Then she added, "You can keep a third of the take. Griffin says you like to cook."

That was true. And I'd learn how to tell the safe ones from the unsafe ones. "All right, but you'd better not make me regret my generosity."

As soon as we disconnected, I texted Ronan: *Want to go morel hunting sat pm with me Griffin and Ivy?*

I watched the phone for maybe a minute before I set it down beside my keyboard and picked up the cookbook he'd given me to look for recipes with morels. Fifteen minutes went by before I saw, *No, thanks.* I wondered how many different responses he'd gone over in his mind before sending that short one.

It was what I'd expected. *No, thanks.* But that didn't stop it from hurting.

Saturday around one, I picked Ivy up. This was our way of making sure her father believed that I'd be with them. As I drove, she asked, "Do you have a recipe picked out already?"

"I do. I have a cookbook a friend gave me with recipes for local produce. There's a soup recipe I have in mind." I didn't mention Ronan; didn't want to go into that with Ivy.

She laughed. "Griffin said you would. He respects you a lot, Jesse."

I tried not to smile and failed. "I like him, too. By the way, are you allowed into the village itself now?"

"I am. Oh—you're not."

"Not yet. Working on it. I'll drive in and drop you off. Then I have to park across the highway and walk in through the woods. Tell Griffin I'll meet you guys at the path at the southeast corner of the clearing."

By the time I got there, Griffin and Ivy had had time to practically entwine themselves together. Ivy seemed like a good name for the way she was clinging to him. I did my best to put a friendly smile on my face, wishing for you-know-what with you-know-who.

I had to clear my throat to break the spell between them. They pulled apart but held hands, revealing a canvas bag slung across Griffin's body that I hadn't been able to see until then. Griffin thanked me for agreeing to watch over them and then led the way into the woods. Partway down that slope to the funeral site he veered to the right along yet another path I'd never seen.

Once the path leveled out a little, he said, "Look for downed trees almost anywhere, but I'm heading toward the spot where we've found the most in the past."

We tramped through the woods, following no trail anymore as far as I could tell, and we spread out a little to widen our search.

After about ten minutes I heard Griffin's voice. "Here!" He was stooped over a jumble of fallen tree branches, poking gently at the ground. Before we got to him, though, he said, "Wait. Nope. False alarm. False morel, in fact." He held it toward Ivy and me as we got close. "See this stem? Morel stems aren't this bright white. And the head of this one has this irregular shape to it. Morel heads are kind of oval, and they're very symmetrical. Some people eat these, but you never know how much it has of this certain chemical that causes vomiting and diarrhea. It might even kill you, if there's enough of that poison in it. And anyway, it's probably carcinogenic." He dropped it back to the ground and the hunt went on.

Maybe another fifteen minutes went by before Ivy called out, "Griffin? What about this one?" She held it up so he could take a good look at it.

"That's it! Are there more there?"

THROWING STONES

As soon as he said that, he looked up at the sky, barely visible through the trees. "Wow. Looks like some weather moving in. Better hurry."

Fortunately Ivy had found a great spot, and there were lots more there, and still more a little farther on. We scoured the ground around where some small trees had fallen maybe a couple of years ago. Griffin dropped the bag where we could all throw morels into it, and within a few minutes we had enough mushrooms for each of us to take home a good haul. I picked up the bag and poked around in it, and an earthy, musky aroma floated up.

Suddenly Griffin's phone made a sharp, unpleasant tone.

Ivy said, "What is it?"

Griffin looked at the screen and then, sharply, up at us. "There's a tornado on the ground, south of here. We have to get out of here, now." He took the bag, wrapped it closely around himself, and turned to lead us out. "There's a storm shelter underneath the meeting house. You'll have to come with me."

As we headed back through the woods, I called home. Mom answered, and I told her, "There's a tornado south of town. I'm safe, but you need to get into the basement. I'm calling Dad now. I'll call you again as soon as I can."

"You're *not* safe! You're running!"

"To a storm shelter. Get downstairs!" I heard the town's tornado warning start to wail.

"I'll call your father. You just get to the shelter." And she hung up. Our house was to the north, so she'd have time to call *and* get downstairs.

While I'd been on the phone to Mom, Ivy had called home, too.

When we broke out of the woods into the labyrinth field, people from the village were heading to the meeting house. I'd never been inside before, and it was kind of hard to appreciate it in the crush. Someone took my hand, and when I looked I saw it was Ronan. All he said was, "Thank the Goddess you made it back." And he let go.

There was a large trap door in the corner of the room with stairs that went underneath the building. The shelter was a finished room with rugs all over the floor, and there were large bottles of water all along two of the walls, folding chairs along another, and piles of blankets along the fourth wall. There weren't any shelves or bookcases, I guess so nothing would fall on anyone. The ceiling was supported by thick beams that could probably have taken the weight of almost anything falling on them.

Ronan pulled me down onto the floor beside some people I don't know, and everyone else sat as well, forming a kind of spiral pattern with Eleanor in the center. Spiral... that was the symbol for eternal life, right? Let's hope. I saw Griffin and Ivy a couple of rows away, almost across from me. He raised his chin to let me know he saw me, and that he saw Ronan was with me.

The woman next to me took my hand, and I realized everyone was taking the hand of the person next to them all along the spiral. Most people had closed their eyes, and individual conversations were getting quieter. Then there was silence. And then I heard Eleanor's calm voice.

"Goddess of life. Goddess of death. Goddess of air and earth and water and fire. Allow this storm to do as it must, but cast a shield around the grove. Cast a shield around the town. Cast a shield around all people. Cast a shield around all animals. Cast a shield around trees and plants. Send the storm where it can be free. Send the storm where it can be what it is and cause least harm. Protect us as the storm lives and dies. Help us protect those who will not ask for protection. Help us protect those who do not know how to ask. With your strength, make gentleness possible. Allow peace to return to all. Blessed be."

Everyone echoed, "Blessed be," and then they began to hum. So I did, too. We swayed gently, side to side, and I allowed myself to go fully into that trance state I'd barely tasted spying on the grove at Samhain, and at Mr. Ward's funeral. We swayed. We hummed. We existed as one. And there was some power, some strength that I didn't recognize, that I'd never felt before, and it wrapped all of us in it together.

Time passed; I don't know how much. At some point I was aware of a roaring sound that I knew to be the winds of the storm, and then all I heard was humming again. Gradually people stopped humming, and the swaying slowed and then stopped. We were all still holding hands.

Then Talise Alexander, the woman Ronan had said doused for the labyrinth site, stood. "The village is unharmed. But someone's hurt. Wait… two people. I don't know who or where."

I was expecting everyone to get up and leave, but no one moved, and we were all still holding hands. But I needed to make sure my family was okay, so I let go and moved over to a corner. First I called to be sure Mom was okay, and she was. She'd already spoken to Dad, and everything was fine at the garage, where both Dad and Stu were today. But I had to call anyway. I wanted Dad and Stu to know I cared about them.

I was on the phone with Dad when it occurred to me to ask, "Patty?"

There was a beat or two of silence, and then he said, "Stu can't reach her, but maybe she's just not picking up." I knew he meant she might not answer when Stu's name showed up on her phone.

"I'll call her now."

"Good idea." This simple phrase from my father right now felt great.

Patty didn't answer for me, either. It rang several times and went to voicemail. I left a short message, but I was worried; she must have known there'd been a tornado, and she must have known I was calling about that. So—why not answer *my* call?

Ivy and Griffin had left the spiral, too, and they were standing there waiting for me to finish the calls. I told them, "I can't reach Patty. Stu's fiancée. Sort of."

Griffin glanced around quickly and located Talise, waving to her to come over to us. She did, and softly, he said, "Can you follow Jesse's energy to his brother's fiancée? We're worried about her."

Talise smiled at me. "So this is the famous Jesse. Of course."

She took my hands in hers. "Jesse, what's her name?" I told her, and she said, "Concentrate on Patty. Hold her image and her energy in your mind. Don't speak."

We stood there for maybe thirty seconds, and I felt Talise's hands jerk in mine. "Do you know anything about where Patty is?" I shook my head. "I don't know what's going on specifically, but I can tell you she's in trouble."

I turned to Griffin. "I have to find her. She's pregnant."

"Oh!" Talise's eyes got wide. "Oh, Jesse! Then—two people..."

OMG. Talise had said two people had been hurt. Was that Patty *and* her baby? My niece or nephew? Everyone in the room was now looking at us, but they were still sitting on the floor.

Griffin said, "I'm coming with you." To Talise, he said, "I'll let you know something as soon as I do."

Ivy and Griffin ran with me up the stairs, out of the building, and toward my truck. There was a huge branch on the ground, blocking my way. Thank the Goddess Griffin was there, because it took both of us to move it out of the way. We all climbed in, and I threw the truck into gear and tore up the highway, barely noticing the arboreal carnage on the west side of the road, thinking Patty might be in her apartment, not knowing where else to start. But almost immediately I heard a horn blaring, and then I saw her car.

Griffin beat both of us to the car. "She's inside. She's

unconscious."

The car was in the road, and there was a tree on top of it. It wasn't a huge tree, but it was big enough that it had crushed the roof onto Patty's head and must have knocked her out. She was leaned forward on the collapsed airbag, and that was why the horn was blaring non-stop. The driver's side door was kind of popped out of its frame just enough to be completely in the way, hanging at an odd angle on bent hinges. Griffin pulled on it, but it wouldn't budge. I joined him, but still, no movement.

I pulled out my phone and called 9-1-1. Griffin called Todd Swazey, who said he'd be right there. My next call was to Stu. I told him where the car was and what I knew, which wasn't much, and he rang off without a word. I knew he'd be here as soon as he could.

Griffin struggled to get his arm into the car and laid a few fingers on the side of Patty's neck. He nodded; there was a pulse. Then he said, "Just look at all the downed trees! It's amazing they aren't blocking the road. Just all up the west side, like Eleanor asked. If only the funnel had missed this one."

Now we waited—more waiting!—and I felt so fucking helpless. I wanted to reach in and pull Patty out, but even if that were something I should do—which it wasn't—that stupid door was in the way. Her face was toward me, eyes closed, jaw kind of slack, mouth open a little. She almost looked dead.

Todd got to us before Stu or the ambulance, and then cars started to collect around us on the road. Griffin and I did our best to wave them on; I wanted the ambulance to have a clear path. This meant I couldn't watch Todd very well, but I saw him bring some equipment from his truck, and pretty soon he had the car door off.

Griffin jogged over to me. "He doesn't dare move her, but the EMTs from the ambulance can get to her now."

The ambulance arrived in minutes that seemed to take

forever, with a police car hot on its tail. They managed to get Patty out of the car and onto a stretcher with padding around her head so it didn't move. I told them, "She's a couple of months pregnant. Is she breathing?"

They nodded and moved with her toward the ambulance.

Suddenly Stu was beside me; I hadn't seen him arrive. "I need you to get my truck home. I'm going in the ambulance. I'll call her folks from there." He tossed me his keys and dashed to the ambulance before they could close the doors.

I went over to Todd's truck to thank him, and a police officer came over to me. "You know the victim?"

Victim. Wow. "Um, yeah. She's engaged to my brother. Patty Arnold." I figured it wasn't worth going into details about the state of the engagement. They asked a couple of questions, like how we came across the accident, what else we might know about it, and who took the door off. They looked hard at Todd, who was just standing there like a statue, huge and powerful and silent. I figured the police knew he was from the village, and they might have suspicions they didn't even know how to express.

But then one of them said to Todd, "Might have saved her life, getting that door out of the way so quickly."

Todd smiled and nodded, and then he got into his truck and headed home.

Griffin was on the phone with Talise, letting her know what had happened. When he hung up he said, "She'll let the others know so they can send a different energy. They don't have to keep trying to see who was hurt."

"They were doing that?"

"Why do you think everyone stayed in the spiral? They wanted to start casting energy out right away for whoever was hurt."

"Even though they knew it was no one in the village?"

He looked at me oddly. "Jesse, haven't you figured out

yet that we aren't the ones who hate?"

"Sorry. Yes, I have figured that out. It's just..." I didn't know how to finish.

He did. "It's just that not very many people of the town would concern themselves if they knew two villagers had been hurt."

We locked eyes for a second, but not in anger. It was more like frustration at this cold war in place between his people and mine.

Griffin said, "Come on. I'll help you with Stu's truck. You drive Ivy home and I'll meet you at your house. Then you can give me a ride back."

I handed Griffin my keys, and Ivy and I climbed into Stu's truck. She'd already called her folks, and everything was fine at home.

"Don't wait, Jesse," she said when I pulled up to let her off. "Go be with your family." I didn't wait.

At home, Griffin stayed out front in my truck while I went inside to be sure Mom was okay and that she knew what had happened. She said Dad had called her.

"Were you there when the ambulance got there?"

"Yeah. Stu was there pretty quickly, too. He went with her. So I drove his truck home. He's calling her folks."

"How is she?"

"She was breathing, but unconscious. I told them she's pregnant."

She gave me an odd look. "How did you know that?"

I shrugged. "I heard something the other night."

She must have thought this emergency was more important than quizzing me further. She said, "I'll call your father, and then I'll call her parents."

She glanced outside to where Griffin was sitting in the passenger seat of my truck, parked along the road in front of the house. "Who's that in your truck? He's been out there for some time."

"Griffin Holyoke. I had to drive Stu's truck home, but

ROBIN REARDON

mine was at the accident site. And we'd given another friend a ride, so I had to go there first. So Griffin drove mine. Now I need to give him a ride back. I'll be home right after that."

She was still looking at Griffin. "Have I met this friend?"

"Don't think so. He's not… he's not gay. He's just a friend, Mom. And Ivy's boyfriend, like I told you. Wanna meet him?"

She shook her head.

We were halfway to the village when Griffin said, "I hope you'll tell them about Todd. About what the policeman said."

I grinned. "Are you kidding? I'm going to tell everyone I know about that." Then, "Ronan came to me. In the shelter."

"Yeah. I saw. I, uh, wouldn't read too much into that. He really cares about you, Jesse, but he's determined not to get involved."

I would change his mind. *I* was determined, too.

Back home, there was a note from Mom saying she'd taken Mrs. Arnold to the hospital, that Patty's father would meet them there, and that she'd call me as soon as there was anything to report. I sat at the kitchen table, the silence of the house weighing on me in a really odd way. Something inside me was shivering uncomfortably. I was sure it had to do with the accident, but I couldn't make it stop. I wanted to get up and put on some music, or turn on the TV, but I felt like I couldn't move. There was a lump in my throat, and I was blinking back tears that didn't seem to have any reason to be there.

Finally I picked up my phone, and I called Brad to make sure he was okay and to let him know about Patty. We chatted for a few minutes, but there was nothing much to say, so we rang off again.

More silence. More shivering. More waiting. I hated

this. I had almost managed to get out of the chair when my phone rang.

It was Mom. She was crying. "Patty's going to be all right, Jesse. But—the baby!"

Now the tears had a reason. I wasn't weeping, but there were moisture trails all down my cheeks. There was nothing to say. I almost asked if it was a boy or a girl, but what difference did it make? Maybe Mom thought it mattered, because she said, "It was a little girl."

I swallowed a few times so I could manage to get some words out. "Is Patty conscious? Does she know?"

"Yes. Stu's with her." She took a deep, shuddering breath. "Patty will have to stay here until they're sure she's all right. Concussions, you know. At least she doesn't seem to be bleeding internally. But they have to watch her."

"That makes sense." What else to say? Why was this so hard?

"I'm going to call your father now, Jesse. He wanted to stay at the garage unless Patty… unless she didn't make it."

That kind of made sense, too, but I didn't say it again. "Okay. I'll get supper started, if you want, and you can stay there as long as you need to."

"Thanks, sweetie." She told me what she had planned. "I'll let you know if I'm going to be here much longer. I think Stu will stay, and probably the Arnolds."

We rang off. I texted Griffin. *She'll be okay. Concussion. But she lost the baby.*

I know. I'm so sorry. We're all sending grounding and healing energy to her.

He knew. These people amaze me. *Thanks.* Then I texted Ivy to let her know.

I had no idea what time it was. My watch said it was almost four, but that felt irrelevant. I had to force my brain to focus on logistical things, like how soon Dad would be home expecting dinner, and whether I should try to keep something warm for Mom if she didn't get home until late.

Zombie-like, I went through the motions of pulling things out of the fridge and cabinets. I barely remembered what Mom had said she was planning, but she'd left the recipe card out. Meatloaf. This was a family favorite, so we had it often. Usually if I was doing this, I'd add stuff depending on my mood and on what was in the house. This time, I just followed her recipe.

More to provide some noise than anything else, I turned the kitchen TV on. It was a news station, and they were talking about the tornado, so I stopped working to listen.

It wasn't a very big funnel. They thought it formed several miles south of town and followed the edge of the highway north, and then just below town it headed west across some plowed fields and roped out. There were a couple of experts on the phone who said this was an unusual pattern. Someone else said that road crews were out making sure there weren't trees or other debris blocking the road, but there was not much for them to do. Somehow no power lines went down. There was no mention of Patty.

I went back to my task, but I almost didn't see my own hands. Rather than focus on Patty's baby, I let my mind go back to the shelter in the village, and to what Eleanor asked the Goddess for. Of course I couldn't know what would have happened if it hadn't been for that prayer or whatever it was, but the fact was the storm did just what Eleanor asked, with the exception of Patty's car.

Meatloaf in the oven, I worked on the potatoes and the vegetables. Mom already had an apple pie ready for dessert. As I was adjusting the water temperature so the potatoes wouldn't boil over, it occurred to me to wonder what had happened to my morels. I figured Griffin had them. If I wanted to make that soup, I'd need to collect more. Not high on my list right now.

Mom got home around five thirty and immediately wrapped me in her arms. We stood there like that for a minute or two, and then she sniffled and released me to grab a tissue.

"Thank God you were nearby," she said. "How did you find her so quickly?"

I hadn't told her details about my plans for the afternoon before I left, and I wasn't sure how she was going to take the truth. I decided to risk it, even though I left a few things out. And maybe twisted a couple of facts, just a little.

"I was with Ivy Gilman and Griffin Holyoke in the woods south of the village. Griffin was harvesting morels, which he does every year. We'd just found a bunch of them when Griffin got a call about the tornado. The safest thing to do was go to the storm shelter in the village, which is below their meeting house. So Ivy and I went with Griffin. After the storm passed I started calling around, and Dad said Patty hadn't picked up Stu's call. So I decided to try, and she didn't answer. Ivy and Griffin went with me to see if we could find her. I was gonna head toward her apartment first, but I saw her car right away and called 9-1-1."

Mom slumped into a chair at the kitchen table. "Did she hit a tree?"

"No. Actually, a tree hit her. It fell on the car. She was slumped over the wheel, unconscious, and her door was hanging partway off the car." Here was my chance to sing Todd's praises, so I told her what he'd done.

Mom sat there, rubbing her hairline with her fingers. She looked done in. I asked, "How is Patty? Other than... you know."

Mom exhaled a long breath. "She had a concussion, of course. It doesn't look like there will be a problem, but as I said earlier, they're keeping her overnight for observation. Stu's still there, with her, and her folks. I don't know whether he'll come back with them tonight, or if he'll crash in a waiting room someplace."

I was dying to ask if it looked like they were back

together, but the only way I'd know about a rift at all would be my eavesdropping, which I didn't want to admit to.

When Dad got home, Mom had to go over all of it again. He didn't pay much attention to me—par for the course lately—until it became clear to him that it might have saved her life that I'd found her so quickly.

When we sat down for the meal, his first question for me didn't give me a warm-and-fuzzy feeling. "What were you doing in the village? You said you wouldn't go there without permission."

"I wasn't in the village. I was with Ivy Gilman and her boyfriend in the woods south of the village."

"Doing what?"

I wondered how many scenarios were playing themselves out inside his head. "Harvesting morels. They're a kind of edible mushroom that grow in the woods this time of year."

"But you went into the village shelter."

"Well, yeah. It was that or hang out under the trees with a tornado on the loose."

Mom passed the bowl of potatoes around. Dad said, "How long were you down there?"

"Just until the funnel passed. We could hear it roaring, so we knew when it was safe."

No one seemed to have any more invasive questions, and talk turned to the path the funnel had taken. Dad used to watch that TV show, *Storm Chasers,* so he started throwing terms and factoids around like he knew what he was talking about. Then he said he agreed with what he'd heard on the radio about it being an odd track for the storm to take, following the side of the highway as long as it did, and for some reason that seemed good at the time but that I regretted almost immediately, I talked about what Eleanor had said in the shelter.

"They prayed for the storm to go where it would do the least damage."

Dad stopped eating and stared at me. "Are you telling me they prayed for the storm to hit us instead of them?"

"What? No! That's not what I said at all. They prayed for it to miss the village *and* to miss the town. They prayed for us as much as for them. Like I said, they asked it to go where it wouldn't hurt anyone."

"But it did hurt someone! It hurt Patty, and it killed my grandchild! Are you telling me that's their idea of not hurting someone?"

"That's—look, wouldn't you have prayed something exactly like that? Didn't you pray?" He glared at me and stabbed at something on his plate like that was a ridiculous question, but what it told me was that he hadn't prayed. "Dad, you might not fall on your knees and talk to God when you need something badly, but that's what the villagers did. They asked for people and animals to be protected." Probably not a good time to mention the Goddess. But I came really close to telling them what Talise had said about two people being hurt. I stopped myself in time, though; in this mood, that might confirm his suspicions.

The side of his hand hit the table edge. "I prayed to keep *everyone* safe!"

"So did they. You *all* failed."

"*I* think," Mom said, in a gentle voice that calmed things down, "we owe them a debt of gratitude. Jesse tells me Patty was trapped in her car, unconscious. The medics couldn't have opened the door. Someone from the village took the door of the car off, so that as soon as the ambulance arrived, they could get to her immediately. That might have saved her life, Gene."

Wow. I had to force myself not to stare at Mom. But you can believe I filed that support away for future reference.

Maybe feeling more subdued than he looked, Dad diverted the conversation, at least a little. "How big a tree was it that hit her car?"

I told him, "Not very big, just heavy enough to crush the roof. And it popped the driver's door part-way open and then jammed it. That's why the blacksmith had to take it off. And it did save her life. The police even said so." And I reached for the potatoes like that was an end to that conversational point.

Dad went back to talking about rear flank downdraft and EFT, whatever that means. All I knew was that it has to do with the strength of the storm, and ours was only an EFT1.

We were nearly done with our pie when a car pulled up in front, and then Stu came in. He said it was Patty's folks, dropping him off.

"I'll drive back up in the morning and stay with her until they release her, and I'll bring her home." He fell into his chair at the table, and Mom brought him a plate full of food. She set it in front of him and then gave him a quick hug around his neck from behind the chair.

I didn't know what to say. Should I have said I was sorry about the baby? Or would he rather not be reminded? And how was the relationship now? Would she take the ring back? And if she did, would that mean Stu hated me less?

Halfway through his meatloaf, eyes on his plate, Stu said, "Sounds like your friends there might have saved her life." Guess he'd heard what had happened.

"They did. The police even said so. Todd Swazey took the car door off so the EMTs could get her out."

"How did you happen to be there?"

So I told that tale all over again, again being careful to leave out details that might be disturbing to my audience.

He took a mouthful of buttered carrots and watched me as he chewed. Then, as I was taking a drink of milk, he asked, "Do you know a Mrs. Coulter?"

I nearly choked on the milk. When I could speak, I said,

"Sorry; swallowed wrong. Um, I don't know her, no. But her son is in some of my classes at school."

"Patty knows her."

OMG. The potion.

That got Mom's attention. "Why is that?"

Stu shoved a forkful of food into his mouth and shook his head. He ignored her question completely. Around the food he said, "Patty feels like it was her fault she lost the baby. Like God is punishing her, or something."

"What for?" Mom sounded annoyed.

What I wanted to ask was why God would kill an innocent baby to punish Patty for *anything.*

But again, Stu didn't answer. He looked at me. "The good news is we're back together again." And he started talking about getting wedding plans underway, which seemed to distract Mom, and even Dad, enough that no one followed up on Mom's questions not getting answered.

Chapter Eleven

Tuesday after school, I called Patty to see if she needed anything, if she was up for a visit, and she said she needed nothing and to come on over.

I'd thought about stopping to get flowers or something, but when I got there I was glad I didn't. I'd have bet she didn't own a vase that wasn't full of flowers. They were everywhere, and she said most of them were from Stu.

She loved it. "It's like a private garden. I only wish…" Her voice trailed off, and I knew she'd been about to say she wished there'd been no need for a garden at all. I wrapped my arms around her, and she cried a little before pulling away and reaching for a tissue. "I'm sorry."

"Oh, Patty, you've got nothing to be sorry for." Even if she thought she did, which is sort of what Stu had said.

She blew her nose rather juicily and then said, "I haven't had a chance to thank you. I might have died, too, if you hadn't been so close, and if you hadn't come looking for me."

"It was really Todd Swazey, from the village. He's the one who got the door of the car out of the way."

"Stu told me you were there. In the village, I mean. Are you sure that's a good idea?"

This, from Patty? Really? "Patty, for crying out loud, they saved your life! Might have saved mine, too, because the tornado was really close to where I was, and they have an underground shelter they took me into. And I wouldn't have been so close to your car if I hadn't been there. There's nothing dangerous there, Patty." Just in time I stopped talking before pointing out that she'd gone there, herself, for that love potion. She didn't reply, just got a kind of pursed look on her face. Time to change the subject. "Anyway, can I ask about something else?"

"Of course."

"Um, how is Mary doing? Since—you know. Is she okay?"

Patty shook her head. "Not really. She's in pretty bad shape. I—I can't really talk about it. But thanks for asking."

"I get it. So... now that you and Stu are back together, does that mean he's changed at all about the gay issue?"

"We're engaged again, conditionally. I've told Stu I want him to put some effort into understanding what things are like for you. He needs to convince me that if you were our child, he would love you as much as I would."

I was thinking that right now, he needed to convince me he loved me at all, even as a brother, when someone turned the front door lock. We both looked that way, and Stu came in, a loaded grocery bag in his arms.

To me he said, "I didn't expect you to be here." I couldn't tell much from his tone. He went into the kitchen and put something into the fridge.

"And I didn't know you'd be here in the middle of the day," I said, loud enough to carry.

Patty said, "You two are not avoiding each other, I hope."

"Not exactly," I told her.

Stu came into the living room and kissed Patty's forehead. He took a seat in a wooden rocking chair, looked at me, and said, "I, uh, I've been reading that stuff."

Knowing he meant the research I'd printed, I waited, but he didn't say more. So I prodded, "And?"

"And I'm trying, Jesse, I really am. It just all seems so wrong. I can't get to where it doesn't kind of make me sick."

"Stuart Bryce!" Patty's head snapped up.

"No, it's okay," I told her. "I don't want him lying to me." I wanted to be really clear with Stu. I searched the ceiling, trying to remember something I'd read online about how a gay person might stand up for their rights without being antagonistic. "Okay, so when you and Dad say you want me to change, you're asking me to be like you. That's not bad, on the surface, but here's the thing. You're really asking me to live a life that isn't mine. I need to live *my* life, not yours. If you can see how that makes sense, all by itself, whether I'm gay or not, *then* maybe you can get closer to feeling like it's okay for me to be who I am. But, Stu, I bet it's always going to feel wrong for you, because you're not gay. What you need to remember is that who you are feels just as wrong to me."

"And that's what I can't get."

"Then I guess you'll just have to believe me. I guess you'll just have to trust me."

Patty looked at him with a tilt to her head, like she didn't want to be confrontational. Her voice was gentle. "Can you do that, Stu?"

He rubbed his face with his hands. "It's not like I think you're making it up. But—I don't know. I'm trying. I'm really trying."

"That's enough for now, then," I told him. "Just don't give up on me, and I won't give up on you." I decided it was time to leave, even though I'd hoped to have more of a conversation with Patty. But with Stu here, that was too difficult. "Patty, let me know if you need anything."

"I will. Thanks."

Enough for now, I'd told Stu. But it wasn't enough for the long haul. More waiting for someone else.

Ivy called me after dinner to tell me the town meeting was scheduled for the Sunday almost two weeks from now. Seven o'clock at the church function hall. It would be announced in the paper, and her parents would call church members directly. She must have helped write the announcement, because the next thing she told me sounded practiced: Her father would also be in touch with the ministers of the other two churches in town as well as the rabbi at the synagogue to make sure they knew about it and to ask for their support and participation.

I asked if she'd be there, and she said yes, but added that her mother thought it unlikely that there would be a lot of non-adults there. I told her I'd be there and that I'd be willing to bet the other TVA members would go, as well.

The idea of this town meeting made me nervous. As far as I knew, I had no role to play, but when I remembered how Ronan had described what had happened when Eleanor had tried to speak to the mayor, it seemed as though anything could happen.

As I pictured Reverend Gilman on the small stage in the function hall, it hit me that I'd heard nothing from him about the stone circle repair. He'd said he knew where the stones were, and suddenly I wondered if I could find them. I opened my laptop and went to Google Earth. I scoured the area south and east and west of the village, looking for small clearings. One or two that I found were just open areas in the woods. But then I found one that seemed to be the top of a small hill, and there were little dots on it. Zooming in as much as possible, I decided that was it. I'd found the stone circle.

At the end of our last morning class Wednesday, Griffin approached me. We walked out of the classroom together, which—despite the success of the TVA—was pretty much a first, because it was just the two of us, not the whole group.

"Sit with me at lunch?" he asked. "I have something you'll like."

We chose a table off to the side, but we still got a lot of looks, some uglier than others.

Griffin handed me an envelope that had already been opened. It was addressed to Eleanor, but when I pulled the letter out, that was addressed to Staci. I shot a glance at Griffin's smiling face and then devoured the letter with my eyes.

Dearest Staci,

It's been nearly ten years since I saw you. In my mind, you're a smart, talented, stunningly beautiful young woman, and it saddens me so much to know that you grew that way without my being able to witness it.

I don't know whether you know about all the letters I wrote to you and your mom. But she was so angry with me for the choice I made that she returned them, unopened. Eventually I stopped trying.

Now I find that another avenue of communication is open, and in case your mother is still as angry as ever, I'm writing directly to you, because you deserve to know what happened and why.

The marriage I called off would not have been a good one. Jeffrey was a good man, certain to be a good provider and a good husband for someone. Just not for me. I have no idea what he's like today, but once we were engaged I had the chance to see how very rigid his attitudes were, how very judgmental he was, and how very intolerant he was of anyone who thought or believed or lived differently from how he thought things should be. This is the purpose of the engagement period: to see if you're as compatible as you need to be. Our engagement had started to fall apart before the day of my flat tire.

I won't say I fell in love with Zayne at first sight, though there was a definite spark. At first there was the thrill of having a young man from the mysterious village stop to help me, but that changed quickly into something more substantial. He probably could have changed my tire in ten minutes, but instead he worked very slowly, stopping frequently, because once we started to talk it was obvious

270

we were both cut from the same cloth. We had so very much to talk about.

I've heard that there was a rumor that the villagers did something to manipulate my feelings and actions. Nothing could be further from the truth. If anything, they met my interest in Zayne with suspicion at first, and it was made quite clear to me that if we were together my life would change radically. And what they meant was not that they would consume me in some way. No. What they meant was that my own people would reject me. And that's what happened.

For my benefit alone, Zayne sought out another Pagan community where we could live, far enough away from my former life that I wouldn't be constantly reminded of the rejection, constantly having to face people who saw me as just this side of the wife of Satan. That's why we moved away.

I'm happy, Staci. I'm so, so happy. Zayne and I have two children, a boy and girl, and our community is thriving. We have excellent relations with our non-Pagan neighbors; in fact, we don't even live in a separate area as the people in the Himlen village must do.

I hope you can see your way to writing back. I'd love to know anything about your life you'd care to tell me. Losing contact with you was probably the worst part of my exile. I would so much love to hear that you still consider me your

—

Loving Aunt Donna

There was a mailing address, an email, and a phone number.

This was *exactly* what I'd hoped for! It could not have been more perfect.

There was a second, short note.

Jesse,

I can't thank you enough for taking this step. Please accept my heartfelt gratitude for your courage, your open-

mindedness, and your love.
Donna Downey

Griffin said, "We're all cool here with giving it to Staci. What's your next step?"

Oddly, I hadn't thought that far ahead. All that time waiting, and I hadn't used it very well. "I guess I can't just go up to Staci and hand this to her. She doesn't even know that I know about her aunt, let alone that I reached out to her."

"Maybe start with Brad?"

"Good idea." I texted Brad to meet for a few minutes after school, out by the athletic field. Then I told Griffin about the date for the town meeting and asked if he would be going.

"Oh, Eleanor's all over that. Lots of folks from the village will be there, including Ronan's parents. Ronan won't, I expect, but yeah, I'll be there. And Selena, though Parker probably won't. Wren and her mom will, and the Fishers, but not Violet. Todd will go, and—"

I laughed. "Okay, that's what I wanted to know. Ivy and I are asking the TVA members today. I already got to Phil, and he'll be there whether his folks go or not."

"Will your parents be there?"

"Good question. I think my mom will. But I'm not saying anything at home about it until Reverend Gilman calls them. I'm still on my dad's shit list, and I'm not sure where I stand with Stu."

When Brad showed up at the appointed spot, he wasn't alone. I watched from my seat low in the bleachers as he and Staci approached, which gave me a little time to think about how to modify the script I'd been working on in my head all afternoon. I was determined to go forward despite this curve ball.

Staci eyed me suspiciously, like she thought I might

lash out or something. I nodded at her like I wasn't at all surprised to see her.

"S'up?" Brad opened.

"Did you happen to mention to Staci that we talked about her Aunt Donna?"

Staci's head snapped toward Brad. His voice a little threatening, he said, "Jesse..."

"Wait. It's actually good, really." I reached into my book bag and pulled out Donna's letter, which I'd already typed into a file on my laptop in case Staci got really pissed off and tore this one up. I decided to talk directly to Staci. I wasn't the one who changed things up for this meeting, but I was going to be the one to take advantage of it.

"Staci, I know you've been given this idea that the people in the village do things to interfere with us, here in the town. And you think they did something to get your aunt to break off her engagement and run off with one of them. But it wasn't quite like that." I stopped, wracking my brain for where to go next.

Staci just glared. Brad said, "What's your point, Jesse?" His tone was not friendly. He moved closer to Staci, protectively.

To Staci, I said, "You know Ivy and I started the Town Village Alliance. We want things to be friendlier between us and the village, and we know there's nothing about them we need to be afraid of. I asked Brad to join, but he's loyal to you, and he knew how you felt about what happened with your aunt. So he said no. Anyway, if what you'd been told was right, that would be pretty bad, and maybe it would mean Ivy and I were doing the wrong thing. So I decided to see what I could find out."

I handed her the letter without the envelope; I didn't think she'd like seeing Eleanor's name. She looked at it, glared at it, really, before slowly reaching out to take it. Brad moved behind Staci so he could read along with her. When she finished reading, she let it fall to the ground.

Brad picked it up.

"This proves nothing," she told me. "They could have forced her to write this."

"Well, I have to say, I've gotten to know some folks in the village pretty well, and the way Donna describes them jives with what I've learned. I even know of someone from the town who went to the village for a love potion and was turned away."

She crossed her arms over her chest and leaned onto one leg, her face stony.

To Staci, Brad said, "Jeff married someone else. They're friends with my folks. I don't like them much. Maybe Donna's right. Maybe they wouldn't have been a good couple."

As soon as I saw that Brad was coming over to my side, I was tempted to join forces and push on Staci. But something told me I should back off and let Brad take over. So I said, "Anyway, I'm convinced the TVA is on the right track. And I really hope you connect with your aunt again." Nodding to Brad, I walked around them and toward the road, listening as I went. Neither of them spoke until I was out of earshot. I'd just have to trust the Goddess. And Brad.

Friday night after dinner I was up in my room watching *Captain America The Winter Soldier* on my PC when I got a Skype invitation from Brad.

"That was a ballsy move, dude."

"I know. I was gonna talk to you first, but there she was, with you. So I had to take a chance. It bothered me a lot that she had all that false information about her own aunt."

He nodded. Then, "She's not ready to drink the Kool-Aid just yet. But—how would you like to be the canary in the mine?"

"Meaning...?"

THROWING STONES

"Come rockhounding with us Saturday. She's never been, so she asked me to take her. And after your bold move this afternoon, she said to bring you along so she could get to know you better. Those were her words, but I get the feeling she wants to make sure you haven't gone over to the dark side."

"Rockhounding will prove that one way or the other?"

"I think it's being alone, just the three of us, someplace where if you glow in the dark she'll be able to see that. And I'll be there to protect her."

I wasn't sure whether to laugh or not, but in the end I couldn't help it. Brad chuckled, too. I said, "Okay, then. You're on. I'll be at my most satanic so she can see how bad it can get."

When we rang off, I felt happier than I would have expected. Maybe I wouldn't so much gain my best friend back as I'd gain a sister. I liked that idea.

I picked them up at Staci's in my truck and drove south; the place Brad had in mind wasn't car-friendly, and his dad was using their truck today. I teased him that the only reason he'd asked me to come along was my wheels.

Staci, between us on the pull-down seat, was pretty quiet. Brad and I chatted on and off until he pointed me off to the east, then to the south, and then east again onto a dirt road I'd never been on before. We rumbled along this for at least a few miles before Brad pointed to the left, toward an even more obscure track. "Think this baby can handle it?"

I braked and looked as far ahead between the trees as I could. "How far are we going? Have we crossed into Arkansas?"

"Yup. Go another half a mile, maybe. It doesn't get any worse than what you see here. My dad's truck was fine."

That sounded like a challenge, so I pulled forward slowly, then a little faster but not much, until Brad pointed to a spot off to the side that barely looked like a pullout.

Brad and I each took one of the two packs he'd brought, and he led the way down a path that was almost indiscernible, but it led very soon to a massive outcropping of rock. No caves today, I gathered. No chance to assess the degree of my phosphorescence.

Brad took the lead. "There's a few ways to tackle something like this." He swept an arm wide, taking in the length of the outcropping from where it started on the left, at about knee height, to where it went steeply uphill to the right. In places it was as high as, maybe, forty feet. He pointed to the right, to the top of the tallest section. I saw a kind of opening there, and there was a depression at the top that turned into a very dangerous-looking, not-quite-path down part of the rock wall.

"That's one option," he said, "but it ain't for the faint of heart. I did bring a rope in case anyone wants to try it there. You'll have to tie it onto a tree at the top and then around yourself. I can show you how. Or," and he waved his arm to the left, "you can just meander along the ground here and see what you can find. In that case, you start where we're standing, to get the overall picture of how the hill is formed, what different layers you can see, that sort of thing. Then you get up real close and personal, inches away, and start chipping at something you think you want, or that you think might expose something you want."

He pulled a few things out of the pack he'd carried from the truck. Head down, eyes on the inside of the pack, he said, "Jesse's already had this lesson before, but since he's not very bright I'll go through it again, for both of you." Staci smiled at that, the first smile I'd seen today.

Holding up a strap-like item, Brad put it on like a belt. "This is a pick holster." He lifted a tool and held it where Staci and I could see it. "This is a hammer pick, two tools in one. It's all one piece, so the head can't fly off." He settled it into the holster on his belt and picked up something else. "Chisel." Another item: "Goggles, so you don't get rock chips in your eyes. I didn't bring hard hats today, but if we were going into caves we'd use them."

Another dive into the pack resulted in a handful of chisels in different sizes and styles. Brad pointed toward the pack I'd carried from the truck. "My dad's equipment is in there. It's all the same stuff, only fewer chisels. They come in different sizes. We just need to decide how to share all of it."

Staci asked, "Are we looking for anything in particular?"

We all turned toward the rock face, and I noticed a thin, black line that sloped down to the left, following the slope of the hillside. "What's that vein?"

"That black vein is obsidian. It's not actually a rock. It's a kind of natural glass. Comes in a few different colors, all dark. One kind, very rare, has a kind of opalescence on it. This here is kind of an unusual formation for obsidian." He went on for a while about how he thinks it got here, using terms like lava and igneous rock.

Staci decided she wanted to try to chisel out some of the obsidian, so we carried our tools close to the rock face and followed the black line down to the left until it was about chest height to Brad. He demonstrated how to work above and below the vein to expose the glass without damaging it, and Staci and I both took tools and worked at it a few feet apart. It was slow going with not much to show for our labors, so after a while we decided to take a break and dig into the lunch basket Staci had put together for us.

I was doing my best to appear as normal as possible, as un-village-like as possible, to put Staci's fears to rest, but she headed right for the proverbial lion's den.

"So, tell me about this club of yours, Jesse. I've heard some pretty strange things about it."

"Really? Like what?"

She shrugged. "You know. The usual stuff. You chant

strange words in dim light and stick pins in dolls." She took a bite of her sandwich.

I stared at her, totally in shock, and then I started to laugh. I laughed so hard I couldn't eat or drink for maybe two minutes. It must have been contagious, because both Staci and Brad gave in and laughed along with me.

As soon as I could, I gave her a realistic report of what went on in our meetings, and why. "Maybe you don't know this, but Ivy Gilman—yes, the reverend's daughter—is dating Griffin Holyoke."

Her eyes widened. "Does the reverend know?"

"He does. Griffin asked him for permission."

"Shit." Brad's deep voice spoke for both of them. "That's a development."

"You do know," I told Staci, "that Reverend Gilman is involved with the club? He comes to our meetings. So I guess if anything other-worldly were to happen, he'd be there to perform an exorcism." I winked at Staci to let her know I was pulling her leg. She obliged me my shoving on my shoulder in a friendly way.

This actually might be working.

After we ate, Brad stretched his long frame out on the blanket Staci had brought, and she curled up against him. I doubted they intended to leave me out in the cold, but that's kind of what it felt like. And I know they didn't mean for it to hurt, but it did; it made me want Ronan with a sudden, searing kind of burn I hadn't felt in a few days. I decided to strike out on my own.

I shouldered Mr. Everett's pack and said, "Where's that rope, Brad?" He scowled at me like he wasn't sure what I meant. "I'll need it when I get to the top of that thing."

He pointed to where he'd left it. "Do you know how to wrap it around your waist and your thighs so you don't kill yourself if you fall?"

I grabbed the coil of rope and my arm sagged; it weighed more than I'd expected. "I'm sure I'll figure it out." I grinned, saluted, and headed toward the lower end so I could get onto the top of the outcropping there and follow the slope up to the higher part.

"Jesse," Brad called, "you be careful. I don't wanna have to carry you outta here."

I was breathing hard by the time I got to where Brad had pointed. Gazing down from the edge, I could see where other rockhounds had been; there was even a boot print, so it couldn't have been very long ago. This wasn't the spot for me, then; I wanted a road less traveled. I resettled the pack and kept going. Below me, Brad called, "Where are you going?"

"Just scouting around. Call me if you need to." I figured, you know, give the love birds some time alone, away from me, away from where their happiness made me aware of that hollow spot where I wanted Ronan to be. I reminded myself I was doing this for Ronan. For us. I was building bridges, spanning gaps, mending fences—pick a metaphor.

The land was level for a while, and underfoot it got more grassy than rocky. I had no idea where I was going, but my mood had turned to a kind of self-pity that I didn't like but that somehow I felt the need to allow, at least for a while.

After about fifteen minutes it occurred to me that I wasn't following anything like a trail, and I could easily get lost out here. I turned and found a sight-line to where I came from and took a mental picture of the surroundings. Just to be on the safe side, I hung the rope coil in the limb of one of the few trees around there so it would point the way on my return.

Before long, the slope headed downward again, and I followed it for want of anything better to do. Just ahead there was another rise, another outcropping. I circled around to the left of it for no particular reason, and the next thing I saw, on my right, was a cave. It wasn't huge, but it wasn't tiny.

I froze, trying to remember what Brad had done to be sure he wasn't about to get ambushed by a cougar. I couldn't have the cougar I wanted—not yet, anyway—and the others were dangerous in their own way. So I checked the ground for scat, and sure enough there was a little pile of hard turds over to one side of where I stood. I didn't know whether the size was more appropriate for a bobcat or a cougar, but by the time I poked it apart with a stick I was sure it was a carnivore. There were tiny bones in it.

Crouching near the ground, I looked around, watching for any sign of movement. Nothing, and no sounds except a little breeze in the grasses and the few trees nearby. I looked back at the scat. What would a bobcat eat? Mice? Voles, maybe? What about a cougar? A cat that big would probably not even notice a tiny rodent, and I really thought its turds would be much larger. So this was most likely bobcat scat. As long as I didn't startle a bobcat, I should be okay, right? I dug into the pack and felt a huge sense of relief when I found a can of pepper spray.

I looked all around me and then at the cave. Then I picked up a few rocks and started throwing them, calling out nonsense sounds. Then I waited: nothing. Closer to the cave, I heaved rocks and called out again, then closer, and closer still, until I was right at the mouth of the thing. It was maybe three feet high at the highest point. I hollered into it and heard a bit of an echo, nothing more. A few heaved rocks later, and I was feeling like I could actually go into it.

I dug into the pack again, and although there was no hard hat, there was a headlamp, and goggles, and leather work gloves. I hung the hammer pick from the belt holster, fit the headlamp onto my skull, put the gloves back into the pack, and then inched my way into the cave, dragging the pack along behind me.

I was not the first person in here, either. There were

signs of picking and hammering and chiseling all around me. But maybe I could get farther back into the cave than they had. It got narrower and lower the farther in I went, and before long I was belly-crawling into crevices that would have been completely black if not for the headlamp. I flipped over onto my back in one of those crevices, and looked around.

It was gorgeous in here. Everywhere I looked I saw flashes of light reflecting off of tiny projections, tiny little teeth. There was nothing large, nothing I could see that was worth digging at, but the sparkles fascinated me. I lay there, transfixed, letting the beauty fill me. It was almost like the night sky at Samhain, that diamond-studded cloak overhead.

Eventually, moving slowly, I inched my way out of that crevice and backed out to where I could follow a different one. Back on my belly, I worked my way into another crevice, grabbing the rock on either side with my hands to help move myself forward.

Suddenly something tore at the back of my right hand. I strained my neck turning it to try and see what had happened, and there was blood there. Not a lot, but enough to notice. I scanned the side of the crevice where the pain had happened, and there was a sharp point of something sticking out. Must have been that. Should have put the gloves on before coming in here.

I backed out carefully just far enough to get a better look at that point, and when I did, I knew I have to have it. It was a quartz point, like one of the ones in that large cluster of Brad's, but smaller, and there was something dark on one side. Working slowly and carefully, I got out a couple of chisels, put on the gloves and the goggles, and holding the pick near the head I tapped oh, so gently at the rock around the point, hoping there might be even more of the stuff I could pull out. Maybe this tooth was part of a cluster.

I guess it takes more than just listening to Brad's explanations to do a good job of this, and in the end I didn't get any more than the bloodthirsty tooth. It was about an inch and a half long, just over half an inch thick, and shining the headlamp at it I could see that in addition to that black streak along the side, there were very tiny lines of black inside the tooth, all going different directions. Too bad it wasn't clear like Brad's, but it was still mine. My find, my tooth.

Once I was back in the larger part of the cave, I went back into the pack and found a plastic storage container with a soft cloth inside. I wrapped the tooth in the cloth, but then I jammed it into my pocket, not into the pack. Not sure why, but I didn't feel like doing a show-and-tell with Brad and Staci. I could always give the cloth back to him another time, maybe even without him knowing I'd taken it.

Outside the cave again, pack on the ground at my feet, I was looking around trying to decide where to go next when I heard my phone ring. *Ronan?* I grabbed for it so fast I nearly dropped it.

It was Brad. "Hey, Jesse, where are you, man? We're about done here. Kind of frustrating, and Staci's ready to go home."

"Yeah, sorry about that. I'll head back now. Maybe ten minutes?"

On the trek back, something stirred inside me, something that didn't feel good. Mentally I chipped away at it as I walked, chiseling around the edges to get a good look at it, to see if it was really something substantial. Suddenly it revealed itself. And I knew that I had been hiding it from myself, deep in some subterranean cavern.

It was doubt. Doubt that all my efforts would change Ronan's mind. Doubt that we'd ever be alone in the treehouse again. Doubt that anything would change between his people and mine, doubt that anything I could ever do would make any difference at all.

282

THROWING STONES

I feared that this love affair with Ronan had lived only long enough to cause me a world of hurt before it died a premature death. Fear that this was the only love affair I was likely to have for years. Maybe, if I managed to get into college, or if I managed to get far enough away from home for some other reason, I'd be able to be myself someplace. And maybe then I'd be able to find someone to love. Someone who'd be able to love me the same way.

But it wouldn't be Ronan. It wouldn't be my fascinating, exciting, consuming Cougar.

I was breathing hard, almost gasping, and not from exertion. Suddenly I was on my knees. I held my breath to avoid crying. I squeezed my eyes shut and craned my neck to hold my face up to the sky.

All my life I'd felt broken, or defective. I was a total disappointment to my father and brother, and source of worry for my mother. And in a couple of weeks Ronan had made me feel whole again. New. Fully myself. Even if I found someone else to love, how could I ever hope for that kind of feeling again?

I took a few shuddering breaths and then let out a yell that might have reached as far as Brad and Staci. Or maybe it would just echo inside me forever.

By the time I got back, Staci was not in a good mood. She'd decided rockhounding was no fun at all, not worth the trouble to chisel away and ruin her nails in the process. She pointed to a paltry showing of bits and pieces of shiny, black bits nestled in a chamois cloth.

I was facing away from the rock wall where the vein was, but something told me to turn around. Then it pulled me toward the rock, and then a little to the left. I dropped the pack and the rope, and almost by themselves my hands reached out and touched the vein of black, now about at my waist. I closed my eyes.

Something inside me pulsed. It almost seemed to come up from the ground as it moved through my body and out into my fingers. And I could see, as clear as day behind my closed eyelids, a large, oblong shape of black glass. I could feel how long it was, how wide it was, and how high it was. I even knew that three inches into the rock from where my fingers rested was where the shape began.

I dug into the pack for tools, gloves, and goggles and began to chisel away at the rock above and below the vein in the place where I knew the shape was. Then Brad was beside me, tools in hand. He didn't say anything, and I just pointed where he should work. Within ten minutes we'd cleared away enough rock to see the swell of the shape begin.

Brad stepped back and said, "Holy shit. Holy shit." And then we went to work with a vengeance while Staci watched.

By the time we stopped, we'd cleared most of the shape, and the back part of it was embedded in something harder than what we'd been clearing away. Brad and I glanced at each other and nodded, and he showed me which chisel to use for what we wanted to do: crack the glass shape from the top and get as much of it out as we could. When we stopped, grinning and a little breathless, we had one large chunk of obsidian—maybe five inches by six—and eight other chunks, a couple of inches each. Some of them had sharp edges that would have sliced meat.

We lifted our goggles over our heads, and Staci said, "Okay, Jesse, how did you do that?"

I didn't want to say what I thought had happened. The rush of energy I'd felt could have come from only one source: Ronan. It was Ronan who had known about that shape, Ronan who had guided my hands, Ronan who pulsed through me like a magic life force.

"Just lucky," I told her. "We couldn't leave here with you feeling like it was a waste of time, could we?" I grinned at her, then at Brad. I held up the large chunk. "Is this piece mine or yours?"

"Oh, bro, that one's yours. Do you want any of these other ones?"

"Maybe one." I chose one with a fascinating concave curve in it that formed a sharp edge along one side.

On the drive back, we didn't talk much. Staci leaned against Brad, and I let my mind focus on what had happened. I was still convinced that Ronan had been behind that pulsing energy, that somehow he was the one who'd seen that black shape and guided me toward it. I just hoped that my response to Staci's question, that I'd made a lucky guess, had been enough to keep her from feeling like maybe there was something freaky about me after all. I needed to believe that today's mission had been accomplished and that she'd feel like she could reconnect with her aunt, or at least let Brad join the TVA.

After dinner, up in my room, I arranged the obsidian piece and the tooth from that cave on a shelf over my desk. Then I picked up my phone and stared at it. And stared at it. And stared at it some more. And then I texted Ronan.

Find any obsidian lately?

I stared at the phone some more while I waited at least two minutes for a response.

I need you to stop contacting me.

You contacted me this afternoon with no phone

I mean it.

We can't even be friends?

There was no further response.

That night I had this dream. It almost felt more like a hallucination. There was a tree, kind of like Griffin's tattoo, but there were things all over the branches, like little gems, and a straw doll, nonsense kinds of things. Somehow I was supposed to retrieve them, and I did, but every time I took one more thing in my hands it got harder to carry them all. For some reason, the things I had to take got bigger and bigger. There was a pillow, and a length of rope that kept uncoiling and getting tangled in the branches. I realized I was stupid not to have brought something to put everything in, so I took my shirt off and used that for a kind of satchel. Still, it kept getting harder to hang onto everything, and I started to panic. And then I started to drop things. I was yelling for help, only there was no sound.

Suddenly there was a bobcat in the tree, glaring at me, mouth wide open and teeth bared. Its crystal teeth looked like the one that had stabbed me in the cave. I tried to scream, but again there was no sound, and then I was wide awake. I was panting like I'd run a race, and my heart was pounding. Somehow I knew that in my sleep I had stopped breathing. I sat up, chest heaving, lungs desperate for air. Finally I recovered enough to turn a light on, and then I couldn't stand being in bed.

At my desk, I picked up that quartz tooth from the cave. Holding it up to my desk light, I could see tiny rainbows in the clear part of the quartz, and they appeared and disappeared with the smallest change in how the light hit them. And those thin black lines shot all through it... what on earth were they?

Brad would know exactly what the black is, and what the lines were all about. Without him, though, and without Ronan, I had no idea.

I figured the Internet would have some information about this; why did I need Brad *or* Ronan? After a number of searches, I did manage to find something like my tooth. It was called rutilated quartz, and the black thing on the side (which, upon closer examination, seemed to have a reddish tint) as well as the threads shot through the tooth, were most likely titanium oxide. This size wasn't worth much, but really large specimens were.

On a whim, I looked up the non-geological properties, the sort of things Ronan might have said about it.

Rutilated quartz can be used to illuminate the soul to promote spiritual growth. It helps you let go of the past, understand the reasons for your current problems, and make the changes you need to make. It lightens your mood, relieves fears, phobias, and anxieties, and it promotes forgiveness.

I set it back on the shelf beside the obsidian. With no light directly on it, it looked dull, especially next to the shiny black obsidian. And yet if it could do even half of what it was supposed to be able to do, it seemed powerful.

But I hadn't felt Ronan guiding me to that tooth. Which stone was more powerful? I looked up obsidian.

Obsidian is used to clear out the energetic fogginess that results if you've been exposed to multiple energetic influences at one time, or to many strong energies over a short period of time. Obsidian is also good if you need to expose yourself to energies that might not be good for you. It protects you to some extent, and then after the exposure you can cleanse your energy with it.

I picked up the small piece of obsidian with the sharp edge and held it up to the light. Where the stone grew thinner toward the edge, the color was more like a reddish brown than black. Holding it with the fingers of both hands, I closed my eyes and concentrated on clearing out the strong energy that had taken over my hands and mind this afternoon. I wasn't ready to give up on Ronan, despite his text message, but if I had to wait for that, too—along with everything else on the list of things I was waiting for—then I wanted to clear his energy from mine.

Then, obsidian in my right hand, I picked up the rutilated quartz with my left hand and closed my fingers around each. I closed my eyes and waited to see if I felt anything like that dizzying sway when I'd held the malachite and the lapis in the treehouse.

At first there was nothing. But then it began to feel as though the two hands were fighting each other, like they couldn't get along. They couldn't exist in the same place at the same time. That place would seem to be me. So I couldn't both clear Ronan away and forgive him at the same time? That was okay with me; I wasn't ready to forgive him. I set the tooth back on the shelf and gazed at it.

Forgiveness. There were two other people in need of that from me: my father, and my brother. But I wasn't quite ready for that, either.

Chapter Twelve

During the service the next morning, the Bible reading and sermon were all about loving one's neighbors, about not judging others, about all the things that supported town and village getting along. Then Reverend Gilman spoke about the town meeting and why everyone who could come should be there.

Sunday afternoon I was deep into math homework, which I almost sort of like, when I heard a loud crash from downstairs. Dad and Stu were both out someplace, so I dashed down to see if Mom was okay, and I found her sitting on the floor in the kitchen, her back against the fridge, and sobbing. All around her were cobalt blue shards, obviously the wreckage of that bowl I'd used for the butternut squash last Thanksgiving.

She tried to wipe the tears away when she saw me, but there was no use pretending. She didn't even try to get up.

"Mom?" I sat, too, moving a few shards out of the way. "What happened? Is it just the bowl?"

"Just the bowl, Jesse? *Just* the bowl?"

"What else, then?"

Her breath caught, and when she scrunched her face, more tears leaked out of her eyes. She picked up a large shard and held it toward me. "This bowl," she paused and opened her eyes, "this bowl was me. This bowl was the only thing I had that represented who *I* am. This bowl is who I wanted to be."

I felt my head shake once or twice in confusion. "I— what does that mean, exactly?"

"I'm saying that I had to leave the creative part of myself behind. I'm saying I wanted to *create* beautiful ceramic things, not buy them."

She started to stand up. I helped her to a chair, and then I picked up all the shards carefully while she watched. I fetched a plastic storage bag, set all the shiny blue bits into it, and zipped it shut. Then she said, "Will you make me a cup of tea, Jesse?"

Anything. I'd have done anything for her right then.

As I started the water heating, I noticed her gaze was on the case of Hummels in the living room. Her voice quiet and sad, she said, "That bowl was the last thing I made. I was an art major at college, and I made the bowl in a ceramics class there."

"I didn't know you went to college."

She let out a sound that was almost a laugh, but there was no humor in it. "It didn't last long. I left when I got pregnant."

"What?"

"I fell in love, Jesse. And so did your father. And we started a child by accident. We decided to marry, because we were headed that way anyway, but then I miscarried. By then I'd come back to Himlen, and the effort of getting back into school and back into art, especially with a home and husband to care for and the very real possibility of getting pregnant again—and both your father and I wanted a family—and everything about art fell by the wayside. Mind you, I wasn't very good at thinks like figurines, like those Hummels. But," she watched as I poured boiling water into her tea mug, "I did very well at functional things like that bowl. I got really interested in glazes and different ways of firing things. And that bowl... that bowl was the most beautiful thing I made. It made me willing to leave my unrealistic idea of making figurines behind." She sighed. "And then I got pregnant."

"So... I had an older brother or sister who died? And

you lost sight of your dream?"

She smiled at me, a sad smile. "That's about the size of it, Jesse."

"Well, why don't you do something now? Stu and I don't exactly need you at home any more. And Dad doesn't. You have time now. You could still do bookkeeping for Dad and work in ceramics."

She shook her head. "It's too late for that, Jesse. I can't go back to school now."

"Wait here." I dashed upstairs again, grabbed my laptop, and scrambled back down. She watched me as though sure I was wasting my time even though she appreciated the effort, while I searched. In no time at all, I said, "Aha! Look at this."

I turned the laptop so she could see the screen, and I pulled my chair up close to hers. I scrolled and clicked and moved from page to page on the site, a center for ceramics education about three hours from here. "See? They have classes, and retreats, and workshops. You can learn about clays and colors and firing techniques, and how to sell your stuff. Mom, it's all here! You can make all the bowls you want!"

"All that costs money, Jesse. I'd have to stay overnight a lot."

"Well... not that much though, I bet." But she was right. "Hang on, I haven't given up yet." And in another minute I'd found an artist in McAlester who offered classes and workshops. "Here. This is no farther than Stu goes for his auto mechanics classes." I bookmarked the site and turned the laptop over to her. "See what you think. I'll just sweep the floor to make sure there aren't any bits I missed."

When I'd finished, Mom was still browsing, but then she pushed the laptop away from her on the table.

"It's less money, but it's still money. My piano lesson income wouldn't cover enough to be worth it." She sighed and closed the laptop. "You go back upstairs, Jesse. Finish your homework so you can go to college and have the career you want. Follow the dream that's yours. Because if you have to give up your dream, even though you might find a substitute," she glanced toward her Hummel case, "you'll never be able to get enough of it."

Dinner conversation was pretty discouraging for me. Dad and Stu were both there, and they talked about the town meeting as though it were a fool's errand. At one point Dad said, "Stupid idea. How can we hope to feel neighborly toward people who worship trees?"

I'd been trying to stay out of it; if they already disrespected me for being so stubbornly gay, why would they listen to me about this? But I couldn't help it. "They don't worship trees, Dad. They believe in the same things Jesus talked about. Like loving each other, and forgiving each other for things."

His chin rose a little as he glared at me. "So what do they worship then, if you know so much about them?"

"They have a god-figure. It just happens to be female."

Before I could say any more, Dad let out a loud, barking laugh. "There you go! That's worse."

Mom's quiet voice said, "How is that worse?"

Both Dad and Stu looked at her and then down at their plates. Dad stabbed at the last piece of his pork chop and said, "I don't think we need to discuss this any more."

But Mom wasn't done. "I'm going to the meeting. I think we should all go."

Stu wouldn't look up, but he shook his head. "Oh, no way I'm going to that."

Mom stood and lifted her plate from the table. "You're forgetting that the villagers saved Patty's life, and probably Jesse's as well. Seems to me they have more Christian spirit than you have." She reached over and swiped Dad's almost-empty plate away from him.

"I wasn't done with that!"

She ignored him.

I whipped Stu's plate away from him, which made him yell, and took it along with mine over to the counter.

Dad nearly whined, "What about dessert?"

Mom wheeled on him. "I think you'd better come back for that later. I'm not in the mood to serve you right now." And she turned her back on him and began to move dishes and pans around as noisily as possible without actually breaking anything. Dad and Stu stomped downstairs to watch TV.

Mom and I were still doing cleanup when the house phone rang. I answered it, and it was Mrs. Gilman. Listening as I washed out a couple of pans, I could tell it was about the town meeting. Mom promised she would absolutely be there, and I wanted to hug her.

That week at school felt weird. Our TVA meeting on Monday had been all about what we could do to support the town meeting, though both Mrs. Knapp and Mr. Duncan said it would be better for us not to call attention to ourselves until we had some idea how the meeting would go.

"There'll be plenty of time to get more involved later," Mrs. Knapp told us. "For now, just go with your parents, or with the parents of a friend if yours aren't going. We'll discuss the outcome at our next meeting."

Tuesday at school I asked Brad if his folks were going, and he said he didn't think so. I didn't bother to ask about Stacy's parents, and I wasn't sure I dared ask about Staci. I said, "My mom and I are going. Do you want to come with us?"

"I'll get back to you on that." At least it wasn't an outright "no way."

Every so often, in one class or another or in one hallway conversation or another, I'd hear some comment about whether someone was going or not. The sense I got was that although there were definitely some parents planning to go, mostly the kids were not. This confused me enough that I stopped beside Janice's locker when I heard her friend Deanna say that she wasn't going, but her parents were.

I said, "Sorry. Eavesdropping shamelessly. Um, why is it you're not going if your folks are?"

Deanna said, "My dad says things might get nasty. He doesn't want me there if that happens."

"Why would they get nasty? What do you think he meant?"

She shrugged and made a face like, "How would I know?"

As soon as I could find Ivy, I told her what Deanna had said. "I know," she told me. "I've been hearing things like that, too. I've told Daddy. You should probably tell Mr. Duncan."

So I did. He nodded like he wasn't surprised. I asked, "What can we do about it?"

"Not much we can do, Jesse. Except maybe to remain as calm as possible, ourselves. There will be a few police officers there just in case, but I doubt they'll need to take any action."

When I got home, I told Mom what I'd heard. "Are you sure you still want to go?"

She stood very straight. "I'm going to take a stand on this, Jesse. Maybe you shouldn't go, though."

I shook my head. "We're going together."

Next I texted Griffin. *Are you worried about the town meeting*

We're all worried but we're going

Mom and I will too

Thank you

Next I called Brad. "I know I asked if you wanted to go to the meeting with me and my mom, but I've been hearing there might be trouble. Maybe you shouldn't go."

"What's that supposed to mean? You think I'm some kind of sissy?"

"What? No, that's not what I meant. I was just thinking Staci wouldn't forgive me if I dragged you into a fray."

"Staci doesn't tell me what to do and what not to do."

Oh, my. Did they have a fight? "I—um, I wasn't trying to say she does. But I know she's not exactly—"

"Doesn't matter."

"Are you two okay?"

"We're taking a little break."

"Brad, spill. What happened? Did it have anything to do with Saturday?"

I heard a long exhale. "I know she didn't show it much at the time, but she was a little freaked out when you found that obsidian. Started saying things like how they'd gotten to you. Some such nonsense. I thought it was pretty cool, and I told her I wished I could do that. Find deposits like that. Um, how did you do it, anyway?"

"It was some kind of energy; it pulled me forward, and I could see the shape inside the rock. I don't really know. Um, Brad, look—I feel shitty about this."

"No need. She just needs some time. We haven't broken up or anything. But I might just go to the meeting. Phil asked if I wanted to go with him and his folks, too."

"Well, if you're going, I'd really appreciate your coming with me and my mom. Dad's not coming. Or Stu. So I could really use the support."

"Done." He chuckled. "Just don't tell Staci. I'll tell her myself at some point."

And just like that, I had my best friend back again. See, Ronan? Sometimes things work.

All this talk of who would go and who wouldn't made me wonder whether Patty was going, even if Stu wasn't. So

I called her.

"I don't know, Jesse. I'm not sure I'm ready to make a statement about that."

"What statement?"

"You know. I'm not quite sure how I feel about the village."

"No one's asking anyone to have anyone else over for dinner. It's just a way of saying that we don't like how the village has been treated. We don't believe idiotic rumors, we don't think they're all Satanists or that they have orgies in the woods or cast spells on anyone or—"

"Are you sure?"

"What?"

"Are you sure they don't do any of those things?"

I was a little surprised to realize that beyond that dinner where I'd brought up porphyria, and the brief conversation after she'd lost the baby, I hadn't said much to Patty about my own connections with the village. "I was with them the day of the tornado. I'm good friends with Griffin Holyoke and his girlfriend, *Ivy Gilman*." I let that sink in. Then, "I've talked with Griffin, with their leader Eleanor Darling, and with Griffin's friend Ronan Coulter," let *that* name sink in, too, "and I've learned a whole lot about how they *do* worship. It has nothing to do with the devil or orgies or spells or anything like that."

"Do your folks know all this?"

I skirted around her question. "Think about it, Patty. Mr. Ward tried to protect Mary Blaisdell and died for it. Griffin Holyoke saved a beautiful black cat from being mutilated last Halloween. Violet Fisher, who takes piano lessons from my mom, is a sweet little girl who loves Hummels. They took me into their tornado shelter without a second thought. Todd Swazey saved your life. And nobody, nobody at all, can come up with anything provable that's bad about them. The bad stuff comes from the town, from bullies who call them names and kill cats themselves and spray things like 'Vampire' on school lockers. They never do anything to retaliate. All they want to do is make friends. Don't you think we should meet them half way?"

She chuckled. "Don't be shy, Jesse. Tell me how you really feel."

"Mom and I are going, and my friend Brad from the football team will go with us. You probably already know Stu and Dad won't be there, but will you come with us?"

She hesitated just a second and said, "Ask me after church on Sunday. I won't make other plans for that evening. Fair?"

Fair enough, I supposed. It would have to do.

Sunday at church it was obvious something big was going on. There were probably only about two-thirds the normal number of people in the congregation, and of course the sermon was once again on topic for making nice with your neighbors. I had to say, though, that the people who were there seemed to *want* to be there. That is, it wasn't the usual go-to-church-because-it's-Sunday crowd. And it included my entire family, Patty, her parents, and all the Elliotts.

On the way home, beside Mom in the back of her car, I texted Patty. *Come with us?*

You bet.

Yes!

Over lunch, Mom informed everyone that we'd be having dinner on the early side so she and I could get to the town meeting. Dad grumbled, and Stu said something about going to Patty's for dinner. It was hard not to throw a questioning look at him; obviously he was taking it for granted that Patty would feed him whenever he wanted. This would be a good lesson.

And, sure enough, Stu was with us for dinner.

As soon as Brad showed up, Mom drove us over to

Patty's, so the four of us walked into the function hall together. We weren't the first, and in fact there were already enough people there that it was obvious the townsfolk were mostly on the right of a center aisle, and the "freaks" were on the left side. There had been a couple of police cars out front, kind of on display, and there were some officers inside, seemingly trying to walk a fine line between keeping things calm and keeping a low profile.

Mom came to a halt inside the door, and I could tell she was unsure where she should sit. Before she could make a decision I disagreed with, I said, "I see the other TVA members over there," and I pointed to the left where I could see Phil and his parents, Mr. Duncan, Mrs. Gilman, and Ivy. I started to move in that direction when Mom grabbed my shoulder.

"Jesse, I think I'd rather sit over on the other side."

I turned sharply to her. "Why?"

Patty intervened. "Diane, I'm going to sit with Jesse. I think this effort needs all the support it can get. And I don't want to be aligned with the people who were too holier-than-thou to come to church this morning. What do you say?"

"But—*they're* all sitting on one side together. Why shouldn't we?"

"Mom, it's up to us to make the first move. They don't pick on us or call us names or—" I almost said knock over our sacred buildings, but towns people weren't supposed to know about that stone circle—"or beat us up because we're Christians."

She heaved a deep sigh and turned toward the left. Brad, who'd been quiet during this exchange, shrugged and followed me.

Griffin had been watching us, and he gestured toward someone on the right side. Griffin's mom, and a man I didn't recognize who must have been Mr. Holyoke (and who looked as "normal" as Mrs. Holyoke), stood; so not all the villagers were on the left side, after all. I knew Griffin wanted me to introduce my mom to his folks. So I did.

Then Mrs. Holyoke said, "Mrs. Bryce, Patty, won't you come sit with us? I'm sure Jesse and Brad would prefer to sit with their friends. We're right over there, next to the Fishers. Oh—I bet you'd like to meet them! Violet's not here, but let me introduce you to her parents."

So at least two village families had broken ranks and mingled with the non-Pagans, and Mom got to sit on that side after all.

As Brad and I moved toward Mr. Duncan and the TVA crowd, I glanced over at the town side, and there seemed to be another line of demarcation there between people who'd been at church earlier, where the Holyokes and the Fishers were sitting, and those who hadn't. I figured it was possible that latter group was here to make trouble.

Conversation in the room got a little louder as more people came in, and the room filled up pretty well, but it still wasn't loud when Reverend Gilman and Eleanor walked onto the small stage area at the front. At the same time, the mayor went to sit in a chair off to one side of the reverend. Then everything got very quiet.

The reverend spoke first. "Welcome! I'm delighted to see so many people here tonight. I know many of you agree that it's time for all residents of Himlen, regardless of where they live, to be more neighborly toward each other than we've been in the past. I have with me Ms. Eleanor Darling, representing the village community."

Eleanor, who looked unremarkable except for her long hair, which she'd piled high on her head, smiled at the crowd and nodded. Her turn to speak.

"For anyone who doesn't already know, this effort Reverend Gilman and I are supporting tonight was inspired by two students at the town high school: Jesse Bryce and Reverend Gilman's daughter, Ivy. It's called the TVA, or Town Village Alliance. It has members from the town and from the village, and for the last several weeks they've made a sincere effort to get to know and understand each other better. They've been very successful."

She turned to Reverend Gilman, who took the vocal baton back. "It's often the case that parents learn from their children. I think the example of this TVA is one of those times. What Ms. Darling and I are proposing is that—"

He was drowned out by some man on the town side. "What you want is for us to pretend those people should be encouraged in their heathen ways!"

The reverend waited patiently while a few other people shouted their agreement. Then he said, "For my part, Mr. Dwyer, I am asking those of us who call ourselves Christian to turn our hearts to love and our minds to Godly actions. We should follow the example of Jesus himself, who extended his offer of love to people from many backgrounds."

Eleanor's voice rang clear; she was almost as used to public speaking as the reverend. "And for my part, I ask that people of the village put behind us the actions that have caused us to feel persecuted, looking only forward and working toward common ground, understanding, and mutual respect."

Again from the right, a woman's voice, perhaps Lou Dwyer's mother this time: "We can't respect people who worship the devil!"

This time it took a little longer, and two of the cops stepping forward, for things to quiet down.

Eleanor spoke again. "Allow me to respond to that. As it happens, my people don't recognize the type of spirit you refer to as the devil. Please set that idea aside. It does not pertain to us."

"Liar!" That was Lou's father again, I was pretty sure.

Reverend Gilman stepped forward, trying to ignore that last accusation. "As you can see, there are many things that we in the town don't understand about our neighbors in the village. Throughout history, we see that when people of good will make an honest effort to understand each other, strife ends and friendship begins. So here's what Ms. Darling and I are asking: Any family or individual in the town who would like to be introduced to a family or individual from the village should contact me in the next few days."

Eleanor said, "And anyone from the village who would like to get to know someone from the town better, let me know."

Reverend Gilman polished it off. "We'd love for some of these meetings to take place in the next few weeks. Then Ms. Darling and I will set up another town meeting and see what other steps we might like to take."

There was some indistinct grumbling from the area around the Dwyers. I heard the word "freaks" a few times.

"For now," the reverend said over the noise, "Ms. Darling has made an extremely generous offer, one that I hope we can all greet with respect and appreciation. To help people from the town decide whether you'd like to participate in the effort I just described, she has offered to answer questions we might have about the village. So if there is something you'd like to ask, raise your hand and I will call on you so we don't end up in a free-for-all. Again, I ask that your questions be respectful and that you ask them with the sincere intention of understanding each other better."

OMG. I couldn't believe Eleanor had set herself up for this. I couldn't imagine that it would go well.

I was right.

Mr. Dwyer shot his arm up immediately, but Reverend Gilman ignored him in favor of a woman in the next row.

"I have a question for you, reverend. How do you expect us to be all friendly with people who hate Christ?"

The reverend turned to Eleanor, who said, "Please believe me when I say that we by no means hate Christ.

301

Hatred of anyone is anathema to us. We believe in love as strongly as Reverend Gilman does."

I noticed she didn't say, "as strongly as Christians do."

The woman spoke again before the reverend could acknowledge anyone else. "Then why don't you worship Jesus?"

The room got very quiet. I watched Eleanor carefully; how the hell could she answer a question like that without enraging these people who were already condemning her?

"We follow the primary message of Jesus of Nazareth," she said, and that blew me away. "Jesus wanted to renew his people's commitment to love. My community is committed to love, exactly as he exhorted his followers to be. And while we don't specifically call ourselves Christians, we respect the intentions and potential beauty of the religion that sprang up after he died."

"But you don't worship him!"

"And you don't worship as we do. We don't believe that makes you wrong or us right. What's important is for a belief system to be motivated by love."

A number of people shouted different things along the lines of, "But you *are* wrong!" A few of them stood up, and the cops moved forward again. Suddenly something went flying through the air and landed with a loud thud near Eleanor's feet.

A stone.

I heard Brad's voice beside me. "Holy shit." And then another stone flew, and another after that, which brushed the reverend's arm. The cops moved in again, but it was obvious the meeting was over. Even so, both Eleanor and Reverend Gilman stood where they were, looking determined and unafraid.

I turned to look at Mom and Patty across the way, and by their faces I'd have said they both felt some combination of anger and fear.

Then a woman near me whom I hadn't noticed stood.

302

"I'm Clio Coulter, and I'd like to get to know someone from the town."

I thought for sure another stone would go flying, but instead my own mother stood up. Even Brad didn't have words for this surprise.

"I'm Diane Bryce, and I'd like to get to know someone from the village."

The two women looked at each other, and something from the back of my mind shot forward: Mrs. Coulter throws pots. That's what Ronan had said that day in the treehouse when I'd admired the mugs he'd served hot cider in.

And suddenly there was another stone. A large one. It hit my mother's shoulder, and she cried out and sank back into her chair.

I pushed my way out of the row I was in and got to her as quickly as I could, Brad on my heels. He and I surrounded Mom and Patty and pushed through the crowd and out the door to the street. I took the keys from Mom's bag, and Patty got into the back with her. Beside me in front, Brad called his folks to let them know what had happened and to say he was fine and would be home a little later. Meanwhile I was preparing myself to do battle with Dad and Stu. I expected they would blame me for starting this whole thing, and Mom for being "foolish" enough to get pulled into it.

But there was no battle. By the time we got home, Mrs. Gilman had phoned already, and Dad and Stu were furious. But not at me, and not at Mom.

Mom insisted that she was all right, but there was a nasty bruise forming on the bone of her shoulder, and it hurt her to lift the arm very far.

Barely containing his fury, Dad asked, "Who threw it, Jesse? Did you see?"

"Honestly, no. I didn't." I had my suspicions, based on my knowledge that the stone had come from the direction of where the Dwyers were, but I couldn't be sure, and I didn't want to have to bail Dad and Stu out of jail for whatever might happen if they went charging out in a vigilante mood.

Stu took Patty by her shoulders and then touched her face gently. "Are you all right, babe? Did you get hurt at all?" When he was sure she was fine, Stu turned to Brad and held his hand out. "Thanks for going with them. I should have been there."

I was so shocked that I didn't have to try very hard not to agree out loud.

Dad decided to take Mom to the emergency room for an X-Ray, and I have to say I thought that was a good idea. I called Griffin to make sure no one else got hurt, and then Brad sat with Stu and me in the living room, shell-shocked and not quite sure what to say. I did my best, when Stu asked, to describe the meeting and what Mrs. Coulter and Mom had said just before the stone hit, and he didn't interrupt with any of his usual disparaging comments.

He turned to Patty. "What was your take on this?"

"It was pretty bad, Stu. I mean, most of the towns people were there for the right reasons. To learn, I mean. But the ones who were there to make trouble did exactly that. I couldn't believe how calm Eleanor Darling and Reverend Gilman were! They never seemed afraid or angry. And the things Eleanor said sounded positively Christian. I think a lot of people were as surprised as I was. But obviously some people didn't believe her. Didn't want to."

Brad's phone rang, and he moved into the kitchen. I could tell the call was from Staci, but I couldn't tell how the conversation went.

Brad came back from the kitchen and gestured toward the front door. I followed. He said, "I'm gonna head out, Jesse."

"Are you and Staci okay?"

"We're gonna have a talk. I'm going over there now."

"Thanks for going with us. And for helping me get Mom and Patty out."

He stood there for a few seconds, looked at his feet, then shook his head. "You, uh, you're doing a good thing, Jesse." He looked up again. "And you got guts, I'll give you that. So does your mom." I lifted a shoulder, an "Aw, shucks" moment. "So, is there still a spot for me in this club of yours?"

I grinned at him. "Mondays, right after school. You can walk over with Ivy and me tomorrow."

But there was no TVA meeting the next day. Instead, each member got a note during home room to go to Mrs. Knapp's office after classes instead. I let Brad know, and he came with me.

When everyone was there, standing in the crowded office, Mrs. Knapp turned to me. "How is your mother, Jesse?"

I told her what she'd learned at the ER. "It's a bad bone bruise. Nothing broken or chipped. It hurts to move her arm very far, and she's taking an anti-inflammatory. It's going to cut into her piano playing, and she'll need some help in the kitchen."

"I know you'll do what you can. Please tell her I'm concerned about her. And now." She took a breath. "I don't like having to do this, but I've been informed by the regional school board that we need to call a temporary halt to the TVA."

She held up a hand when we all started to protest. "It's because of the violence at last night's town meeting. We weren't surprised by some of the attitudes, but the throwing of rocks was not expected. We all knew that there might be some push-back, both here at school and in the community, but last night's reaction was extreme enough that there's a question of your safety. So for now—and I stress, *for now*—the TVA is on hiatus. Thanks to all of you for your sincere efforts, and you'll hear from me if and when the club can start up again. That's all."

Outside, the little group seemed reluctant to break apart and go separate ways.

Ivy said, "What if we meet at my house instead of the church? We're just a group of friends, right? I can have friends over if I want."

Interestingly, Griffin was the voice of reason, even if I didn't want to hear it. "Let's give you a chance to ask your dad first. Maybe plan for next week, if he's okay with it. Let's you and I go talk to him now. How's that?"

We all agreed on this plan, and Brad suggested Phil and I go with him to The Pig for a consolation ice cream. I sat across from Brad in a booth, with Phil beside me. While we waited for our orders, I asked Brad, "Is this a bad time to ask how things sit with Staci?"

"No. It's fine. She, uh, she was pretty upset about the rocks. Said she was glad she wasn't there. So was I, as things turned out. I told her how it went, and she didn't chime in with her usual comments about the 'freaks,' so I'm hoping she's thinking about things. Hard to tell. She still hasn't decided whether to contact her aunt." He gave Phil a thumbnail sketch of that situation.

I asked, "Does she know you were ready to throw your lot in with the TVA?"

He grinned. "Yeah, I told her. Let's just say she'll be thrilled that they've stopped it."

"For now," Phil said.

"Yeah. For now."

The air felt heavy, like there was something we all knew was in front of us but that no one would acknowledge. And it was this: We were sure the TVA was dead.

I was pretty quiet the rest of the time we were there.

THROWING STONES

Didn't know what to say. Didn't want to say how I was feeling, which was angry and sad and, on some level I couldn't explain, betrayed. While talk went on without me about summer football practice, I tried counting in my mind the good things that had happened. Like, how Mom and Patty both went and were now firmly on my side of this debate. Brad had taken a stand with me. Ronan's mom and mine might actually get to meet, and maybe—just maybe—ceramics were in my mom's future again. Most of the townsfolk last night had not been outright antagonistic, though of course I couldn't really tell how they *did* feel. Eleanor had said some really great things that people needed to hear, but I didn't know how many of those people believed her.

And there was no denying the bad things. Right up there on top was my mother being stoned. I was responsible for that. I was the one who got this ball rolling. I was the one who convinced her to get involved. Now Patty was involved, too, and who knew what Dad and Stu might do to protect their own family? What might happen to some of the village families, especially the ones who stuck their necks out last night?

This was all my fault. And Ronan had been right.

Chapter Thirteen

At dinner that night, after Stu finished saying Grace, I stood and tried to look around at my family, but in my shame I just stared down toward my plate.

"I want to apologize to all of you," I told them, sensing rather than seeing the startled looks on their faces. "This whole thing about trying to make people in the town and people in the village get along better was such a bad idea, and I pushed forward even when people said I shouldn't. And what's happened now is my own mother gets rocks thrown at her. And I don't even want to guess what might happen to the woman from the village who stood up last night, or to the other village families who were there. It was bad before. I've just made it worse. And I'm really, really sorry."

Before I could sit down again, Mom was on her feet. She wrapped her undamaged arm around me. "Oh, sweetie, you weren't alone in wanting that." She stepped back but kept a hand on my shoulder. "Reverend Gilman was right there with you, and Eleanor Darling. Don't blame yourself."

When I did manage to look at Dad and Stu, I wasn't sure they agreed with Mom. I wasn't sure I did, either.

Upstairs in my room after dinner, I tried to keep my mom's words going in my head. I would much rather have believed that I'd done what was right. But how could it be right when it caused so much bad stuff to happen? And now there was something else Dad and Stu might never forgive me for. I might not be able to forgive myself, either.

Forgiveness. I reached up and grabbed that rutilated

quartz tooth, the one that was supposed to help with spiritual growth. Help you let go of the past. Lighten your mood. And then there was the forgiveness.

But it had bitten me. It had drawn first blood.

Desperate to be anywhere but in my own head, praying that an escape from wherever I was would help, I grabbed my wallet and keys and thundered down the stairs. "Back soon," I called on my way out to my truck. It wasn't until I went to fasten the seat belt that I realized I was still holding the tooth. I shoved it into my jeans pocket.

I drove to Wister Lake, to my spot, to where I could stand on the narrow shore and stare out at nothing. Where I really wanted to go was the treehouse. I missed Ronan so much. I felt like I owed him an apology, too, for being stubborn, for making him feel like he couldn't be with me, and now for maybe getting his mother into a pile of shit she didn't deserve. I wanted to be with Ronan, feel his arms around me, ask for his forgiveness. Forgiveness for trying to build a bridge that was doomed to fail.

In fact, I'd burned that bridge, through my own stubbornness. In my fucking certainty that *I* knew best, that I was smarter than everyone else, I'd isolated myself. I was already isolated, after I came out, but this was different. This was my own fault.

FUCK!

I heaved a rock into the water.

Maybe it wasn't such a bad thing to be wary of what you didn't understand.

I heaved another rock.

Maybe staying with what you already understand, what you're born into, what's been true for you in the past, is wiser. Maybe I shouldn't have trusted the scorpion, that tempting idea that all could be well, and that I could make it be that way. And now, as the frog, I was taking everyone down with me.

I'd thought I was in a bad spot before, banned from a

place where I would be accepted, for want of permission to be there, permission withheld by a place where I wasn't accepted. But what had I done? I'd betrayed that place, the place that accepted me. I'd just made their lives even more of a living hell than my people had been making it before I came along and fucked things up.

I stood and heaved a large stone into the water.

It was all about love, was it? Really? Because it sure felt like it was all about hate. And all about the fear that causes hate.

I shoved my hands in my pockets and nearly cut myself for a second time on that bloodthirsty quartz tooth. I made a fist around it and pulled it out of my pocket, clenching and unclenching my hand around it like I didn't know whether I loved it or hated it more. My eyes fell on what I was sure was the same spot I'd seen Ronan's cougar eyes in the water a lifetime ago. I got ready to heave the tooth at that spot. But it bit me again! I dropped to the ground. Keeping my eyes on the cougar spot so I wouldn't lose track of it, I squatted down and picked the crystal up again, and this time I heaved it into the water, hard.

My cougar would never forgive me.

Back in my truck, I was most of the way home when something happened, that's the only way to describe it, and instead of taking the turn toward town, my truck turned south. In my head I had a picture of the track I'd found on Google Earth that led off the highway about half a mile below that wreck of a barn that Ronan said the village kids played in. When I got to it, the track was not so much a track as it was a path through the woods. But I figured if Lou and Chuck could do it, so could I. In four-wheel-drive, I bumped and jostled my way through the woods as light faded, and things got harder still when the path started to climb more steeply. But this meant it was the right way to go. I was on the right path. For a change.

Very soon the woods ended, and in front of me was an exposed knoll with eerie, unfamiliar shapes on it. I'd found it. The grove's stone circle.

I stood beside my truck for a minute or so, telling myself I just wanted to be sure no one else was there, but really feeling like crapping my pants. There was something about this place that was undeniably different from anyplace else I'd ever been in my life. Pretending it was just a little spooky being out here under the darkening sky didn't work for long. I gazed up the last part of the slope at the oddly shaped monoliths, and the ones that were still upright seemed to tower over me, like living creatures watching me from another world that had somehow intersected with mine at this spot. This was not just a bunch of rocks someone had stood up on their ends. No; this was a very, very special place. Just like Ronan had said.

There was no way these stones were friendly. But were they malevolent? Why would they be? I decided that the feeling I got from them was that they were indifferent to me. I could have been a bug or a coyote or a mushroom. The stones didn't care about me at all.

Walking first in a wide circle around the stones, I assessed the damage. Like Ronan had said, three of them had been pushed over, and four were still standing. Even in the fading light, the starkness of the obscenities scrawled on them in red paint was a shock, an insult to top all insults. I wondered if the stones cared about that, either. My sense was that they didn't. But the grove did.

An owl nearby hooted, and I smelled the sharp pang of my own fear.

"Stop it, Jesse," I whispered to myself. "If they don't care, then they don't care. Nothing to be afraid of here."

Still on the outside of the circle, I walked toward the toppled creature nearest me, which hadn't quite fallen all the way over. It was on the opposite side of the circle from the track I'd followed, and it leaned away from me, toward the center of the circle. The hole where it had been rooted was at least two feet deep—hard to tell for sure in this light—and the stone itself was partly in it and partly not in it, leaning precariously at an odd angle. The other two toppled stones lay horizontal on the ground.

An urge to touch one of the stones came over me in a powerful wave. I didn't want to touch one of the vandalized ones, and the toppled ones seemed like they wanted to be left alone. So I reached out and set the tips of my fingers on the outside of this partially-toppled creature and waited.

What should I feel? Should I feel anything? Should I expect to be whisked back in time like the woman in that TV show, *Outlander?* Should this stone pulse or buzz or tremble? Should I be able to see what was inside it, like with the obsidian?

Nothing. I felt nothing. Could it be that these stones had magic in them only when they were rooted firmly in the earth?

I stepped closer. First with one hand and then the other I worked my way around to the part of the stone that was leaning forward, toward the inner part of the circle, sort of over the hole it had been yanked partially out of. I looked up; it was maybe ten feet tall, this stone, and unbelievably heavy. What would someone have to do to get it back into place? And would whatever magic it used to have be restored once it was upright once more?

Hands pressing on the stone at a spot just over my head, I planted my feet firmly and gave a slight shove to see if I could get a sense of the practical issue of moving this thing. I might as well have pressed against the rock face where I'd found the obsidian; there was no more sense of movement than that. So I pressed harder, and again, trying to rock the thing a little.

Suddenly one hand slipped, my left foot went deep into the hole beneath the stone, and I hit the ground hard, knocking some of the wind out of me. I gasped for several seconds, terrified that either I would never breathe again or that the stone would fall completely over and crush me. But I did breathe again, and the stone remained unmoved.

I pulled at my left leg, but the foot was stuck. Really stuck. There was no pain in my foot or my leg, and I could wiggle my toes. So I twisted and turned and pulled and yanked, thinking a least I should be able to get my foot out of my running shoe, but nothing worked.

Shit! Fuck!

Breathing hard, I rested for a minute and tried to picture what was going on under there, tried to figure out which was the best way to turn the shoe and dislodge it. It was almost dark, now, but I didn't know how much that mattered; I couldn't have seen into that hole at noon. I was going to need some help.

Automatically I reached for my phone. And there it was, gone. Or forgotten. How could I have left the house without it? Sure, I was in a state, but—fuck!

"Don't panic, Jesse. Don't panic. Don't panic."

Guess what I did. I panicked.

"Help!" My shout disappeared into the night and went absolutely nowhere. I shouted again, and again. Nothing. So I shouted it at the stone. But it didn't care. It really just didn't care.

I was having trouble breathing, and my chest felt horribly tight. I almost got dizzy from the frantic darting around my eyes were doing. I forced myself to lie back and breathe evenly and deeply. I'd heard somewhere that to calm yourself down you should count, and breathe out for almost twice as long as you breathe in. I won't say I managed that immediately, but I kept going and finally got there.

I went back to picturing my foot and how it was wedged. Maybe if I just kept wriggling, I could dig down into the dirt, which would give me more room, and maybe I

313

could maneuver my way out. It was worth a shot, and what else did I have to do?

The problem with this plan was that I couldn't move my heel very well, and that would have been the best part of my foot to dig with. Whatever; I'd do what I could.

So I lay there, wriggling, freeing maybe a millimeter of space every ten minutes, until my leg muscles began to cramp. I worked the muscles with my hand as much as I could and rested for a few minutes, willing myself not to shiver, and then tried wriggling again.

This was going to take all night! I tried to remember how cold it was supposed to be tonight. In the fifties, maybe? I would survive that okay, but it wasn't going to be any fun. And then what? Who the hell would think to look for me here tomorrow, or the day after, or the day after? Maybe I should be hoping Lou and Chuck would come back for more destruction so I'd have some hope of rescue. It seemed unlikely they'd actually kill me.

I had plenty of time to think. How, exactly, had I got myself into this fix? Why had I come here? For sure I felt like I'd made everyone's life worse. And knowing that what had happened to the circle had been Ronan's final straw, maybe I'd had some vague idea of helping to fix things. Plus, I'd gotten tired of waiting for Reverend Gilman to get back to me with ideas.

Waiting. Well, shit, I was waiting now, wasn't I?

I gave up my wriggling and collapsed onto the dirt, about ready to cry. But that feeling passed, and an odd calm came over me. I calculated I'd been stuck here maybe an hour and a half so far. And I'd been away from the house for nearly an hour before getting here. My folks were probably wondering why I wasn't back yet. The thought of Mom calling my cell and hearing it ring upstairs came close to sending me into a panic again, but—hell, there was nothing I could do. At what point would they start calling around to my small circle of friends? At what point would they call the police?

It was unsettling to think about my family, and I couldn't do anything to reach them, so instead I turned my thoughts to something pleasant. I treated myself to reliving my memories of Ronan, starting with the day of the labyrinth build and his curt response to my infantile attempts to impress, moving on to his description of dousing, to what he told me about sensing my energy.

I was about to move on to that first visit to the treehouse when I came to a screeching mental halt.

Ronan can sense my energy.

I had no idea how to go about getting him to see me, to sense where I was and that I was in trouble. The only thing I could think of to do was to concentrate on Ronan himself. I pictured his eyes, those deep, animal eyes. Mentally I placed my hands on either side of his face to keep him looking at me, and I concentrated.

Time stopped. Sound went away. I forgot that I had to pee. All that existed in the world was whatever connected me to Ronan.

Something jerked my eyes open; I didn't even realize I'd closed them. There was still nothing to see, but I knew something had changed. I just couldn't tell what.

I tried concentrating again, but nothing else happened. Maybe it had been a waste of time even to try. Maybe he sensed me but couldn't tell what I wanted and was pissed that I'd reached out to him that way. Maybe all kinds of things.

I really had to pee. It was getting worse, but I wasn't quite ready to let go, stuck here.

I went back to my memories, and this time I started with the second treehouse visit, the one where we'd had sex for the first time. This was not only distracting in a good way, but also the muscles that allow you to release piss contract automatically when you're aroused, and that made the urge to pee less intense.

I got about as far as him getting me off before the dire aspect of my situation slammed into my brain again, surprising me with its intensity. That's when I heard the sound of a vehicle climbing up that slope.

Of course, I was facing the other way, helpless and blind. I craned my neck anyway; would the truck be red? And would I even be able to tell in the darkness? No use; I'd just have to wait—again—and learn my fate when it presented itself to me.

Two doors slammed, and I heard a metallic sound like someone lifting shovels or equipment out of a truck bed. I held my breath, not wanting to give myself away until I knew what I'd be giving myself away *to*.

Footsteps, movement through the grass, flashlight beams. Then, "Jesse, how the hell did you do this to yourself?"

"Ronan! Oh, my God! Shit, but I'm glad you're here!"

"Todd and I have come to rescue you."

"But—how did you know..."

"Silly question. Todd? What do you think?"

Todd chuckled as he hefted a mysterious piece of equipment off of a wheeled dolly. "I do seem to keep rescuing your family members from one disaster or another. Quite a fix you've gotten yourself into. Is your leg or foot hurt at all?"

"No, just wedged. I was trying to dig into the dirt, but my foot isn't positioned very well for that. I made a little room, just not enough."

"Good thought, anyway." He moved away and I lost track of what he was doing.

As Ronan settled on the ground near my head, the flashlight beside him, I asked, "What is that thing?"

"A hydraulic jack. By the way, I take it you don't have your phone?" I shook my head, and he handed me his. "Here. Call your folks. I'm sure they're panicked."

Dad's voice sounded strained when he picked up the

316

house line. "Dad? It's Jesse. I—"

"Jesse!" I pictured him looking at Mom, and then I heard her voice. She must have picked up the other line.

"Oh, Jesse! Where on earth are you? We've called all your friends, and—"

"Mom, listen. I'm fine, I just got myself into a bit of a bind. Fell into a hole in the woods. I'm in the process of getting out now." Dad tried to speak, but I talked over him. "I'm not sure how long it will take, so I'll give you another call in a bit. Sorry about all this; I forgot my phone, so I'm using someone else's. I'll call again soon. Bye." I hung up before they could go into any more detail about their worry; they'd tell me all of it again when I got home anyway.

I looked at the phone, before handing it back, to see what time it was.

"Ronan! It's after one o'clock in the morning!"

"So it is. You woke me up, y'know." I could see the grin on his face. Exhausted, I let my head fall back onto the dirt. "My mom told me what happened Sunday night. Is your mom okay?"

"Bad bruise. Hurts to move her arm very much, so I'm helping around the house."

"Especially in the kitchen, I imagine."

"Your mom was very brave."

"Yeah. She's a trooper. Dad and I stayed home like the cowards we are."

I had no idea what to make of that. "Ronan, I need to tell you something." But before I could get anything else said, Todd called to Ronan.

"Bring the crowbar and come help me with this."

Not being able to see much, I had to wait to get a sense of what they were doing. Using the bar, they managed to roll a large rock from someplace over to where I was trapped. Somehow, using the crowbar and the jack, Todd wrangled it into a position beside my leg and wedged it against the stone that kept me captive. He positioned the

317

jack on the other side of me and settled it under the monolith. Then he disappeared.

"Where's he going?"

Ronan picked up a coil of rope and kneeled beside me. "Can you shift from side to side at all? I need to get this rope under you." In a different context, I thought to myself as Ronan was pushing the rope underneath my back and getting ready to tie it around me, this could be fun. I knew I was getting giddy, and that wasn't good, so I focused on my foot and what I was going to have to do to move quickly after being stuck for hours on the cold ground. When Ronan had the rope tied securely around my chest under my arms, he sat back on the ground and answered the question I'd already forgotten I'd asked.

"He'll move the truck around the outside of the circle and secure this stone as best he can, with webbing attached to the truck. He won't pull the stone upright this way, but if it falls, you'll have a fighting chance to get out before it hits the ground. If the webbing holds, I think he'll use the jack to move the stone up, even if it's just a little, and this other stone that we moved over will break the fall if the jack lets go or the stone falls off of it. Again, just a fighting chance, but you look like a fighter to me."

"Shit, Ronan. I'm so sorry about this."

"You're a lot of trouble, Jesse Bryce. You've been a lot of trouble since the very beginning." He got up onto all fours so he could hover over me, and then he did something unbelievable. He kissed me. Then he kissed me again. "Feel better? Now, you had something you wanted to say to me?" He sat back down.

Wow. My brain spun. What did those kisses mean? "Um, what I was saying was that I've been a total idiot. A stubborn idiot. And you were right. This whole fucking plan of building bridges and getting people to make nice with each other and forget about years of bad feelings? Bad idea. Bad, shitty idea. From a fucking idiot. That would be me."

"A fucking courageous idiot. Let's talk more once Todd's done." He got up and Todd reappeared.

"Jesse, I'm going to see if the jack will shift the stone just enough for you to pull yourself out. It's not designed to work on an uneven surface like this stone, and I don't know how well it's going to hold. So as soon as I start pumping, you'll need to get yourself out from under this thing and several feet away as quick as you possibly can. Ronan's going to pull on that rope, and that should help with the first part."

"Um, you really can't just pull the thing up with your truck?"

"If I pull up on the top of the stone, the bottom could slide forward and crush your foot."

I nodded. To prepare myself for sudden action, I tensed every muscle I could, released, tensed again. I found places to put my hands where I could push hard, and I got my free leg bent and positioned where I could push away with that foot. Ronan pulled from the other end of the rope so it was taut.

Todd said, "Everyone ready?"

Ronan and I said "Yes" together, and Todd began pumping the jack. Almost immediately I felt a shift in the hole. "Pull!" I shouted to Ronan, and I scrambled for all I was worth. My legs were not working very well, and I was glad of Ronan's rope. I didn't trust my legs enough to stand, so I started rolling as soon as I could. When I looked back at the monster rock, Todd had released the jack and was moving it away quickly; guess he didn't trust the stone not to shift farther. And, in fact, it did shift down farther, onto that rock they'd placed under it.

I lay on the ground, panting, almost hysterical with something like laughter that wasn't really any fun at all. Ronan stood over me, rope slack in his hands, grinning, panting a little, too, as he undid the rope. By the time I felt able to get up into a sitting position and massage my left foot, Todd had removed the webbing and moved his truck back around, headlights illuminating the scene. The jack reloaded, crowbar retrieved, he came over to me.

"All's well?" he asked, holding a hand out to me.

I grabbed on, and he pulled me up, his other arm around me for support, which I needed more than I would have thought. I moved my foot in a circle, telling myself it didn't hurt as much as I was afraid it did. "It'll be fine soon," I told him. "I just need to be able to drive home. Clutch, you know."

"Ronan, you drive Jesse's truck. I'll follow you and drive you back."

I started to protest, but Ronan put a hand over my mouth. "Not your choice. You're the idiot, remember?"

Todd helped me around to the passenger side and opened the door. But I knew my bladder wasn't going to last another minute. "Is there someplace I can take a leak that won't hit sacred ground around here?"

Todd threw back his head and laughed. He told Ronan to get behind the wheel, and then he helped me move several more feet away from the circle toward the trees.

"Can you stand on your own?"

"I'm not sure."

So Todd stood behind me and wrapped his arms all the way around my chest. I couldn't have fallen if I'd tried.

"Let loose, kid." And I did.

Ronan handed me his phone again once we were in the cab, and I called home. Mom answered this time.

"Jesse, what on earth is going on?"

"I'm on my way home. A good friend is driving me because my foot's a little sore, but it'll be fine. Mom, I'm real sorry. None of this was supposed to happen. I'll tell you all about it when I get home. Okay?" This time I waited to see if she had anything more to say.

I heard her exhale through her nose. "You've got some

explaining to do, young, man."

"I know. I will. See you soon."

We were half-way back to the highway. "Ronan, what can I tell them about the stone circle? And how am I going to explain that you came looking for me?"

He laughed and then shook his head. "Maybe you should just tell them the truth about how I found you. But about the circle... We're already talking about what it means that someone who would vandalize it had to know where it was. It's location is already known; we just don't know to what extent, and we aren't quite ready to say, 'Sure, go ahead and tell everyone about it.' Maybe for now, just don't say exactly where the circle is, or how you found it. And if you can, avoid letting on how important it is."

"Did you know that Reverend Gilman knows where it is?"

He glanced quickly at me and back at the path in the headlights. "I did not. How do you know that he does?"

"I guess I'll just tell you the truth, too."

"Never ever do anything else, Jesse. I'll know."

My turn to laugh. "I believe you. Anyway, I was beyond pissed off about the damage up there, and I had this supposedly bright idea that maybe we could get a bunch of people together to help you clean up the paint and resettle the stones. In my idiocy I saw only two problems. One was to figure out where the circle was. The other was that anyone who helped would know where it was, and it wouldn't be a secret any more. So after one of my ill-advised TVA meetings, I asked the reverend if he had any ideas. He said he already knew where it was, and that he'd give the idea some thought. I never heard any more about it from him, so I guess he's not as stupid as I am."

"And you found out where it was how, exactly?"

"Google Earth."

"I never thought of that." Ronan turned north on the highway. "Up there, at your near tomb, you told me

something important. Now I need to tell you something."
He hesitated and then went on. "I wasn't right, Jesse. You're
the one who was right. This thing that's started, this bridge
of yours? It's working. I know it looks bad right now, but
you should see how much everyone in the grove is rallying
around the effort. My mom was the first one to stand, but
the fact that your mom stood, too, was huge. Huge! And I
know of at least seven people who've told Eleanor they
want to participate in the individual meetings. I don't really
know what's going on from the town side, but Eleanor
does, because she's been in touch with your reverend. The
only connection I've heard about specifically so far is my
mom and yours, but I know there are others under
discussion."

I watched the side of his face, unable to believe what I
was hearing.

"Shit, Jesse, you've done it. We have a long way to go,
but—" he looked at me briefly. "I'm so fucking proud of
you. And I hope you'll forgive me for being such a
Cassandra."

"Cassandra?"

"You know. Like Chicken Little. 'The sky is falling!
The sky is falling!' Only it isn't. You were right, Jesse. You.
Not me." The only sound for ten seconds was the tires on
the road. "So, will you forgive me?"

I was still feeling stunned, but all I could say was, "I
forgive you."

His voice so soft I almost didn't hear, he said, "And can
we be together again?"

My smile almost hurt my face. "When do we start?"

He laughed. "That's one truth you might not want to tell
your folks tonight. Now, I'm not sure which house is yours,
so—"

"What, you can't just close your eyes and let your
psychic senses guide you?"

He reached sideways and punched my arm. So I told

him where to turn.

Mom and Dad came out of the front door as soon as Todd pulled up behind us. I'd gotten my door open, but my foot was still unsteady; I was beginning to think all that twisting and straining had sprained something. Dad stepped forward and put his arm around me to support me out of the truck and into the house. I couldn't remember the last time he'd touched me, and I nearly wept.

Behind us I heard Mom ask Todd and Ronan to come inside. Stu came downstairs in a bathrobe, and we all sat around the living room while I did my best to tell the story of my brush with death. I downplayed the importance of the stone circle, referring to it only as a pile of stones that had looked interesting from a distance, and not mentioning the vandalism. And I skipped entirely over how Ronan and Todd happened to find me; if someone asked about that later, I wasn't sure what I was going to say. I mean, *Well, you know, the usual. I beamed thoughts over to the village and Ronan picked up on them*wouldn't go over very well.

When I got to the part about Todd lifting the stone, Mom got up, and Todd and Dad stood like gentlemen, and Mom hugged Todd and started crying. He helped her back to her place on the couch, and Dad shook Todd's hand.

"Seems like you keep saving our lives, Mr. Swazey. I don't know how to thank you."

I did my best to swipe away tears without letting on I was crying, too. My father. My own father, shaking the hand of a "freak," of someone who believed in goddesses and, for all Dad knew, had one of those "heathen" symbols hanging from the rear view mirror of his truck.

Stu was next. He stood and offered his hand to Todd. "I never thanked you for saving my fiancée's life. Patty Arnold."

Todd nodded. "I heard about the baby. We were all real sorry."

I had to bite my tongue; Talise Alexander had known

about the baby before anyone else.

Ronan, sitting on the piano bench, had said nothing to that point, and I'm sure he would have kept it that way if Mom hadn't addressed him.

"Ronan? Clio Coulter is your mother?"

Stu's head snapped in his direction, and once again I remembered that love potion, and Stu's questioning me after the tornado.

"Yes, ma'am."

"I'm hoping I'll get to meet her."

I was terrified that someone was going to ask Ronan why he'd been with Todd, so I tried to stand. My foot went out from under me. Everyone stood at once, but Ronan was closer, and he helped me onto the piano bench where he'd been sitting. "That's sprained, Jesse. You should probably see your doctor."

Mom was on board with that. "Indeed, he will. I'll call first thing in the morning." She laughed. "I mean, a little later *this* morning." Todd and Ronan took that as their cue to leave. Mom held onto the door as they stepped out. "Good night, and thank you." She watched them get into Todd's truck, waved once, and shut the door, leaning against it hard. Before she could speak, Dad did.

"Young man, this little escapade of yours showed a remarkable lack of good judgment. You could have died, do you realize that? You've made trouble for a lot of people and worried your mother and me nearly to death. And now, if that foot is badly sprained, you won't be able to get to school without help, and you won't be able to help your mother as much as you have been. Do you have anything to say for yourself?"

He wasn't wrong. In addition to everything he'd said, it had been an incredibly stupid thing to do, with night coming on, and no permission to be on the grove's land, and—though Dad wouldn't know this—running the risk of offending the entire village by trespassing in that sacred spot the town had already desecrated. But I couldn't help smiling a little, if only internally, that Dad thought it was a good thing for me be helping Mom—a one-eighty turnaround from the day I'd come out to him.

Like I hadn't already taken enough risks lately, I jumped in for another. "I have no excuse, Dad. And I'm also sorry that I put you in this position. I know you don't like those people."

He scowled like he didn't quite know what to make of that or how to respond. Maybe *whether* to respond. What I was going for was getting him to see for himself that "those people" are really good people, and I was doing it by reminding him what he'd said about them in the past.

Finally he said, "I suppose they have their good side. But as for you, I'd ground you except that you can't drive anyway."

I nodded and looked as submissive as I knew how. Which wasn't difficult; now that the crisis was over and the rush of adrenaline from being rescued by my boyfriend (!) was draining, I felt so exhausted I didn't know if I could have climbed the stairs to my room without a foot injury, let alone with one. Before I escaped, though, Mom fed me some ibuprofen and a glass of milk. Then she handed me a bag of frozen peas.

Stu, of all people, surprised the hell out of me as soon as I handed the glass back to Mom. "Come on, Jesse. I'll help you upstairs and into bed." I was so tired he almost had to carry me.

Stu had an ulterior motive, though, which I should have realized but didn't until I was flat on my back on the bed with him undoing my shoelaces. "I have a question for you. How did Todd and Ronan know where you were, or that you were in trouble at all?"

I'd nearly fallen asleep already, but this question jolted me awake again. I was about to panic, but then I remembered that Ronan had said just to tell the truth.

"Ronan has a gift. Somehow he senses these things. I don't know how he does it. And there are a few other people in the village who can do that. One of them knew two people from the town were hurt after the tornado, and when I couldn't reach Patty, this woman knew immediately that Patty's baby was in serious trouble."

Shoes and socks were off now, and Stu was tilting my bedside light to shine on the ankle. "This does look swollen, but I don't think it's too bad. Where's that bag of peas?" He positioned the cold, limp thing on my ankle, and I hissed with the shock. "So does Ronan's mother have this gift?"

"I don't know. She's not the one who knew about Patty. But she's the one who stood at the town meeting, and I think she and Mom will be able to get to know each other. I really want that to happen, because Mrs. Coulter throws pots."

"Sounds dangerous. What does it mean?"

"She makes ceramics. Like Mom used to do. Like she'd love to do again. Especially after she broke that blue bowl."

"What blue bowl?"

I lifted my head off the pillow to look at him. "Can we talk about this another time? I'm dyin' here."

"Just one more for now. Are you—is Ronan—who is he to you?"

My defenses were down, my shields weren't functioning. "My boyfriend."

Stu stood. "Thought so."

I half-sat up quickly, leaning on my elbows, realizing what I'd just done. Making it sound more like a statement than a question, I told him, "And you won't say anything, will you?"

"Don't know. Might."

"Mutually assured destruction."

"What?"

"I have one word for you. Potion."

THROWING STONES

Even in the low light of the room, even in my wasted state, I could see him blanch. He turned out the light and left.

I was dead to the world within five seconds, and if I had any dreams about being buried alive or crushed under tons of weight I didn't remember them. I hadn't even thought about setting my alarm, so it was around nine when I woke up and hobbled my way into the bathroom, hanging onto anything stable enough to hold me upright. The left ankle was more swollen now.

Mom heard me and came upstairs. "You're not going to school today, though I suppose that doesn't surprise you. We're due to get X-Rays at eleven. As soon as you're cleaned up and dressed, come downstairs for some breakfast and more ibuprofen."

I went down the stairs one at a time, sliding on my butt. After my toast and eggs, Mom wrapped my ankle in an ACE bandage, and together we hobbled out to her car.

On the way to the hospital, she told me, "I had a call from Mrs. Coulter this morning." She waited.

"Oh? Are you getting together?"

"Yes. But she also called to see how you're doing. I happened to ask her something I didn't think about last night. That is, how anyone knew where to look for you." Again, she waited.

I could have gone into the explanation I'd given Stu, but what if it was somehow different from what Mrs. Coulter had said? "What did she say?"

"I think she was trying to be circumspect, but there's no way she could avoid saying Ronan had sensed you out there. When I asked if he could do that in his sleep, she had to admit that you'd reached out to him in some way I don't understand. I need you to tell me about that."

So I repeated the story I'd given Stu, which was true enough. But maybe she didn't think so.

"Why Ronan? Why not the woman who'd sensed that

327

about Patty?"

"I don't know her very well. Ronan's in my classes at school."

"How, exactly, did you reach out to him?"

Stalling for time, I reached down and rubbed my ankle. "Well, I mean, you know. You just concentrate on the person, hold them in your mind in a really focused way."

"Is this something they've taught you to do?"

Ah; so that was it. She thought I was being indoctrinated. "Nope. I just tried it out of desperation. It was all I could think of to do."

"Is Ronan in that club you started with Ivy?"

"No. He didn't think it was a good idea. But he might be changing his mind. He told me his mother's not the only one in the village who wants to get together like you'll be doing. Um, did you know Mrs. Coulter throws pots?"

Her head jerked toward me and quickly back to the road. "What?"

One lie, a white one, was called for here. "I can't remember how I heard about it, but—yeah. She does." I decided to let her chew on that herself rather than point out how cool it would be if the two of them got together over this common interest. And she must have chewed it into mush, because she didn't say anything else until we got to the hospital.

In the waiting room, I got a text from Brad.

You okay? R told me what happened.

Getting an X-ray in a minute. Will be fine.

UR one crazy dude

Yup

Ronan had been right; the ankle was just strained, almost certainly by my frantic attempts to dig out the dirt underneath that foot. I left the hospital with a new bandage, a prescription for something called ketoprofen to put on it, an ankle wrap with insertable cold packs, a pair of crutches, and instructions to elevate it for two days and avoid stepping on it. So until the ankle was better, I couldn't drive my truck. Whose idea was that standard transmission, anyway?

I called Ronan that evening from my bed, foot on a bunch of pillows, to find out what he'd told Brad and—hell, just to talk to Ronan.

"Yeah," he said, "I told Brad pretty much what you told your folks. I thought you did a good job of walking that fine line between truth and fiction. How are you feeling?"

I gave him the details of my diagnosis and treatment and asked him to thank Todd again for me. After that, we both kind of ran out of things we wanted to say on the phone. Acknowledging the elephant in the room, I said, "I don't know how long it will be before I can walk that path through the woods to the trees."

"Well," he replied in a warm, silky tone I loved, "if you can't go to the treehouse, perhaps the treehouse can come to you."

"I have no idea what—"

"You're lying down, I think. Close your eyes. Breathe deeply, slowly, and allow your facial muscles to go soft." He waited, then continued. "You're on the path in the woods, and you've just taken that left fork that leads to the cliff. It's dusk, and the tree branches look dark against the sky. There's a light breeze that lifts your hair and brushes against your face. The path grows steeper as it rises toward the top of the cliff, and the swinging bridge comes into view. You grip the rope railings. The rope is rough against your palms, solid but flexible, supporting you but allowing you to find your own balance. Walk across that bridge. Come to me."

"You're standing in the doorway."

"Yes."

"You're smiling."

"I am. Can you see the look in my eyes?"

I concentrated for a few seconds and then smiled.

"Yeah. You want me."

"All of you."

I'd never had phone sex before, and I have to say this was nothing like what I would have thought. Ronan talked us through it, taking his time, focusing on how things felt but also why they felt that way. We were well into foreplay before I realized that Ronan was not in human form. He'd said nothing specific, but I knew. He was Cougar. I laughed out loud.

"What's so funny?" He was smiling, I could tell.

"You just put the tip of your tail into my right ear."

His turn to laugh, but it was sultry. "And did you enjoy that?"

"Yeah. Do it again."

By the time he'd used the pads of his front paws—nails sheathed—to bring me to ecstasy, I could have sworn I had light claw marks across my shoulder blades and down one side of my chest. His cat's tongue, rougher than a human one, was so deep inside my mouth I could almost swallow it.

Somehow I'd managed to grab a handful of tissues in time to avoid making a mess of my underwear. Until that point, I hadn't touched myself. But Ronan had.

"Curl your back against my belly," he told me, and I swear I could feel the warm fur against my naked back, even though I wasn't naked, even though I couldn't lie on my side and still keep my foot elevated. I felt his furry arms wrap around me from behind.

"Now, Jesse, my treetop lover, sleep. And dream of me."

My injury kept me out of school on Wednesday, so when Brad texted me that he and Phil were on their way for a visit to the invalid I had no idea what had been going on.

Brad propped himself on the footboard of my bed, and

330

THROWING STONES

Phil sat in my desk chair.

"I'm certain you're faking this whole thing just to get out of a few days of school," Brad said. "But in the process, you're missing all the fun."

"And that would be—?"

Brad just grinned, so Phil picked up the story. "The TVA might be the only club in school to get new members while it's not in session. We have three more town kids who want to join."

That confused me. "Why? What happened?"

"You!" Brad poked at my foot pillows. "*You* happened. I grilled Ronan for details of your rescue, and he gave me a blow-by-blow account of it. Some pile of stones in the middle of nowhere, and one of them falls on you. The truck holding this boulder in place, and the hydraulic jack, and pulling you out with a rope—man, that's the stuff of legend. And now lots of kids know about it. The only thing Ronan wouldn't tell me is how he and Todd knew you were there."

Still confused, I asked, "But why would that make anyone want to join the TVA?"

"Are you kidding me? They're convinced there was something magic, and somehow someone in the village knew you were there. That is some cool shit, dude. And they want to know what it is."

Phil said, "We figure, you know, it doesn't matter why they join, really. It's just great that they aren't afraid to, and that they think something about the village is cool."

Brad slid off the footboard and onto the end of the mattress. "So do tell. How *did* they know?"

I had two choices, here. I could tell them what I'd told Stu, which had been true enough, or I could play up the mystery. I opted for the latter. "What makes you think I know the answer to that? They just showed up all of a sudden."

"You didn't ask them *why* they showed up?"

"Like they're gonna tell me something they won't tell

331

you? Maybe they enjoy the mystery. I think those new members do. Just something else we have in common."

Phil laughed.

Brad changed the subject. "So are you getting off your ass tomorrow and coming to school?"

"That's the plan. Though I've been a good boy and haven't been on this foot much, so I don't know how well I'll be walking."

"Let's find out." Brad pulled the pillows out from under my foot. "Phil? You get on one side of him, I'll get on the other, and we'll see if he falls."

I couldn't have fought these guys off. They were both football players, and I was not. Plus, I kind of wanted to know, anyway. They hauled me off the bed and let me set the foot down carefully. I was surprised and relieved to find out it wasn't too bad. I definitely needed to limp off of it because it felt a little weak, but the swelling was gone, and it didn't hurt very much at all. I'd be in school Thursday for sure. And Brad was going to drive me, in my own truck.

Chapter Fourteen

By the weekend, the ankle was almost normal, and I could drive again. This meant two great things happened that weekend: Mom went to see Mrs. Coulter's ceramics workshop, and—since she was going into the village, herself—I got general permission to visit friends there, too.

Mom spent that Saturday afternoon in the village while I went grocery shopping and got dinner ready. She got home ahead of Dad and Stu, who were working at the garage.

I did my best to sound casual. "Was it fun?"

She sat at the table and smiled at me as I was putting a pan of brownie batter into the oven. "Clio—Mrs. Coulter—does the most beautiful work, Jesse! Have you seen any of it?"

I wasn't sure whether she had the focus to interrogate me, but I soft-pedaled it anyway. "I think I once saw a mug of hers. What kinds of things do you think you might make?"

"First, I want to replace that bowl. In fact, I want to make nesting bowls, three of them. That means each one will be a different size, and they'll need to sit comfortably inside each other. That won't be an easy project, but I really want to do it. And the glazes! Oh, my goodness. There's nothing I won't be able to do there. And here's the great part: All I'll owe her is materials! She's going to teach me what I need to know."

I grinned at her. "Sounds like you'll be going back, then."

"I will. She even has her own kiln. But—it's wood-fired." She stopped there, almost like she'd walked right up to the edge of a cliff.

I prodded, "Is there something special about that?"

"Firing that kiln is rather a big production. Evidently, she does it only a few times a year, and it goes for a few days. It needs to be tended continuously, so it's kind of a village project when it happens." She stopped again.

"And?"

"And I would need to help."

I almost laughed with joy. My mom, working alongside people of the grove. Does it get any better than that? "I'll help, too, Mom. I'll go with you."

She stood and ruffled my hair. Then she gave me a hug. "Jesse, this was all your doing. I just want you to know that I know that." And she headed upstairs.

My own plans for Saturday also included Mrs. Coulter. The whole Coulter family, in fact. After dinner, I headed over to the village, with permission for the first time—at least, from Mom; I didn't know whether Dad knew where I was going.

Ronan's house was a few doors away from Griffin's, and I felt an odd, fun thrill parking right in front, like I had a reason—and a right—to be there. My ankle wasn't quite stable enough to walk through the woods to the treehouse, but it was going to be a great night anyway. I was going to meet my boyfriend's parents.

As I shook Mr. Coulter's hand, I knew I'd seen him around town in one place or another. He wasn't very tall, and his hair was lighter than Ronan's or Mrs. Coulter's, but I could tell where Ronan got his eyes. The handshake was warm and kind of tingly, like energy passing between us.

The four of us sat around their kitchen table, with Ronan across from me, and Mrs. Coulter offered me a piece of pumpkin pie. I'd had brownies at home, but I wasn't about to turn this down. Plus, she'd made real whipped cream; Ronan made a point of letting me know that. There was also a large pot of something called ku-ki cha tea, which Ronan told me had very little caffeine. It tasted really good with pumpkin pie.

I was all ready with something to talk about. "Mrs. Coulter, I'm so glad you and my mom are going to throw pots together." I loved that odd phrase; I just hoped Ronan wouldn't think I was trying to impress anyone. "Did she tell you how I found out she'd ever even done that?"

"I understand there was a certain blue bowl that shattered."

I nodded and swallowed a mouthful of pie. "I used that bowl at Thanksgiving to serve mashed butternut squash. The orange against the blue? You can picture it."

She laughed. "I can, indeed. I hope you'll be able to do that again next Thanksgiving."

"Is it okay if I help with the kiln firing? Mom says you'll need lots of help."

"I would love that, Jesse. Please plan on it. We'll be setting up a schedule a couple of weeks ahead of the next firing."

As people talked, I looked around as best I could. The house wasn't large, and it was different from Griffin's house in that it looked more like what I would have expected a village home to look like. For example, the kitchen curtains were blue with suns and moons in yellow and white, and the cloth napkins were the same material. In one corner there was a shelf just over shoulder height with a large, jet black, round stone or something like that, on a wooden stand. Ronan noticed me looking at it

"That's Dad's scrying ball. It's made of obsidian." He gave me an arch look when he said "obsidian."

Mr. Coulter asked, "Do you know what scrying is, Jesse?"

"Sort of. Ronan described it to me, and once I saw a cougar in the water at Wister Lake."

He raised his eyebrows, looked at Ronan, and said, "Did you, now?"

Ronan actually blushed. "He knows what my power animal is. Actually, he guessed."

"So I gathered. Jesse, would you like to hold it?"

"Would I!"

He got up and fetched the ball, along with a wooden ring, which he set down in front of me, placing the ball onto it. He sat down again. No one said anything.

Not knowing what else to do, I placed my hands on either side of the black orb, barely touching it with my fingertips, and stared into it.

Mr. Coulter asked, "Can you feel anything?"

"It's... it's shimmering, sort of. If it were a sound, it would be a kind of tinkling."

He looked at Ronan briefly and smiled. "Ronan did say you were a sensitive."

"A sensitive?"

"You're aware of a stone's energy. And it sounds like you've already done a little scrying on your own without even setting out to do that." He looked at me thoughtfully for a second or two. "Feel up to a little adventure?"

I grinned and nodded. He got up and fetched two wooden sticks.

"Sit comfortably, hands in your lap." I did. "Now, Jesse, take a moment to bring something to mind. It should be something you want to understand more than you do, or something confusing that's troubling you, or maybe some message you'd like to send someone. Don't think of trying to bring about some big change or convince someone of something you know they can't accept. And don't confuse this effort with making some kind of wish. This is about helping you live your life in the best way possible."

"Wow. Um, okay, give me a minute." At first

everything that came to me was just like a wish you might make blowing out birthday candles. Then everything was a question about what would happen in the future. Then I thought about living my life, and I knew what I wanted. "Can it be about my brother? I mean, helping him understand me better?"

"What about you understanding him better?" I blinked at him. Why hadn't I thought of that? "Maybe you'd want to consider enhancing the channel between the two of you. Improving the flow of communication and understanding in both directions. How about that?"

"Perfect. Thanks."

"Gaze gently into the obsidian. Take several slow, deep breaths." And he began to tap the sticks together, lightly, over and over. "Think of your brother. Focus on the way you want to feel about him, and the way you want him to feel about you. These should probably be the same kind of feeling."

A couple of minutes went by. I looked at the obsidian, wondering what it meant to look into that intense blackness, and then something about the visual surface of it gave way.

Speaking slowly, Mr. Coulter said, "Now, close your eyes. Hold the image of a powerful tree in your mind. Its power might be from its physical strength or from the energy you feel from it, or both. Follow down the trunk to the ground, and as you picture the roots underground, follow them slowly down into the earth. Move down, slowly, slowly. Breathe deeply."

I was feeling decidedly lightheaded, and I almost opened my eyes to get my bearings. But I was really curious about what would happen next if I kept going. I didn't want to spoil the adventure.

After maybe another minute, and several layers of roots later, Mr. Coulter said, "Settle gently among the roots. Breathe. Focus on the way you feel here in the roots of this powerful tree. Your own energy is centered. Grounded. Fluid, but settled. Focus on this feeling. Become very familiar with it." He kept tapping the sticks. "This is going to ground. This is where you will always come back to. You can't get lost."

A few breaths later, he spoke again, and his voice sounded like it was coming from all around me. "When you feel calm and settled, think of your brother. Feel the energetic connection you have with him. For the moment, just establish a connection."

I breathed several more times, and I noticed that when I thought of Stu, I saw a kind of river between us.

"When you have the connections," the quiet voice said, "begin to pull your grounding energy together. Draw on the earth all around you." A few beats went by, sticks gently tapping. "Now, see your energy flowing from you to him, and see that energy arriving in a way that calms fears and opens minds. Your energy is loving, and warm, and it helps him relax. It opens him up in a gentle way so the love you send finds its way home. Be fully aware of the connection so your energy is received and absorbed. Draw energy from the earth. Create love. Let that flow."

I pictured Stu sitting beside me at Wister Lake, looking across the water, both of us feeling really great with my new truck parked nearby, the truck he'd worked so hard on for me. There was a river flowing beside us, deep and strong.

But then the river changed. Stu and I were on opposite sides now, and there were boulders in the fast-moving river. I tried to get closer to Stu, but it felt like I was struggling upstream, and the current was more than I could manage.

Mr. Coulter must have sensed this, because he said, still slowly, still quietly, "If you feel resistance, allow it to happen. Let it push you back, and then use that push to lift yourself up so you're above it."

When I did this, I could see Stu from overhead. I reached out to him with my energy until I could settle back beside him again. But very quickly that river was between us again, and it was turbulent again.

"I sense frustration. If you can, use the energy of the resistance to rise above it again."

But this time I couldn't get there. I just couldn't. And the turbulence, rushing like mad around the boulders, became scary, like I was going to be washed away and drowned.

"Breathe deeply. Again. Allow the resistance to carry you back to the tree where you started." The stick tapping got faster, and I barely heard Mr. Coulter's voice as it guided me. "Come back. Back to the tree, back to the roots. Follow the sound of the sticks. The resistance you feel will grow weaker as it gets further from the source of your frustration." The stream reduced to not much more than a trickle. And then I heard, "Sink into the ground gently, slowly. Find the tree roots again, and rest there calmly. Breathe slowly and deeply."

It took a while. It worried me, how long it took. The turbulent energy really unsettled me, and I wasn't sure I could get back to that calm feeling I'd had, here in the roots. But I kept breathing deeply, and eventually things got grounded again.

"Begin to follow the roots upward, slowly, calmly, until you're above ground again. When you're ready, open your eyes." The stick tapping slowed and then stopped. As I opened my eyes, Mr. Coulter said, "How are you?"

"I'm okay."

"It's just that I sensed some real negativity. It upset you."

"You—you were following me?"

"I wanted to make sure you didn't get lost, or overwhelmed."

"There was this river. At first it was good. Deep, you

know? And strong. We were together on one side of it. But then it turned into whitewater, with all these boulders. We were on opposite sides, and the water was rushing all around the boulders, pushing against me. I couldn't get through it. I couldn't get back to him."

My voice sounded frantic, and my throat tightened. Mr. Coulter's hand wrapped around my forearm. He said, "Breathe, Jesse. And again. Allow your shoulders to relax."

Something about his touch was immensely calming. I couldn't have said what it was. When he withdrew his hand, I felt much better.

"When something like that happens," he said, "usually the resistance is coming not just from the object of your connection. It's also coming from you. You might want to think about that if you decide to try again. Because if you really want to, if you focus very clearly on your own energy, you can purify it, at least to some extent. Then the resistance would be much less. Do you have any obsidian yourself?"

I smiled at Ronan. "Yes. I do."

"If you try this on your own, it might help if you use that. It doesn't have to be a ball; you can just hold a piece of it. But if you do this again, Jesse, I think you might want to work just on your own energy at first, as I said. And keep a part of your focus on the tree roots. Don't let yourself get agitated. If something is resisting when you're working alone, come back to the roots immediately."

He sat back and exhaled slowly, and the mood around the table changed. Ronan said, "If you like this kind of work, we can do some experimenting with the best medium for you. Dad uses that ball because it works for him. But you saw things in the water once. Some people use other things. A mirror, or a pile of broken sticks. We can test different things if you like."

Mrs. Coulter said, "It's after nine-thirty, Jesse. What time do your folks expect you home?"

THROWING STONES

"No special time, really, though I think they haven't quite gotten over what happened Monday night."

"Then maybe you should think about getting back soon."

Ronan stood. "I'll make sure he doesn't get back too late. Jesse, can I take you for a ride in your truck while you rest your foot?"

I wasn't sure how to thank Mr. Coulter for the adventure he'd led me on, but I did my best. And I told Mrs. Coulter her pie was as good as my own, even though maybe it wasn't quite. Outside, Ronan reached into my pocket for my keys and didn't take his hand out right away. We stood beside the truck for a few minutes, kissing and touching and panting a little. Then Ronan pushed me away, laughing, and dashed over to a sedan parked in the driveway. He opened the trunk, grabbed something, and brought it back to the truck.

"I stashed these blankets in Mom's trunk earlier," he told me. He threw them into the truck bed and climbed behind the wheel.

He didn't drive very far, and in fact he went directly to the pullout across the highway from Woods Way, driving a little farther in than I usually did. No one on the road would have seen us. He killed the engine, grinned at me, and climbed out. I followed after him, into the bed of the truck, and helped him spread one blanket, which we lay on, and we pulled the other over us. In a flash, we were glued together.

We kissed for a few more minutes, and we didn't exactly stop that to pull our clothes off. I reached for his dick and was sent into a whole new level of excitement as my fingers wrapped around it. But he pulled away.

Between breaths he laughed quietly and said, "Let's slow down just a little. I want to enjoy you thoroughly."

He pushed me onto my back and hovered over me, our hard dicks touching just enough to notice, and he proceeded to kiss or run his tongue over everywhere he could reach, and some places I wouldn't have thought he could. It became too much for me.

"Ronan, I—"

In an instant, he'd taken me into his mouth. Oh. My. God. I'd heard this was supposed to be unbelievably wonderful. It was at least unbelievable. He worked me until I came against the back of his throat, and then he swallowed everything that wasn't attached to me. He kissed his way back up to my face, and as I tasted my own cum I thought, "Who *is* this guy?"

He lay back down beside me, grinning. I said, "My turn." And I did my very best to send him where he'd just sent me. Then we lay there, touching all down our sides, holding hands, for several ecstatic minutes.

"When we get really good at this," he said in that delightful, silky tone, "we'll do it together."

"I can hardly wait. I kind of want to do it now."

He chuckled. "But let's save it for when we're not in the bed of a pickup truck."

Overhead, with trees on either side of the truck but nothing directly above it, and with the half moon approaching the horizon as it was setting, I could see a patch of stars framed by leaves. Ronan let go of my hand so he could turn onto his side to face me. With his other hand he stroked my chest, and I felt some part of myself rise up into the sky, floating as if it had no substance. I could almost see the sky shift as the earth rotated beneath it. One brilliant star flamed for an instant across the darkness, a thin trail of light behind it, and disappeared. There was a kind of softness around me unlike anything I'd felt before.

I barely heard Ronan's quiet voice say, "Where are you?"

"Up here."

He lay back and reclaimed my hand with his. A few silent seconds later, I knew I was not alone in the sky. He was right there with me.

I don't know how long it took us to float back down to the truck. I heard Ronan exhale as we settled. Then he said, "I hope what my dad did wasn't too much. He's really deep into this life."

I shook my head and felt the bed liner ridges through the blanket as I moved. Up on my side, I folded the top part of the blanket into a few layers in a makeshift pillow for both of us, and I found Ronan's hand with mine again.

"I don't think so. I guess I went to a tough place right away. Probably should have gone someplace easier."

"You mean with your brother? I take it he's having a hard time accepting you."

"You could say that. He says he's trying. And he did read a bunch of research material I printed out for my folks."

"What kind of research material?"

"Oh, stuff like how we have biology on our side."

"Yeah, well." He lifted his hand, mine with it, and dropped them together in an exasperated gesture. "That really burns me, actually. Sure, it's great that science supports us. But, damn it! We shouldn't *have* to prove it. Why can't they just believe us? We believe *them!*" He exhaled loudly. "My dad says it's not a belief in Christian scripture that keeps them from seeing reason. It's their need to believe that something other than their gut allows them to condemn us. Like the scripture validates what they were already feeling."

Thinking it might be good to change the subject, I asked, "Did you learn about all this grounding and other stuff from your Dad?"

"Mostly. But, you know, it's all around me, in the village. Most everyone practices energy work to some extent."

"How often do you think I should do it?"

"Whenever you think of it and you have a little

undisturbed time. If you don't intend to go really deep into it like you did tonight, it could be as you're lying in bed at night, before you fall asleep."

I grinned. "Nah. That time's for thinking of you."

He looked at me from under his eyebrows, a real sexy look. "After you think of me, then. Once you've, um, calmed down again."

I couldn't resist. "Do you, y'know, think of me at night?"

He let a few beats go by. "I think of you then, and a lot of other times, too." Somehow I knew he wasn't talking about sex. "And when I do, I burn. It hurts, and it's the best feeling, all at once. And I'd rather burn like fire than lose the way I feel about you."

After dinner Sunday, Ivy Skyped me. "Bad news. My dad doesn't think we should meet as the TVA after what Mrs. Knapp told us, and he doesn't think we should meet under false pretenses. So I can't have a fake meeting here, and even if you held one, I couldn't go. Bummer."

"Can't say I'm surprised. It was worth exploring, though."

"There's some good news, though. Daddy tells me he's heard from several people who want to meet someone from the village. Mostly women, but a few of their husbands, too."

"Interesting. So the women are braver than the men."

Ivy laughed. "Not news to me!"

"Very funny. But at least part of our agenda got met, I suppose. We sure got something going outside of school."

"We did. Jesse, I'm very proud of us."

"Me, too."

The very next Saturday, Brad and I went rockhounding,

to yet another place in Arkansas I'd never been. But first, he said, he had something to show me at his house.

Like old times, I went to the kitchen door, and he was there waiting. Instead of heading upstairs or sitting at the kitchen table, he stood there, grinning.

"Dude, to quote you," I told him, "spit it out."

"K. You remember how my dad used to make his own beer? And how he's had to buy commercial stuff since he got hurt?"

"Yeah."

"I haven't told you about this yet, 'cause I wasn't sure it would really work out, but now it has. Follow me."

He turned and headed for a door I'd never been through, which turned out to lead to the cellar. I could hear noises coming from below as we descended, and the smell of newly-cut lumber drifted up. Once we were down I could see what was happening.

All along one side of the cellar was a whole array of equipment on new, clean wooden tables, and there were new shelves mounted on the walls all over the place. Mr. Everett, with his back to us, was busy doing something mysterious. He turned as we got to the bottom of the stairs.

"Hey, Jesse. Haven't seen you for a while." No one commented about why that was true. And his smile looked genuine, so why go there?

Brad's smile looked pretty good, too. "We've been working down here for a while. Got rid of all the old beer stuff. This is all new." He pointed to something in the corner. "That dumbwaiter goes to the back hall upstairs. It's big enough for Dad to get most everything up and down, and I help with anything that won't fit."

Brad started to describe the work they'd been doing, but Mr. Everett couldn't help himself, and he took over. The setup was even more impressive than any mental picture I would have drawn. There were fancy burners whose names I didn't catch, thermostat equipment, tubes all over the place, something that I think he called a wort chiller, whatever that is; I didn't mention the term wortcunning, but I couldn't help but wonder if they had something in common besides the word "wort." There was a huge container of honey and some green stuff I think he said was hops, there was malt syrup, yeast—all kinds of ingredients.

When Mr. Everett finally stepped back, I said, "This kind of reminds me of cooking. I do a lot of that."

"It is cooking, actually," Mr. Everett said. "It's just making beer instead of bread."

"I don't suppose I could get a taste when you have a batch ready?"

Brad jumped in. "Dad said I could have some, as long as it's just a glass here at home."

Mr. Everett nodded and said, "Have to get your folks' permission first, Jesse."

I was trying not to look too enthusiastic about what was going on here in the basement now; that might have made everyone's mind go to why this was such good news compared to the horrors before. Because it was, like, total turnaround. Instead of being thrown down those stairs, Brad would now come down here to help his dad with something fun that had brought them together again. Whatever Reverend Gillman had to say about gay people, he sure must have said the right things to Mr. Everett.

On the way to Arkansas, I decided to take a risk and trust Brad with something I hadn't cleared with Ronan first: the stone circle. After all, Lou and Chuck—or at least someone bent on destruction—had already located it, and Reverend Gilman knew, and even Eleanor was on the verge of throwing up her proverbial hands regarding the strict secrecy around it.

"So, Brad, you know that pile of stones I got trapped in?"

"The one Ronan and his superman friend rescued you from so mysteriously?"

"Yeah. That one. Anyway, it's not just a pile of stones. It's this huge stone circle."

"You mean, like in *Outlander?*"

"Very much like that. They're huge. Ten feet? Twelve? Seven of them, on this hilltop surrounded by trees. It's at the end of an obscure track east of the highway below the village. I didn't even know about them, because no one from the village ever mentioned them, until someone—I think we can guess who—pulled three of them over and scrawled obscenities on the others."

"Oh, my God. For real? Why didn't Ronan ever tell you about them?"

"The village has tried to keep them a secret so nothing like that vandalism would happen. But someone found out, somehow. Anyway, I wanted to see how bad it was, and maybe figure out a way to get towns people to help fix them. Stand them up, clean them off."

"Wouldn't someone just pull them over again?"

"Yeah, I guess that's likely, isn't it?"

"Maybe we could put up a barrier. Not like a fence, but you know those strips of road spikes cops use sometimes? Like on TV? They deflate any tire that runs over them. Then the villagers could pick the spikes up if they wanted to drive in there."

I glanced at him and back at the road. I wasn't sure whether I was more stunned by the idea or by the fact that he'd said "maybe *we*" could do something. All I could say ways, "Wow."

But he was on a roll. "And then—picture this—we could have a battery-powered siren paired with a receiver across the track, and if that's positioned right over the spikes, as soon as the tires deflated you'd hear the siren all the way to McAlester!" He turned a little in his seat to look at me. "Wouldn't that be cool? D'you think they'd go for it?"

I couldn't help laughing, but it was a good laugh, at

Brad's enthusiasm. "You're ready to do this, aren't you?"

"I would love to! I think we should suggest it."

"You know, I think I'll do that. I'll tell them it was your idea, since you think you'd like to help."

"I'll start tonight. Or maybe tomorrow afternoon; date with Staci later. Anyway, I'll see where we can get the equipment and all that, how much it would cost. Dude, this *has* to happen!"

"It's very creative. So, the date. You and Staci are okay?"

"She wrote to her aunt. Didn't quite feel like she wanted to call, after all this time, but she did write. She didn't tell me what she said, but I'm guessing it was good. If they connect again, bro, it was your doing. Thanks, on behalf of Staci."

"Staci is welcome. But I also did it for the village, you know. I didn't like that Staci thought they'd brainwashed or drugged or otherwise made off with her aunt."

"It'll be good for everyone, then. In any case, way to go."

Another bridge built, perhaps?

Not long after, Brad directed me onto a dirt road that got gnarlier over the course of the thirty minutes we traveled until he had me stop. Then we had to walk through the woods for another ten minutes or so. Finally he turned toward me, grinning, an arm out, and gestured dramatically to the side. All I saw at first was a rocky hillside, all green with different kinds of moss. There was a stream coming from someplace ahead, flowing more or less southwest. Then, between some trees, I saw a dark area where the stream was coming out of the hillside.

Brad turned and walked toward the dark area, and as we got closer I saw it was a cave, a little lower than my height. The stream was coming out of it, and there was just enough room beside it to walk without stepping into the water.

Brad told me, "In another month, there'll be too much

water here to go in without wading, until later in the summer. When we get farther in, there's more room away from the water. It gets higher, too." He dropped his pack, opened it, and started pulling stuff out. "Helmet."

I pulled the helmet out of the other pack. "Check."

"Headlamp."

"Check."

"Flashlight."

"Check."

"Extra batteries."

"Check."

"Rope. You don't have that."

"Rope? What for?"

"In case we need to follow it to find our way out, or in case someone else needs to find us from the outside. My dad knows where we are. We'll tie the rope up out here."

Okay, that gave me pause. He went through the rest of the checklist, during which I managed to sneak that chamois into my pack, the one I'd borrowed when I'd found my rutilated tooth. We put on helmets with headlamps, pulled on gloves, hefted our packs, and headed toward that darkness.

"Not checking for cats today?"

"They wouldn't use this. Too much water. And everything's slippery, not just the rocks that look wet. Step carefully. I don't wanna have to carry you outta here."

This was so cool. It was completely different from the cave where I 'd found my rutilated quartz, partly because here we could stand fully upright once we got in a little farther, and partly because it wasn't all sparkly. On the walls in some places, the rock looked kind of rope-like, falling in what Brad said were called drapery formations. It was absolutely gorgeous.

There were a few different openings to choose from. Brad headed to the left. "When you're in a cave, even though you have the rope, if there are branches like this it's a good idea to make sure you always turn in the same direction, so on the way back you always know which way to go. Let's start going left today and right on the way back; I haven't done that in here in a while."

We left the stream behind us. Every so often, Brad took a good look into the darkness overhead. I asked, "What are you looking for?"

"Bats, or maybe someplace where the ceiling seems unstable."

After the second left turn he stopped and pointed to one side. "See that?"

My flashlight didn't shine on anything that looked interesting. "What?"

He moved toward a spot on the cave wall maybe two feet off the floor, feeling around an area with his gloved fingers. "See where the texture changes like this? This curved area is the outline of a geode." He dropped his pack and dug out a pair of goggles. "And we're gonna free it from captivity."

It took us maybe half an hour, each of us chipping carefully from opposite sides of the spot, to work around it enough to lever it out. It was maybe five inches in diameter and sort of egg-shaped. Goggles off again, Brad set it carefully onto a large piece of chamois and stood back, looking at it admiringly, though it didn't look like more than a stone blob to me. I squatted down and took my gloves off so I could feel it better with my hands.

I stood again. "What are you gonna do with it?"

"You mean what are *we* gonna do with it. We're gonna crack it open, right here. I'm expecting there to be some crystal formations inside it, and if so we can both take some with us. Might just be lots of tiny sparkles, or might be something like my quartz piece you like so much."

"Maybe rutilated quartz?"

"Maybe, but that's kinda rare." He looked at me. "Why?"

THROWING STONES

"I found a tooth of it, that day we were with Staci and I went off on my own."

"You never said."

I shrugged. "It wasn't a good day for me. Ronan and I nearly broke up."

He nodded. "I thought something was up. But—if you already have a piece…"

"I lost it."

He just looked at me like someone would have to be insane to loose something like that. Then he put his goggles back on and picked up a chisel and hammer. "Put your goggles and gloves back on, and come hold it steady."

We kneeled beside the geode as Brad felt around it, tapping lightly and listening. "Trying to find the thinnest part." I wasn't sure what that meant, so I just kept holding however he said to. Finally he said, "Okay, hold it steady." And he started to tap the chisel into the thing, then a little harder. It got more difficult to keep it from wobbling as he hit it harder, and then finally it split just enough for him to get the chisel in. I was thinking he'd really give it a whack now, but instead he took off his headlamp and shone it into the geode.

"Good," he said after a minute. "This is the right spot." He got out a smaller chisel, and as I held it, he tapped along the crack to extend it farther around until finally it split wide open. It was broken almost in half, with a few small pieces separating themselves from the rest of it.

"Oh, man!" Brad lifted the half closer to him. "Will you look at that!" He shone his headlamp directly at it, and I saw crystal teeth. They were a beautiful soft white, mostly close to an inch long, all in a cluster about two inches by one inch. "What's in the other half?"

I lifted that one, and his lamp revealed another cluster of soft white, maybe a little bigger, and a couple of smaller clumps of teeth about an inch long.

"You keep that piece," he said. Then he looked at me.

"Don't you lose that one." He examined the smaller pieces, but there was nothing either of us wanted to keep. He put those bits on cave floor near where we'd found the geode. I used a chamois from my pack to wrap my piece up and pack it carefully, he did the same, and we headed out.

Outside, Brad recoiled the rope, looking at me. "Was that cool, or was that cool?"

I shook my head in amazement. "That was beyond cool. Thanks, man." No rutilated quartz, but—hey, it was a great find, and Brad and I spent the afternoon together. I loved my crystal piece, rutilated or not. I couldn't wait to show Ronan.

On the highway back, Brad at the wheel, he said, "So you and Ronan. You're okay again?"

"Yeah." I wasn't sure how I would explain the details, so I didn't try. "It was just a stupid misunderstanding. I apologized, then he did. We, uh, we made up."

He gave me a quick look, like he'd love to hear what that meant, but he didn't ask. And I didn't say anything more, except, "I have a date tonight, too."

Chapter Fifteen

My ankle had finally healed enough to allow me to get to the treehouse, especially since I no longer had to park all the way out across the highway, and I was meeting Ronan there after dinner. I called him as soon as I got home from the cave, my beautiful crystal on the desk in front of me. I wanted to talk about Brad's idea, but I wasn't altogether sure how Ronan might react. I was hoping I could tell Griffin at the same time.

"Listen, is there any way we could grab a little of Griffin's time before we get together later?"

"I've missed you, too, Jesse. How about 'Hello, handsome,' or some other friendliness before you tell me you want to shorten our time together?"

I could tell he was teasing me. "You're right. And I *have* missed you. And I can't wait to see you. All of you, as you're so fond of saying. But this shouldn't take long."

"Good, because I'm pretty sure he's seeing Ivy tonight, anyway. Any hints?"

"It'll be a fun surprise. Well, maybe fun isn't the right word, but at least interesting. Do you want to call Griffin, or should I?"

"I will. I'll text you time and place if he can do it."

I spent the rest of the time before dinner reviewing a few images I'd saved from the Internet. I'd made good use of the time I'd had to spend off my feet, while my ankle healed, browsing for information about how men have sex with each other. It didn't exactly bother me that Ronan seemed so much more experienced than I was, but—well, hell, maybe it bothered me a little. Anyway, I'd found quite a bit of that free gay porn that's there as a teaser for what you get if you pay. Up to this point, Ronan had initiated things, and I wanted to turn that around a little. So lately, I'd been imagining trying out on him some of the moves I'd seen on the web, making a real mess of my sheets in the process. Tonight maybe I'd have the guts to try a few of them out.

We met at Griffin's house, in his room, which I'd never seen. He had posters of tattoos and ear studs and a few other images I couldn't make much sense out of, as well as a small, framed photo of Ivy over his bed. The bedspread had the image of a tree with bare branches, black against a green background. It looked very much like the tattoo I'd seen on his back.

We all sat on the floor, on a thick rug of deep blue, facing each other.

"What's up, oh intrepid voyager into the vampire's lair?" Griffin grinned at me and winked.

I turned toward Ronan. My voice teasing, I asked, "How much do you love me?"

His tone in keeping with mine, Ronan answered, "I love you beyond words. I love you beyond life. I love you beyond reason. Why?"

I chuckled, but I hoped it was at least a little true. "Promise you won't be mad at me?"

"I promise nothing of the kind. That might be a promise I couldn't keep. Again: why?"

I looked over at Griffin. "I told Brad about the stone circle."

Ronan said, "You mean, about its importance?"

"Yeah." And something of the location, too, but I didn't mention that. I looked back at Ronan. "But it might have been a really great thing. Because, like you said, even if we get everything fixed and cleaned up, what's to stop someone from doing it again? But Brad had a terrific idea." I told them about the spike strips and the siren. And then I told them Brad wanted very much to help.

No one said anything right away. I was afraid to look at Ronan, and I was feeling a little like the date where Ivy and I had told these two about the TVA. But Griffin broke the silence.

"That is such a fucking great idea."

And, much to my huge relief, Ronan said, "We couldn't just put it in place, though. We'd really need to have a sign saying 'No trespassing' or 'Proceed at your own risk,' something like that. Maybe both."

"And 'Private property,'" Griffin added. "But we wouldn't need to tell them why. Oh, and Cory—you remember Cory, Jesse? From the labyrinth build? Anyway, Cory knows electronics. So he'd be great at figuring out how to set the siren up." He grinned at me, then at Ronan.

Ronan asked, "Do we know how much this would cost?"

"Brad said he'd look into that, tomorrow afternoon. You don't think it would be a problem, do you? I mean, that he wants to help?"

Griffin shook his head. "No. In fact, I love it. Jesse, can he put together an email or something with the basic information? Maybe a few links to where we might get this stuff?"

Ronan had an even better idea. "I'll bet Todd could even make the spike strips; that would cut the cost. Oh, and I think I'll do a little digging, too. See what our legal liabilities might be." He grinned at me. "We do have an attorney in our midst, here. Bet you didn't know that."

I laughed. "I did not know that. Anyone I know?"

"Andrew Fisher, Esquire."

"Violet's father? Cool."

"And it's what I want to be, too." I just stared at Ronan,

unable to wrap my brain around Ronan Coulter, Esquire. It was so very far from what I would have guessed. Then he said, "Depending on what we find out, we might want to consider something a little less violent. Maybe paintball guns that would go off?"

Griffin said, "Terrific! Ask Brad about both, will you? And have him put that stuff together, and if he could look into paintball guns, too, so much the better. Then Ronan and I can take it to Eleanor, and once we get the village on board we can do it. And, you know Jesse, that was a major concern. I mean, of having someone destroy things again, and maybe even worse next time, if we fixed it. I don't know whether this is a total solution, but at least they'll know we mean business."

I added, "And it might finally get someone arrested."

In the treehouse, after a few minutes of—let's say renewing our relationship without undressing—Ronan had us sit at the table, and he brought out some dark chocolate squares and some strawberries. We'd eaten maybe half of them when he picked up a particularly red, perfectly formed, small berry and rolled it between his thumb and middle finger. "Don't you find these sensual? It's kind of like the slow tease of someone's tit."

This gave me a sharp zing that ran from my own tits to my crotch, and I decided it was time to move on to a different part of the evening. "Might I suggest a different treat?"

"Did you bring something you've made?"

"Nope." I stood and held my hand out to him. "It's an even more sacred task."

I forced myself to move slowly, undressing him, kissing him lightly in various places, teasing his tits with my teeth, loving the way that made him gasp. For his part, he submitted completely, letting me have full control. By the time he was naked, I was wishing I were as big as Brad so I could carry him to the bed. Instead, not wanting to risk injuring either of us, I led him over by the hand, settled him onto his back, and as I undressed myself I allowed my gaze to move from his closed eyes to his open mouth to that sweet dick pointing straight up, no curl, no twist to it, just a perfect erection.

On the bed, I spread his thighs, kissing them as I moved upward, watching his balls get closer, wondering what they'd taste like. We'd gone down on each other in the back of my truck that time, but it had been hurried, almost frantic, and we'd been nearly blind in the dark. Tonight I was going to take my time and take in all of him.

He moaned softly as I wrapped my lips around his balls, poking them with my tongue as I grabbed his ass with both hands, kneading harder as I moved from his balls to the hard shaft of his dick, to the tender tip, inhaling the warmth, which I decided smelled a little like those morels I'd harvested.

Ronan's laugh, and then the near scream when he came, felt like the best kind of reward. Then his whole body went limp, the only sign of life being the deep rise and fall of his chest as his breathing slowly calmed. It was almost like he'd fainted. The expression "like butter" comes to mind; he'd practically melted into the bedclothes.

Despite my own hard-on, I hauled myself over to where I could sit with my back to the wall. My erection deflated slowly, and I wondered how long Ronan would be unconscious, or whatever had happened to him. Somehow it was different from sleep. It fascinated me, actually.

And then he turned his head, eyes open but at half-mast, a smile on his face. "Your turn." And before I knew it, he'd thrown me onto the mattress, and his face was deep into my crotch.

Somehow he saved some of my cum, and he flipped me over while I was still panting. The next thing I knew, he was using that natural lube to slide a finger into me. I couldn't have described what he did, or how it made me feel. But I vowed to relive this feeling every night for the rest of my life.

We lay side by side, hands clasped. His eyes were closed, his face relaxed and almost sweet. "You smell like morels," I told him.

He smiled without opening his eyes. "You smell like shiitake with a note of ginger."

Brad came through on the research. He outdid himself, in fact, and after he sent an email to me, Griffin, and Ronan, Ronan replied that he and Eleanor had already spoken to Mr. Fisher. The upshot was that using spikes would be taking a huge risk. Between the required signs and the liability, Mr. Fisher said that "as an attorney," he didn't recommend it. But then he told Eleanor exactly what the risks were and how to maybe get around a few of them.

Ronan called me after he sent the email to give me a few more details. He said the village had met that afternoon, and they were still talking about whether to do it, but they already had a proposed implementation plan. Along the highway and all along the track, there would be "no trespassing" signs. Then maybe fifty feet into the track, they'd place the first siren system. Then there would be more signs warning of potential vehicular damage to anyone who proceeded. Then there would be another siren system. Then, maybe fifty feet past that, they'd have the paintball guns ready to fire. Then maybe, after another fifty feet, they'd put camouflaged spikes that only they would know how to remove. Mr. Fisher said they'd need to be prepared to compensate anyone who was so determined to get in that they drove over the spikes and damaged their vehicle.

The sirens and the paintball guns could be set on or off

by a keypad with a numerical combination, so the villagers could deactivate them as needed.

The final step they were seriously considering was to send a notarized warning message to the Dwyers and the Armstedts, with a copy to the chief of police, informing them that the area was private property and warning them to stay out. Mr. Fisher said this might not help them if something really horrible happened, but it might. So now we waited while the village decided what to do.

Monday I went to The Pig with Griffin and Ivy. I sat across from them in a booth while we talked about everything that had been happening, including the stone circle, since Ivy's father already knew about it.

I think it was a huge milestone for Ivy and Griffin. Word had begun to spread at school about them being an item, even though they didn't do anything conspicuous. It might have been something to do with the TVA that helped get the word out, and it might also have been because of the TVA's success that there was very little pushback. I expect it would have been worse if they'd walked down the halls holding hands, or if they'd done any of the other things that town couples were unafraid of doing in public with their significant others. Or maybe the fact that Ivy was a minister's daughter had something to do with it, but the reaction so far had been remarkably minor—offhand comments that led nowhere else, a snicker in the hall, that sort of thing. I expected more paint on Griffin's locker, but that didn't happen.

We didn't stay at The Pig long, and although Griffin had told Ivy about potential plans for the stone circle track, we didn't talk about it; we didn't want anyone overhearing anything.

At home, Violet Fisher was still there for her lesson, so I headed into the kitchen to see if Mom had left me a note about dinner. It had been a couple of weeks since the stoning episode, and her arm was much better, but sometimes lifting things was a problem. And besides, I liked the opportunity to influence the menu. So I was peeling potatoes at the sink as Violet was leaving, and I heard what she said to Mom.

"Oh, Mrs. Bryce! Oh, thank you, so much! I know just where she'll live, too."

I turned my head enough to see Violet giving Mom a huge hug. Then she took a shopping bag from the piano bench, lifting it as though it held the most fragile glass imaginable, grinning from ear to ear. I shook the water off my hands and stepped toward the living room, curious about what was going on. Through the open front door I could see a car waiting for Violet, but she didn't walk quickly or skip toward it. She moved slowly and very cautiously. Mom had been standing in the doorway watching, and when she turned toward me I saw a smile as big as Violet's.

"What was all that about?"

Mom walked over to her Hummel case and shut a door I hadn't noticed was open. "I gave Violet the 'First Piano Lesson' figurine. The one with the little girl at the baby grand piano."

"Wow." I didn't know for sure, but I could have sworn all the pieces in that cabinet were worth over a hundred dollars each. "Some special reason?"

Mom's smile turned a little mysterious. "Just because. I wanted her to have it. How are things going in the kitchen? Anything I can do to help *you*?"

So Mom had given little Violet Fisher, the Pagan, the freak child, one of her cherished Hummels. If I had needed any more convincing that Mom was coming around to my way of thinking about the village, this would have been it.

THROWING STONES

The grove moved very quickly once they decided to go forward with Brad's suggestion. Ronan told me that during the week, they had removed the graffiti from the stones, which they hadn't wanted to do before they could be fairly sure of no repeat "artwork" being painted there. They'd also ordered everything they'd need for the entire project, and Todd was in the process of fashioning the spikes they'd need.

Parker Harrison had made another suggestion that tied the whole thing together: photographs. They'd ordered a few of the setups that naturalists use to capture wildlife movements, and the plan was to make sure anyone who got paintballed would be photographed at the same time, with all the warning signage in the frame, and there would more cameras to shoot anything that kept going and went over the spikes, also including the signs with the direst warning.

One thing they decided to do in the near future wasn't in the original plan, and it wasn't something they had wanted to do in the past. This would be to put up one of those lockable, metal swinging gates like you see at park entrances. When they'd thought no one knew were the circle was, they hadn't wanted to draw attention to the track. But now, with the cat out of the bag at least to some extent, and with all those signs posted conspicuously, it seemed advisable.

Ronan kept Brad and me informed about what equipment was arriving, and by Friday afternoon, before school was out, Griffin said there'd be something for all four of us to do if we headed over to the village after school. I called Mom to be sure she was okay on her own for dinner, and I told her I might be a little late for it and not to wait for me.

It was absurd at this point, but Brad still couldn't actually go into the village, because he hadn't let his folks know he might want to, which meant he didn't have permission. So he and I were to meet everyone else along the highway at the track entrance.

Brad and I were the first to arrive, so I decided to drive him up to the circle so he could see what he was helping to protect. We noticed orange ties on several trees and blue on a few others, and I figured that someone had already decided where the planned equipment would go.

I killed the engine a few hundred feet from the circle, and we stared at it through the windshield. I got out first and walked toward the stones, feeling respectful and awestruck and nearly as overwhelmed as on the night of my adventure.

Brad and I didn't go into the circle; we just walked around the outside. With the red paint gone, the sense of mystery, the feeling that anything was possible, was greater. I stopped at the backside of the stone that had trapped me. Even bent away from us at an angle, it looked massive. "This is the one that nearly killed me."

His voice hushed, Brad said, "This place is fucking amazing. And you were here alone for hours? In the dark? Trapped? Man... How long has it been here?"

"No one seems to know."

"What do they do here?"

I knew he meant the grove. "I have no idea."

He shook himself with a few swift jerks as if to shake off something he couldn't see. "I'm convinced. I mean, this is definitely worth protecting. So let's get to it."

Todd, Cory and Parker were already unloading boxes from two vehicles near the track entrance when we got there, and Griffin's car showed up a moment later with him and Ronan. Parker was in charge of organizing the work effort, and he sent Griffin and Brad into the woods to test fire the paintball rifles and the neon florescent ammo, with instructions to help Todd and Cory mount equipment when they were done.

Parker turned to Ronan and me. "The orange ties on trees are for signs, and the blue ties are where siren equipment will be mounted. Your job is to figure out the best camera placement for the paintball spot and the spike spot, farther up. When you get done with that, you can come help me get signs posted. Any questions?"

I had one. "Have you guys thought about someone going up on foot, maybe not even on the track itself? Maybe they couldn't knock the stones over, but a can of paint doesn't weigh much."

"Actually, we have. We'll be getting more camera units, and maybe a few more sirens, and we'll position them just inside the woods below the knoll where the stones are. And we're considering a few more guns, with peppershot ammo, though we'd probably have to put up a few specific signs about that. We plan to reposition things from time to time, in case someone cases the joint, as it were, to figure out where they are. Nothing's foolproof, but now we have a fighting chance."

I think my favorite part was working with Parker's laptop to test and upload digital images. Once we had the camera set up at the paintball spot, Ronan drove through it with my truck, and I uploaded the shots to make sure we'd captured everything we wanted. We repeated this at the spike spot.

I think Brad's favorite part, other than testing the paintball guns, was working with Cory to set up the sirens. When they'd finished testing, he stood on the track, hands on hips, admiring his work. Then he said the same thing he'd said after I'd told him how I'd removed that limestone slab from the woods: "Well, shit. I'm impressed."

By the time we left, everything was set up and working except for the spikes. So if anyone came through tonight, they'd get painted and photographed, at least. I almost hoped someone would try it.

Someone did. It was maybe half past midnight when I

heard the distinct sound of one of those sirens. It was far enough away that it wouldn't have waked me up, but I was just finishing a session of imaginary sex with Ronan when I heard it. I had to know what had happened. I *had* to.

Not caring who heard me start my truck, I threw on a pair of jeans and my shirt from earlier and headed south. When I got there, whoever had broken the siren beam was gone, but not before they'd gotten pelted. And we knew this, because Parker was there and had already uploaded images of a dark truck with bright orange splashes all over it. The camera had captured it leaving, too, backing out, and the time stamp indicated almost no time had elapsed, so the truck didn't go any farther than this. Plus, the other siren hadn't gone off.

Ronan wasn't there, but his father was. He stood next to me as we looked over Parker's shoulder. His voice low and pointed, he said, "That's Mick Dwyer's truck."

Mick. Lou's father. "How do you know?"

"We've made it our business to know who owns the vehicles that might be capable of pulling the stones over."

Parker closed the laptop and handed it to Mr. Coulter. "Todd and I are going to do a little reconnaissance. Would you send copies of these to everyone?"

"Can I have a copy, too?" I asked. Mr. Coulter gave me a heavy look but then agreed. I asked, "Where are Todd and Parker going?"

"Probably to the Dwyers', to take a picture of that painted truck in their driveway."

I started to dash toward my truck; I wanted to see that. But Mr. Coulter caught my arm. "Jesse, this isn't your battle. One thing we don't need is for Dwyer to know you had anything to do with this. We have no idea what the repercussions might be. We're willing to risk it. We're not willing for you to do that. Will you promise me you'll go straight home now, and stay there?"

What a dilemma! I wasn't sure what he'd do if I didn't

promise, but I also didn't want to piss off my boyfriend's father, a guy I really liked into the bargain. And I didn't want to lie to him, but I would so love to have seen what happened next. But—"I promise. Can I at least help reload the guns?"

He smiled at me, but he said, "I think you should go home, Jesse. You'll notice that Ronan and Griffin are not here. This is the dangerous part, and we don't want you involved. Now, go on home."

I sighed and headed for my truck. I knew what he was saying, but didn't he understand the dangerous part was the most fun? Or, at least the most exciting?

Somehow I got back into my room with no one challenging me. And sure enough, my email already had a couple of images of the truck, and it was evident that Ronan and I had done a terrific job of positioning the camera. I could even make out a little about the driver, through the closed side window. I decided to suggest we add another camera to get the license plate.

I texted Brad. *U up?*

Maybe fifteen seconds later, I saw, *Y something happen?*

Sending photos now

Cool!

Maybe one minute after I sent them, I saw, *Holy shit batman we got him!*

They've gone to take a photo of the truck in the owner's driveway

Who is it

They think it's dwyer

Makes sense

Will tell u more when I know probably not till tomorrow

K CU

Saturday, a cloudy and chilly day for May, Brad and I

decided to take a drive to the scene of the crime. We didn't expect to see much of anything, but we felt drawn to it anyway. Just before we got as far as that old barn, coming the other way up the road at a killer speed was the red monster, Lou behind the wheel and Chuck beside him. Brad and I looked at each other.

"See any orange on that one?" he asked.

"Nope. Not sure what that's about. Maybe we'll know when we get there." I stepped on the gas, wondering what mischief they might be able to do in the daylight.

I parked just off the road, and Brad and I got out and wandered around the back sides of where we knew the camera was, and where the siren was, and where the paintball guns were, and we couldn't see that anything had been disturbed.

Brad said, "There must be something. Lou was tearing ass away from here, and he didn't so much as honk at us or flip us off. He was in a hurry to get away. But from what?"

We stood still, puzzled, trying to think of possibilities, when I saw smoke floating above the trees from very near by, back up the way we'd come. I pointed. "What's that?"

Brad didn't answer. We ran to the truck, and he pulled out his phone and called 9-1-1. The old barn was very close, and it was obvious that's where the smoke was coming from. As we got closer, it wasn't just smoke. Now there were flames.

"Shit! Brad, kids from the village! They play in there sometimes!"

Brad passed this information along to the 9-1-1 operator and then followed me as I ran toward the barn. I could feel the heat as soon as I got out of the truck.

I dashed toward the opening on the side of the building, the huge, ancient door sagging on rusted hinges. Over the noise of the fire I could hear screams.

I pulled my shirt off and wrapped it over my nose and mouth. I had to squint to see where I was going, and I was

366

almost knocked over by a boy, maybe ten. Then a girl about the same age approached at a run, screaming in fear, streaks of tears running through the soot on her face. I grabbed her.

"Who else is in there?"

"Violet! And Dion!" She jerked away and ran before I could ask where they were.

I moved forward between pieces of flaming wood falling from overhead.

"Jesse!" Brad was right behind me. "Are there still kids in here?"

"Yeah! Two!"

Over the roar of the fire and the groans of the dying barn, I barely heard someone calling for help. Brad and I moved that way, about halfway into the building and over to our right, and through the smoke I saw Violet Fisher. She was pulling on something, something that was burning, and I could barely make out another child trapped underneath.

Suddenly there were flames on her right arm, and she screamed in panic and pain. I pulled on her other arm, threw her down on her right side, and rolled on top of her, desperate to put the flames out, barely aware of the noises Brad was making as he lifted the debris off of the other child. By the time I succeeded, Violet was nearly unconscious. I'd never seen anyone in medical shock before, but I was pretty sure I was looking at it. The sweater she was wearing was now missing its right sleeve, and the skin on Violet's arm looked horrible. Just horrible. I could smell her burned flesh right through the fabric of the shirt that still covered my face, and it nearly made me vomit.

Something on the other side of the barn fell hard, something on fire, and the heat intensified beyond anything I'd ever felt. I picked Violet up and ran, Brad and the boy who must be Dion right behind me.

My truck was far enough from the fire, so Brad opened the back, and I set Violet down in the truck bed. Dion stood there, crying but apparently unhurt. I could hear sirens approaching.

As I put my shirt back on, I asked, "Are you Dion?"

He nodded.

"I saw another boy and another girl. Is there anyone else in there?"

He shook his head as the first fire truck showed up. A paramedic ran over to Violet, who was moaning. I prayed that she was unconscious, but I couldn't tell. Brad and I backed away, taking Dion with us, and a little way past my truck, near the side of the road and watching in terror, were the other two children, also crying but they didn't look hurt.

An ambulance arrived, and then two police cars, and then another fire truck. The EMTs got Violet onto a stretcher and into the ambulance. I must have been in a kind of shock, myself, because all I was thinking was that this wasn't far from where Patty's baby had died.

A female officer and her male partner took the three uninjured kids, and another officer was sent to notify the Fishers. Brad started to say something to me, but before he could get it out I heard my name called. I turned toward it and saw Todd Swazey and Talise Alexander running toward us.

Talise said, "I knew something was wrong, but until we saw the smoke I didn't know what it was. Who was hurt?"

I told her about Violet, and her hands flew up to cover the lower half of her face as tears began to roll out of her eyes. Todd put an arm across her shoulders as I said that someone was going to notify the Fishers and that no one else was hurt, and before I could say anything else, Brad and I were surrounded by police officers. For sure the first thing I told them was that Brad and I had seen that red truck hauling ass away from this direction, even though I couldn't truthfully say that I'd seen it stop here at the barn.

THROWING STONES

The officer I was talking to went over to his car and, I was pretty sure, radioed this information in to someone.

Todd and Talise stood and listened as the police asked Brad and me more questions, Todd on his phone, probably telling Eleanor what was going on. We couldn't be as helpful as we'd like to have been, or no doubt as helpful as the police would have liked, but we told them everything we knew. The tricky part came when they asked how we'd happened to be here at all, to rescue anyone. I had to force myself not to look at Todd.

Brad saved us from having to say anything about the grove's track or the stone circle. "Jesse and I do a lot of rockhounding," he said in a tone that was more casual and relaxed than I could have managed. "Sometimes we just take a drive to scout out new locations. So we weren't actually looking for rocks today, just for places to go."

"Why wouldn't you look for rocks at the same time you're finding the locations?"

"I, uh, I have a date later today, and I didn't want to get all grubby. Plus, I mean, once Jesse and I get into it, it's hard to pull us away. My girlfriend wouldn't be happy if I was late, you know?" And he grinned like only a straight guy can grin at another straight guy about the fairer sex. I didn't actually know whether Brad had a date or not, but at that moment, I believed him. So did the cops. I had a date later, too, for after dinner, but only Brad could have handled this explanation so well.

"Okay, so we've got contact information for both of you." The cop glanced down at his notes and then up at me. "Bryce. Isn't that the woman who stood up in that meeting?"

"Yes, sir. That was my mom."

He nodded and half smiled. "Brave lady. Hope it comes to something."

I let out the breath it felt like I'd been holding for too long. "It already has, actually. She's working with a woman from the village—the other lady who stood up—to get back into ceramics. She stopped years ago to have a family, and now she's back at it."

He nodded again, smiled more broadly. "You boys did a marvelous thing here, today. Saved one life for sure, and most likely two. Get on home, now. We'll be in touch if we need to."

He turned to Todd next. "This isn't your barn, is it? The village's, I mean?"

"No. It belongs to Jeffrey Conroy."

I glanced at Brad, and he nodded once; this was the Jeffrey that Staci's aunt left for Zayne Downey.

The officer took Todd's contact information and then looked at him a little harder. "Say, you're the one who saved that girl's life, aren't you? The day of the tornado?"

I answered for Todd. "Yes, he's the one. She's engaged to my brother."

The cop turned back to me and grinned. "You're in the middle of just about everything around here, aren't you?"

I shrugged; didn't know what to say to that.

They let us all go after that, and Talise hugged first me and then Brad, tears streaming down her face. Brad and I didn't get on home, as we'd been instructed. As I started my truck's engine, I asked him, "Any reason not to go into the village?"

"I was gonna suggest it."

I knew exactly where to go: Eleanor's house. As Piper, Eleanor's daughter, let us in, I saw a crowd had gathered in a circle around that huge kitchen table. All the chairs had been pushed against the wall.

Ronan came over to me. "Are you all right?" I nodded, and he hugged me.

Brad let me tell the story, and even though I hadn't actually seen him shift that fallen beam or whatever it was off of Dion, I made sure he got as much credit as I could give him. When I had finished, without anyone saying

370

anything, everyone moved into a circle around the table. There was silence, and then someone began to hum. I joined them; I don't know whether Brad did. As I felt Ronan, beside me, take my hand, I knew the whole circle was joining hands, and I reached for Brad's. The humming grew quieter but continued, and the next thing I heard was Eleanor's voice.

"Goddess of all life and all death and all rebirth, we pray to you. Be with our precious daughter Violet. Soften her pain. Heal her wounds. Make her whole and well again. That will be the easier task." She paused and took a deep breath. And then another. When I'd heard her pray in the past, she hadn't done this. At first I didn't know if she'd go on or not, but after yet another deep breath, I felt just a little tension flow away from the circle of people. Then she continued.

"Goddess of love, Goddess of forgiveness, we ask that you come into our hearts. We beg that you help us to release the anger, the fury, the hatred, and any unloving feelings we have for whoever caused this fire that damaged our little girl, for whoever might even have sought to kill our children. We know you understand these feelings. We know how easily these feelings come into our hearts through those who have no way to rid themselves of hatred and fear except to push it onto others. But the true pity, the true sadness, is with those who hate, with those who fear. Goddess, we pray you to help us from becoming the pitiable, the truly sad, the hateful and fearful. We pray that as you open our hearts, you pour into them all the love they can hold. Only in this way can we heal.

"Goddess of love, Goddess of forgiveness, we ask that through us you send your infinite love to those in most need of it. To those who hate, to those who fear, to those who are truly in need. Blessed be."

We echoed, "Blessed be." I sensed rather than saw a gentle squeeze move from Eleanor around the circle, accepted and passed on by each person to the next, and when that squeeze made its way back to Eleanor, the humming grew quieter still, and then stopped. Then everyone laced arms around the next person's waist and we stood around that table as though it were a bonfire, heads bowed, many people quietly sobbing. My own throat was tight, and my eyes stung with unshed tears.

Here it was. Here was the love, the togetherness, the belonging I'd craved. It seemed both very wrong and perfectly right that it had happened because of the most horrible act by someone of the town against the grove. My tears spilled over and ran down my cheeks, and it felt both painful and ecstatic at once.

Slowly I became aware that Eleanor had been taking more slow, deep breaths, and others in the group were doing the same. So I did, and gradually people's arms released, and everyone stepped a little back from the tight circle. Individuals hugged and quiet conversations began. I turned to Brad, and he turned to me, and I saw his tears. We hugged, not long, but hard.

When I turned to Ronan, he was smiling through his own tears, and we hugged. As we began to let go, Ronan said, "Have you called—"

Before he could finish, my phone rang. It was Mom. Ronan smiled at me, and as I answered the phone I stepped outside.

"Jesse! Where are you? Is everything all right?"

"I'm fine, Mom."

"I heard all the sirens, and I know you and Brad were out driving someplace. Your father even called to see if I knew anything. Do you know what happened?"

"I do, yeah. Listen, I'm fine. There was a fire south of the village. I'm going to give Brad a lift home, and then I'll be there to tell you about it. Okay?" I waited to make sure she agreed.

Back inside, I found Ronan. "You knew she was

worried, didn't you?"

He grinned. "Sort of. Are you headed home?"

"Yeah. I'll call you later. I don't know whether I'll be able to—"

He took my hands in his and shook his head. "Don't worry about it. Just let me know one way or the other. You might better stay with your folks. There'll be time for us." He stepped forward and kissed me once, lightly, sweetly, let go of my hands, and turned to join his people. I watched him disappear into the small crowd and wondered whether I was fooling myself, thinking this bridge would ever be built, and if so whether it would last.

But there was love here. All things were possible.

At home I made Mom sit on the couch before I told her what had happened, which proved to be pointless, because as soon as I got to the part where Violet's sweater caught fire, Mom jumped up. Hands at her throat, she listened to everything I had to say, and by the time I was done she was weeping shamelessly. She stepped forward and wrapped her arms around me. I held her until her sobs lessened, then grabbed a box of tissues, and we sat side by side on the couch.

It was maybe a full minute before Mom could speak. And when she did, her words—said more to herself than to me—surprised me. "Oh, my little girl. My sweet little girl."

I'd known Violet had found a soft spot in Mom's heart, but I hadn't known how very deep the feelings went. Maybe Mom hadn't known, either, until this moment. And in an odd rush, I was hearing again Mom telling me that Patty's baby, killed by the tornado, had been a little girl. Feeling almost like the parent, I said, "Let's call the hospital and see how she's doing. Okay?" But I wasn't quite the parent; internally, I was begging Mom to stop crying, to shake off this profound grief, to surface once more as my own mother. But she didn't respond to my suggestion.

I'd heard someone mention Eastern Oklahoma Medical Center, so I looked that number up. They told me she'd arrived but had been airlifted to the Integris Burn Center in Oklahoma City.

I glanced at Mom, hoping she was still in enough of a funk that I wouldn't have to tell her this news, but she was watching me. I told her what I knew.

Mom nodded. "That's good. I didn't want to think of her being treated by someone who didn't really know what they were doing. I want that little girl playing piano again."

She stood and held a hand out to me. In another hug, she said, "Oh, Jesse. Thank the Lord above you were there. And you might have been hurt! Oh, my sweet boy. So brave. So brave. And Brad, too. I'm so, *so* proud of both of you."

She released me and went to pick up the house phone. "I have to call your father." But she just stood there, staring at the phone.

"Mom? Did you always want a daughter?" It was a variation of a question I'd asked weeks ago, for a very different reason. She smiled at me, looking very sad, but didn't answer. So I said, "Do you want me to call Dad?"

Without a word, she handed me the phone. I told him as little as possible, and he was silent for several seconds. Then, "Jesse, why are you calling instead of your mother?"

I looked at Mom and mimed for her to talk, but she shook her head. "She's kind of upset right now, Dad. She's very fond of Violet."

"Right. I'll be there in a few minutes." The line went dead, and I held it at arm's length and stared at it. Dad never, and I mean never left the garage in the middle of the day. I knew Stu was with him, so the place wouldn't be deserted, but—man.

I told Mom he was coming home, and she sat quietly back on the couch. Then, "Jesse, would you call over to

Reverend Gilman and let him know? I think he might like to offer what comfort he can."

I blinked at her; that seemed odd at first, but when I thought about it, it made perfect sense. So I did. Mrs. Gilman answered, and I asked for the reverend. When I'd told him what happened, he thanked me, and I got the impression he would go to the village himself. I hoped he would.

The rest of the day was a series of odd moments and intense emotion. Dad sat with Mom for a long time as she cried quietly. I'd never seen him like this, or seen them together like this. It gave me a whole new perspective on them as a couple, and I loved seeing it.

Ivy called at one point and demanded a full accounting. She said her parents had both gone to the village to visit Eleanor; the Fishers were both on their way to Oklahoma City.

Somehow Patty heard about it and came over, and I had to go through it all again. When I finished, she called the burn center, insisting on information they obviously refused to provide. But she managed to get through to Mr. Fisher, identifying herself as my future sister-in-law, and he told her that Violet was on oxygen support, pain medication, and antibiotics. The primary specialist felt sure she would regain normal use of her hand and arm, although the scarring would probably be with her for life.

She grinned at me as she told us what she'd learned. "The only reason he was willing to talk to me was my connection to you, Jesse Bryce."

It was at this point that my dad got up, walked over to me, reached out his hand, and when I took it he pulled me to him and hugged me hard. "I'm proud of you, son."

I didn't know whether to be embarrassed, shocked, or thrilled. I chose thrilled.

Not long after this, a call came in on the house line for me: Mr. Duncan. I had no idea how all these people were hearing about this, and I was getting tired of repeating the story, but in a way it seemed like a really good thing. It seemed unlikely that there would have been this much attention from the town if this had happened a year ago. The bridge building was going as planned.

I didn't get to the treehouse that night. It just seemed wrong to leave. But my cougar and I had, like, the best phone sex ever.

Chapter Sixteen

Church the next day was unlike any service I'd ever attended. Reverend Gilman looked tired but also grim and determined. His sermon was an odd mix of the wages of sin, loving our neighbors, and being willing to commit fully to what we know to be true and righteous. At the end he stood there, silent and kind of intimidating, and then he looked directly at me.

"Jesse Bryce." He looked over at Brad. "Brad Everett. Please, stand."

I had no idea what was going on, but tentatively I got to my feet, and Brad did the same. We glanced at each other, confused.

Reverend Gilman spoke again, his words as clear as bells. "These young men saved the lives of two children yesterday. They risked their own lives and entered a burning building, dodging flaming beams, inhaling smoke, shouldering aside heavy debris to free one child and using their own bodies to put out the fire that had taken hold of an innocent little girl. These young men are heroes." And then he did something I'd never seen anyone do in church. He started to applaud.

Suddenly my dad was on his feet, and then Mom, both applauding. Brad's parents did the same. Patty, sitting with Stu and her parents, jumped up, and Stu stood as well, and pretty soon, all around the church, everyone stood and applauded. Despite my embarrassment, I glanced around, and I didn't see anyone still sitting. Reverend Gilman hadn't specifically said the children were villagers, but I was sure everyone knew. I didn't know whether to laugh or cry, so I sort of did both. I glanced at Brad again, and we saluted each other, and then I just took in this great feeling until everyone sat down again.

As everyone was filing out later, lots of folks shook my hand and Brad's, and we got lots of friendly slaps on the back. Reverend Gilman asked me to wait until the crowds had left, and then he asked me, Mom, and Dad to come back into the church. He had us sit in one of the pews, and he sat in the one in front of us.

He turned to face me. "Jesse, I think the time has come when we can take some action regarding the stone circle. And I want to begin by inviting your father to help."

He told my folks the truth about the stone circle and its importance, explaining why I'd had to be vague about it until now. He told Dad that Eleanor had given him permission to conscript a few men from the town who had the means and the strength to join together and help the villagers reset the toppled stones. He said that Lou Dwyer and Chuck Armstedt had been arrested for setting the fire, and that the police had warned Mick Dwyer to stay off of the villagers' land or face legal action. He didn't say anything about the paintball evidence, but I suspect he knew.

I watched Dad's face carefully. Would he be willing to do this? But, again, he surprised me, in a good way.

"I'm sure Jesse's looking forward to getting back at that stone that nearly crushed him. Would it be all right if I ask my son Stu to help?"

Reverend Gilman smiled. "I think that's a great idea. And I wish I could include Mr. Everett, but I don't know if he would be able to help, but I also don't want him to feel left out. Perhaps you can guide me there. So, I'll be calling a meeting to get the team set up, probably in a few days. We'll be in touch again then." We all stood, Dad shook the reverend's hand, and then the reverend shook mine.

THROWING STONES

I said, "Dad? Mom? I need another minute with Reverend Gilman. Can I meet you outside?"

Once they were gone, I looked directly at this man I forced myself to think of as Ivy's father rather than the reverend who'd preached against who I was. "There's something I want you to know about me. I don't know what you're going to make of it, especially after today's service, but—here goes. I'm gay."

His eyebrows shifted just enough that I could tell he hadn't known. He looked briefly down at his hands, folded on the back of the pew. "Have you told your parents about this decision?"

"It's not a decision. It's who I am. You didn't decide to be straight. And, yes, my folks know."

"And why did you want me to know this, Jesse?"

"Because I'm building bridges. I don't like it when people misunderstand each other, or mistrust each other, or hate each other. I guess this is the next bridge I want to build, because I don't think you respect people who are gay. I don't think you like us. I don't think you believe God loves us."

"Oh, Jesse, that's not true. I know God loves you. And I love you."

I wanted to stop him before he said what I expected was coming next. Maybe all the praise and applause had gone to my head, but I felt absolutely no fear at all. "Then don't tell me you love me but hate the sin in me, as long as you think being gay is sinful. Because it isn't. It's just being who I am, being who God made me. Love me, love who I am. Can you do that?"

He looked at me for several seconds, more thoughtful than anything else. "I think you were aware, after that TVA meeting where Phil and Griffin acted out their skit, that Griffin asked me if he could date Ivy. But I'll bet you don't know the first thing that went through my mind. Now, I think the world of Griffin, and he treats Ivy like the gold she is. But what went through my mind was, 'Why couldn't it be Jesse Bryce asking me this question?' Of course, at the time I didn't know you were gay. And even now, I wish you would change your mind, and that you and Ivy could get together. So I'll tell you what, young Mr. Bryce. I'll do my best to meet you half-way on this new bridge of yours. I'll do my best to understand you if you'll do your best to understand me. I can't make any sense out of a young man like you not wanting to love someone like my daughter, but I'll do my best to believe you. You'll need to do your best to be patient with and old man like me, trying to lead a congregation through changing times without losing touch with what's true and Christian. Do we have a deal?"

In a perfect world, this wouldn't have been enough. But we don't live in a perfect world, and I knew that I'd have to get the reverend half-way across this bridge before I could convince him to come fully to the other side. And I knew Ivy would help. So I held out my hand. "Deal."

I knew that after lunch, Dad was going to drive Mom to see the barn and then into the village to meet the Coulters, because of Mom's working with Mrs. Coulter. I'd been stealing looks at Dad ever since they'd told me this last night, wondering when he'd begun to soften about "those heathens." In one way I wanted to go with them, but they didn't invite me. Plus I still hadn't told them about Ronan, and I didn't know if I could act normally. I'd made sure that Ronan knew to tell his parents to keep our secret for now.

Stu had sat with Patty and her folks at church, and he'd gone with them for lunch. I didn't expect to see him at home that afternoon, but he showed up around two thirty. "I need to talk to you. Can we drive out to the lake?"

Out to the lake. Whatever this was, it was serious. "Sure."

Stu led me to his truck, saying he needed to drive. I was

thinking that he needed to be in control right now. I just didn't know why.

We rode in total silence until we were about half way to the lake, and suddenly Stu said, "So what's going on with Mom these days?"

"Not sure what you mean."

"Every time I see her, she's smiling. Well, until this fire. She was even humming the other day when I stopped by to get some warm weather clothes to take to Patty's." He chuckled. "Guess I'm gonna have to stop referring to it as Patty's, huh? Anyway, Mom's different somehow. I figure you know more about things at home than me, these days."

Smiling. Humming. Yeah, I guess he was right. It had kind of snuck up on me. "You know she's into ceramics again, right?"

He didn't even remember the vague reference I'd made, the night I'd told him who my boyfriend was. So I told him everything. I wanted him to know all of it. I wanted him to know that she gave up a huge part of herself to take care of her family, and I wanted him to know she was getting it back, and I wanted him to know how much of it was thanks to the generosity of people in the village. The Pagans.

When I stopped, finally, he was quiet for a minute and then said, "You really like these people, don't you?" I looked hard at him. His tone was more like he was a little confused than like he was condemning anyone. Then, "Are you still Christian?"

"Of course I am. No one's trying to make me change my mind, either. By the way, my boyfriend's mother is the one who's helping Mom get into ceramics again. That's why they're going to visit the Coulters this afternoon. Mom wants to show Dad Mrs. Coulter's work."

I watched as he ground his jaw, but he didn't say anything right away. I decided to wait him out, which took all the way to the lake.

We walked along the shore for a bit, near where I'd

seen the cougar in the water, that day oh, so long ago now. We sat on some rocks, and Stu picked up a few pebbles and tossed them. Finally he started to talk.

"We've been pretty rough on you. Dad and me, anyway."

"No argument."

"I'm sorry. I still don't understand it, but I'll just have to live with it for now. Maybe it will get clearer."

I nodded, not sure how to respond to that. All I could think of to say was, "Thanks for trying. Really."

A few more pebbles hit the water. I focused on the plopping sounds and almost missed Stu's next statement. "Patty and I are planning to get married in July."

"Big wedding? Small?"

"Very small, actually. Family, a few friends, that's all."

This made sense to me, though I really hoped Patty hadn't been hoping for a bigger event. I didn't want her to end up like Mom, giving up too much without really knowing what it would mean.

Then Stu said, "I told you once that Patty knows Mrs. Coulter. Your boyfriend's mother."

I strained my ears for any note of disdain or worse, but his tone seemed totally flat. So I said, "I do remember, yes."

He waited maybe another thirty seconds before saying, "And you've made it clear that you know Patty went to her for a potion. I guess Mrs. Coulter is supposed to know about these things."

"Wortcunning," I said, and when he turned a shocked face toward me I told him, "It's just knowing about plants. Medicinal properties, things like that. So she wanted to use a love potion on you?"

I thought he'd shrug, or grin, something like that. Instead, he looked surprised. "Uh, no, not so much. She asked for a potion to cause a miscarriage."

My turn to be shocked. "What?" *Get rid of the*

baby? And here I'd assumed it was a love potion Patty wanted. "Patty wanted to get rid of her baby? Why?"

"What? No! No. It wasn't for her. She was trying to help a friend."

"Oh, my God. Mary Blaisdel."

"Anyway, Mrs. Coulter wouldn't give her anything, and Patty was pretty relieved. She said she hated the thought of helping Mary do that, but Mary was desperate. But then— well, the night Patty and I had that fight, when she told me she was pregnant, it ended up being only partly about how I was having trouble accepting you. It started there. But I raised my voice, and she got angry about that, too. Said she wouldn't marry someone who yelled at her. Said maybe she'd go back to Mrs. Coulter and get a potion for herself." He waved a hand in the air as if to brush something aside. "Anyway, of course that only made me madder. It was... it was a bad night."

I was speechless. I just sat there like a lump and stared at the side of my brother's face. I'd known it had been a bad night, but what he was telling me made it sound much worse than I'd imagined. Honestly, you just don't know people. You just don't.

"Why did Patty tell you about the potion, Stu?"

"It all came out in the hospital, after she lost the baby. She kind of feels like losing the baby is her fault, like she's being punished for being willing to help Mary that way."

"That's crap." It was out of my mouth before I could stop it. "Sorry; I didn't mean that the way it sounded."

Stu's tone of voice was heavy. "Then how did you mean it, Jesse?"

"There's no way God would punish Patty by killing an innocent baby. That would make Patty's punishment worth more than the baby. And that doesn't make any sense."

Stu looked at me, scowling, but not in a bad way. More like he was confused. "Is this something you're hearing from your friends in the village?"

"No. If anything, it might be something I would tell *them*. I don't think I'd be willing to worship a God who'd do that."

He threw his next pebble at the water. I threw one.

"Stu? Why did you want to talk to me about this?"

Two or three more pebbles later he said, "You have a different way of looking at things. I know I can get stuck in my own thoughts."

Wow. Another wow. "Are you mad at Patty because she asked about the potion?"

"I was for a while. Now I guess I'm mad at me. I'll get over that. But what I need you to do is keep an eye on me. Let me know when I'm getting stuck in my own head, when I can't get out of my own way and listen to what Patty's trying to tell me. Because I don't want to lose her again." He turned to look at me. "Will you do that?"

If I was shocked before, I was dumbstruck now. What to say? What to think? What to feel? "Well… I'm not sure I'll know."

"You'll know. Maybe it has to do with being gay."

"What are you talking about?"

He shrugged. "Aren't gay people more sensitive about emotions and things? *You* always have been."

A kind of snort escaped me, but I didn't snap at him about that stereotyping. It seemed more important to maintain this connection with my brother. "Okay, first of all, I'll help you any way I can. But, look, Stu, gay people are just people. We're all different from each other just like you're not exactly the same as Brad, or as Griffin Holyoke. And Mom's not the same as Patty or Mrs. Coulter. So I don't want you thinking I have some kind of magic power because I'm gay, or even that I'll act a certain way because I'm gay. If I have insight, if I'm sensitive, that's just who I am." I waited, but he said nothing, just looked down at his hands, worrying another rock.

Something about it captured my attention. And I was in

for another shock. "Where'd you get that?"

He looked at me. "This? Just picked it up." He lifted his hand like he was going to throw it.

"Wait! Can I see it?"

When he handed it to me, I saw that it was my rutilated quartz. "I—this—oh, my God! I found this in a cave, rockhounding with Brad. I thought I'd lost it." That day I'd thrown it at the cougar, I had dropped it, and I'd kept my eyes on the water when I bent over to pick it up...

"What is it?"

"Rutilated quartz. It's supposed to have a lot of great properties, but most of all it has to do with forgiveness."

"Forgiveness." He looked back out over the water. "I guess we could all use a little of that."

"I think we could all *give* a little of it, too."

I stood and moved to face my brother. I held the tooth out to him. "Here," I told him. "You keep this."

He took it, looked into my face, and nodded. Sometimes you don't need words.

It was going to be a long haul for little Violet's recovery, but there were plans for physical therapy, and her doctors liked the idea of her getting back into piano playing when she was ready. But Mom wasn't willing to wait as long as they were. She wasn't going to wait for the injured right head to be ready.

"Look at this, Jesse," she said to me one Saturday as I was about to head over to Brad's to work with him on his father's new beer brewing setup. Mom handed me a kind of booklet, and on the cover it said, "Grand One-Hand Solos for Piano."

I looked up at her and grinned. "You don't give up easily, do you, Mom?"

"I don't give up at all. And I found more music, too. Violet is right-handed, and sometimes right-handed players short-change their left hand. By the time she's ready to use her right hand to play again, her left will be so much better than my other students. It might just be better than mine!"

Mom also started a GoFundMe account for the Fisher family, to help defray the costs of Violet's medical expenses. I watched it grow, and grow, and grow.

And Dad took the lead on the town team of people helping to fix the stone circle. He included Brad and his father, with Mr. Everett consulting, as a miner, about the best way to handle the stones. And Mr. Everett was able to drive, so his truck was one of the vehicles doing the pulling. The team worked on the site two weekends in a row.

Brad was finally able to go into the village without getting kicked out like I had, so he finally got to walk the labyrinth. I hadn't even known that it was Cory's father who was the stonemason, but Brad found out, and they talked for nearly an hour about the stonework needed for the labyrinth.

The Sunday after the stone circle was fully repaired, as I was walking into church with my folks, and with Stu and Patty (who were sitting with us that week), I saw Ivy Gillman ahead of us, with her mom as usual. And, as usual, it looked like they were headed for one of the front pews, where they sat every week. But beside Ivy—holding her hand!—was none other than Griffin Holyoke.

O.M.G.

All up the aisle, heads turned to stare at the tall, black-haired, body-pierced boy holding their preacher's daughter's hand, obviously accepted by the good reverend's wife. The normal quiet rustle of conversation before the start of services changed gradually into something more pointed, but it didn't sound critical. Just, maybe, confused.

It seemed extremely unlikely that Griffin would ever convert to Christianity, but you never know. And anyway, I

386

placed myself in the middle of the Pagans' sacred ceremonies. Why can't Griffin join mine?

I was beginning to think that this bridge I'd started didn't need me to do anything more. Maybe it was already finished; there were people from both sides all the way across it now.

The kiln firing happened just after school let out for the summer. Mrs. Coulter's schedule, which had teams of two people monitoring the wood fire around the clock for three days and two nights, had Ronan and me taking an overnight shift on Sunday. We got our assignments a week ahead of time, and I took this as an opportunity to tell my mom about him.

"You like Mrs. Coulter, right? And Mr. Coulter?"

"Jesse, of course. You know that."

"And you met Ronan again, the day you and Dad went to the village after the fire."

"Yes. Jesse where is this going? What—oh." And I knew she'd gotten it. She knew. "How long?"

"Since the middle of February."

"Valentine's Day?"

Oh, yeah. It had been. "Sort of. It wasn't really about that."

"Do his parents know?"

"Yeah. Nobody in the village cares if you're gay, so for him it would be just like Stu telling you he had a girlfriend."

She blinked hard. "So—how many people in the village know?"

I shrugged. "Just about everybody, I'd guess. Look, Mom, I didn't know if I could tell you or not. And if I told you, even if you were okay with it, how could you not tell Dad? And obviously he can't keep a secret from Stu, and you saw what happened when I came out."

"I see." And I was sure she did, even though she looked a little hurt. "And why is it that you're telling me now? Does it have to do with the kiln schedule?"

"Yes. I wanted to be able to tell you that Ronan and I will be tending the fire together. And that's all we'll be doing. Well, maybe a little more, but we'll be there for the kiln, not just to be together. You can see that his mother trusts us to do that, or she wouldn't have put us on the same shift. And I guess I didn't think it was fair to give her a chance to trust us and not give you one."

She let out a long breath, and then she smiled. "I couldn't quite tell what to make of Ronan, the day I was there. He seemed aloof, somehow. Almost unfriendly. Maybe he was afraid of giving something away."

I chuckled. "Maybe. But he strikes a lot of people as arrogant. And I guess in some ways he is. But he's also a really terrific guy. I hope you get to know him better."

"I'm sure I will. And—Jesse, thanks for telling me."

The very next thing I did was text Stu to tell him to pretend this revelation, which I expected he'd hear from someone soon, was a surprise. His reply surprised the hell out of me. He'd already told Dad, who didn't blow a gasket, and who hadn't told Mom. So now I was gonna have to talk to Mom again and break the news that she hadn't been the first in the family to know. But I wasn't too worried about that.

One day, when Ronan and I had taken a picnic lunch to Wister Lake, I asked him if he knew who owned The Flying Pig. It was a bit of a surprise when he said that the village owner was Mrs. Ward, Allen's widow. But the town owner threw me for a loop. It was Mrs. Knapp.

So I'm watching the kiln. It's Sunday night, or really Monday morning, maybe around three? I can't see my watch at the moment.

THROWING STONES

Ronan and I did do a little more than just feed the fire. Mrs. Coulter had set up a special tent with sides made out of netting, with lawn chairs inside, so kiln watchers could keep rain showers off of themselves and keep mosquitos to a minimum, and there were a couple of blankets in case the night got chilly. Ronan and I spent a little time earlier in our watch using those blankets for something other than keeping the chill away, though we didn't dare do much; one of the assignments is "night watchman," and this is someone from the village who walks by the tent a few times to make sure someone is awake. Open minded as the grove might be, Ronan and I don't really want to get caught with our literal pants down.

He's asleep now, his head on my chest, his hand in mine. My head is propped up on pillows so I can see the kiln. I'm not worried about falling asleep. I'm way, way too happy for that.

My mind has been busy thinking over how things have changed since last summer. So many things are different now. And not just these bridges I've been so busy building, either. For one thing, Brad, my best friend in the world, has decided for sure that he'll go to school for auto mechanics. And then—this is so cool I have to shake myself when I think of it—my dad is going to hire him. So there will be two "sons" to turn the business over to, after all.

As for me? If anyone had told me last September that before a year was out my own family would be okay with the fact that I was spending all night in a secluded location in the middle of "freak" territory with my Pagan boyfriend, I would have laughed in their face. As recently as April, I'd been sure that my family would never accept me, that they'd never accept my boyfriend or his family, and that I'd have to go far away from home to be myself.

You just don't know people. You just don't. I'd said this to myself the day Stu had found my rutilated quartz tooth, and I'm sure I'll be saying it for the rest of my life.

Whatever people show you up front, they reveal themselves slowly, over time, and you get see who they really are only if you chisel patiently away around them, protecting yourself with gloves and goggles as necessary, trusting that behind the hard surface you can't see through is a core of something with special properties. Sometimes you're disappointed, and you can't find that precious core, and you don't know whether you've used the wrong tools or looked in the wrong place, or if there wasn't anything brilliant in there at all. But you have to try. And if you're patient enough, if you trust enough, you'll find it.

Sometimes you have to perform this patient chiseling on yourself. And sometimes, when someone else chisels on you, you learn as much as they do.

Something else I've learned? Fear is like the really hard, worthless rock that can hide rich obsidian or beautiful crystals. So maybe my next bridge—the one I told Reverend Gilman about—isn't a bridge at all. Maybe what I need to do is figure out how to chisel away at fear. This would be my own, but also the fear other people use to avoid thinking about what they don't understand. If I can figure out how to do that, I'll be able to help people realize that this thing about me that scares them—this thing they can't see, this thing they don't understand, this thing they just have to believe is there because I tell them it is, this thing called sexual orientation—isn't anything to be afraid of. You can't see gay. You can't see fear. But you can't see joy, either. And you need love. Life's full of things you can't see, so you need love to figure out which ones to trust.

I've decided that I will go to college, if I can get in. But now it feels different. Now it feels like I want to chisel away at myself a little, find out what's really inside. And maybe after that I'll come home again.

Author's Note

During the funeral ceremony for Allen Ward, a version of an untitled poem written by Mary Elizabeth Frye is spoken aloud. Frye almost certainly based the poem on an unattributed Native American prayer. She circulated the untitled poem privately and never had it copyrighted or published. It has been used in many different circumstances, occasionally altered for those circumstances, and there is no confirmed definitive version.

Some of the characters in *Throwing Stones* hunt for cyrstals and rocks in the Ouachita National Forest. Please note that while there are some areas in the US where collecting specimens is allowed, in many locations the collection of rocks, minerals, and other natural artifacts is prohibited.

If you enjoyed this book, please consider posting a review on the online sites of your choice. This is the best way to ensure that more titles by this author will become available.

If you would like to be notified when new titles are released, you can sign up for Robin's mailing list at robinreardon.com/contact.

About the Author

Robin Reardon is an inveterate observer of human nature, and her primary writing goal is to create stories about all kinds of people, some of whom happen to be gay or transgender—people whose destinies are not determined solely by their sexual orientation. Her secondary writing goal is to introduce readers to concepts or information they might not know very much about. On her website, robinreardon.com, there is a section on each individual novel's page called "Digging Deeper" that links to background information and research done for the novel.

Robin's motto is this: The only thing wrong with being gay is how some people treat you when they find out.

Interests outside of writing include singing, nature photography, and the study of comparative religions. Robin writes in a butter yellow study with a view of the Boston, Massachusetts skyline.

Robin blogs (And now, this) about various subjects that influence her writing, as well as about the writing process itself, on her website.

THROWING STONES

Robin Reardon

ABOUT THIS GUIDE

The suggested questions are included to enhance your
group's reading of Robin Reardon's THROWING
STONES.

DISCUSSION QUESTIONS

Note: The questions below contain spoiler information. It is recommended that you finish the book before reading through the questions.

1. When Jesse comes out to his best friend, Brad, the reaction is better than expected. But Brad also says he feels as though he now needs to get to know Jesse all over again. While this proves not to be true for Brad after all, can you understand why he was concerned? If you suddenly found out a close friend you thought was straight turned out to be gay, how would that make you feel? What if you had been certain that friend had been gay and they turn out to be straight?

2. Jesse isn't sure what's pulling him toward the Pagan community, or "grove." At first he thinks it's his crush on Griffin Holyoke, but when that wanes, Jesse's fascination for the grove remains strong. Over time, as he learns more about the grove, his interest increases rather than diminishes. If you were in Jesse's place, how much would the feeling of mystery be the source of fascination for you, and how much might that abate as you became more familiar with the grove? Would it become less mysterious? Would it matter if it did?

3. Griffin's sister, Selena, is involved with Parker Harrison, who identifies as gender queer. Parker was born apparently female, but he presents himself to the world as male. How does this differ, in your opinion, from a transgender male? If it's different, what are those differences? If it's the same, what would gender queer mean to you?

4. At one point, Jesse finds out that Ronan Coulter is bisexual, when he had assumed Ronan was gay. Jesse is troubled, because his idea of bisexuals is that they want both men and women. Ronan corrects Jesse, saying bisexuals who want to commit can do so with either a man or a woman. There is another aspect of bisexuality that Jesse doesn't discuss or even consider. If a gay man is involved with another gay man, and that first man has some insecurities around relationships, he might find reason to be jealous of other gay men. But if he's involved with a bisexual man, he now might find reason to be jealous of almost anyone. If you're not bi, and you fell in love with bi person, how secure would you feel? Would you be able to discuss it openly with your partner? Or do you think you would avoid romantic involvement with a bi person? If so, why?

5. When Eleanor Darling tells Jesse the grove can't allow him in the village without his parents' permission, Jesse is devastated. He loves his family, but he needs the grove. And now, not only can he not be with his new friends who accept him completely, but also he's been forbidden to be with them by the very people who won't accept him, who make him feel shame for who he is. He feels caught in a gulf of hated and fear. Have you ever been in a similar situation, where what you most want is thwarted by something you really need?

6. Ronan plays a song for Jesse, Loreena McKennitt's The Stolen Child, the lyrics of which are the W.B. Yeats poem of the same name, about "faeries" who steal children away from a world where "the world's more full of weeping than you can understand,"

away from troubled people whose sleep is anxious. Ronan says if this description is what's pulling Jesse toward the village, he's in for a disappointment, because it doesn't describe the village at all. Do you agree with Ronan? Or does the grove have more in common with Yeats' faeries than Ronan is willing to admit? Would a community of faeries as described by Yeats appeal to you or scare the willies out of you?

7. When many people hear the word "Pagan," they don't know what it means. They might think the term means something other than Christian, or something other than religious. As Jesse discovers, this is far from the case. Having finished the book, how much has your concept of Paganism changed? Do you understand why it should be capitalized in the same way as Christianity or any other religion?

8. What do you think of the prayers Jesse hears Eleanor Darling lead? How far are these sentiments and intentions from those of your own belief system?

9. There are a number of events that begin to shift the Bryce family's attitude toward the village. Can you recount some of them? Do you think their final acceptance was brought about by one or two events in particular, or was it more a case of critical mass? Do you think Staci will reconcile with her aunt? Will Stu and Patty have a gay child? Will Jesse and Ronan maintain their relationship during their college years? Will Griffin convert to Christianity? After efforts to protect it, will the sacred stone circle remain safe?

10. Had you heard of scrying before reading this book? Does it appeal to you? Would you be willing to try it yourself? If so, what might you want to find out through this channel?

11. After a fight in which Ronan breaks up with Jesse, Jesse drives his truck down a track so deep in the woods that his only light is from his headlights. He drives into the unknown darkness, hearing unseen things scrape against the sides of the truck. How well does this describe how Jesse approaches life in general?

12. Throughout the book, Jesse learns more and more about rockhounding, or hunting for minerals and crystals, from Brad. He learns about the various tools, how to protect yourself when you use them, how a brilliant crystal might be hidden inside a nondescript lump of rock. By the end of the book, he sees how this process applies to getting to know people—other people as well as himself. How much chiseling have you done so far in life to uncover your own brilliance? What tools have you used? Have you protected yourself? Enough? Too much?

13. What do you think Jesse's power animal is? What about yours?

Other Works by Robin Reardon

Novels
A SECRET EDGE
THINKING STRAIGHT
A QUESTION OF MANHOOD
THE EVOLUTION OF ETHAN POE
THE REVELATIONS OF JUDE CONNOR
EDUCATING SIMON
(Published by Kensington Publishing Corp.)

* * *

Essay
THE CASE FOR ACCEPTANCE: AN OPEN LETTER
TO HUMANITY
(Published by IAM Books)

* * *

Short Stories
GIUSEPPE AND ME
A LINE IN THE SAND
(IAM Books)

CPSIA information can be obtained
at www.ICGtesting.com
Printed in the USA
LVOW11s0731091117
555624LV00001B/343/P